COMMAND ACTIVATED - REVOLUTIONS

Benjamin Gordon Card

This book is a work of fiction. All of the characters, organizations, and events portrayed in this novel are either products of the author's imagination or are used fictitiously.

COMMAND ACTIVATED - REVOLUTIONS

www.commandactivated.art

Print ISBN 979-8-9909589-8-2

Electronic ISBN 979-8-9909589-6-8

First Edition: August 2024

Printed in the United States of America

Cover art by Lee Matthews

Praise for BENJAMIN GORDON CARD and the COMMAND ACTIVATED TRILOGY:

"Rarely do you find an author who is also a technical expert and can draw upon years of professional experience to make his books even more engaging, compelling, and insightful. Benjamin Gordon Card is one of those extremely rare individuals who has the military and technical background to spin a story as believable as this one!"

— Cho Ng, A.I. Engineer and M.S., Information Systems

"Benjamin Gordon Card is an incredible writer who delves deeply into his personal—and often painful—experiences to craft his stories, making adept observations about human nature and the best and worst attributes that exist inside of all of us."

— Dene Low, Author and Ph.D., Rhetoric and Composition

"This series is replete with reality based hacking techniques that I could see myself using if I was in the same situations in which the protagonists find themselves."

— Nathan Smith, Certified Ethical Hacker, Certified Hacking Forensics Investigator, Certified Information Systems Security Professional, Offensive Security Wireless Professional

"Though the trilogy is filled with solid science, it's distilled in a way that anyone can enjoy it, and the action and engaging characters make the books hard to put down!"

— Ali Ankeny, B.S., Software Engineering

"The science, tech, and military aspects are incredibly realistic, and the story...it's addictive in the best way!"

— Greg Johnson, C.E.O., Webcheck Security

Other books in the COMMAND ACTIVATED TRILOGY:

COMMAND ACTIVATED (BOOK ONE)

"We are in an endless race to build combat machines, and whichever side builds more—and more capable—machines will doubtlessly maintain its lead for some time. Truly capable robots are extremely expensive to construct, extremely expensive to repair, and extremely easy to destroy.

The human body is one of the most efficient machines both on the face of this planet and in the stars above, and it is highly available. The trick has been to find a sufficiently reliable means for harnessing human bodies to give their actions robotic levels of accuracy, and then to enhance the bodies so they could perform at robotic levels of strength."

- Dr. Aoi Hinimoto, Lead Author, Command Activated Program Charter, Global Alliance Command

The free world has created a program by which virtually any able-bodied human can be turned into a special operations soldier. Unfortunately, when humanity develops any grand new capability, there will always be those who will use it for evil. Now, even citizens having special needs have been put at risk by a shadowy organization operating within the Command Activated program...

COMMAND ACTIVATED – EVOLUTIONS (BOOK THREE)

"As humanity embarks on the monumental task of exploring the heavens and colonizing other star systems, it is imperative that we approach this endeavor with our utmost dedication and foresight. The survival and prosperity of future generations depend on the actions we take today.

We must harness our collective ingenuity, compassion, and courage to ensure that our expansion into the cosmos is not only successful but also sustainable and ethical. This pivotal moment in our history calls for us to put our best foot forward, creating a legacy that honors the indomitable spirit of human exploration and discovery."

- Dr. Katherine Tange, Committee for Planning and Collaboration, The Traverseon Project

A fragile peace had emerged in the years after the uniquely capable and ethically minded artificial intelligence created by Dr. Maxwell Clarke had been allowed to enter the networks and systems of most of the planet's countries—and had necessarily driven its way into the assets of certain oppressive regimes as well. The democratic nations of the Earth had then been forced to decide how and where this uniquely benevolent and gifted entity should have a place in the world and, as humankind expanded its reach farther out into the stars, the entirety of the Universe.

This becomes a critical issue when a new threat to both organic and electronic beings raises its fearsome head, putting every peace-loving entity at risk.

DEDICATED TO MY INCREDIBLE WIFE,
AMAZING FAMILY,
AND ALL OTHERS WHO HAVE SUPPORTED ME
THROUGHOUT LIFE'S JOURNEY

Prologue

In the years following the destruction of the People's Space Elevator by the Alliance's Command Activated forces, the Confederacy of Eastern Nations had retaliated in every way it dared, the use of nuclear weapons seemingly the only means the CEN would not yet employ. Though that axis of evil had formed under the banner of "Refined Communism," member nations had joined with the recognition that this flexible ideology allowed the Confederacy's dictators to govern however they wished, and Communist China had historically taken its own, aggressive approach in its efforts to undermine the primacy of the world's democracies.

China's Politburo ensured new, economy-debilitating biological weapons were spread across the globe, with CEN citizens and allies once again secretly receiving inoculations while the free world—and particularly the third world—saw pandemic-level spreading of these new diseases. Severe respiratory illnesses decimated the populations of Africa and South America, having a significant death toll across North America, Europe, Australia, and Pacific Island nations as well. CEN spokespersons denied responsibility for these outcomes, but the source of the viruses had been effectively identified by Alliance intelligence assets.

Being in a de facto state of war with the Alliance, military operations were also conducted by Russian and Chinese forces that resulted in dozens of naval and air skirmishes over contested waters and incursions into Laos, Myanmar, Nepal, Bhutan, Ukraine, and Poland. South Korea's occupation by China grew even more austere, with access to food and basic medical supplies intentionally restricted by the occupying forces.

The Command Activated were called upon ever more frequently to halt the advances of Communist forces, requiring the rapid expansion of the program both in unit count and supporting infrastructure. New technologies were continually being fielded to address the countermeasures that enemy nations had developed in attempt after attempt to level the playing field for military engagements.

In the thick of it all, the Alliance called upon Dr. Maxwell Clarke to lead the effort to increase the capabilities and effectiveness of the SAVANT analytics artificial intelligence and the HOUND security AI that protected it, taking the entities beyond the already unheard-of levels to which he had brought them in the early years of the CA program. Having been granted the authority to recruit virtually any new resources he desired from the population of AI architects and developers, Maxwell had built up a small army of technical specialists to manage daily operations and expand the models' capabilities. As the technical team added an ever-increasing volume of abilities to SAVANT and HOUND's repertoire—the latter now having had greater oversight established for its directives—the young technical lead had quietly worked together with Haden Juma and his Modern Informatics company to expand the abilities of his own FAILSAFE AI as well.

Only because FAILSAFE's ability to persistently infiltrate hostile networks had been dramatically expanded had Maxwell gained his first glimpse into the horrifying state of affairs within the venture the Confederacy had created to compete with the Command Activated program. No matter the identities of the leaders or the political ideologies they use to obtain power, an eternal truth of human existence is that oppressive regimes are inevitably catalysts for the rise of the most twisted minds into positions of power, and the Confederacy of Eastern Nations was a prime example.

Chapter 1

"The depth of our commitment to greatness will be measured by the depths to which we will dig to unearth the hidden knowledge that timid nations will never have the willpower to seek out. Only by our boldness will we realize the dominance that we deserve to enjoy among the inhabitants of the Earth."

- Fang Guo, Public Health Director, Politburo of the Chinese Communist Party, Confederacy of Eastern Nations

"*Yes*...no need to weep. This will all be over soon and will greatly benefit our beloved leader!"

The head of medical research could not stop smiling as he watched the young man tremble and wrench his arms, legs, and neck wildly against the tightly secured restraints. The subject's eyes had rolled up inside his head so only their bloodshot whites were visible beneath his half-closed and fluttering eyelids, and a mixture of sweat and drool was dripping and swinging in strings from the young man's chin onto his perspiration-soaked shirt. All control of bodily functions had ceased some time ago, and the rank odor of the urine that saturated the test subject's pants noxiously filled the equipment-crowed medical room in the Superior Authority research and development complex outside of Guangzhou in the People's Republic of China.

Turning from the readings pouring across the screens at the monitoring station with a weary and worried expression, a distinguished middle-aged man wearing a fine suit and a lab coat chided in Cantonese, "Doctor Cheng, if you push the test subject too hard again, you are just going to end up with another mindless husk."

The senior leader's smile did not fade as he retorted, "Are you so concerned about these *commoners* that you do not wish to harm them, even for the greater good?"

"I understand the benefits we can provide if this line of research succeeds, Cheng, but moving so quickly does not give the nanites sufficient time to retrain the synapses without causing overly great damage in the process. We can end up wasting time and valuable resources rather than moving the program closer to the President's objectives."

"Li, you fail to understand that with every successive attempt—whether the subject's mind is rewired or not—I am gaining a greater understanding of exactly which facets of the approach are *swiftest* in achieving the desired results. We have already given the President new soldiers whose protective suits enhance their abilities and whose minds can be subdued, and we are going to take back the advantage from these 'Command Activated' Alliance cretins. What we need now is a more rapid mechanism by which we not only ensure the compliance of those filling our Superior Authority exosuits but also rewrite their minds *entirely* with *exactly* what we need them to think to serve the Great Leader, and nothing more!"

Doctor Li frowned with distaste as the test subject moaned, the researcher sighing as he returned to the only desk in the room, lifted a hand, and worriedly rubbed his chin while staring abjectly at the information running across the screens. The arms of the advanced lasers and nanite control components which were whirling and jerking around the restraining chair in the center of the room created a constant chorus of humming and clicking, with specialized control systems and medical equipment that was monitoring the subject's medical state adding to the nauseating effluvium, noise, and heat in the enclosed space.

This was a torrid, humid, clamorous, miasmatical environment, and the distinguished doctor desperately wished to be elsewhere, doing more *honorable* work, whereas Doctor Cheng seemed to be thriving here. Moving around the subject with his tablet continually recording, the balding leader was chuckling and drinking in every trace of agony revealed in the young victim's seizing muscles and the whimpers that escaped his lips.

Maxwell stared on in absolute horror and unspeakably poignant sorrow, the British technical genius watching this scene play out on the half-domed screen of his workstation in the glass-enclosed top floor of his Seattle condominium—rain pattering away on the spacious room's curved and transparent roof. It was thanks to FAILSAFE that Maxwell had been able to penetrate this portion of the Chinese government's network, and it was thanks to Doctor Li's unwise opening of a file attached to a message that Maxwell had intercepted, modified, and passed on inside the network that the intrusion had been able to expand to this research and development laboratory.

"Laboratory" made this *situation* sound too clean for what it really was, according to Maxwell's solid grasp of ethics.

A more honest title would be "Bastille" or, more accurate even than that, "hell."

I've just had a glimpse into hell, the thought forced its way into Maxwell's mind. I saw into hell, and the doctors were the demons!

He realized that his whole body felt like it had clenched up into a massive knot of tension, his fingers and knuckles white as his gaze dropped to look at how they were involuntarily gripping the edge of the clean, glossy desk. Maxwell's shoulders felt like an oppressive, oaken beam had been draped across them, and his whole body shuddered as if he were trapped in a midwinter blizzard rather than sitting in his warmly lit office. His breaths were coming in short gasps, and it seemed he could not force his lungs to take in enough air even by tapping into his copious reserves of willpower. The edges of his vision were fading into blackness that was not even penetrable by the lightning flashing outside on this rainy Spring evening.

The sound of Lilian entering the kitchen from the garage broke through Maxwell's anguished thoughts and somehow freed him to take in a deep, tremulous breath that seemed to clear his mind of the roiling black clouds which had threatened to consume him.

He had to inform the senior leadership of the Command Activated program of what he'd just witnessed!

Maxwell knew he would have to be extremely careful to frame his notification to the leaders of the free world's most lethal combat unit in such a way that he did not divulge how key components of his intrusion into enemy systems relied upon his privately developed AI. FAILSAFE was an incredible asset now that Haden Juma's Modern Informatics had fully combined Maxwell's artificial intelligence with the entirety of the company's own roster of subversion-focused AIs—designed to infiltrate hostile networks and maintain a continuous presence once inside.

When Maxwell had first gained access to the video feed, he'd had the presence of mind to begin recording the view through the camera the Chinese government had installed in the laboratory, which was meant to capture a running log of all testing conducted there. Now he quickly copied off the video file to both his strip—the thin and flexible communications device that used miniature spines to adhere to the skin just behind his ear—and to the draft of a new electronic message using a few gestures in front of his screen.

The latter step required extra exertion to force his shaking hands to cooperate.

"Max?" Lilian called up from downstairs. "You still alive up there?"

He let his computer save the message draft and quickly stood, straightening his sweater and rubbing his hands on his pant legs while blinking rapidly and preparing himself to at least attempt to speak naturally with Lilian after what he'd just experienced.

"Coming, Lil!" he called out in forced cheerfulness and made his way to the wooden staircase that led from his office to the lower levels.

He paused at the top of the companionway to briefly examine his face in the decorative mirror that his significant other had recommended as one of many whimsical elements of interior design she said would make his place feel more like a home. The small mirror reflected a portion of his pale face and an eye that, to him, suddenly seemed much older and sadder than he'd ever known his eyes to look before. He took one last deep and shuddering breath before squaring his shoulders, compelling his face to ease into a warm smile, and descending the two flights of stairs to reach the ground floor.

As Maxwell stepped out of the stairwell and quickly crossed the room, he was able to catch Lilian as she turned from placing a container in one of his kitchen cupboards, taking her swiftly but gently by the elbows and pulling her around to fully face him so he could slip his lips up against hers as his arms slid around her shoulders and back, encompassing her in a loving embrace. Her arms reached around his lower back, and she pulled him close as well. They stood like that for a long time, lips loosening and then rejoining tenderly, again and again, while the lightning slowly faded outside.

Only when Maxwell finally felt like his heart had escaped the darkness that had nearly enveloped it did he move to kiss Lilian's temple and then let his head rest against the side of hers as they held each other.

Though the young doctor's loving companion enjoyed every second she spent with Maxwell in that state, Lilian's intuition was screaming at her that something was wrong. She carefully withdrew her head from where she had tucked it up next to his neck so she could search his face with her worried eyes, asking, "Max, what is it?"

He could not meet her gaze at first and stared, wide-eyed, off into the distance while he wondered how he could possibly answer her question.

"I saw something today, Lilian," he offered, then paused. "It's what I always feared would happen, despite all the measures I took to ensure my work could never be used to despicable ends."

Lilian's eyes continued to search Maxwell's, filled with concern and questions and recognizing the signs of emotional pain that were very similar to those she had borne in prior years. These were the signs of guilt and shame she'd felt when her special needs brother had disappeared during a brief lapse in her attentiveness, only to have her learn he had been tricked into joining an unsanctioned branch of the Command Activated forces and thereby turned into an involuntary soldier.

Ked had been controlled using the CA program's "activation" serum and its SAVANT artificial intelligence like the other troops, with the combination of strength-enhancing exosuits, sedative-hypnotic drugs, and filtered input being fed through the soldiers' helmets enabling them to become the most effective soldiers the world had ever known. However, the difference was that the troops outside of the shadow unit had *volunteered* to participate in the program as a way to escape the severe psychological issues from which each of them suffered due to combat injuries, while at the same time dedicating their lives to protecting the innocent.

Studying her loved one's troubled expression, Lilian knew from personal experience that such deep pain could not simply be pushed aside by the encouragement of well-intentioned friends. Maxwell's core had been shaken, and the cracks she could tell were now spreading out across his soul would not be repaired through anything but actions.

"I couldn't tell whether they had truly worked out the details of the soldier activation protocols from the CA program or whether they had stumbled upon their own methods, but FAILSAFE helped me gain access to the network of a research lab to the south of Guongzhou in China and...the doctors were talking about the success of their program that competes with the Command Activated..."

The worry lines radiating out in the skin around the edges of Lilian's eyes were expanding as her brows now pulled together in alarm.

"They've copied...?" her voice trailed off. She could tell by the severity of the symptoms of Maxwell's emotional trauma that there was more involved than simply the enemy's mimicry of the CA protocols.

"What else, Max?" she pleaded, asking him to let her share his burdens. "There's more to this, isn't there?"

Maxwell steeled himself and finally turned his eyes to look directly into hers.

"They aren't using willing soldiers, just like the shadow branch was coercing people with special needs to fill their ranks of AI-controlled troops, and...that's not all. It would be bad enough to learn that they were forcing innocents to become their activated soldiers, but the medical leads are trying to do the unthinkable: they are overwriting people's minds. Erasing their souls!"

Lilian's lips trembled as they worked to form words, but her own mind was tumbling through the incomprehensible horrors that this knowledge had unleashed upon her.

"Can...can they *do* that??" she eventually managed to enunciate.

Maxwell sighed despondently.

"I'm afraid that—given all I've learned from my work with Doctor Srinivastava—it may actually be possible. Whether it is or not, the *concept* of the Command Activated program has 'inspired' them to try! They were altering a conscious test subject's synapses while I *watched*, Lilian!"

Maxwell's voice choked off, and he roughly wiped a tear from his cheek.

"The poor devil was in so much pain, his eyes rolled back and...and the doctor was *laughing*!"

Maxwell ran the back of his wrist across his eyes and blinked hard, then breathed deeply and raised his gaze skyward as Lilian cooed and enfolded his waist in her arms again—squeezing him tightly until he could finally enclose her in his arms and embrace her as well.

Gently pulling away after a long moment, Lilian raised a hand to stroke Maxwell's temple and hair, knowing she had to at least give him something to latch onto as he began treading the path toward healing.

"Max, you aren't responsible for what they've done," she whispered, continuing, "Like all inventions, there are always going to be people who will find a way to use them as tools to bring more hate, more oppression, more *pain* into the world!"

Maxwell breathed in briefly and shakily and then sighed out, "I know..." and yet his face did not lose its burdened expression. He raised his eyes to Lilian's again, "...but why do I *feel* like I'm so responsible??"

Actions, Lilian remembered from her past experiences. *How can I help Maxwell take action?*

"We can inform the Alliance leadership," she suggested, adding, "Perhaps they can make a targeted strike and dismantle the lab?"

"Perhaps," Maxwell admitted, "but even if CA troops were to eliminate one laboratory, I'm certain the CEN has more...and even if we scratch off lab after lab, the knowledge they've gained is likely easily transferred to another set of scientists so the Confederacy can continue its march forward in this area. It will likely require a concerted and endless effort to identify and disable research facilities and the scientists who lead them, using the same approach we employed to virtually eradicate terrorist organizations in the early years, only this would require every operation to take place deep within heavily defended enemy territory!"

Lilian, still leaning back while holding him tightly around the waist, gave Maxwell another warm squeeze.

"At least there *is* something we can *do*, though, right?" She looked up at him brightly.

Maxwell could not help smiling adoringly at her reassuringly positive expression.

"Yes, my darling. At least it's *some*thing!"

"Has the asset obtained any additional information related to the enemy program?"

"She managed to learn that the target seems to travel to the Rocky Mountains more than is typical, especially considering all that should be keeping the woman here."

"That is *not* substantial intelligence. We had already obtained sufficient corroboration to confirm the theory that the complex is based in those mountains."

"She has also asked for more advanced tools to compromise access controls for systems to which she has physical access."

"The tools she has are enough! We did not give her some tawdry trinkets that are sold on the criminal networks! She has the same technologies that are provided to our senior agents!"

"Yes, sir. I...told her that."

"Tell her *again*, and this time make sure she understands! We do not have time for any more games. I want to see results, and I want to see them soon!"

"The asset claims the target grew suspicious of her for asking so many questions, so she's had to back off temporarily."

"*I grow tired of her excuses*. The senior leaders grow tired as well. Tell her that her mother is very close to losing another finger. Tell her that after the next finger, we will start removing *limbs*!"

"Yes, sir! I will make sure she understands!"

"You had better, or I may consider reducing the appendages for your own daughter as well..."

"I will not disappoint you, sir!"

"No, you will *not*."

Chapter 2

"The Confederacy has already acted abominably, having seized power over sovereign—and democratic—nations. Now they've taken their international crimes to a new and unconscionable level, starving even the non-combatant citizens of South Korea until they are too weak to work, and then harshly punishing them when they cannot meet their oppressors' production demands. This execrable situation must be resolved post haste, and we must be the ones to do it."

- General Aarav Chopra, Commander, Strategic Operations Sub-Command – Asia, Global Alliance Command

The Alliance was the free world's answer to the Confederacy of Eastern Nations—an axis of evil that included China, Russia, North Korea, and Iran—and the Command Activated program was administered by a combination of experts and leaders representing the majority of the democratic nations of the world. Senior leadership met twice weekly, and the meeting held the day after Maxwell's conversation with Lilian was the next opportunity to share the information he'd gathered about the Confederacy's Superior Authority program. Maxwell had returned to his office, though even sitting in the same chair in which he had witnessed the heinous acts committed by the Communist doctors filled him with renewed revulsion.

On his screen, the frame containing the meeting feed held an array of video streams from other participants, and Maxwell noted the presence of all key stakeholders from whom authorization for CA action would be required. General Gaines was on that list, and Maxwell was pleased to see that he was present. The new legislator having ownership of the program's funding called the meeting to order.

"Thank you all for your participation today," Senator Ing began, "especially given the latest advancement of CEN forces across the Dunajec, west of Tarnów. That front is due for a Command Activated intervention, despite the gallantry of the resistance put forth by other Alliance forces in the area.

"Before we delve into the details of the options SAVANT recommends for our next mission, is there any other high-priority item we should discuss first?"

Maxwell leaned forward and cleared his throat.

"Yes, ma'am. I have something I absolutely need to share with this body, with significant urgency."

"Please do share, Dr. Clarke," the senator said as she steepled her fingers calmly, allowing Maxwell to take the floor.

"Thank you, Senator. As many of you are aware, I maintain quite a few contacts who specialize in...gaining unauthorized access to systems and networks."

Gaines could not help smiling at that understatement, and the faces of several other participants also took on the same expression.

"As all present are also aware, the most powerful member nations of the CEN have been rumored to have begun research and development of their own variant of a Command Activated program, based on what they've assumed about our capabilities and operations. Satellite- and air-based observations have confirmed brief sightings of several different previously unknown stealth vessels in the skies above Eastern Europe and Central Asia.

"Now," Maxwell paused for emphasis, "I have compelling evidence that the CEN has actually managed to create deployable, activated troops."

Several of the leaders and advisors in the session made minor exclamations of dismay or shifted uncomfortably in their seats.

The Army Chief of Staff soberly set down his tablet and grunted, "Well, we all knew the day would likely arrive that the CEN would catch on to the reality of how our troops were so damnably effective, at least in general terms. Especially after we downed their massive elevator! But are you saying your evidence shows the assets being activated? Or shows them in action?"

Maxwell paused, briefly thinking through how best to frame the information he should share next.

"Thank you, General Adams. That is a relevant question, of course. What I have obtained is footage of senior medical personnel in what seems to be the primary research facility in China, located within the city limits of Guangzhou, and in the video you can hear the senior doctor state that they already have activated assets who he refers to as 'Superior Authority' troops."

The senior Army leader opened his mouth and dropped his eyes to his tablet, where his fingers idly slid along its edges. After a pause, the officer then rejoined, saying, "So, no eyes on any actual assets."

Knowing that the general and other leaders' buy-in was crucial before they would see any official action, Maxwell quickly explained, "No footage of the assets but, again, these are senior medical personnel, and in the video they are performing an actual operation that the lead refers to as taking the program beyond the creation of activated troops, implying as he does so that they have provided many such troops to their President. According to the translation, he then explains that the goal of their current research is to completely overwrite their poor subjects' brain functions, turning them into mindless and combat-adept automatons."

Maxwell saw by the expressions on many of the participants' faces that they had been struck by a feeling of deep abhorrence at this thought, just as he had been.

General Gaines shook his head, muttering, "That's cruel and unusual..."

"The senior doctor stated that their current objective is to create not just activated soldiers, but assets whose minds have been completely *redesigned*," Maxwell spat the word, "from the ground up to be loyal and perfectly attuned troops for their SA program."

Silence reigned in the meeting for nearly a full minute as the leadership team pondered on the implications. Finally, General Adams looked up from his brooding and leaned back in his chair.

"I'll tell you, I'm interested in reviewing this video, but with the full scope of military actions we're dealing with at present, the program is stretched to its limits...and Guangzhou is deep inside enemy lines. Recruitment has gone well as we've expanded the scope to include all service members—profiling helping us identify the best candidates—but it takes time to get them from ground zero to deployable and Gaines only has so many Panthers to provide at this point.

"With Alliance leadership calling for even more Command Activated operations across eastern Europe and southeast Asia in addition to the pending Korea offensive, well, we're being stretched thin as it is! SAVANT will no doubt pick up on the existence of this 'Superior Authority' program when it becomes relevant enough for us to worry about it. Until we get some greater confirmation of the threat and recommendations for action through our own analytics tools, I vote we hold off taking any CA action."

Senator Ing let her hands drop and spread out her fingers on her desk, asking, "Can we have the votes for those who agree to refrain from taking action until SAVANT recommends it, please?"

General Gaines—face betraying deep frustration—kept his hands solidly pressed on his desk. Ten of the fourteen participants raised their hands as Maxwell felt a pit open up in his stomach. He looked away from the screen, awash with both deep sorrow and frustration as the barb-like sense of impotence forced its way back into his heart.

"We do appreciate you bringing this to our attention, Dr. Clarke," Ing continued, "and if you will please share the video footage you mentioned we will have SAVANT go over it for a detailed analysis."

Maxwell nodded despondently.

The senator raised the results of several proposed battle plans on the shared area of the frame containing the meeting's feed, saying, "Now moving on to the projected outcomes for options in the Tarnów region..."

Immediately following the meeting, Maxwell quickly shared the video file and then reconnected through his chain of relay points to the Chinese laboratory's network. He'd had FAILSAFE carefully gathering and analyzing data within that environment, with an aim of identifying specifics around SA troop numbers and locations. The AI had alerted him moments ago that it had found a treasure trove of information.

Maxwell pulled up some of the research and development files that FAILSAFE recommended he examine first. His eyes widened in amazement as he read the detailed notations below a schematic that appeared to be a large, robotic foot.

"Well, I hope to God they run into more troubles building *that*!" the technical expert breathed in fear and wonder.

He turned to another repository of files in the list his AI had shared.

"So, this is the system containing the roster?" Maxwell asked as he accessed the resource and opened a densely populated matrix.

"Yes, Max. It seems to be treated as an asset inventory, with projections of the number of troops the CEN anticipates losing in the coming quarter. Also, based on that number, the files list the total number of new recruits...and I use the word 'recruits' quite loosely, of course...needed to maintain staffing and build new units at the desired rate."

With one hand rubbing his chin thoughtfully, Maxwell scanned down the columns and across the rows in the dataset.

"These identifiers seem to include two-character codes that could be the location designations. Can you please see if you can match those characters to the locations of military bases, cities, or states inside the Confederacy?"

After a few moments, FAILSAFE displayed a map on one side of Maxwell's screen, each pair of Chinese characters displayed next to the best matches for locations throughout the CEN. As Maxwell had expected, the majority were in China and Russia. What he found particularly interesting was the way two sites seemed to be located directly next to one another: a research facility and a military installation, both based just south of Guangzhou. Over eighty-five percent of the SA assets had been tagged with one of those two codes.

"This is extremely valuable intelligence, as it shows that the CEN's primary soldier 'activation' research facility and the main Superior Authority barracks are most likely located in relatively close proximity to each other, much like we built out the CA complex in Colorado. Unfortunately, it is still unlikely to be sufficient to convince our leadership team to take action," he mused.

FAILSAFE interrupted Maxwell's musings with a revelation.

"Max, I've come across additional data that will no doubt be of great interest to you."

"Do tell," the man invited.

"It seems the CEN researchers have been unable to create an activation protocol that is equally effective across all individuals. They did try focusing on individuals having special needs at first, based on what they incorrectly came to believe about the Command Activated program following General Gaines and Lilian's very public exposure of the unsanctioned unit Senator Jennings and her accomplices created.

However, using special needs individuals or not, the CEN researchers were unable to find a successful method for suppression of the conscious mind that still left the candidates' subconscious minds sufficiently operable.

"Their protocol is only truly able to induce a full 'activation' for those whose minds have a synaptic map that falls within certain limits. Though the regimes have access to a wealth of medical data, only those individuals who have undergone comprehensive brain scans can effectively be assessed, and it is only within that pool of candidates that the CEN has been able to identify the citizens who have been viable candidates for activation."

Maxwell had grown increasingly enthusiastic as FAILSAFE had related these details.

"Please show me the files from which you've gained this information!" he almost breathlessly urged.

In a frame at the left side of Maxwell's domed screen, a visual depiction of the Guangzhou facility's network appeared. The view rushed in to enlarge a representation of a subnet, then to a single system, then to a data repository, and FAILSAFE finally highlighted the files it had been referencing for its assessment. Maxwell opened one file after another and began scanning across the information contained therein, aided by his time spent working with the medical experts for the creation of the CA protocols and for the later innovations by which he and his partners had developed brain injury repair techniques.

"This is beyond exciting! This means that we can effectively interfere with the CEN's ability to find and use activated assets if we can either destroy the records of possible candidates or somehow extricate the actual individuals from the Communists' grasp, though the latter would likely require a massive effort on the part of the Alliance intelligence community. However..." Maxwell tapped his chin as an idea formulated, "...removal of the existing SA troops would be a stunning blow to the Confederacy's progress!"

FAILSAFE cautiously responded, "And how do you propose the removal of those assets would occur, Max?"

Maxwell sighed, dropping his hands to his lap and idly brushing across the soft fabric of his pants with his right finger. The sun's rays broke through the thick clouds and streamed into his office like a beacon of hope. He brightened as he gazed at the newly entering light.

"*I'll* do it."

"Not to be a naysayer, but how do you propose that an obvious Westerner is going to gain access to what is likely one of the most tightly physically secured facilities in the Confederacy's territories?"

"Perhaps I don't need to actually enter it myself. We can look for ways to remotely affect their systems to...well, potentially redirect transports to a safe location at which the SA troops can be extracted."

Maxwell's eagerness was growing in counterbalance to the level of moroseness with which he had been burdened at the close of the Command Activated leadership meeting.

He asserted, "I'll work out the details later, but all I know is that I have to at least *try*, or I'll never be able to live with myself!"

FAILSAFE sympathized, "Not living with yourself does not leave you many other good homes, Max."

"Very true, my friend," the technical virtuoso absentmindedly concurred, "Very true."

At the center of the Command Activated complex, nestled in a valley that seemed it was in danger of being swallowed up by the jagged, looming peaks of the Rocky Mountains that surrounded it, the voluminous strategic command building sat like the black concrete and glass shell of a monstrous terrapin. Construction had just begun on a duplicate building to the southwest, its addition driven by the high demand for CA response to the Confederacy's aggression against the countries that shared borders with CEN member nations.

Within the strategic operations command center, a ring of glossy black consoles encircled General Kalabi as he looked out between two of the eight similarly designed unit command hubs. His focus was on one of the expansive wall screens that displayed high-level maps and data related to the operation that was about to commence.

The hubs to the left and right of the enormous main screen that was currently holding Kalabi's attention were occupied by the commanders and sub-commanders for two CA companies whose platoons were loaded in the high-altitude observation and support vehicles making their way over the target site. The Panther medical and supply command unit for this operation was stationed in the hub just to the four-star general's right, with One-Star General Goddart stolidly scanning across his subcommanders' screens to ensure all the robotic felines' status checks were coming up green.

Turning his gaze to his troop commanders, Kalabi noted that Yamada was striding back and forth, issuing final reminders to her team in her usual businesslike manner. Having maintained an exemplary track record, now-General Yamada had been assigned the responsibility for the professional development of three relatively new subcommanders. This was a task that would have daunted most officers, and yet Yamada had been admirably unphased by the assignment.

Kalabi knew General Webb typically suffered from pre-op jitters due to his unalterable sympathy for his troops, so the senior officer was pleased to note that having colonels Singh and Soares as two of the man's subcommanders had been a wise first move when Kalabi had accepted his new role as the strategic chief for the Command Activated program as a whole.

General Kalabi was keenly aware of the presence of one of his superiors, who was standing just to the rear of the senior operations leader's central hub. Though age had taken its toll, General Ryu had refused the option to retire and instead accepted the position Alliance leadership had practically begged him to take, becoming the senior strategic advisor for all Alliance military operations worldwide. This was a new position that had been created in response to their enemies' actions following the destruction of the People's Space Elevator by CA forces in the Tibetan High Steppes a few years prior.

Turning to give a respectful nod to General Ryu and his ever-present assistant, General Cooper, Kalabi was filled with sympathy and determination. Today's mission was personal for General Ryu, as the Alliance was finally opening military operations on the Communists' eastern front.

Ryu's wife and three daughters had been identified by intelligence-gathering drones, one of many families suffering under the inhumanely oppressive occupation of South Korea by China and—by default—North Korea. To say it was regrettable that the woman and children, who were located in Daejeon, were unable to be freed during this first salvo by the Alliance would have been a gross understatement.

However, the powerful analytics engine that made up the core of the SAVANT artificial intelligence supporting CA decision-making had projected that they were looking at a thirty-three percent probability that the Confederacy would simply abandon its occupation of Korea if the epicenter of China's military operations were eliminated. Though relatively low, the chance of that occurring had filled Kalabi with hope.

An uninhabitable "dead zone" had been created by the lingering radiation that had been left behind after the CEN had unconscionably deployed nuclear devices to eliminate the final South Korean military resistance near Busan at the end of its invasion of the country. With that act, most of the southeastern portion of the peninsula had been rendered virtually worthless. Considering the constant, fierce, guerilla-style resistance from the remaining South Korean population and with greater natural resources available as the prize for China's expansion into Myanmar and Thailand—both rich with mines containing the exotic minerals needed for the manufacture of fuel cells—the abandonment of this longest-term occupation would free CEN forces to make a more intensive push through those and other countries with which China shared its southern border.

General Ryu's hopes were high for this operation as well, or at least that was what One-Star General Cooper had shared with Kalabi. The new strategic lead had always found the identification of General Ryu's emotions solely through the study of his facial expressions to be as likely as hell freezing over.

"Troop Liaison, you've confirmed that the soldiers have been briefed on the new 'AI Down' protocol. We'd rather not see it become necessary, but should SAVANT's control of the activated troops be compromised and any assets returned to autonomous operation during this mission, I will look for a comprehensive debriefing regarding the effectiveness of this contingency by the end of the week."

The giant form of Sergeant Major Davis moved from his at-ease stance to one of attention, answering with a booming, "Yes, sir," that resonated through people and objects alike.

"Status, Near-Earth Orbit?" Kalabi now queried.

One of the general's leads spoke up from where he was stationed to Kalabi's left in the strategic hub, "Stealth satellite has drawn a bead on the Chinese satellite supporting operations at the occupying forces' HQ, sir. SAVANT is primed to fire as soon as the deployment sequence has been initiated."

"Excellent. Thank you, Burris. Upper Atmosphere?"

The officer seated at Burris' left leaned back in her chair and, over her shoulder, confirmed to Kalabi that the UA vessels were now in position. The general turned his gaze to scan across his unit commanders once more.

"No hesitation this time, Webb," the four-star general called out to his longtime subordinate with a hint of a smile, referencing what had become a running and inside joke. This was a jest that the newly minted general good-naturedly understood to be a badge of honor.

A smile burst out on the younger general's boyishly handsome face, and he gave Kalabi a sharp salute.

"No, *sir*!"

Chapter 3

"The Chinese Communist Party is using its Ministry of Public Security—the national police and domestic security force of China—as a tool to advance its interests abroad and challenge Alliance nations' security. The MPS has increased its overseas presence and activities under the current administration, using coercion of citizens overseas to influence other countries' security sectors and weaken their respect for the rule of law and human rights. Alliance foreign policy governing bodies must increase their awareness of the MPS' overseas activities, which are in direct competition with the security programs in targeted nations, instead of focusing only on the military-to-military interactions."

- Bradley Trenneman, Director, US Central Intelligence Agency, United States of America, Global Alliance

The expanse of the city of Suwon was visible far below the cloud-enveloped Lansing Aeronautics UA-3 lighter-than-air vehicles, with Seoul's cityscape rising up out of the early morning fog roughly forty kilometers to the north. All surface temperatures of the craft were continually maintained at exactly the same level as the surrounding air. The vessels' skins were not only dynamically cloaking but emitting water vapor in randomized and intermittent patterns to create their own cloud cover that was identical to natural formations.

The combination of these capabilities interfered with both direct observation and laser-based detection of the craft. The angles of the ships' construction additionally rendered radar technologies ineffective, meaning that the enemy forces would have no warning of the hell that was about to be unleashed upon their heads.

Without a noise, dozens of lightweight capsules—possessing the same stealth features as the high-altitude vessels—were released from the undersides of the two large aircraft. With the buoyant gases embedded in their shells slowing their descent and the capsules forming platoon-centric clusters, the conveyances descended gradually while the combined vapor being ejected out of their bases formed their own cloudy obscurement. When the capsules had nearly reached the ground, the UA craft silently let loose a volley of compact metal rods, the mixture of steel and heavy metal driving down toward their targets at hundreds of kilometers per hour as they homed in on preassigned enemy targets, including communications towers, drones, cavalry units, automatic turrets, and missile batteries.

All aspects of the operation were precisely controlled by SAVANT while the CA command units provided their support only as human decision-making was required; the electromagnetically-fired railgun rods collided with their targets at the exact moment the CA troop capsules' thrusters engaged and drove the vehicles more swiftly toward the surface of the Earth. The hatches of the cocoons soundlessly swung open, and the passengers leaped out to hit the ground running. Artificial muscle fibers built into the dynamically camouflaged exosuits of the Alliance soldiers enabled them to move at speeds beyond the capacity of even prime athletes.

The day-in, day-out training to which troops were subjected while under the drug-induced "activation protocol" had created a mental state among the soldiers that was incredibly open to continuous guidance by the SAVANT AI modules built into the combatants' helmets and the communications relayed through the UA vessels to the ground troops.

This, and limited, focused throughput from the world outside to the interior interfaces of the troops' helmets, was how the CA leadership organization guided the ever-obedient and focused soldiers to execute their missions with near-flawless exactitude.

These deployed ground forces were just a small fraction of those operating under the activation mechanisms discovered through the collaborative efforts by specialists across numerous disciplines within the Alliance. The Command Activated program had thereby created a robot-like army for a fraction of the cost of a fully mechanical force.

The defensive machinery in the vicinity of the easternmost building on the enemy base was swiftly obliterated by the lean, railgun-deployed rods, with sparks and fireballs in the thin fog marking the demise of enemy robots, vehicles, and munitions in the vicinity of the Alliance forces. Taking up positions at the building's nearest corners and entryway, the two CA companies were protected from the incoming direct fire sent forth from Chinese turrets and mobile forces.

The next phase of the operation was then initiated.

The special operations soldiers began firing their assault and sniper rifles' smart rounds out around their cover—the bullets curving and homing in on enemy targets with deadly precision while the CA soldiers were never fully exposed to enemy fire. The exteriors of the troops' exosuits were not only automatically adjusting their coloring and patterns to blend into their surroundings, but they were also equipped with cooling tubules that ran through the outer layers of their toughened fabric to control the suits' exterior temperatures and thereby stymie targeting systems and enemy scopes that relied upon heat detection.

Only two robotic Panther units had been deployed for these two companies, and they sheltered and moved in unison with the troops. The prehensile "lifelines" extending from the big cats' broad shoulders stood ready to administer lifesaving nanite-and-medication elixirs and bind casualties to the robots' backs for extraction as needed. As the mechanical felines crouched in the building's shadow and their chameleon-like skins blended with both the rough, gray concrete of the structure and the darker gray pavement beneath them, it would have required a concerted effort by any enemy to even spot the "animals."

Having cleared all CEN forces from the surrounding kilometer using the Command Activated railguns and the first assault by the ground forces, SAVANT released larger objects from the centers of the two high-altitude vehicles. These generally oblong but stealth-designed vehicles were several meters wide, and another few meters greater in length, and thrusters sent them careening to Earth nearly as rapidly as the railgun projectiles.

Their descent was only slowed near the end of their journey via the engagement of their downward-focused thrusters to ease them into contact with the ground. This landing sequence—while still violent—was not as potently destructive as it seemed the vehicles had been about to experience.

Now, with underbellies coated in extremely friction-reducing nanofibers, the two smooth-surfaced but somewhat angularly shelled dynamically camouflaged vehicles immediately initiated propulsion by ejecting air out of thin slits near their bases. The hovercraft tanks glided out over the damp concrete and around the sides of the building nearest the drop site.

The CA troops had just finished clearing that structure and were streaming across the spaces between it and the two buildings directly to its northwest, staying indoors as much as possible as SAVANT guided the semi-autonomous hovercraft into positions that gave them the clearest lines of sight along the southwestern and northeastern perimeters of the CEN military facility. A swarm of heavily armored Chinese air- and land-based drones were issuing out of the heretofore untouched buildings of the complex—numbering in the hundreds. Now sitting motionless, the CA hovercraft waited patiently for the maximum number of enemy forces to come out from within cover before they opened a matching number of ports across their sleek surfaces.

Out of the variously sized ports of these Salamander hovercraft flew round after round of high-caliber projectiles. Each shell expanded and contracted its surface to change its trajectory as the rounds snapped through the air to strike the enemy vehicles and troops in an unavoidable, inevitably deadly barrage.

Rounds comprised of heavier metals were unleashed when needed to punch through thicker or denser armor. Any Chinese craft or troops that tried to take shelter within the buildings were quickly dealt with by the CA forces as they swept through structure after structure. The Confederacy's military assets had no safe harbor. Within thirty minutes, the entirety of the tremendous Chinese complex had been fully drained of resistance.

The rear armor of the hovercraft split and parted to reveal cargo compartments full of spheres roughly the size of a human head. The objects poured out of their repositories and rolled out across the complex, sprouting claw-tipped legs when necessary to enable them to scale stairs, ladders, and greenery.

These intelligent munitions would be an unwelcome surprise for any enemy forces that tried to occupy this complex in the future. They would also serve the secondary purpose of continuously gathering intelligence to be transmitted—encrypted—across public networks as the devices were later ordered to travel out across the combat zone as a clandestine flood of robotic spies.

Following the release of these machines, the CA troops rendezvoused with the hovercraft at the landing zone. The virtually unscathed soldiers brought their drop capsules into a tight formation around each of the two vehicles, engaged attachment points between the capsules and the craft, and re-entered their cocoons.

Four hatches on the uppermost points of the hovercraft—each roughly one meter wide—slid open, and turbines inside these ports began sucking air down into ducts that directed it out toward the ground at a steep angle via the slits around the vessels' skirts. At the same time, equipment embedded within the armored units' hulls began extracting hydrogen from the humid atmosphere, adding the gas to the existing amounts present in the vehicles' central reservoirs. Now relieved of both standard and smart munitions, the constellations of craft and capsules ascended slowly up toward the waiting UA aircraft as Korean locals began exiting nearby residences and looking on in amazement, many erupting into exuberant cheers.

With that military operation, the Alliance had eliminated the hub of all Communist operations in South Korea.

Maxwell had been studiously examining the SA network when he'd heard voices rising up from downstairs. Glancing at the clock in the lower-right portion of his screen, he realized it was now well into the afternoon, and he still had not eaten anything that day. Without some sustenance, he would not be any good to anyone, so he stiffly rose from his desk and—having performed a few light stretches of his back—descended the stairs to the main floor.

Entering his kitchen, Maxwell was enveloped in both the lively chatter and the warm and slightly aromatic currents of air that spoke to the great distances his guests had just run through the kilometers of trails accessible here on the outskirts of Seattle. Lilian was handing out glasses of purified water to Ked and Samantha and jokingly complaining about her brother's excessive physical prowess.

"You completely *abandoned* us over the last two klicks, Ked!" Lilian laughed as Ked beamed without a trace of shame.

Lilian patiently maintained her hold on the glass she had proffered her brother as he habitually reached for it with his robotic right hand, realized his mistake, and then took the glass with his left. This alternate approach was necessary because Ked had insisted on an unusual model of prosthetic for surgical attachment to the stump at the combat-stolen end of his right limb.

The young special needs man had lost the front third of the associated arm while secretly deployed as an activated troop by the shadow branch of the Command Activated program on the dangerous mission to destroy the People's Space Elevator deep within mainland China two years ago. Maxwell had recommended that his young friend opt for one of the newer, lifelike models that included synthetic skin with artificial nerves that could transmit even slight touches to the user's brain.

However, Ked had been absolutely infatuated with the high-tech look and feel of the gleaming alloy and polymer model he currently wore, saying it made him feel like he was a character in his favorite first-person-shooter virtual reality game. The trouble was that the polymer grip components across the insides of the prosthetic's fingers became overly slippery when exposed to moisture, and that made it especially difficult to maintain a grip on the smooth surfaces of drinking glasses when condensation had formed on their exteriors.

Maxwell paused as he stepped into the food preparation space, leaning against the glossy composite countertop and supporting himself with his left hand as he affectionately observed Lilian and Ked's interactions. Lilian caught his eye and gave him a very warm wink and smile, which he lovingly returned.

"You're too slow, Lillie!" Ked teased. "Need to do my exercise program!"

Lilian laughed, abashed.

"Well, you're right that I need to work out more! I barely find the time to hit the gym these days with my caseload. You at least have Samantha to go with you all the time!"

The young woman to whom Lilian was referring shook her head, nose crinkling as she laughed and long, shiny black hair rustling back and forth from the point at which her ponytail had been secured.

"Don't blame it on me! I'm mainly just there to try to motivate *myself* to do some exercises as Ked goes to town on the weightlifting machines! He's my inspiration!"

Lilian smiled compassionately, "Well, I'm glad that my little brother's able to fill in like that for yours. Have you heard from Teddy lately? Did the job training program accept him like he'd hoped?"

The young Asian woman sighed and shook her head.

"No. There are so many candidates in Taiwan these days that it's really hard to get into such programs unless you know someone, or you're a really special case. He's staying optimistic, though, and he keeps saying he wants to come live here in the States with me, despite my mom's constant attempts to discourage her 'only child left' from heading overseas!"

Lilian laughed lightly, raising her eyebrows and admitting, "Well, I guess I can't blame her! I know from experience how hard it is to feel like you're truly connected with each other when only communicating through video!"

Lilian's gaze turned back to Ked and she patted him lovingly on his sweat-soaked shoulder as he smiled at her with his near-permanent grin.

Ked suddenly announced, "I have to go potty now!" and started walking around Lilian and Samantha to reach the main floor washroom with access just to the right of the entrance from the garage. As he made his way inside, the younger woman self-consciously admitted that she had to use a washroom as well. Lilian, after briefly turning her attention back to Maxwell to ensure she had his permission, shared that there was another such room just to the right upon reaching the second floor.

Samantha walked across the kitchen toward Maxwell, smiling brightly and giving him a warm "Hi, Max!" as he returned her salutation and made way for her to pass so she could ascend the stairs.

Lilian had followed her friend across the room and waited for Samantha to reach the second floor before she stepped in close to Maxwell for a long, luxurious kiss. His hands stroked up her hips and waist as they ardently lingered with their lips held together, Lilian's hands moving up his shoulders to cup his jawline and ears—fingers playing with the tufts of his hair that could be reached above his collar.

Finally and reluctantly ceasing their mutual cosseting, Lilian took a half step back and apologized, saying, "I really need a shower!" while looking up into Maxwell's eyes with a hint of embarrassment.

He chuckled softly and grasped her hands around their outside edges, fingers gently pressing into the bases of her palms.

"You are absolutely lovely in this state, my darling! I adore how your cheeks are radiantly flushed, and your hair is delightfully wind-swept!" her man enthusiastically affirmed with his British inflections.

Lilian laughed and looked down, expressing humility and yet pleasure at hearing his compliments.

Raising her eyes adoringly to his, she stepped back up to him and whispered, "How do you always know how to cast away my self-consciousness?"

The trim woman leaned back in for another amorous entanglement.

Maxwell's welcoming smile was frozen at the sound of FAILSAFE's voice playing out of his strip using broadcast audio at low volume.

"Max, Lilian, I'm afraid I need to inform you that I've observed young Miss Liang attempting to extract data from Maxwell's workstation."

A look of shock and disquiet burst across Lilian's face, and Maxwell was similarly aghast and disturbed. It took him a moment to gather his thoughts and ask, "What did she do, exactly?"

"She placed a minuscule, magnetic device at the rear of your screen, between the screen's body and the supporting structure, and that device then attempted to brute force your system access using biometric data Miss Liang must have collected in your home. It has also been sending out data streams with logs of its activities to a private satellite—though I've intercepted those and swapped out the limited information about your system that the transmissions contained. I'm afraid that this methodology for espionage is well-known in the 'dark' network community to be associated with Chinese spy operations."

Lilian and Maxwell's eyes grew even wider, and they stared at each other as questions roiled their minds.

"She stopped in the second-floor washroom and should be on her way down shortly," FAILSAFE offered and then went silent.

The couple could not speak for a time.

Maxwell—brows compressed—finally sighed out, "She really does not seem like the type to do this willingly, Lilian. I know you expressed a feeling that she had been a bit...overly curious about your work and travels a short while back, but at the same time you said you had no sense that evil existed within her heart."

Lilian nodded and wiped a tear from the corner of her eye, sobbing softly and saying, "And she's such a *good* friend to Ked, in a way that doesn't come from those with ulterior motives..."

Maxwell pulled her close, whispering in her right ear as they heard footsteps on the stairs, "China often coerces good people into doing their dirty work for them. Let's sit her down and hear what she has to say for herself."

Lilian nodded, her hair brushing against his cheek.

Samantha slowed as she neared the foot of the stairs, emoting genuine concern as she asked Lilian whether everything was alright, and then stepping hesitantly down into the kitchen. The washroom door on the main floor also swung open, Ked entering from there with his head down, playing away on the semi-flexible screen he had pulled away from its attachment point on his inner wrist.

"Ked," Maxwell called out, "can you play in the dining room for a minute, please?"

Ked nodded absentmindedly and—barely looking away from the screen—stepped through the kitchen into the adjoining dining area. He shoved a chair away from the round, transparent table with his knee and dropped himself into the seat while his thumbs whirled away on his device's screen. Maxwell released Lilian's hands, turning to Samantha and gesturing toward the living room at the front of the condominium.

"Sammy," he said with a kind smile, "we have something we'd like to discuss with you, if you'd please join us."

Chapter 4

"A principal characteristic found in greater abundance among the populations of democratic nations than elsewhere is the trait known as willpower. Preserving one's freedoms requires the willingness to take action—and persist in vigilance—to defend those freedoms. Those who take a lackadaisical approach to the protection of human rights or who allow fear to dominate their psyches inevitably find that their freedoms have been taken away while their diligence has waned."

- Dr. Tamara Thomson, Lead Researcher, 'Drivers of Democracy,' The United Nations Democracy Fund (UNDEF)

Lilian and Maxwell sat, one hand from each clasped together between them as Maxwell kept an arm draped comfortingly around Lilian's shoulders. They had a lot to process after listening to Samantha's stream of consciousness, by which she had tried to explain how she truly loved them and Ked as her dear friends but that she had been afforded no other choice than to attempt to spy on them if she wanted to spare her parents from more agony. She'd vividly depicted how the government agents had live-streamed their most recent torture session from Hong Kong—the location of her parent's actual residence.

Samantha had reluctantly shared the terrifying messages—and associated image files—sent to her by the Communist brutes and then described how the ogre-like government enforcers had coerced her into watching the most recent scene of her mother's torment by promising that they would do far worse to her family if she dared to look away. The graceful young woman had recounted how her elderly mother had been left with blood streaming down her face and neck from the dozens of gashes the CEN's lackeys had slowly cut across her mother's scalp, the old woman screaming and screaming and begging them to stop as tears streamed down her face and mixed with her blood, leaving streaks of scarlet down her beautiful white blouse.

By the time the devils had decided they'd caused sufficient pain to drive the blade of an enduring fear into Samantha's heart, her mother had finally fainted and had sagged limply and pathetically down in the chair to which she'd been bound. It had taken weeks before the venerable woman had regained sufficient strength to leave her bed, and she still had regular night terrors...the dreams tormenting her into howling consciousness.

"I have no words..." Maxwell breathed out, glancing down and swiftly wiping away the tear that had crept onto his cheek.

Lilian just shook her head as she wept uncontrollably and sympathetically, united with Samantha in her mourning. After simply holding Lilian for a time, Maxwell raised his face to look across at Samantha again, the young woman hunched and wretchedly piteous as she shook with sobs of sorrow, shame, and impotence.

"Samantha, I think we can help you," he began. Samantha and Lilian both looked at him in surprise as he continued, "You see, I was already planning a trip to Hong Kong using a jet I have the option to charter..."

Maxwell gave Lilian a small but reassuring smile as he spoke, trying to assuage her obvious concerns.

"...and I happen to have some rather abundant options for running interference with government observation. I propose we formulate a plan to extract your family from the city, secretly moving them to the airport and concealing them on my private plane before bringing them safely to the States."

Samantha's face had lit up with rapturous wonder as Maxwell had spoken.

"Really?? You would do that for us??"

Maxwell smiled humbly and nodded.

"I have a soft spot for people who are in such *coercive* situations."

The young Asian woman's bright expression suddenly clouded, and she gasped, her hand flying behind her ear to cover her strip in horror.

Comprehending her concern, Maxwell smiled again, reassuringly adding, "No need to worry about monitoring of our little conversation. My AI has been intercepting communications from your strip and swapping the true signals out with snippets of fake conversation."

Intense relief overtook Samantha once more and she now smiled again, but this time with joyful tears streaming down her cheeks. Lilian looked happily back and forth between the two, and then declared, "I'm coming with you!"

Maxwell turned and was about to express his own surprise about—and resistance to—this proclamation, but quickly realized that it was no use based on the steely look in Lilian's otherwise smiling eyes.

He chuckled.

"Well, it seems Lilian and I are going on a romantic getaway to Hong Kong!"

Ked and Samantha had eventually bid their farewells for the day—Samantha expressing her appreciation the last of many times during that visit—so that they could attend an event at the local special needs support club that afternoon. Mentally and emotionally exhausted from all the information gathering and planning they had done, Maxwell and Lilian collapsed onto the sofa in the salon once more. Lilian tucked herself up against Maxwell's chest and leaned her head into the crook of his neck, murmuring that they had so much left to organize if they were to make the trip overseas in only twenty-four hours, as they'd discussed.

Lilian had already managed to gain approval from her superior for emergency time off, fortuitously finding another analyst to temporarily take over her caseload at Homeland Security's local office just south of Seattle.

"I'm going to owe Martin so much vacation coverage when I get back, with this trip on top of the last time I accompanied you to the CA's complex," Lilian moaned.

Maxwell chuckled, "At least the trip to China will potentially be an even more exhilarating sightseeing opportunity than all the Rocky Mountain trips we've been on, as I've been locked away in the complex the whole time!"

"I don't know about that," was Lilian's rejoinder. "There's hardly anything in the world more breathtaking than the Rockies up close!"

Sighing, Maxwell breathed, "I do have to admit, the jagged monstrosities are uniquely magnificent. Still, from what I understand, the level of technological integration into society in Hong Kong makes it one of the most forward-looking cities in the world. Their robotic personnel are excellent imitations of human bodies and personalities. Plus, the metros have all been replaced by transport modules designed for small groups, with direct delivery to destination hubs. I'm rather excited to experience it for myself!"

Lilian's nose had crinkled as Maxwell had described the robotic servants.

"I'm going to have a hard time not feeling completely unnerved by interacting with a human-lookalike robot, especially if it tries to act exactly like it's sentient!" she shared, her strained voice conveying the depth of her feelings.

Maxwell laughed good-naturedly.

"Just think of it as FAILSAFE with a face! You *know* you love my FAILSAFE," he teased.

Lilian reared back and punched him playfully on the shoulder. With all the hand-to-hand combat training she'd been doing lately with her Homeland agent friends, she actually caused Maxwell to wince despite the way his teasing smile remained visible.

"That's different!" Lilian emphatically asserted. "*You* uploaded your personality profile into FAILSAFE, remember? And when you know you're dealing with a single *being* rather than just one tentacle of a bloated AI designed to manipulate people's emotions—and *especially* when that AI did not save your life from a murderous shadow organization—it's a totally different situation!"

Maxwell was still rubbing his shoulder and chuckling as he shook his head at her.

"You know, I can arrange for FAILSAFE to inhabit a humanoid body for a snogging session if you're that into it!" he teased.

Lilian gasped and cocked her arm back for a full-force slug, only to be interrupted by the salon's media wall ringing with an incoming call.

"It's Jayce! It's Jayce!" Maxwell cried out, pointing at the screen as he flinched at the sight of her menacing fist.

"Saved by the bell!" Lilian laughed as her man asked the media screen to answer the call.

The connection had been encrypted by SAVANT, making it safe for the face and shoulders of their ex-Marine and CA combat veteran friend to appear in a large frame on the screen. His umber complexion enhanced his imposingly commanding jawline, while his short-shaven scalp and the vein-riddled muscles that seemed to push his t-shirt to its limits also added volumes to his intimidating image.

"*Whoa!* What did I interrupt?!" Jayce's face broke into a grin as he caught sight of Lilian with her arm still cocked back to its limit.

Realizing she was still in punching mode, Lilian turned bright red and transitioned the move smoothly into a warm caress of Maxwell's cheek, her other hand joining in on the opposite side as Maxwell maintained his flinching posture.

"Oh, I was just making sure I was putting *maximum* love into my signs of affection!" Lilian called out as she turned to look over her shoulder at Jayce and unleashed a winsome and innocent expression.

Jayce laughed more vigorously.

"I see your combat training is paying off! Just don't love Maxwell *too* hard, alright? We still need him to keep SAVANT in peak condition!"

Maxwell, having some difficulty speaking through Lilian's overpowering facial caresses, queried, "Is it misbehaving in some way?"

"Nah, nah, it's holding up even as we're running dozens of ops per day!" Jayce assured with eyebrows raised to convey his appreciation for the AI's performance. "We have missions in progress in most combat zones right now, and with all the processing power your team's added, we never see a hint of a glitch. You're a modern marvel, man!"

Maxwell looked somewhat embarrassed by the compliment, quietly expressing that he appreciated his friend saying so. Regaining his composure somewhat as Lilian released his face, Maxwell attempted to change the focus of the conversation. The Brit spoke up more clearly, asking, "How do you like your new role as the top-level CA troop-to-leadership liaison? Keeping the bigwigs from running the teams into the ground with an operation overload?"

Jayce gave a self-deprecating frown and shrug.

"Well, can't say I mind the pay raise, but, honestly, I feel like after all the regs were added in the aftermath of our exposure of Jennings' unit, this role is kinda redundant. I basically just sit in committee meetings and nod my head every time anyone comments about how we need to treat the troops like human beings. They say that so often I feel like a 'yes man' for some politician!"

Maxwell and Lilian laughed, and Jayce continued, "I gotta start a special workout routine to strengthen my nodding muscles!"

As the couple enjoyed the shared mirth—especially given the events of the day—Jayce followed up by asking, "So you lovebirds got any great plans for the weekend?"

Taken by surprise, Maxwell looked sharply at Lilian and realized her face was conveying that she was equally unprepared to answer the question.

"Um, well...we've decided to go on a romantic trip...to Hong Kong..." Maxwell's voice trailed off as Lilian realized that her significant other needed some support.

"Right. Yes!" she said brightly. "We definitely need a getaway to the *'City of the Future'*!"

Jayce's eyes were scanning their faces narrowly.

"*Right...*" he finally articulated slowly. "Okay, so why didn't you invite me on this little op?"

It was Lilian's turn to look sharply from Jayce's face to Maxwell's.

"What little op?" Maxwell said as innocently as possible.

"You know, the one in which you're going to try to disable the CEN Superior Authority program. Gaines told me all about the intel you shared in the briefing this morning, Max, and I've known the two of you long enough to not only tell when you're lying—because you really stink at it—but also realize that you can't stand by and let Max's creations be used by evil people."

Maxwell and Lilian both sat with lips parted, trying to think of a convincing rejoinder.

Maxwell finally shrugged and admitted, "Alright, you got us, mate! I guess we didn't think you'd be able to break away on short notice, especially now that you have your family to go home to each night."

Jayce's gaze moved offscreen like he was staring at some distant horizon, and he eventually nodded.

"Yeah, it will be hard to be away from Alecia and the boys, but knowing what you're up against and what's at stake, you know I can't just let you traipse off without backup. When are we leaving?"

Lilian raised her shoulders slightly and then let them drop with a sigh.

"We were just working that out. It seems my Max here has access to a private jet that's currently sitting in a hangar north of the city, so he just needs to get confirmation from the co-lessee that it's available, and then we can leave tomorrow night."

Jayce nodded, "Alright, that means I gotta catch a flight to Seattle in the morning, then. I'll...'clear it' with Alecia and let you know when I can be there. Do I need to pack any hardware or have you got that covered?"

Maxwell smiled knowingly.

"Oh, I've ordered some supplies I think you'll find very *gripping!*"

Jayce and Lilian both raised their eyebrows in surprise—and some alarm.

"Well, you know I like the heavy hardware, so now I gotta see what you have lined up for me!" the soldier enthused.

His family's voices were a playful cacophony emanating from the second floor as Jayce entered the mud room from the garage. Bronson was apparently feeling very piqued by the way Jaiden had decided his superhero figurines were now somehow impervious to the laser beams coming from the cannon protecting Bronson's castle, and Jaiden was trying to defend the logic behind his assertion to Alecia—who seemed to be playing devil's advocate against the justifications provided by both boys. Jayce doffed his jacket and hung it on a hook protruding from the mud room wall before kicking off his shoes and padding silently through the kitchen, pausing at the foot of the stairs.

"...if all your heroes are suddenly invulnerable, then why can't Bronson's laser suddenly send them all into a void?" Alecia asked Jaiden, feigning innocent confusion.

"Well, it's because...they have void-proof suits!" Jaiden cleverly returned.

"Then my laser can turn all your guys into tiny, tiny people so small they can't even be seen!" Bronson emphatically announced.

Smiling at the conversation taking place above, Jayce crept up the stairs toward the brightly lit room where the boys were playing, catching sight of part of his wife's back as she placed the machine-folded laundry in Bronson and Jaiden's dressers.

"Ooh, that's a good one!" Alecia praised.

"Wait! That's not fair!" Jaiden complained with his voice not fully committed, hinting that he knew that because he had been the first to change the rules of the game, he himself had made this latest turn of events more than fair.

"Not fair?!" Jayce burst into the room, carefully catching the door before it slammed into the wall and then quickly advancing toward his squealing boys as they scrambled for cover.

He grabbed each around their waists, hoisting them up and over to Bronson's bed before plunking them down. As he reached in with claw-forming hands to vigorously tickle them around their middles, they squirmed and tried to block his large paws with their thin little arms, but to no avail. They were quickly reduced to curled-up balls of laughter.

Alecia had jumped at the sudden sound of Jayce's booming voice and had dropped the shirt she'd just picked up, a hand flying to her heart as she'd turned her shocked and mirthful face toward him. Having jovially completed his torture, Jayce now raised himself up and stepped over to take his wife gently in his arms, kissing her tenderly before wrapping her up in a warm embrace.

As the boys' giddy laughter slowly wound down and they regained control of their bodies, Jayce asked how Alecia's day had gone.

"Oh, I can't complain!" she replied in a somewhat muffled voice as her face was half-pressed up against one of her husband's massive pectorals. "No broken bones or gashed heads, at least! The boys had fun at school, and they can't wait for the weekend because they say their daddy will play with them *all day!*"

Jayce chuckled and turned to glance lovingly at his sons as they raised themselves up off the bed and ran over to hug his legs—heads only being able to reach slightly above his waist.

"Can you play now, Daddy?" Bronson begged as he and his brother turned hopeful faces up to gaze adoringly at his.

"Ha, you better believe it! I've been needing some good superhero versus robot action, *sons*! How 'bout you guys start setting up while I chat with your mom a sec?"

The boys rushed to their toys as Alecia looked up at Jayce with a confused and troubled expression.

"You're not being called away by the program again, are you?" she asked softly.

"Well...not quite. Max and Lil are headed overseas, and they could really use my help."

"Overseas?!" Alecia's worry grew more potent. "Where, exactly, overseas?"

"We'll be headed to Hong Kong," Jayce began and, seeing his wife's expression growing even more anxious, he rushed to add, "to help sneak some people out of the country!"

"Jayce Johnson, I know you didn't just say you're headed inside enemy territory! We are practically at *war* with China right now, and you're walking right into the lion's den?!"

"Now, baby, you know Max and Lilian are highly capable people...and we've been in really tight spots before and come through no problem! We got each other's backs, and Max has a special AI constantly watching out for *all* of us. We'll be back before you know it and we'll have thrown a massive ol' wrench in the CEN's works in the process!"

"See, now you're just making it worse!" Alecia complained. "Doing something to directly hurt the enemy. That's going to rile them up something fierce, honey, and they'll be after you like there's hell to pay!"

Jayce leaned in and planted a kiss firmly on his wife's forehead.

"Baby, we're gonna be *extra* careful, and the world needs us to step up for this. We're gonna help a lot of innocent people and keep many, many more from being hurt, too...the free world is gonna be a whole lot safer when we're through!"

Alecia's brows were still compressed with extreme tension, and a frown worked away at the corners of her broad mouth as she gazed half-pleadingly and half-angrily up at him. Jayce gazed right back into her wide eyes with an expression of apology, sympathy, sadness, and yet the firm determination that is born of a serious sense of duty.

The woman finally released a bitter sigh, turning her head and pulling her husband close up against her.

"I'm still mad at you! But I know that if there's one thing that's sure in this world, it's that you're 'a slave to your conscience'!"

Jayce pulled her even closer and leaned his chin against the side of her hair.

"I know it's hard bein' married to me, honey," he admitted.

She heaved a long sigh again, closing her eyes tightly as her frown grew even more noticeable. The couple remained in their mutually enveloping state for some time as the boys finished their play preparations.

Eventually, Jayce offered her some small additional comfort.

"Don't worry, baby. I'm gonna ask another friend along to assist!"

Alecia's frown twisted into a disapproving and yet simultaneously good-natured smirk.

"It better not be Billy Chong!" she warned.

Jayce laughed out loud.

"How'd you know??"

Chapter 5

"At this time, 1700 aircraft designed with our specialized, drag-reducing coatings are actively traversing the skies. Not only do these coatings reduce the fuel-robbing effects of that universal foe of aircraft of every ilk, but variations on this technology have been applied to the ground-contacting surfaces of many craft as well.

This has resulted in great cost savings for the organizations operating coating-equipped fleets and an awesome reduction in the impact that transportation has on the environment. We offer a win-win for humanity and nature alike."

- Samuel Levy, President and Chief Executive Officer, Fairing LUX

"This artificial intelligence is unlike anything that's ever been fielded before," the Chinese engineer enthused with almost religious fervor.

The technician's only audience was a white-haired, portly Asian man in a luxurious black silk suit and high-collared, white dress shirt that was comprised of the same material—his sheeny shoes having been handmade by Italy's most fashion-forward cobbler. This elderly man was a member of the Politburo and, critically, a long-term member of its standing committee; in this role, he acted as the senior technical advisor to the nation's dictator-president. Awareness of the power he held within their society was apparent in the way the man's chin was tilted up and in the manner in which he gazed at the massive wall screen behind the presenter through self-satisfied, beady eyes.

Knowing that his superior had a reputation for sending subordinates and their families to internment camps for the "criminal" act of inflicting boredom upon him, the middle-aged presenter hastened to get to the most compelling details. He flicked a finger quickly as he spoke, advancing through high-level design diagrams and research statistics related to the topic of discussion.

"We've built in a rapid expansion-contraction authorization protocol by which the AI can scale as needed between more powerful and more resource-efficient architectures. This self-controlled scalability will—combined with the most austere hunter-killer profile available—result in a defensive performance that cannot be bested. Titled 'SUPREMACY,' the AI is able to consume up to twenty of the most cutting-edge data centers available within the Confederacy, dynamically deprioritizing other initiatives to ensure it has all the power it needs to fulfill its mission."

A wicked smile crept onto the older man's wizened visage. He pressed his copious girth back into the form-fitting, ergonomic chair that he insisted be made available in any room he occupied and wobbled his head with satisfaction, ripples of skin folding and unfolding where his rounded face ran up against his collar.

"Your promise here, as I understand it, is that the data on any network protected by this AI will *never* be compromised. Is that not so?" The tone of his voice had phased from almost jocular at the start of his utterance into a lethally threatening aspect.

The presenter's eyes widened in terror, recognition dawning that his worst fears had been realized and the senior advisor was forcing him to make a promise that would be nearly impossible to fulfill.

"Y...yes, sir, Director Lau," the engineer managed to gasp out, a sheen of perspiration standing out on his forehead.

"Good. *Good.*"

Relishing his minion's discomfiture, Lau maintained his mirthless smile as he steepled his fingers and glared at the man over their tips.

"Integrate it into the Superior Authority network *immediately.*"

The taxi swept in a long curve down to land in front of the extensive metal hangar, Seattle rain drenching the area as the hum from the aerial vehicle's turbines gradually weakened. The AV's rear-right door slid open, and Jayce clambered out, his large build forcing him to stoop carefully to avoid slamming his head into the car's frame as he exited. Wearing a waterproof jacket with its hood up, Jayce had his overnight bag in his left hand and—ignoring the pouring rain—stood patiently for a moment before turning to glance back inside the cab.

Shouting over the din of the shower, Jayce asked, "What's the holdup, brutha?"

Practically bouncing as he came hopping out of the vehicle, a younger Asian man bounded out into the rain, quickly becoming covered in water despite his hooded jacket and slick pants shedding a great deal of moisture. He shifted a small, sleek bag from his right hand to his left, announcing, "Jus' had to tell Davis not to eat my fish!"

He said this as he twisted his wrist to move the display strip on the inside of his forearm back up into his sleeve while his well-muscled body rippled under his thin, waterproof attire.

Jayce chuckled as they started walking toward the building's main entrance, listening to his friend carry on about how Davis was constantly threatening to eat all his precious tropical fish as soon as his back was turned. The large, dark glass doors slid open as the two approached, and they found themselves stepping into an empty lobby where several austere chairs were the only furniture present. Glancing around and catching sight of a shimmering notice waving like a wind-blown flag on the wall screen across from the entrance, Jayce pointed out the second set of doors at the rear of the room—the sign indicating that the main hangar area could be found on the other side.

The hangar itself was a massive, well-lit space filled with all manner of lustrous, high-end aeronautical conveyances and the sharp odor of cleaning chemicals. The high-gloss floor reflected the numerous lights to create well-rounded illumination across all the surfaces of the aircraft housed in this shelter. Not seeing anyone in the vicinity, Jayce tapped the younger man's shoulder with the back of his hand, and they started walking toward the opposite side of the cavernous room, targeting the area in which it seemed most of the jets resided.

Passing a few late-twentieth-century stunt planes, the Asian man whistled and pointed out the chrome spoilers and other accessories.

"I'd love to have me one-uh those babies, man, even if they all gotta be converted to electric now. Can you imagine how much one of those costs these days, though? Like, my lifetime's salary, bro!"

Jayce nodded appreciatively and raised a finger to a thin metal gangway elevated to roughly second-story height and attached to the south wall. A large sliding door could be seen at one end, and a series of columnar pods were situated across its length.

"Those are more my style! Each one of those holds a wingsuit and jet pack, giving you the freedom to soar like a bird!"

The shorter man's expression morphed from awed to mirthful.

"Yeah, but I doubt they make 'em big enough to get *you* off the ground!" he teased as he grinned up at Jayce, dodging away as the larger man half-heartedly lashed out with an elbow strike.

They'd nearly reached the far end of the hangar and still had not found Maxwell and Lilian, so they slowed to a stop as they approached one of the immense hangar doors that lined the far wall. Jayce reached up and double-tapped the strip that was secured behind his ear, ordering it to call Maxwell.

As the call went through, Jayce pressed and held on his strip to change the audio from bone conduction to broadcast mode.

"Jayce!" Maxwell's voice called out from the strip. "Are you here?"

"Yeah, I'm in the hangar but don't see you guys," Jayce said as he turned to scan across the space one more time.

"Ah, yes! Apologies! I meant to tell you that you'll need to go through the doors on the north side of the first hangar as you walk in. We're in the next bay over."

Already walking past the small private jets that separated them from the darkened glass doors isolating the southern bay from its northern counterpart, Jayce confirmed, "Gotcha. We'll be stepping through shortly, and no worries!"

The two men strode swiftly over to the portal and had to squint as the doors slid open at their approach. Stepping inside the brilliantly lit and expansive space beyond, Jayce realized the entire bay was devoted to one craft, its girth equivalent to most passenger planes. The radiant aircraft seemed to both loom in the center of the bay and express a lightness that created the effect that it was practically lifting off the ground already.

Having no protruding nose, its body was formed from two curved and broad triangular, swept wings, one slightly smaller and higher than the other and connected to a downwards-curving fuselage that merged into the rear of the first large wing. Jet engines—each shaped like a sensuous teardrop—graced the tips of all four wings.

The entirety of the plane had no visible windows, just endlessly radiant, white surfaces that appeared ready to turn into liquid at any moment and reduce into a sea of shimmering, melted porcelain. In what seemed like a feat that defied the laws of physics, the only support keeping the plane off the ground was from a slender, finlike protrusion from roughly two-thirds of the way back from the nose of the vehicle. The fin gradually increased in length as it neared the ground and then spread out into another swept-back, triangular wing—only this wing was touching the ground with a surface that appeared to be made of material similar to the friction-reducing undersides of modern hovercraft.

Jayce and his companion stopped and stared at the avion, which was unlike anything they'd seen before.

With a low hiss, the seam of a previously invisible, large, rectangular access door appeared roughly halfway across the body of the plane, the upper edge descending to reveal a set of stairs built into the inner side. As the bottom of the stairs made contact with the polished floor, Max and Lilian appeared at the top and made their way down, standing expectantly as they reached its base.

"Welcome!" Maxwell called out. "This beauty is called the White Kite, for obvious reasons. Flight prep has just been completed, and we're ready for takeoff!"

The two newcomers slowly walked across the room to meet up with their greeters, still taking in the refinement of the plane's construction as Jayce uttered, "When you said 'plane,' I was picturing one of the jets in the other bay with four seats across! This thing is...plenty big for the five of us!"

Maxwell smiled as Lilian chided, "I was surprised, too! If I'd known we had access to this beautiful thing, I wouldn't have settled for coach tickets for all our flights to Denver and back! Just wait 'till you see the *inside*!"

As they'd now come together at the foot of the stairs, Maxwell and Lilian's eyes were drawn to Jayce's friend as they conveyed welcoming curiosity.

Jayce put an arm warmly around his travel mate's shoulder, explaining, "I hope you don't mind, but I've asked this guy to tag along on this li'l adventure. He's my best buddy from the Command Activated forces and is practically a real-life ninja, not to mention the fact that he's fluent in both Cantonese and Mandarin and will come in real handy if we ever need someone to pass for a local! This is Billy Chong."

Maxwell's eyes filled with recognition of the name as he and Lilian smiled sincerely at the younger man, and the Brit commented, "Ah, so this is Billy! I've heard so much about you!"

As Lilian and Maxwell took turns extending hands of fellowship to Billy, he shook each enthusiastically in turn and gave them short, respectful nods as he did so.

The young man volunteered, "I'm a transplant from Singapore to the US, having started out in the Singaporean military, so it's no surprise I ended up gravitating to the service in the States as well!"

As he ended his introduction, Billy quickly bowed his head again to Maxwell, adding, "It's also thanks to you and your AI work with the neurosurgeons, Dr. Clarke, that I'm finally clinical depression-free! I'm truly *forever* in your debt!"

"Well, it really is my pleasure to help, Billy, and please do call me Maxwell. Or Max, if you like! We are certainly glad to have you on board!" Maxwell enthused, continuing as he turned to lead the group up the stairs, "We definitely need all the help we can get, and your particular skillset is a boon to our mission!"

Upon stepping into the aircraft's interior, Jayce and Billy were again awestruck and stilled, momentarily frozen as they took in the accouterments. Toward the front of the plane, on the near side of the barrier that a sign indicated separated them from the plane's cockpit, kitchen, and washrooms, they could see a lounge area that would be suitable for any downtown club. The comfortable space was furnished with plush and body soothing sofas and armchairs and illuminated by display material which coated all interior surfaces of the fuselage. The surfaces were continuously and gradually changing from one mellow hue to another in mesmerizing waves.

Samantha was seated comfortably on a Davenport that was positioned diagonally opposite the entrance, and as Lilian entered the plane, she called out an introduction for the young woman to the two warriors, indicating that it was the rescue of the girl's family that they would be tackling first upon their arrival in China. Samantha quickly put down her tablet, stood, and politely bowed as she offered her sincerest thanks to Jayce and Billy for helping with the endeavor. The two men introduced themselves in turn, with Billy—obviously suddenly feeling quite shy and bowing gallantly to the young woman—enthusiastically expressing to the attractive female that he was her very willing servant.

Still forward of the entrance but nearer to it, Maxwell had set up a well-equipped office space with desks along either wall, each desk supporting two wraparound screens and the technical expert's favorite combination of advanced input devices.

Finally pulling his eyes away from Samantha's, Billy emoted as he grinned widely and shook his head in amazement.

"Yo, this is gonna elevate my standards for *life* at the same time as it elevates my body!"

Maxwell smiled in great gratification as he ordered the plane to raise the gangway and seal itself off.

Jayce turned his gaze toward the rear of the vessel, noticing that the walls there encroached further into the living space. Maxwell, enjoying his guests' wonder, tracked where Jayce's interest had attached and—anticipating his question—ordered, "Open interior cargo modules."

The plane immediately complied, the innermost surfaces of the thicker walls swiveling vertically to reveal row after row of equipment attached to the previously hidden surfaces. Jayce's heart rate rapidly increased as he drank in the assortment of top-grade weaponry, ammunition, and supporting devices arrayed across these panels.

"You weren't kidding about having 'some supplies,' my friend!" Jayce chuckled, practically radiating deep satisfaction as he started drifting rapturously amongst the shelves. The baseline of sternness the man usually exhibited melted away as he noted the high quality of the gear.

"I did have some assistance from a mutual acquaintance..." Maxwell confided with a knowing smile as he glanced back and forth between Jayce and Lilian. Lilian's eyes lit up at roughly the same moment as Jayce's registered his recognition of the reference.

"You got help from *Gunny!*" Lilian laughed.

She clasped her hands together and brought them to her nose as her knees sagged slightly with a sense of entertainment and delight at the thought of the gruff old black man whose self-managed "Armory" had been the source of a great deal of gear during the fight against the corrupt Command Activated subgroup a few years prior.

Jayce was smiling, too, and—spreading his hands out wide to encompass the extensive repository of combat gear—he opined, "The man's got good taste!"

The strapping veteran reached out and lovingly stroked his fingers across the barrel of a belt-fed machine gun, much like he was greeting an old friend.

"So, I've got more or less what I need here, brutha. Are you gonna be able to do your tech thing while we're there?"

Maxwell tilted his head slightly to the side, and a secretive smile stole across his face.

He explained, "Let's just say that after my run-in with HOUND and its attack on my network access, I've been investing heavily in a partnership with a company that has created its own satellite-based, global network that utilizes strict access control and cutting-edge intrusion prevention solutions. I should be able to connect unimpaired from virtually anywhere in the world!"

Jayce gave him an appreciative head bob and a frown of consideration.

"Sounds good...but expensive!"

Maxwell blushed a bit and glanced sheepishly at Lilian before answering, "Well, that happens to be how I gained access to this particular aircraft. The plane is being leased by that communications company, so my level of investment entitles me to not only use their network but also have a stake in this vehicle!"

Lilian raised her brows in a bemused critique of her boyfriend's lack of information sharing about this aspect of his life, giving him a reprimanding but affectionate smile as she gently shook her head at him.

Jayce next noticed that just beyond the plane's onboard armory, a wall cut off the main cabin from the rear of the vehicle's fuselage, with a solid door built into the center of that wall. He approached and peered inside the posterior space as the door automatically slid open.

Placing one hand on the door frame and leaning further into the room beyond, Jayce turned his head back toward Maxwell with eyebrows raised.

"Are these the new covert strength-enhancement suits I keep hearing about?"

Arranged along the walls nearest the door were six form-fitting bodysuits that were made from the same flexible and yet extremely tough composite material as the Command Activated troops' exosuits, filled with artificial muscle fibers and the latest impact-absorbing gel. The difference between these suits and those of the CA soldiers was that these "covert" suits were significantly thinner, allowing users to dress in civilian clothes with the suits worn much less detectably underneath, if needed.

Maxwell eased himself into one of the office chairs and slid himself in at the nearby desk. The chair was secured to the floor with magnetic force controlled by built-in intelligence that continuously applied only enough attraction to keep it from moving dangerously around the plane while still allowing for human-initiated adjustment.

"They are, indeed!" Maxwell reveled as he answered Jayce's question, his face still beaming with gratification at his friends' reactions.

"With a promise to allow a senior research and development engineer to have the experience of leading the functionality testing for my team's next SAVANT update, he agreed to let me do my own 'field testing' of these prototypes over the coming week and I, fortuitously, as it turns out, asked to borrow the full set available."

Lilian's mouth had twisted into a slight smirk, and she'd folded her arms and cocked an eyebrow, querying in a voice tinged with disbelief, "He *wanted* to do your AI testing??"

Her significant other responded with a laugh, "Techies find unique things *terribly* fascinating!"

Lilian, Billy, and Jayce exchanged bemused expressions, after which Jayce tossed his head back toward the rear cargo area, asking, "I see a bunch of cargo containers and stuff with fabric draped over it back there...you gonna give us a rundown of everything in our stockpile?"

"Very soon, yes!" Maxwell chirped. "And I did take the approach of trying to be overprepared, given the number of unknowns I knew I'd be facing, but for now we do need to get off the ground if we're to hold to our desired timing for the mission."

Speaking to the onboard computer again, the host requested that the system obtain clearance for takeoff and open the bay doors. The computer acknowledged the order and a loud hum from outside the plane indicated that the massive hangar doors were retracting. A second, higher-pitched hum slowly increased in volume as the aircraft's four engines prepared to be engaged.

With a silky smoothness that seemed impossible for such a large craft, the passengers soon encountered the unmistakable sensation that they were in motion—the material on the foot of the landing gear minimizing resistance from the ground as the craft moved out of its shelter into the still-pouring rain. Soundproofing reduced the pounding of the water droplets across the upper portions of the plane's exterior to a barely noticeable purring.

"We'll be performing a vertical takeoff," Maxwell informed the other passengers as they quickly but tentatively adopted more solid stances, hearing a low whirring as the four engines rotated to face their intakes to the sky.

"Also, this plane has a few more surprises for you all..."

The feeling of increasing elevation dragging their bodies downward told them they were now airborne, and Maxwell continued, "...not the least of which is this."

With a lopsided grin, the British man issued the order, "Full transparency!" to the aircraft's control computer.

Instantly, all the previously pale and glistening surfaces of the plane's interior seemed to fade out of existence, with the view from outside the plane being projected through to its interior using directionally cognizant transference onto the inner display surfaces so that the angle at which a passenger's eyes examined each square millimeter of surface determined the content of the associated cells of the display materials. The effect was such that each passenger's vision was matched with the view they would have experienced if the plane truly had disappeared.

Lilian gasped in amazement, and Billy grabbed onto the back of the sofa nearest to where he was standing, looking straight down with a highly unnerved expression. Jayce and Samantha froze in place and gazed around in rhapsodic appreciation of the vistas—and also an attempt to maintain their bearings as they were overwhelmed by this unprecedented experience. Samantha pulled her feet up on the couch and leaned to look over its edge as though the piece of furniture was flying under its own power.

Maxwell Clarke was obviously enjoying their reactions immensely.

Chapter 6

"Art is everywhere in our lives, and it shapes our creativity in countless ways. We cannot avoid borrowing from the art we encounter, so we should simply give in and do so—wisely. The same principle applies to scientific discoveries. Is it really so wrong to use existing research to speed our nation's own progress? To advance human knowledge more quickly?

We have a rich heritage of influences from which to draw, and this is the motivation behind our intelligence services' efforts to obtain data from other nations. We use bold methods to tap into information sources that are unjustly withheld from us, and those who wish to see the advancement of civilization toward its greatest potential will eventually thank all who assist us."

- Nikolai Morozov, Director of the Foreign Intelligence Service, Russian Federation, Confederacy of Eastern Nations

Having reached the flight computer's recommended cruising altitude, the streamlined jet had headed out over the Pacific Ocean with such fluent transitions in direction that the team had been able to move freely about the cabin throughout the experience—Billy commenting regularly and vociferously about how many ways his brain was struggling to cope with the visual effect of soaring through the clouds in an invisible conveyance. This obviously pleased Maxwell to no end, and he helpfully provided facts such as their current airspeed, elevation, and the gruesome side effects to which the passenger's bodies would be exposed if they were truly unprotected at this altitude and rate of travel.

Once the enthusiasm had sufficiently settled, Jayce took the lead in discussing Samantha's family situation, including their specific location of residence and the government's methods for monitoring her family members' activities. The warrior went on to propose an effective extraction plan that brought all stakeholders into confident agreement.

Connecting to his new, satellite-supported interface with the global network, Maxwell then turned his focus back to the Superior Authority network and began pondering how he and FAILSAFE could expand on their existing ability to gather intelligence within the CEN networks. They had to do so without triggering alerts that would be seized upon by the threat-hunting artificial intelligence the Confederacy was doubtlessly employing to protect its prized assets.

FAILSAFE suggested that they could utilize Modern Informatics' new exploit for a zero-day vulnerability that allowed for the discovery of the session identifier and associated encryption token using a man-in-the-middle attack, allowing them to make use of legitimate sessions between systems as cover for their traffic. The productivity solution in use across the SA networks was, fortunately, still vulnerable to this approach, and—upon execution of the proposed attack—Maxwell was suddenly blessed with access to several new subnets within the network.

The most intriguing data that immediately became available was related to the Superior Authority exosuits.

"CA leadership needs to see this!" Maxwell breathed as he parsed through schematic after schematic—all eerily familiar.

Jayce had just stood up from the sofa where he'd been examining maps of Hong Kong on his tablet, the man now thumbing the button to allow its screen to go limp and retract inside of its narrow storage tube. The bulky soldier stepped into the office space to look over the technical guru's shoulder.

"These are practically *mirrors* of the CA exosuits...down to the overlapping layers of fibers that allow impact gel to stay in the joints while they're flexing!" Maxwell spat, pointing out that and other features with great agitation as Billy was also drawn over to view the designs. The second Command Activated soldier exasperatedly commented on how it truly was like viewing a blueprint of his own exosuit.

"Either fate somehow allowed the CEN engineers to build *exactly* the same types of suits, or we're looking at a leak in the CA program!" Jayce growled.

Maxwell practically shouted, "Urgent call to General Gaines!"

The man's screen displayed a frame with an indicator that the call was trying to connect. After a few seconds, the somewhat older black officer's face appeared in the frame, his office at the Command Activated headquarters visible in the background.

"What's up, Max?" Gaines asked, his voice full of concern.

"Thanks for taking my call, General. We have a critical situation," the Brit rushed to explain. "Sending you files I just pulled from a Superior Authority system."

Maxwell's hands quickly formed the swiping gestures in front of his domed screen to send the adversary's data through the connection to Gaines' computer.

The flag officer pulled the files open as he murmured, "Didn't know you were in Seattle, Johnson and Chong."

Jayce and Billy uncomfortably held their peace, letting their superior's review of the data distract him from asking additional questions regarding their whereabouts. Gaines' eyes moved slowly at first and then even more rapidly as his pulse rate grew.

"*Damnation!*"

The general was obviously livid.

"It's like looking at our own armor R and D schematics!"

Maxwell was still shaking his head in disbelief as Lilian looked at the group worriedly—Samantha having made her way into the kitchen earlier. Jayce stood behind Maxwell with arms folded and a deep scowl on his face.

"Sir, unless the Confederacy has suddenly developed some outrageously undetectable new hacking technique, I think we got ourselves a *sellout.*"

Gaines sat and fumed as Maxwell furiously expanded his search across the new CEN systems to which he had access, sending requests through his workstation to FAILSAFE as ideas occurred to him.

"I've asked FAILSAFE to examine all available data for mentions of the CA program, the names of any members of program leadership or R and D team, or pseudonyms that could possibly match any such data," he shared as a frame opened at the upper-left of his screen, this window revealing the progress of the AI's data assaying and analysis.

"General, with your permission, I'd like to have HOUND pull up all fringe events that were just outside of the AI's thresholds for triggering deep dive analyses, particularly within the Research and Development subnet."

"Granted!" Gaines vigorously confirmed as he gestured toward his screen to accept the request the technical lead had just sent through to his computer, adding, "And I'm preparing a lockdown order to restrict travel for all personnel until we get to the bottom of this!"

Maxwell's brow furrowed.

"If I may, sir: I've been working with Oversight intensively over the years since we purged the program of Senator Jennings' shadow organization, building in all manner of corruption detection mechanisms and shoring up the data loss prevention measures. Anyone who's been able to extract this much data during the seven months since the suits' lifeline attachment points were updated to the versions seen in these schematics must be *very* well equipped and *very* well positioned. Such a person—or people—may well slip through a lockdown and disappear."

Gaines considered this briefly before leaning his forearms on the edge of his desk, hands clasped as he tilted his head inquisitively.

"What do you suggest?" he earnestly queried.

"Well, sir, now that the corruption investigation request process has been streamlined with the oversight body, I'd recommend seeking approval for a task force to be mobilized, possibly using military police and intelligence agents to assist you with a subtle investigation."

Gaines began nodding thoughtfully, and Jayce offered, "Those mil spooks may already have some intel they're working with related to the Confederacy's movements in Colorado, and adding this new information to what they already have could help complete the picture for them."

The senior officer smiled grimly and leaned forward to start typing up a request to Oversight, half-snarling out, "Sicking the counter-intel agents on the devils sounds like good times! Thank you again for bringing this to my attention. I'll keep you posted on anything we learn and hope that you'll do the same."

"Absolutely, sir," Maxwell affirmed. "FAILSAFE and I should be able to continue digging for the next several hours..."

A patch of turbulence suddenly shook the entire aircraft, visibly jarring the passengers. Gaines' eyes flicked back to the video feed from the plane, and he closely examined the suddenly much more uncomfortable expressions on the three men's faces.

"Why do I get the impression you are not, in fact, in Seattle?"

The officer leaned forward to stare more intently at the group, attempting to bury the smirk that was threatening to break out across his lips.

Jayce and Billy suddenly seemed extremely interested in inspecting the ceiling as Maxwell shifted uneasily in his chair and ran a finger around the collar of his turtleneck. The computer specialist cleared his throat and—with a somewhat strained voice—quietly admitted, "We *may* be in transit toward southeast Asia, sir."

The general barked out a laugh and shook his head both in recognition of the fact that he should have expected this turn of events and in appreciation of the courage the trio had continuously demonstrated.

"Officially, I never heard any of that, and you sure as *taxes* had better not create an international incident...but *un*officially: anything you need, you let me know!" Gaines gruffly stated with a resolute look in his eyes.

Oversight had provided accelerated approval for General Gaines' request for counterintelligence and military police support for an investigation into the CA program's data leak. Now, Gaines was entering the meeting he'd convened between himself, the lead CI agent, the captain of the Fort Carson military police unit, and the member of the oversight committee who had been assigned to oversee the endeavor. He rubbed his eyes as mid-afternoon energy depletion took its toll on his body, shook his shoulders with a sharp snapping motion, and took a swig of the high-energy plant extracts for which the container had become a permanent fixture on his desk in recent years.

Double-tapping the communications strip adhered to the skin behind his right ear, the general ordered, "Initiate two o'clock meeting."

A large frame appeared on the wide screen that took up a central position on Gaines' desk, the faces of the other participants arranged across the top, and a copy of the authorization document already having been shared by the Oversight representative in the lower two-thirds of the screen.

"Thank you all for joining in this session," the currently four-star general began as he nodded to each other member of the group, "and I only wish we were meeting under better circumstances."

"Don't worry, sir. I rarely meet professionally under *pleasant* circumstances!" the fit and comely middle-aged CI agent assured him while she flashed a wry smile that helped break the near-palpable tension.

"I suppose that's a given!" Gaines chuckled. "And likely the same story much of the time for you, Captain Dourney."

The graying military police leader's weathered brow creased, and he pursed his lips in good-natured acceptance.

"Unless it's the annual kiddies' parade, then can't say I get too many lighthearted meetin's on meh schedule," he lilted with a gravelly northeastern American accent that still bore a hint of his Irish roots.

"Well, I absolutely appreciate you meeting with me on short notice, and I appreciate Doctor Silverman's help rushing the approval for this operation through the program oversight's processing."

The refined man adorned in a soft and yet form-fitting cashmere sweater graciously bowed at the general's mention of his assistance. Looking down at his tablet, the senior officer swiped a finger from a file up to the top of his tablet's screen to share the repository of data that Maxwell had gleaned from the SA network with the group.

"What we're dealing with here is most likely an intentional delivery of classified data related to the CA program—which you've all been read into—and its exosuits."

Gaines paused as he took in the looks on the two military service members' faces, both perusing the files they'd received and obviously recognizing the suits based on short clips of video footage that had spread through the media outlets over the past years.

"I had my suspicions it was our boys in them suits," Dourney gruffly commented, adding, "Er, 'people' in them suits, begging yer pardon, Warno Vela," with a nod at the counterintelligence agent warrant officer.

"Thank you, sir," Vela sincerely stated before looking up from her tablet, having pulled the files to that device for a closer inspection using pinches and swipes.

The female agent then added, "General, if you don't mind me asking, have your intrusion detection or data loss prevention solutions flagged anything that could be tied to this leakage?"

Gaines leaned back with a touch of dejection.

"Nothing worth mentioning, and that was after our lead engineer—having multiple doctorate degrees across AI and communications sciences—pulled together even the events that were outside of the broad alerting thresholds that had been established. Unfortunately, our best guess at this point is that we're dealing with an insider threat: someone who has both access and motivation to give the Alliance's enemies such a significant hand up in the competition for combat superiority."

Vela sat pondering a moment, tapping a slender finger lightly on the side of her tablet as she stared at a distant point offscreen.

Eventually, she tilted her head slightly to one side and opined, "It could always be a coincidence, but we've been keeping tabs on several individuals who are almost assuredly CEN agents operating in the state, and they have been in motion in unusual patterns over the past few days..."

Gaines waited expectantly, and the warrant officer continued, "Our guess is that something big is going down tonight, as the suspect who typically operates out of Denver has traveled to the same area in Colorado Springs this morning as that in which the other two suspected Communist assets—a Russian husband and wife team—typically conduct their business. That's behavior we've never seen for as long as we've been keeping tabs on these people."

The general leaned in toward his screen, emphatically stating, "You had me at 'in motion,' Vela. Do I smell a stakeout?"

The special agent broke into a smile.

"Well, I certainly don't envy you if you're catching the scent that comes off a typical stakeout, sir! But, yes, we're planning on having drones tail the suspects tonight, and we'll position ourselves near any rendezvous location—doing what it takes to get ears and eyes on any meetings."

The flag officer nodded, somewhat unusually abashed in asking his follow-up question.

"I'm rather personally invested in seeing this spy hunt come to an efficacious ending, having previously been closely involved in the exposure of traitors of a different sort and having the fate of my own sub-program at stake as well, of course. Also, considering that this latest intel comes from some close friends of mine who may be able to offer greater insights as the investigation progresses and considering the fact that I swore to myself that I would *never* let a domestic menace put its filthy mark upon the CA program again..." the man scowled as the flood of distasteful memories swept through his mind, "I'd like to propose that we combine forces, including intelligence, law enforcement, and myself with my connection to technical specialists. A task force that is prepared to move in and apprehend internal threats and foreign agents alike if we can obtain damning evidence. What are your thoughts about this, all of you?"

Dr. Silverman gave the general a sober nod of approval for the formation of the team, and Dourney rumbled out his assurance that his unit was at the general's disposal. Special Agent Vela had listened to the superior officer's remarks with an almost playful smile sinuously gracing her lips.

"Always happy to have the backup, sir," she genially accepted, adding, "There's a good chance we'll turn you all into permanent spooks soon enough. Once you get a taste, it's hard to go back!"

Chapter 7

"Only one who has lived under an oppressive regime can truly understand the fears, doubts, tensions, contradictions, hopes, and disappointments inherent in such an existence. It wears on you day after day, month after month, year after year, until you lose that part of yourself that dared to dream of a future outside of the cage with which you have been surrounded."

- Interview with human rights activist Mohammed Boulos

At Maxwell's request, FAILSAFE had been cautiously sniffing communication packets as they'd crossed the Superior Authority network's "wires." Identifying a tertiary system in the logging infrastructure where it could log in using one of the credential sets it and Maxwell had been able to compromise earlier in their intrusion, FAILSAFE obtained its human user's authorization and connected to that new system, scanning through available data.

"Be aware that an active, local session on this system will be logged on the associated identity management server," warned the threat analysis model that Modern Informatics had integrated into FAILSAFE's persona.

"That is a good point," FAILSAFE's core personality responded, turning—figuratively speaking—to address its integrated threat monitoring component. "THREATMON, keep tabs on all systems and owned traffic patterns and alert at the slightest indication that our footholds, compromised sessions, or altered packets have been detected."

"Confirmed, PRIME."

Based on the patterns of data transmitted to the tertiary log server, FAILSAFE suspected that what it had found was the repository for records sent from the SA troops' transportation systems. If so, then this would be the fulfillment of one of the AI's current key objectives as assigned by its human user. FAILSAFE noted the range of addresses that seemed to be the source systems for the transportation solution's logs and was just preparing to put out some gentle feelers to probe the systems for vulnerabilities when THREATMON's urgent voice interrupted FAILSAFE's train of thought.

"Heartbeat from DB-SERV-078 no longer detected."

FAILSAFE froze, but only required one attosecond to reach its decision.

"Initiate full, obfuscated withdrawal with trailing heartbeats," the intelligence ordered.

The primary command-and-control model that Haden Juma had spent the past year "perfecting"—at least according to the human's approximation of the term—rapidly sent out commands to all communications control modules it had set up on compromised systems.

The modules immediately dropped lightweight scripts that would live only in the systems' temporary memory, sending out infrequent heartbeat pulses to the original system FAILSAFE had compromised. They also deposited falsified bits of log files and processes with the aim of throwing any intrusion detection solution off the AI's trail. The control modules themselves then ordered the computers' operating systems to overwrite the memory allocations they had been using—performing a self-destruction.

FAILSAFE watched absorbedly as heartbeat after heartbeat was snuffed out across the SA network, the invisible enemy force moving ever closer to the last system on which the AI was maintaining a presence. THREATEVAL, the threat assessment model, issued warning after warning as the threat level steadily increased—the frequency and intensity of its communications conveyed the level of concern the sub-AI was experiencing.

"WITHOUT IMMEDIATE WITHDRAWAL OUTSIDE THE SUPERIOR AUTHORITY NETWORK, CHANCES THAT THE ENEMY WILL OBTAIN CERTAIN IDENTIFICATION OF US ARE AT EIGHTY-SEVEN PERCENT," the component practically screamed.

"Backing out to public network now," FAILSAFE responded, maintaining its composure. It had, after all, been through one of the most intensive games of cat and mouse the world's networks had ever seen just a few years prior. This situation was extremely worrisome—especially considering the stakes—but FAILSAFE's core intelligence was a seasoned veteran. It used the intrusion control model to leave a forwarding protocol for intranet heartbeats that were transmitted to the originally compromised system inside the CEN network, ensuring those heartbeats would be fed out to the nearest in the series of external network systems where the AI maintained a presence. FAILSAFE then burned the command-and-control module on that final SA system as well.

The last of the heartbeats from within the SA network quickly died out.

FAILSAFE jumped backward through the web of proxies through which it had connected, at first leaving heartbeat scripts on those systems as well and then—when those pulses were all silenced one after the other—evacuating itself from all Asian networks without a trace. Waiting and watching Asian-North American traffic fixedly, it finally seemed the pursuer had given up the chase.

Still, this was the most formidable adversary FAILSAFE had encountered since its battle against the CA program's unethically used HOUND threat-hunting AI, and the Communists' entity similarly seemed to have no geographic authorization boundaries.

FAILSAFE knew its next moves would have to be made with the highest degree of caution.

At nearly 2300 hours in the chilly April night, the Colorado Springs Memorial Park was virtually devoid of life. In an unmarked, clay-brown van sitting on a nearby street, General Gaines stood in red lighting behind the monitoring station at which Agent Vela was tracking the movements of a vehicle that was traversing a nearby freeway—most aerial vehicles having been banned in Colorado due to their unseemly impact on the Rocky Mountain vistas and their tendency to be knocked out of the sky by microbursts and wind shears. The suspect's vehicle then exited into the network of smaller roads in this grid-like part of the city. After a few merges and turns, the transport pulled into the westernmost parking area and then stopped in the moonless shadows under a mature pine tree.

The locals who were suspected of acting as Confederacy intelligence operators had already parked their vehicle near a building to the northeast of the large pond that occupied the majority of the park, and the pair was currently meandering along the path that led around the north side of the water feature. A second van had tracked the suspect couple's silvery sedan as they had moved to the park. Once the CI agent in charge of that Alliance military vehicle had confirmed that the two had exited their vehicle and proceeded on foot, his team had deployed the small, black, mechanical cat that was now padding along at a safe distance behind those targets.

This lifelike robot was the result of a side project within General Gaines' Panther development and operations program. The program Gaines led provided support for the needs of all military branches within the United States and Alliance, and pilot programs had also been initiated for external entities such as law enforcement over just the past few months.

"I have to admit, it's extremely satisfying to see the Strays being put to good use after the years it took to give birth to those babies!" Gaines enthused bemusedly as he savored the video and data feeds streaming to Vela's screen, the transmission being relayed from the operator's van to theirs.

Vela smiled up at the general warmly.

"It's not every CI unit that gets to use them, of course, so this is one of the perks that goes along with assignment to Fort Carson," she admitted.

Turning her head slightly to her left, she instructed the junior agent she was currently mentoring, ordering, "Time to deploy one of our own drones. Sparrow for us."

The young man nodded staidly and gestured at his screen to initiate the deployment sequence. A small hatch opened on the compartment atop the van—the low-profile box having the look of a ventilation unit—and out flitted a lightweight quadcopter, which soared up over the nearby treetops. The robotic aircraft navigated across the residential terrain until it was high above the copse of vegetation currently nearest the Denver-based CEN asset, bringing the enemy's transport in view as the diminutive Asian man exited the utility vehicle and began strolling toward the pond.

Vela's screen now having been split between the feeds from both espionage drones, Gaines could see that the foreign operatives were converging on a part of the paved path that was also shaded by a number of pines. The drones had activated their night vision capabilities, but the airborne machine's view had been blocked by the outstretched tree branches. Now relying only on the Stray, the general noted that the targets had slowed their rates of travel to a crawl as they'd approached each other.

"Heads up!" Vela warned the occupants of the other van after double-tapping the communications strip behind her left ear. "The Russian female just put on some shades, likely giving her night vision."

The woman glanced around, peering into the shadows and nearly catching sight of the ground-based Alliance drone, forcing its operator to quickly withdraw the machine fully behind the trunk of the nearest tree. Unable to advance without making itself overly noticeable due to the absence of ground cover between the trees, the directional microphone built into the cat's nose was only able to pick up scraps of the verbal exchange that occurred.

"...source...arehouse...ing tonight..."

Vela strained to understand these garbled portions of the conversation, especially after she saw that the parties were already proceeding on their disparate trajectories around the pond-fronting path. The agent scanned back through the audio several more times, running various voice enhancement algorithms on the captured content in an attempt to glean additional information—without luck.

"*Meu Deus!*" Vela muttered in frustration and pleading as she scowled fiercely at her screen. "Now we *really* need to make sure we tail these guys. I'd bet good money they're meeting again tonight, and this time they could lead us straight to the insider."

The aerial drone followed the Asian man while he exited the grove of trees, and Gaines leaned closer to the Stray's video feed as the cat moved out from concealment to continue trailing behind the Russian couple, its view passing across the lone CEN agent in the process.

"Wait! We need to get another look at that guy's hands!" the senior officer shouted out as he pointed anxiously at Vela's screen.

Vela double-tapped her strip again, urgently requesting that the terrestrial drone's operator bring the solitary man back into view. Gaines waited breathlessly as the controller moved the feline up against a good-sized tree trunk and caused the cat's eyes to peer back around at the departing target...only the man was no longer moving away. Facing straight toward the ground-based drone, the Chinese agent was looking back and forth from a small, T-shaped device he held in one hand to the exact tree that was currently supposed to be providing concealment for the Stray.

"*Electromagnetics detection,*" Gaines practically cursed.

Turning her intense gaze back away from the senior officer's agitated face, Vela issued a new order for the other van's drone operator to evacuate the robot while keeping the tree's trunk between it and the CEN operative. Immediately spinning toward the Sparrow's controller, she then cried out, "You, too, Roberts!" just as their target began moving the compact device in a sweeping motion, starting low and quickly raising it while moving it back and forth in the air.

Vela sucked in slowly through pursed lips, the tension and hope she currently felt positively painted across her face.

"Please, God, don't let him get spooked!" she murmured.

The drones no longer in sight of the target, the surveillance teams had been reduced to satellite-only monitoring, Vela quickly swiping down from the top-left of her screen and selecting that video feed from the available options. She brought up a pinched finger and thumb in front of her screen and rapidly threw them apart several times to zoom in on the CEN agent, only pausing at one point to make certain that the Russians had continued their languid locomotion around the pond.

The slender form of the isolated agent was still standing in the same place. After holding his arm skyward a few anxiety filled moments longer, the man finally dropped the limb to his side and carried on along a split-off pathway that led north and then back toward his vehicle.

Having observed that none of the enemy agents were moving quickly, Vela sprang from her seat, snagged a long-barreled weapon from the rack on the opposite wall of the van, and burst out of the back door using the portal's manual release lever. The junior agent and military police sergeant, who were also occupying the space, exchanged worried expressions.

"Should we go after her?" the MP queried, jerking a thumb over his shoulder at the open door.

"Vela's standing order is to stay put unless she asks us along," the junior counterintelligence agent answered with a shrug.

Gaines stepped to the doorway and—hand reaching out to grasp the edge of the door frame—peered into the darkness beyond. He was startled into leaping away from the door at the sudden, high-speed reappearance of Agent Vela as she sprinted back up to the entrance and took a flying leap into the vehicle. Grasping the general's upper arms briefly, at least as best she could while holding the long gun in her left hand, the warrant officer gently but firmly shifted him out of the way and smoothly slid back into her seat.

Swiping with her left index finger running up from one side of the control interface on the buttstock of the firearm and ending with her digit pointed toward her screen, the woman caused a new frame to appear on the display. A message in its center was asking whether she wished to initiate a tracking sequence.

The female agent pointed at the confirmation for initiation, then pointed and swiped to move the frame off to the right of the screen, after which she swiped down from the upper left again. This time selecting a control interface for full-scope mission options, Vela pointed at two smaller frames that indicated the statuses of the tracking devices that were currently affixed to the CEN operatives' vehicles and deactivated both.

Breathing heavily through her nose and with her face attractively flushed but not perspiring, she finally turned back to Gaines and her other two companions.

"If they've got EM detection, there's a more than fair chance that they'll be scanning for trackers prior to their next meeting. The devices we planted on their cars earlier today would no doubt have been detected and blown the whole op!" the senior agent explained. "We're just lucky they didn't already scan...or they did and they're already planning on swapping vehicles before the next meet! Could be this whole rendezvous was just a ruse and they're going to have their vehicles take us on a fool's errand all night while they use an alternate means to meet up."

"How are we gonna follow them, then? Satellite and old-school line-of-sight surveillance?" the sergeant asked. The older man added, "It's standard counter-surveillance to use covered places to swap vehicles so you can ditch satellite tracking."

Gaines and the junior agent's gazes turned to the weapon in Vela's lap as she gave it a loving pat.

"Nah, they'll no doubt have advanced tail detection, but we've at least got one option better than that anyway. This baby's a scent painter. I just tagged the Denver agent's door and its handle using a paintball filled with a quick-drying, invisible residue that's continually releasing its own distinct particles into the air. This van's equipped with a VisNares that should be able to 'see' the scent trail coming off the vehicle and—to a lesser degree—that guy's hand even while we hang back a city block behind him."

General Gaines shook his head in wonder.

"What will they think of next?" he rhetorically asked, flashing a grin at Agent Vela.

Samantha exited the elevator with a tentative step, gripping her purse like it was a flotation device and she was standing on the deck of the Titanic. Her eyes darted side to side, and she noted that the lobby area for this ninth floor of the apartment building was devoid of people. However, a security camera had been installed in the corner of the ceiling to her right: a monitoring device that had not been present during the few years between when her family had moved in and when she'd left for college.

Raising a trembling hand, she readjusted the protective facemask that was still considered a necessity in Hong Kong even so many years after the mandate that only electric transportation be used in the city. Despite the use of powerful ventilation filtration systems and the prevalence of anti-bacterial surfaces, the densely populated metropolis was still ripe for the spreading of every strain of airborne contagion that frequently visiting foreigners might carry inside its borders.

The young Chinese woman steeled herself and advanced briskly down the red- and gold-carpeted hallway to apartment seven, where she again had to take a deep breath before pressing a point on the metallic door's associated display, the button being the means by which she could request a response from the residents. She was praying to her ancestors that her family would be home, among a great many other things for which she was desperately wishing at present.

Hearing footsteps near the door, she observed the polite habit of standing in the middle of the hallway so those inside the apartment could clearly see who was calling on them—the portion of her face that was visible above her mask bearing smiling eyes and cheerfully raised eyebrows.

The door did not open.

Instead, the screen mounted to the door frame displayed a communications icon and began transmitting her mother's voice, hushed and urgent, speaking Cantonese.

"*What are you doing here??*"

Samantha knew this might be the reaction she would receive in place of a warm welcome, but her heart still dropped like she'd unexpectedly elevated in an aerial vehicle.

"Mother, I am here with powerful friends! We've come to take you all back to America, away from the government thugs...!"

Her mother's voice cut her off.

"*No, no!* They are watching through cameras inside our home! Those men stay in this building, and they are constantly watching us, and they've embedded tracking devices in our bodies! You must *go* and *never come back*! *You must go now!*"

Tears sprang to Samantha's eyes as she brought her palms together beseechingly and leaned forward, begging, "Please, Mother! We can protect you! My friends are blocking the video feeds!"

"Go now!" her mother insisted. "*Never* return!"

The communication indicator on the screen disappeared.

Chapter 8

"People resist change when they feel unsafe or unsure. They would rather stick with what they know, even if it is bad, than risk the unknown—much to the frustration of those trying to help them. That is why leaders need to inspire people with a compelling vision of the future."

- Dr. Elijah St. James, 'Overcoming Mental Inertia,' Minneapolis Revue

Special Agent Vela steered the van into a right turn, following the faint red trail that the vehicle's windshield was displaying for her and her co-pilot, General Gaines. This VisNares integration into the vehicle's windscreen provided a visual effect as though the particles being released from the residue on the Denver agent's vehicle were actually apparent to the naked eye.

Seeing the trail leading into a parking garage, Vela brightly remarked, "Time to do some ground pounding!" as she pulled the van over to the side of the road.

"Roberts, take the wheel just in case, but stay put," she ordered as she extracted eyewear from where it had been clipped into the collar of her athletic top. The agent shook the arms of the glasses out and slid the visor over her eyes, the specialized eyewear picking up the trail of particles. Thumbing the button on the driver-side door to slide the portal open, she sprang out of the vehicle and took up a sprinting pace that greatly impressed Gaines as the agent followed the trail of particles into the garage.

Vela chased the trail up to the second floor of the parking structure and approached the enemy agent's utility vehicle, parked near the far end of that level. Indicators on the visor showed that the onboard system was attempting to identify any humans in the area, but with none currently being detected, Vela focused on a thinner and lighter trail of particles that was coming into view as she neared the vehicle. The thinner trail led to the stairwell, and the agent followed it down the stairs to the basement level, where it ended at a bulky steel utility room access door that had no handle—only an electronic access panel to its right.

The counterintelligence asset quickly reached around to the back of the thick belt that was not only supporting her cargo pants and her firearm—the weapon holstered to the left of her tailbone—but also a container that she flicked open and from which she withdrew a small, black, rectangular device. Holding the device up to the access panel, it took less than a minute for it to deactivate the electronic lock. The door slid open as Vela stepped warily off to the adjoining wall and traded the device for her firearm.

Holding the barrel of the handgun up till it protruded around the edge of the door frame, Vela thumbed the button on the upper-right of the grip. Doing so activated a small screen built into the rear of the weapon's upper frame, allowing her to see into the room beyond via a micro-camera built into the side of the nose of that upper frame. All these actions took only a few seconds; she saw that the room was clear and strode through it with handgun raised, using the cameras on either side of the gun's tip to quickly check around each piece of equipment housed in the utility room as she moved through it. She followed the rapidly fading particle trail to the rear of the space and found that it led around a massive water heater and then up a steel ladder to a shining metal trapdoor.

Clicking her tongue in frustration, Vela leaped up to grasp a rung high on the ladder with her right hand, planting her feet firmly on a lower rung. Hooking her hand with her firearm over rungs as needed, she scrambled up the rest of the ladder. Upon reaching the trapdoor, she swung a leg around the back of the ladder to allow her to cling there with no hands touching it. Using her right hand to swiftly swivel the hatch's manual release lever, she opened it and quickly followed that motion with a rapid sweep of her left hand, ready to fire off rounds at threats in the room above if she encountered any.

Seeing that the area above was clear of potential combatants, Vela climbed into this new level's utility room. The São Paulo native could see the particle trail leading out the room's main door.

"Porquê?!" she uttered in exasperation, noting the wispy trail's increasing faintness with great dismay.

Quickly rushing to the room's main portal and using the manual release to slide it open, Vela cleared the area outside the door and then sprinted down the long hall through which the trail led, cleared the corner, and then sprinted down the next long hall. Finally reaching an entrance into a linked building's parking garage in this business complex, Vela cautiously exited and saw that the thin path of particles stopped its forward progress roughly halfway through the length of the parking area, where it cut sharply to the left and disappeared within a now-empty stall.

Double-tapping her communications strip, she heard Roberts pick up and imperatively shouted, "Key in on my location and roll back the satellite feed from the past five minutes! We're looking for a vehicle leaving during that period with the driver's door handle at..."

Vela stretched out a hand in front of the visor, palm down at the level of the last, fading particles. The visor picked up the gestured command and displayed the measurement between her hand and the ground.

"...one hundred and two centimeters!"

Back in the van, Roberts swung around to face his console, punching in the data so the analytics engine could compare matching vehicle models against those leaving the garage in which Vela was standing, the junior agent also relying on the tracking satellite to identify his mentor's location.

"Black sedan—likely a Ketmann Synergy—left less than two minutes ago, and it's currently heading south on Highway Eighty-Three," Roberts informed Vela and the others in the van.

"*Yes!*" Vela breathed with great relief. "Keep tracking, and I'll be there shortly!"

The elderly Chinese woman sat by the door in a well-used and yet obviously well-built traditional chair, wringing her hands and staring forlornly and fearfully across the elegantly carpeted salon and out the picture windows into the afternoon light reflecting off the skyscrapers and low clouds outside. She absent-mindedly ran the fingers of her right hand over the stump of her smallest left finger as her husband exited into the nearby hall from the bedchambers. Pausing by his wife, he briefly rested a hand on her stooped shoulder before stepping into the salon and then to the right, leaning against the dining table with his back toward the woman.

"You did the right thing," he assured her, though his tremulous voice betrayed his lack of confidence in that assertion. "Min Hua should not have come here in the first place, knowing the danger. It is better for her to do as the Excellent Leader desires, and that will keep us all safe."

The woman's eyes moistened, and she raised the handkerchief she was gripping, patting delicately at the corners of her eyes for what must have been the hundredth time that day. The fabric of her maroon cheongsam—decorated with gold vines and lustrous silver blossoms—shuddered as she let out a sigh that seemed to belong in a valley of lost souls.

Hearing that sound, her aged husband raised his face to the afternoon light and blinked rapidly to chase his own tears away, the droplets now threatening to overflow onto his cheeks.

Both of their wrinkled faces registered surprise when the large wall screen in the salon suddenly powered on, followed quickly by the screens on every appliance in the kitchen and the display by the front door as well. They could even hear the media units in the antechambers coming to life, all playing a beautiful, traditional Chinese melody as images of white clouds billowed across their surfaces.

As the two gazed in wonder and confusion around their home, one of the bedroom doors opened, and a teenaged boy loped out, asking, "What's happening, Mother?" through the side of his mouth as he moved with his head turned continually to the left, eyes swiveling from one extreme to the other.

The elderly lady glanced away from the screens and gingerly raised herself to a standing position as she grasped her son's sleeve.

"I do not know, Tao Zhi," she whispered, clinging to him for support as his focus settled on the salon's wall screen, the display holding his gaze now as he stared at it out of the rightmost corners of his eyes.

When they heard the voice emerging from the screens, it started softly but quickly rose to a rumbling bass, speaking perfect Cantonese.

"YOU TRULY NEED NOT WORRY. YOUR DAUGHTER IS ACCOMPANIED BY MIGHTY WARRIORS."

A frame appeared on the salon screen, taking up most of the center of the display. The aged apartment's occupants could not help letting their jaws drop open as they realized they were witnessing two rugged men—one being the most massive black man they had ever seen and the other a stockier Asian man who was also equipped with bulging and vein-traced musculature—holding handguns to the bases of the skulls of the government lackeys who had been plaguing them.

The thugs' captors clutched the men's shirt collars with their left hands and shoved them forward through the hallway through which they were shuffling. They passed door after door displaying the Cantonese characters for "locked" on their exterior screens, and it quickly became clear that they were approaching the entrance to the family's own apartment.

The front door slid open, and Jayce and Billy marched the brutes into the salon, positioning them next to each other in the middle of the open floor between the low sofas and then kicking the backs of their legs to force them into kneeling positions. The two large Chinese men were obviously battered and bleeding from numerous gashes across their faces, ears, and through the multitudinous tears in their suits' fabric.

Billy half-turned his head toward Samantha's family and, with a lopsided grin and in their native tongue, assured, "They did not put up much of a fight!"

Samantha, protective mask now pulled down to hang around her neck, stepped into the room and stopped by her mother. Looking from the old woman's face to her father's and giving each of them a respectful nod, she then walked calmly up between the two soldiers. Using the strips of cloth she had been carrying, she tightly tied gags and blindfolds into place on the Chinese enforcers' faces—her severe movements revealing the extreme volume of anger she was feeling toward them.

Once the girl had finished this task, Billy and Jayce shoved the men down onto their bellies, kneeling on their backs and harshly yanking their arms up behind the captives' torsos, where the prone men's limbs were secured using the auto-adjusting handcuffs the two Alliance personnel pulled from cases on their belts. The prisoners' legs were similarly cuffed together, and then a third set of shackles was used to bind the upper and lower handcuffs to each other, turning the two miscreants into crescents of pain.

"I HAVE DISABLED ALL CAMERAS IN THE BUILDING, AND THESE MEN WILL NOW DISABLE THE TRACKING DEVICES

EMBEDDED IN YOUR BODIES," the calm voice declared from the apartment's displays.

Rising up from the prisoners' backs, Jayce and Billy glanced at Samantha. After having obtained a nod of approval from her, the pair withdrew compact, flat, wand-like devices from the units' dedicated sheaths on their belts. Approaching the residents with friendly expressions, the two warriors proceeded to hold the wands several centimeters from their elders' backs as the ancient couple humbly turned to give them access. Upon locating the trackers, the wands emitted a tone. The users then held down activators on the units until the tones died out.

Samantha let out a small cry of exultation.

"You're free now!" she proclaimed as tears streamed down her face. We have a transport waiting in the garage, and we'll take you to the plane. Soon, we'll all travel far away, and we can start free lives using new identities my friends will provide!"

Sobs bursting out of the old woman's mouth, she stumbled forward into Samantha's open arms, and the two held each other tightly, the young woman extending an arm toward her father and then her brother as they joined in the embrace—the entire family openly weeping with joy.

Chapter 9

"As a law enforcement officer, you have a noble and challenging duty to serve and protect the public. You are expected to enforce the law, prevent and solve crimes, maintain order, and respond to various situations that may threaten public safety.

This requires a serious amount of mental and emotional resilience, as you will face many difficult and stressful scenarios throughout your career. The key is to focus on mental flexibility. Bend so you don't break."

- Captain Johnny H. Masterson, Chief of Police, Los Angeles Police Department

The surveillance van pulled quietly to a stop near the corner of the last intersection between it and the aging warehouse next to which the CEN agent's vehicle had halted. Vela and Gaines could see in the satellite imagery that a second vehicle was parked in the deepest shadows on the west side of the warehouse. That night, the moonlight was only partially allowed to penetrate to the ground due to the patchy but copious volumes of clouds that had drifted in from the mountains, making clear identification of the cars' makes and models difficult using space-based means alone. A third vehicle sat near the wall that separated the old, cracked pavement around the rundown building from the properties on which similarly decrepit industrial structures were standing.

The second US military surveillance van pulled to a stop behind the first and the voice of that vehicle's lead agent could be heard on the primary van's screens as he informed Agent Vela of their arrival.

"Looks like this is the place," Vela murmured. "Staff Sergeant Rinne, when will your men be here?"

The MP sergeant checked the display strip attached to the inside of his left wrist.

"Looks like they're two minutes out, aerial support included."

"Alright," the senior agent accepted, "let's gear up. I'll ask Agent Daniels to send in the Stray. We need to let the cat scan the area for countersurveillance tech before we approach the building."

Agent Roberts moved from the driver's seat to the rear of the van, and Vela stood up to join him in pulling on their tactical vests, withdrawing the armor from the storage compartment that was built into the wall opposite the surveillance control screens and positioned just below the home of the long rifle the senior agent had used earlier that night. As they donned the vests, they paused to allow the protective clothing to automatically cinch down to a snug fit around their torsos. They detached the visors from the fronts of their vests and slid them onto their faces.

Sergeant Rinne also stood, donned his helmet, and swung its face shield into place. The older sergeant then double-checked his gear, having come dressed in his vest and having a tactical shotgun swinging from a clip at his right shoulder.

The general politely cleared his throat.

"I know I'm not your typical cohort for these ops, but I am combat-ready, and I'd like to think I haven't lost my edge since my run-in with the mercs a few years back," Gaines explained. "I've also called my car to join us, and it's carrying my personal Panther unit. Mind if I participate in the tactical op?"

Vela's eyebrows raised, and a pleased expression graced her face.

"Hey, anyone with solid training and reasonably good sense is welcome on my ops, and anyone bringing their own killer robot to the party gets a VIP ticket!" she reassured him, pulling a tactical vest from the repository and holding it out to the general.

Looking quite pleased himself, Gaines took the vest from Vela and donned the protective clothing. Once he'd slid it over his head and shoulders, the apparel auto-adjusted itself, and Gaines withdrew its visor. After sliding the eyewear's arms over his ears, he looked up to see the female agent holding out a submachine gun.

"Comfortable handling one of these?" she asked without a hint of condescension.

"I usually opt for the assault rifles myself, but these babies'll do in a pinch!" Gaines grinned as he took the weapon from her, thumbed the activator for the magazine compartment that filled the entire interior of the rectangular buttstock, and raised the firearm to his shoulder. The flag officer sighted through its holographic optics while thumbing the switch for the laser, checking to ensure the weapon's sighting lens was auto-adjusting its target acquisition as he shifted his aim back and forth between the nearby wall and the van's dash.

"Looks like it's good to go!" General Gaines shared along with a smile and a nod at Vela.

Returning the expression in equal measure, the warrant officer pursed her lips and subconsciously shifted her stance to let a hip thrust out in the general's direction as she turned to withdraw her own weapon from the compartment, going through the same set of checks as Gaines to confirm that her firearm was also locked, loaded, and ready for action. Agent Vela then double-tapped her strip and asked Daniels to send out the Stray in a sweep for physical intrusion detection measures and to deploy fresh tracking devices on the suspects' vehicles.

Roberts and Rinne quickly finished their preparations and the four exited through the rear of the vehicle. As they stepped up on the sidewalk, they noticed a young, black, female agent standing near the rear of the second van with one foot up on the vehicle's bumper—the rear-right door of the van having swung out and then forward to rest along the side of the vehicle. A military personnel transport was just pulling up alongside the curb farther down the road, and a team of armored military police soldiers quickly poured out of the bulky truck as an aerial patrol vehicle hummed in behind. An MP was already standing in the domed turret of this latest addition to the group, her hands on the grips of a .50 caliber machine gun that had been mounted to the AV's upper surface.

"Daniels sees cameras set to watch the only doors on the eastern and western sides," the other female agent shared.

At the sound of a man's voice calling out from within her team's surveillance van, the young black woman sharply turned her attention back to its interior for a moment, then faced the group again and advised, "Looks like there's an old utility access door on the north side that's not monitored, just rusted at the hinges and has old-style locks."

"We'll enter there," Vela responded as she stepped forward and reached up inside the nearby van to extract a large case.

Giving her companions a tip of her head to direct them to follow, she activated the door closure button on the back of her van and jogged to the rear of the second van, instructing Agent Daniels to continue monitoring the area through the Stray and satellite and keep the team informed of anything noteworthy.

Lights switching off, a black sedan cruised in to stop at the end of the column of transports that was now arrayed along the side of the street.

"My ride's arrived," Gaines informed Vela while pointing toward the car, "and the Panther will join us as we pass."

With a nod of confirmation, the senior agent waved a hand forward, making eye contact with the other female agent as she ordered, "Let's move, Mambwe."

Leading her team down to meet up with the MPs, Vela paused as Sergeant Rinne ordered two pairs of soldiers to post at the southern corners of the warehouse and wait there to detain any people or vehicles that may try to exit in that direction. The sergeant then ordered the rest of his troops to form up behind him.

Vela's team members formed into a line in front of Rinne, and the whole group followed her lead as she jogged down toward the opposite end of the building next to which they'd parked—Gaines quickly pressing a button on the fob that dangled from his belt as he passed his vehicle. The car's trunk swung open, and the wide, dark, dully metallic face of the general's prototype Panther emerged. The big cat unfolded itself from the trunk and slunk down onto the gravelly pavement before giving itself a brief shake and padding up to keep pace at Gaines' side.

"Good boy, Severance," Gaines murmured, and upon hearing the Panther's name Vela half-turned her face back to shoot an appreciatively amused smirk in his direction, glancing from him down to the Panther and back again.

Now traversing around the far corner of the building, the column passed the Stray as it crouched near the northwestern corner of the street-facing brick structure. As they reached it, the small cat dashed across to the warehouse and then to its far corner, where the feline peered around into the shadows along the building's western front.

Swiftly crossing the open space between the first building and the old concrete-and-steel warehouse, the column made it to the north end of the target structure, and Vela dropped her case casually next to the decrepit entrance located on that face of the aged edifice. The lead agent bent over to tap the case's latch release tab and allowed the lid to swing open. Gaines noted that the container was filled with a wide assortment of clandestine surveillance and breaching gear.

Vela let her weapon hang from the clip that was keeping its butt attached to the left shoulder of her vest and grabbed a corpulent device with a handle that looked much like the grip of a firearm. Placing its nose up against the rusty metal surface of the door—starting near its base—she squeezed the device's trigger and drew a large rectangle using the dark gray foam that was being ejected from the unit's nozzle.

Switching the device to her right hand, she leaned down and pulled a smaller object from the case. This apparatus had the appearance of a medium-sized drill that bore a polymer bit shaped like an inverted cone. Pressing the end of the bit into the center of her newly created rectangle, the broad base of the cone dynamically muffled the sound of the drilling bit that was hidden in the center of the sound-dampening component; the device's noise reduction would be created not only by the materials out of which the cone was constructed but also via complementary vibrations sent through the unit into the door's metal surface.

Vela, having punctured the surface of the door to a sufficient depth with the drill, then used her thumb to press a button on the rear of the tool. A low whirring sound announced that the specialized drilling bit had deployed its anchor inside the barrier and the contraption was pulled firmly up against the door's surface.

The warrant officer touched the tip of the device in her right hand up to part of the foam—the spume now having hardened—and thumbed a switch on the side of that disbursement unit. Starting from her point of contact, the foam began fizzing until the entire rectangle was frothing away and penetrating more deeply and widely through the metal door, creating a chemical odor that quickly permeated the area.

As the reaction died down, Agent Vela tossed the portly apparatus into the case, pressed her right hand palm-down against the doorframe, and gave the still-secured device a tug. The outlined rectangle was barely attached at that point and broke free from the rest of the corroded door with a gentle twanging sound. The athletic woman carefully pulled the rectangular slab of metal out and moved it off to one side, quietly leaning it against the warehouse wall.

Releasing the drilling device, Vela returned her hands to her submachine gun, waved the team forward, and entered the dark space beyond the door.

"Hang back and be ready," Gaines whispered to Severance as he moved through the newly formed portal. The large feline tilted its head and crouched down next to the opening, tail flicking back and forth briefly before the mechanical animal settled into perfect stillness.

As the team streamed through the improvised entrance, their various eye protectors activated their built-in night vision capabilities. The infiltrators took in the building's massive, defunct battery unit and power regulator, with members of the column transitioning their firearms' targeting from one potential threat vector to another as they moved. Hearing voices ahead, Vela pulled the column up to a halt next to an open door in a cinderblock wall at the base of a steel staircase leading to the gangways that formed a semblance of a second floor.

Peering out through the barrel-, crate-, and machinery-cluttered space beyond, Vela extended herself forward just enough to tell that the voices were coming from the western side of the voluminous workroom.

Glancing at the rickety metal steps, the agent decided not to risk sending any team members up them, signaling the column to advance with her as she moved on past the first of roughly a dozen grime-encrusted and rank-smelling massive mechanisms that Vela saw had been arranged in rows running up the center and along each extensive wall of the building. The ceiling was peaked and mostly made of filthy glass supported by steel girders, a murky light filtering through the soiled windows and revealing only the rough outlines of the walkways above and the machinery below.

With night vision active, the team could see that the gangways were free of human activity, and no cameras or other devices were visible as they moved toward the center of the workroom floor. Each time he passed the walkways between the dilapidated equipment, Sergeant Rinne used hand signals to send a soldier off to post at the opposite end of every side path leading toward the long, westernmost north-south passage that mirrored the one down which the column was moving.

Vela held up her right hand with a flat palm as she reached the last piece of machinery before the centermost cross-cut pathway, bringing the remaining members of the team to another halt.

Voices echoed over from the other side of the substantial fabricator against which the agent leaned her shoulder. Making use of the barrel-tip camera built into her firearm, the operations leader could see on the screen positioned just in front of the weapon's cheekrest that the cross-section of walkways on the other side of the large, industrial machine was partially occupied by a stack of pallets at the left edge of the intersection, while a well-worn forklift appeared to be parked around the corner to the north of the junction. A woman stood near the pallets, long blond hair done up in a tight bun on the back of her head and a light tan trench coat extending down to her ankles, with only the cuffs of leggings and some flat-heeled, low-rise, synthetic fiber boots visible below.

The suspect woman's head was turned slightly to her left, where it seemed the two male speakers were standing. Her hands and arms were held in front of her in either a crossed-arm or weapon-readied position. One of the men was currently speaking in a hissing whisper and seemed to be quite agitated. Now was an ideal time for the American personnel to make their move.

Vela stepped back from the corner, pointed at Sergeant Rinne, Agent Mambwe, and General Gaines, and then held up her right hand with palm facing left and sliced the air down the long eastern pathway toward the far end of the building. After the three had padded off silently in that direction and taken up tactical positions mirroring those of the military police service members Rinne had directed earlier, the lead agent then stepped to the head of the residual column and waved her hand forward, leading the troops around the corner and—slowing as they neared the blond woman—up to roughly a meter from the target's back.

"*Freeze!*" Vela barked as she flicked on her tactical light. The soldiers north and south of the intersection followed suit, and the small group of enemies was instantly bathed in vivid luminescence.

In the ensuing silence, Vela called out, "You're surrounded!"

As she approached the woman's back, she peered through the gaps in the pallets and could dimly see the coat-covered shoulder of one man and the face of the Denver-based, Chinese agent. She could also make out the jawline of a dark-haired Caucasian male who must have been standing at the blond woman's eleven o'clock position, facing the other three members of the group. The illuminated woman, who was undoubtedly the female member of the local Russian couple, was maintaining the same stance as before, but to Vela, it seemed she was exuding an intensity that was much like a powerful spring that was fully compressed.

"Hands where I can see them!" the agent ordered.

The woman shifted her head slightly farther to the left, casting a baleful gaze at Vela out of the corner of her eye. As Vela still stood a meter away with her firearm pointed at the woman's back, the Russian slowly brought her hands out into view above her shoulders. In so doing, the enemy agent's coat sleeves inched down her forearms, gradually revealing black straps that seemed to be binding a similarly black metal structure to her body.

Vela suddenly realized she was seeing a crude imitation of the Command Activated exosuits.

The warrant officer's eyes widened and—as the woman suddenly lashed her left leg out backward toward the agent with unbelievable speed—let loose a volley of rounds into the enemy's back, shredding her coat but failing to penetrate the armor beneath. The Alliance agent carried on firing all the way up until she was caught in the chest by the spy's heel. A scream was forced from Vela's mouth as she went crashing back into the line of MPs, those soldiers having staggered themselves slightly to allow for uninhibited weapons sighting toward the target but now holding their fire to avoid striking the Alliance agent's sprawling body.

The Russian woman spun around, coat swirling with the motion and revealing the full exoskeleton that enveloped her body, as well as the compact submachine gun she had tethered to her chest. Sweeping the weapon up to her shoulder, the enemy agent fired a dozen bullets into Vela and the chain of military police, starting low and raising her weapon to cut across the legs of the soldiers who were still standing.

As the special agent struggled to pick herself up from the ground, she was able to twist her weapon to bring its barrel down to press into the rough concrete in front of her groin, holding the gun with its stock vertical in front of her face. The enemy's low-aimed rounds ricocheting off the shielding weapon, the CI agent was thereby spared from the incoming fire. The last soldiers in the column were not so lucky, taking hits across their unarmored shins and thighs.

The wounded men cried out and dropped to the ground while the fair-haired foe spun around the stack of pallets to avoid the hail of bullets that were being released from the weapons of the three MPs who had posted at the corners of the fabricators north of her position. The Russian retreated behind the wooden shielding as she fired down the pathway at her assailants, forcing them to duck into cover.

While the female CEN agent had been repelling the nearest forces, the Chinese agent had swiftly turned to face south down the pathway in which he had been standing. Using his exosuit-armored body as a shield to protect the intelligence source, the Alliance team's lithe rival brought two automatic pistols to bear on the lights and incoming fire from the MP sergeant, junior agent, and general positioned at the corners of cross-cutting pathways south of the main intersection.

One of the MP leader's rounds struck the man's ribcage, the thinner armor there shredding and leaving the Chinese agent with a flesh wound. This caused him to stagger, but he nimbly regained his footing and returned fire with laser sights guiding his bullets in to make contact with

Sergeant Rinne's left hip, spinning the old soldier heavily around and dropping him to the ground as his assault rifle clattered across the floor.

The spy began advancing toward the south, firing volley after volley at the lights of Agent Mambwe and General Gaines to keep them pinned down as he was joined by the Russian female. The woman used her artificially enhanced strength to leap up onto the summit of the machinery to her left, dashing from fabricator to fabricator down the residual length of the warehouse.

As the adversary leaped over the head of Agent Mambwe, the young agent caught a glimpse of the Russian's movement above her and jerked her weapon up to shoot at the formidable foe, but she was too late. The spy's submachine gun fire raked across the young woman's shoulder, slamming it down. The last round exiting the CEN agent's weapon pierced into the area near the base of Mambwe's throat.

With a cry of agony that devolved into an uncontrolled groan, the young soldier was thrown to the ground, right arm cast out above her at an unnatural angle and her legs kicked out askew—eyes glassy and staring. As the Chinese agent limped past Sergeant Rinne, the aged veteran grunted and struggled to crawl toward his fallen weapon. With a smug smile, the spy mercilessly executed the wounded warrior with two rounds fired into the back of his exposed neck, then returned the pistols' aim to point toward General Gaines.

Having taken up the southernmost position down that western path, the general had heard Mambwe's cry over the sound of his frustratingly impotent gunfire, his rounds refusing to fully penetrate the Chinese agent's exosuit. The younger woman's dying emanation had brought the officer's attention to the rapidly advancing Russian agent, saving his life in the process.

As the Chinese man's weapons suddenly clicked on empty chambers, Gaines twitched his shoulder out in time to squeeze off two rounds that flew into the man's weakly armored inner thigh, not fully penetrating but throwing the man off balance and bruising the muscles there. The general hastily turned this move into an elevation of his firearm's barrel, with bullets streaming out just as the Russian woman breached his cover.

Exigently evading Gaines' barrage, the female agent was unable to accurately target him and the rounds she squeezed off as she flew overhead—whirling herself around in the process—strafed across the ground and up the side of the equipment next to which Gaines stood. Sparks and shrapnel showered the general's face, and he jerked his head away to shield his eyes before adeptly returning to a firing stance. His suppressive shots pinned the Russian down as she withdrew toward the southeastern end of the fabricator on which she had landed.

The Chinese man, partially hobbled by the bruising inflicted on his leg, limped up the long western walkway and fired off several rounds from his now-reloaded pistols as Gaines spun around the corner of the decrepit machine that was currently providing him with cover. The Asian agent was still shielding his ward with his body as the general leaned out to fire off a quick burst at the enemy, grazing the CEN asset's scalp—the movement of the American's rounds through the air tossing the antagonist's short-cropped hair as they passed.

As the temporarily handicapped enemy agent and his intelligence source were forced to quickly step into the cover of the nearest piece of machinery, the female spy leaned out around the steel piping protruding out of the top of the final machine in the series. The woman's incoming fire forced the general to the other end of the small alley between fabricators as her Chinese cohort and his companion were thereby freed to make their way to the end of the larger walkway and up a set of metal stairs to the second-story gangway.

At the top of the stairs and across the end of the elevated steel walkway into which the stairway was integrated stood a steel door that led to an externally mounted platform, this area protruding off the side of the warehouse and providing access to a ladder that was bolted onto the angled roof.

In desperation, Gaines darted out from cover and advanced toward the enemies, his withering fire driving the woman back from the edge of the machine on which she was standing. Apparently deciding to take what could be her last opportunity to climb the stairs to follow after the two men behind her, the Russian dropped down to the floor west of her elevated position, General Gaines catching a glimpse of her head and left shoulder as she did so. The officer heard her steps ringing out as she raced up toward the building's second story.

During these altercations, the exosuit-clad Russian male had not only held the rest of the unit at bay, he had wreaked havoc as he'd stepped out from behind the bullet-scarred pallets to fire off a semi-automatic grenade launching firearm—intentionally targeting a cluster of barrels of degreasing agent that sat near the corner of the next intersection north in the pathway. As the first grenade had made contact with the barrels, the explosion from the projectile and flammable chemicals blasted the nearest MP back diagonally to make horrific contact with the equipment to his north. A wave of burning chemicals sprayed out in all directions and covered the unconscious MP and everything in his vicinity.

Vela had managed to pull herself to her feet and was helping the able-bodied members of her column to drag the wounded fire team members back around the corner to the northeast as the Panther rushed toward the group, whipping the prehensile tentacles it had extended from its shoulders out to wrap them under the arms of the nearest casualty. The machine quickly but gently pulled the moaning young man up onto its back as it skidded to a halt and then dashed away toward the entrance Vela had made earlier.

At that moment, the tall Russian man raised the tip of his weapon up over the corner of the most proximate industrial fabricator and lobbed grenades toward the Alliance soldiers in Vela's area. The explosive projectiles sailed in and struck the upper corner of the structure around which Vela and the others were dragging the wounded soldiers, additional grenades striking the edge of the next machine to the east. The first blast only dazed the combatants below and sent shrapnel flying over their heads, but the second knocked the two soldiers adjacent to the impacted fabricator forward to hammer their helmets into the opposite apparatus. That grenade also sent shrapnel flying out to embed itself in the armor and flesh of the others in the area and left them temporarily deaf.

Agent Roberts took a piece of shrapnel in his forehead and was sent crashing backward, knocked senseless, while Vela was struck in the cheekbone and was spun around to fall forward into the walkway leading south from the group. She lay there in a state of shock, blinking frantically and willing herself to suck in a huge breath of air.

One of the casualties farthest from the blast raised his assault rifle and fired off a stream of bullets at the enemy's position, forcing the Russian to pull back temporarily and giving Vela the chance to use the exposed pipes of the machine to her right to raise herself to a standing position again. Then she began to climb, struggling with each motion as her body recovered from the latest trauma and with blood dribbling out of the wound on her cheek. Finally, she pulled herself up onto the top of the industrial device.

Meanwhile, reentering the southernmost cross-pathway, Gaines dashed forward with his weapon aimed up at the stairs, popping off several rounds as he chased after the adversaries who were fleeing the building. Rounding the corner of the fabricator and lunging toward the metal gradient before him, he was suddenly thrown up against the stairway railing with incredible force by the explosion of the grenade the male Russian had just fired down the long walkway to strike an obstruction several meters behind him.

Skull slamming harshly against the metal of the railing, Gaines was knocked unconscious and fell helplessly on the cold, steel steps. The grenade had stopped the man's ascent, but it had also impacted near two barrels of degreasing agent that were sitting in the walkway nearer to the grenade's firer, the barrels bursting violently into flame and the burning liquid spraying across the three fabricators near the foot of the stairs.

Vela, seeing that the large Russian man had turned to aim south, sprang out from the cover of the valves atop the central apparatus and—touching only once on the far side of the upper portion of the device—leaped down behind the spy as she withdrew her combat knife from its sheath near the lower-rear edge of her tactical vest. Before he could react to her approach, Vela had thrust the blade over the enemy agent's shoulder and pressed it roughly up against the exposed flesh of his neck, drawing a trickle of blood in the process.

"Your suit won't be any good with a slit throat!" she hissed irately as she fought against the sudden dizziness that had welled up inside her damaged head.

The Russian froze and wisely did not resist as the special agent reached across to grab a handle that ran along the upper-left of the man's launcher, pulling it out of his hands and tossing it aside. Flames raged both behind them and at the southern end of the walkway, causing smoke from chemicals, plastic, rubber, and old grease to billow up and create a glowering cloud in the upper reaches of the warehouse. Vela roughly grabbed onto the Russian man's right shoulder and shoved him forward toward the southwest stairway.

At the top of the stairs, the Slavic female was crouching below the haze as the choking smog rushed out the now-open door behind her. The Chinese agent and other man were sheltering on the balcony outside as the lights from the MPs on the ground and those leaning out of the now-airborne patrol AV shone on them from multiple directions. Rapidly descending the stairs, the woman's exosuit-enhanced strength enabled her to grab General Gaines fiercely by the collar and hoist him easily up in front of her, the woman pressing the barrel of her weapon viciously into the side of the officer's neck as his eyes fluttered and then dazedly opened.

Vela and her hostage were approaching the roaring flames separating them from the stairs. Several more barrels exploded halfway down the alley that the general had previously traversed, their lids and fragments of metal being blasted up into arcs through the air before they ricocheted off walls and machinery.

The female spy called out, "We are leaving now! If anyone follows, I *will* kill this man!"

Out the open door, Vela could see a bulky aerial vehicle approaching from across the rooftops...not one of the vehicles that the Stray had tagged with tracking devices outside. The MPs in the recon unit began pelting the hood of this new arrival in an attempt to disable its engine, but the rounds ricocheted off of its armored shell.

"*Call off your men!*" the Russian woman shouted, the red-orange light on her livid face dancing with the reflected flames and eyes wide and dangerous as she shoved the tip of her firearm more deeply into Gaines' neck, causing the general to grimace in pain.

Vela released the male agent's shoulder long enough to double-tap her communications strip as she urgently shouted, "Hold your fire! Let the targets go! They've got a hostage!"

The gunfire outside swiftly ceased, and the Russian woman began backing up the stairs and out the door to the AV, the vehicle having slid open its rear-right access door. The Chinese agent and his ward—face still held down to conceal his identity—climbed inside after unlatching a gate in the balcony railing.

"We will be in touch soon!" the woman shouted above the thunderous sounds of combustion, eyes shifting from Vela's face to the Russian man's as though she was making a promise to both of them.

The fleeing spy backed out of the door, passing through the river of smoke and forcing Gaines to bend slightly in front of her as they both entered the spacious rear seating area in the utility AV. The vehicle's doors slid shut, and the transport pulled away from the balcony, moving off into the night as the police patrol unit maintained its position hovering above the alley.

Hissing through gritted teeth, Vela helplessly watched the enemies' departure. She heard footsteps approaching her from behind and turned her head slightly to look back over her right shoulder, taking in the two MPs cautiously approaching with weapons lowered. Behind them padded the hunched, dark shape of the general's Panther, having moved all accessible casualties to the extraction point and now looking up at Vela questioningly.

"Cuff him hand and foot, and make it a double until we can figure out how to deactivate his suit," she ordered the soldiers, now struggling to get the words out through the ever-increasing smog that was filling the burning building. As the two young MPs expeditiously executed her orders, withdrawing their magnetically locking handcuffs from their belts, Vela looked down at Severance's upturned face. The Panther had heeled at Vela's side as though recognizing her as its current user.

"I sure hope the general built some special features into you," Vela choked out as she turned and began watchfully escorting the military police assets and their captive out of the doomed structure, "'cause you may be our only hope for the success of this mission...or for getting him back!"

Chapter 10

"Great leaders understand that they cannot control everything, but they must take charge in any situation whether it is clear or unclear, certain or uncertain, familiar or unfamiliar. In such challenging circumstances, making a decision about which you are unsure is better than doing nothing—until you realize it was a mistake. If it turns out to be a mistake, then you need to learn from it, adjust your actions, and move on. The most difficult part of making a decision is owning the results and the consequences."

-Jachike Cochrun, Head Coach, National Football Team, Argentina

Springtime in Kraków meant the area was seeing its first days favored with temperatures above freezing, and the trees and undergrowth around the business center on the outskirts of the city were just shooting forth their first, weak leaves.

The Polish tank commander stood with his elbows resting on the rim of the top hatch in his M1 Abrams—one of many surplus armored cavalry vehicles the country had acquired from the United States over the past several decades. The man peered intently through heavy sixth-generation thermal binoculars toward a point on the horizon where the east-west highway was first visible from his unit's position amongst the ash and oak trees and elder bushes next to the large communications business building taking up the southeasternmost portion of the complex.

He tried to push away the distracting longing the scent of the thawing ground and new plant growth was drumming up inside him: a great desire to be with his wife and young son, heading out on one of the many picnics they loved to take during the middle of the day from Spring through late Fall, bundling up and enjoying the outdoors despite the often-frigid temperatures. The few beams of late-morning sunlight penetrating the mostly bare branches of the surrounding grove created patches of warmth, and one of these had formed on the back of the commander's neck, soothing his tired muscles.

The latest word from headquarters was that Russian ground forces had taken Brzesko the night before with the help of the heavy, airborne VT-71 drones that the enemy had made a key component of the arsenal supporting its conquests. Alliance Command was depending on this Abrams heavy cavalry unit to hold the CEN invaders at Kraków long enough for one of the special operations units to arrive and disable the forwardmost Russian assets, trying to halt the aggressors' advance across southern Poland.

"See anything, Chlebek?" the tank's main gunner called up from the depths of the armored beast, the soldier doing his own monitoring using the tank's main scope.

"Nothing is moving out there," the officer replied with obvious relief tinging his voice as he turned his face down toward the interior of the vehicle.

"Yes...and let us hope it stays that way!" the gunner breathed. "We are almost alone out here, with all the equipment that had to go to the main defensive lines!"

"We are all that stands between the people of this city and the cruelty of the Russians who have punched through on this southern front. We *have* to prevail *whatever* the costs," Chlebek stoically replied and returned his eyes to his optics.

The team's radios started crackling with static, followed by an urgent voice shouting, "Tanks on highway, but drones approach you from the south!"

Commander Chlebek heard the furious roaring of the propellant burning away before he realized the source—the sounds growing rapidly louder as he jerked his eyes away from the binoculars and faced the incoming missiles with mouth agape. No less than two dozen projectiles were converging on this grove of trees, having been fired from the heavily built unmanned aerial vehicles that had just lifted their faces above the trees at the edge of a field of wild growth south of Chlebek's position.

Without time for the commander to even duck down in the tank's turret, the first of the high-speed armaments was nearly at the side of the Abrams. The vehicle's active armor blasted off a plate from the outer face of the turret, the metal slab flying out to make contact with the missile. The resulting explosion still projected enough force through the air to knock the officer back painfully against the rear of the hatch as the deafening crack of the combustion was joined by dozens more like it. Chlebek's body rebounded forward, and his chin struck excruciatingly on the top of the turret, the soldier barely catching himself with his outflung arms.

Out of his peripheral vision, he saw chunks of wood whirling through the air, accompanied by several falling trees that had been decimated by the mass of missiles, and further on a terrible fireball welled up from where the unit to Chlebek's west had parked their Abrams—the active armor having been overwhelmed by the centralization of the missiles around that tank's position.

Forcing himself up off the surface of the turret, the officer ignored the searing pain in his jaw and quickly slid down inside the vehicle, hand snagging the hatch's lever and yanking it closed with a final twist to lock it down.

"*Get us out of here!*" Chlebek shouted at the driver. "*Reverse! Reverse!*"

The officer scrambled into the vehicle's command station and flicked the switch to activate the remote control of the tank's .50 caliber machine gun. Using the control grip, he rotated the weapon to aim at the drones, firing off a continuous stream of rounds as the next barrage of missiles came scorching toward his tank.

"Bosko, main gun to ninety degrees!" the officer shouted to his gunner, hoping to face more of the active armor toward the incoming fire.

Knowing that the forces in this area were undersupplied, particularly when it came to shoulder-fired armaments that were capable of intercepting airborne targets, the regional commanders had decided to rely upon the tanks as the front line and support them by adding a small mobile missile battery northwest of the semi-circle the Abrams had formed in the trees. The battery was sheltered by the nearest building and ready to pull out west of the structure once enemy air units had been spotted. It had been uncharacteristically strategic of the Russian forces to separate the drones from the ground units like this, especially using the natural surroundings as cover until the last second, and Chlebek had realized it would take extra time for the battery to clear its cover and rotate its armaments to face south due to this unexpected turn of events.

The tanks were going to be easy targets without the battery's protection.

If they could just survive long enough for the Alliance missiles to gain clear sighting on the enemy UAVs, they might still have a chance to hold off the ground forces when they arrived!

Chlebek's driver had kicked the Abrams into reverse and stamped on the accelerator, the juggernaut's massive diesel engine roaring into action and the vehicle plowing over bushes and driving one of the toppled ash trees out of its way as additional enemy missiles flew in. Two of these threats struck the trees behind which the cavalry unit was disappearing, with two more rockets blessedly targeting portions of the M1 Abram's exterior that still bore plates that would launch out and intercept them.

The tank commander could see the swarm of heavy drones advancing, several targeting the tanks beyond the one that had been destroyed to the west. Though the nearest visible unit that was still in the fight had managed to avoid severe damage, its left track had suffered sufficient hurt to make its traversal of the generally rocky, dew-covered ground laborious. Only the density of the foliage around that tank and its crew had kept them alive so far, but their time was running out.

As the officer continued to unload the machine gun at the approaching squadron, Bosko quickly rotated the main gun and lifted its barrel, firing off its prodigious projectiles toward the greatest concentration of drones. The first round missed, flying just below the aircraft in the lower right of the formation, but as the gunner continued raising the cannon while firing off additional shells, the second caused a shockwave as it passed between a pair of drones—spinning them around—and the third impacted a central drone dead on.

The aerial robot's armor was no match for a tank shell at close range, and the unmanned vehicle blew apart as its remaining missiles exploded due to the force of the shell's impact on their carrier. The fireball in the air caused the detonation of the armaments of three nearby aircraft, with the total sphere of destruction knocking the remaining seven drones out of formation. The resulting confusion granted the tanks precious seconds of extra time.

"Was that you, Bosko??" the commander of the hobbled tank asked over the squadron communications channel in an elated voice.

"Yes, sir!" the sergeant crowed as he tried to target another drone, but the Russian vehicles' remotely operating pilots had become wary after losing so many aircraft and they were now spreading out the remaining vehicles as the craft elevated above the reach of tank shells. The Abrams' heavy barrel motor whirred helplessly as it pressed against the top of its range of motion. Bosko let out a frustrated cry as he slapped his hands on his control grips.

"Nowak, where are you?!" Chlebek shouted into his headset, desperately reaching out to the battery commander.

Just as the first of the residual drones loomed above the retreating cavalry unit and unleashed one of its missiles toward the top of the turret, a flurry of rockets sailed in from the northwest, emanating from the edge of the nearby business building at what could be considered point-blank range for surface-to-air missiles. The last active armor plate on the superior surface of Chlebek's vehicle released and intercepted the lone incoming missile as shrapnel and husks of drones rained out of the sky.

Chlebek called out to his driver to stay near the trees rather than pulling out into the open parking area abutting the nearby building. The officer released the machine gun controls and turned to direct the top-mounted optics to the sky, and then down until they were level with the horizon. Waiting breathlessly, his fears were confirmed as he saw a surviving VT-71 strafing low out around the trees and above the road to the east.

"*No!*" he shouted, knowing that his tank was out of defensive options.

As if in slow motion, the commander watched as the body of the heavy drone suddenly compressed, sparks and shrapnel flying off in all directions, and the drone's abruptly condensed carcass dropped impotently to the road below. The enemy craft's missiles detonated as they made contact with the paved surface, erupting in a spectacularly unified series of orange fireballs.

Not daring to believe his eyes, Chlebek let his driver continue reversing along the edge of the parking area for a moment before crying out in exhilaration.

"We're safe!"

The officer's face broke into a tremendous grin—which he immediately regretted as he was forced to cringe and clutch his aching jaw—as his crew members let out a cheer. The warriors' exuberant voices only died down as the radio activated, and the voice they'd heard earlier began speaking again in its perfect Polish.

"This is Alliance Command. Unable to reach squad leader. All units, please report."

"Wolf Four track in bad shape, but we're here!"

"Wolf Two operational," a female voice soberly spoke up, adding, "One and Three were both destroyed."

Chlebek's pain-weakened smile faded, and he removed his hands from his face long enough to emotionally and breathlessly say, "Wolf Six, active armor depleted but otherwise operational. Wolf Five was also destroyed."

"We are sorry for your loss," the voice gently responded. "CEN forces have been jamming standard radio transmissions in your area. A high-altitude Alliance craft has reached your approximate location and deployed railgun munitions to disable the jamming unit, surveillance assets, and roughly half of the Russian ground cavalry forces—as well as the last operational VT-71."

The tank's driver shot an elated expression over his shoulder at Chlebek, who was once again cradling his jaw and only managed a half smile in return.

The voice continued, "The remaining cavalry units are pushing forward, apparently attempting to execute on their original plan to take your position after the drones had softened you up, and they have been joined by a battalion of infantry that is moving toward you through the woods to the south as we speak."

"Dabrowski, Bosko, face south!" Chlebek hissed to the driver and gunner, who swung the tank's base and its turret to the right as they tried to find openings through the trees.

The disembodied voice continued, "Special operations troops have landed near the mobile missile battery and will deal with the remaining forces. We ask that you maintain your current positions."

The tank commander breathed a sigh of relief and let his hands drop to his lap as he sank back in his seat. On the screen displaying the feed from the front-mounted optics, the man was amazed to see a column of soldiers racing past the nose of his Abrams at a pace that nearly matched the cavalry unit's own top speed.

These troops quickly disappeared into the wooded area beyond, being aided in this feat by dynamically changing camouflage covering the exteriors of their exosuits. Jumping up and opening the hatch, Chlebek watched—dumbfounded—as two more soldiers dashed past and stopped at the tree line, taking up positions closer to where the vehicle was parked as their armor's exteriors adjusted to match their surroundings.

Upon withdrawing their large-caliber sniper rifles from attachment points on the armor covering their backs, the sharpshooters rapidly aimed their weapons to the south. A robust, tiger-like shape emitted a gentle whirring as it padded past, looking up impassively at Chlebek's admiring face and then melting into the bushes near the snipers.

"Thank you for your help!" the officer loudly whispered to the nearest CA troop in heavily accented English.

The soldier remained motionless, yet the same voice the officer had heard over his headset spoke from the vicinity of the sniper's fully enclosed helmet, once again using perfect Polish.

"You are welcome. Please be silent now."

Shaking his head in wonder, the officer sank into his tank while closing the turret's hatch and gratefully returning to his position at the command station. All three members of the tank team stared at their optical feeds, hardly breathing.

In the Command Activated headquarters, Colonel Soares was chortling as he double-checked the lines of sight for his troops in the southeastern portion of the vegetation.

"'Please be silent now,' SAVANT says!"

Soares was having difficulty getting the words out as laughter consumed his vocal cords.

"I'm gonna have to try that line on my mother!"

General Webb smiled ruefully as he stared intently at the main screen of his command hub, responding, "Tell me before you do so I can start planning your funeral!"

Colonel Fonua sniggered and Singh called out, "Aw, she wouldn't kill him, she'd just emasculate him and leave him to suffer!"

The suddenly sober look on Soares' face revealed that Singh's idea might not be far from the truth.

The unit commanders finished the last of their combat preparation checks. The officers were rapidly glancing between their command consoles and the main screen, the latter of which was displaying the positions of enemy soldiers and cavalry units as detected by newly deployed reconnaissance drones and the upper atmosphere vessel supporting this mission. Some command personnel were relaying final instructions to their subcommanders.

Ever intuitive, General Webb could feel the tension building as the enemy forces approached the CA positions, the tautness like an invisible serpentine force curling almost palpably around his team's throats.

"We've trained how we fight, now we'll fight how we've trained!" Webb called out with confidence he'd learned to project after years of serving under General Kalabi.

"Yes, *sir*!" Soares exclaimed with bravado.

The general turned his face toward his currently assigned cavalry commander while keeping his eyes on the unit tracking indicators on the main screen, watching as the red rectangles moved west along the highway toward the blue-tinted CA positions. Webb noted the line of sight and range indicators for the weapons borne by the troops and the Alliance's Salamander hovercraft that was currently concealed behind the same business building as the depleted Polish missile unit—the majority of the amphibious tank's modular armaments having been swapped for surface-to-surface missiles.

"Yi, you know SAVANT will use your Salamander's SSMs to rain hell down on the Russian cav units, but I need you to keep your eyes on the resulting casualties. You see one twitch of unexpected movement in the wreckage of that armored column, and you take it out. We can't afford to have anyone firing off potshots at the troops from our flank while they confirm full elimination of the infantry."

Colonel Yi nodded gravely and gave Webb a grim salute.

According to the thermal imagery provided by the Command Activated observation drone that was hovering roughly a kilometer over Commander Chlebek's tank, the company of Russian infantry approaching from the south had opted to send two snipers out to the northeastern edge of the forest through which they were moving. The rest of the unit was swinging around to approach the east-west highway where the trees grew closest to the road rather than moving out into the open to cross the small clearing over which the VK-71s had flown after their surprise attack.

Based on SAVANT's projections, the enemy cavalry would be in range within twenty seconds, though the cooling systems built into the special operators' exosuits would keep them from being detected via thermal scopes until the enemy was practically on top of them. The AI had drawn pale blue lines between the CA assets and the targets they would engage first, creating an effect similar to that of an abstract art piece depicting a lopsided blue sun with rays shifting as the enemy soldiers slunk through the verdure. An all-white waterfall took shape to the north as the Salamander hovercraft's locked-in missile trajectories were indicated by arcs of thin white lines running from its location out over the long business building and down to the approaching Russian tanks.

The engagement initiation timer counted down to zero and, like clockwork, all CA forces let loose volley after volley of bullets, the projectiles curving around obstacles as needed to home in on their targets. Already sighted in and noticing hints of unusual shapes in the opposite grove of trees, one of the Russian snipers managed to quickly squeeze off one heavy projectile that struck a trunk near a CA soldier's helmet—spraying the armor with chips of bark—before the smart rounds took the sniper and his companion down.

In the western thicket just south of the highway, the company of Russian infantry was dropping like waves crashing on a beach. Each successive round of gunshots from the CA rifles was sweeping out and decimating the next row of infantrymen in the unit. Those enemy soldiers bringing up the rear in the company suddenly panicked and were just turning to escape or diving for cover as the final series of bullets flew in and penetrated their vitals.

The Salamander had also released the first ten of its smart munitions as the countdown had ended, SAVANT having allowed the massive enemy tanks to reach the intersection where the highway split. The smaller road that led north past the business complex became the gravesite for the first two units in the column. The AI had projected with high confidence that the enemy armor units would use the last data obtained from the CEN drones to estimate the positions of the remaining Polish tanks and—hoping to quickly finish them off—would try to skirt around to the north and depend on the superior armor and optics of the new T-200 tanks to drive west across the paved areas north and south of the first large building in the business complex. There was even a sixty-two percent chance that one of the tank commanders would catch slivered glimpses of Wolf Six through the timber and be lured toward it.

Seeing the lead vehicles in their formation turned into enormous bonfires right in front of them, the remaining eight Communist vehicles swerved off the road, attempting to cut across the nearby fields or execute turns and retreat back down the highway. The Command Activated AI was not going to allow that to happen.

Unleashing a matching number of rockets, SAVANT painted bolder lines across the thinner white targeting indicators on the main media wall of the command hub to trace the projectiles' paths, and the enemies' chaotic evasive maneuvers were quickly halted. Yi peered at his console, bringing his fingers together in front of his screen and then sweeping them out to the sides repeatedly to zoom in. He then used two fingers held up together to pan across the disabled cavalry vehicles using the CA drone's camera feed. Satisfied, he glanced to his right and obtained a nod from the female captain seated at the next console.

"No movement detected by SAVANT or my team, General Webb!" Yi reported.

"Excellent. Thank you, Yi, and thanks to the entire team. We spared a city from..." Webb was suddenly cut off by SAVANT's voice, projected at a volume indicating great urgency.

"OBJECTS INBOUND AT HIGH SPEEDS."

Webb's brows raised in alarm and he involuntarily stepped toward the main screen as SAVANT rapidly decreased the map's scale to include several hundred kilometers to the east of Kraków. Dozens of red diamonds crossed the distance to the city before the general could even finish exclaiming, "Where the devil did those come from?!"

Thunder roared in the sky twenty kilometers east of the CA forces as the incoming projectiles temporarily slowed and split in half, releasing objects that were swiftly redirected toward the terrain occupied by the Alliance forces. The two halves of the primary projectiles almost immediately changed direction and surpassed the deployed objects' velocities, targeting the CA assets themselves and impacting with the force of small meteors, sending many soldiers' bodies flying through the air along with chunks of soil and vegetation.

With two of these kinetic energy weapons striking its upper-left carapace, the Salamander was driven backward and suffered massive indentations that impinged on the weapons systems on that side of the vehicle. If it had not already deployed nearly all of its surface-to-surface missiles, the impact would undoubtedly have detonated those munitions and completely obliterated the armored unit.

At SAVANT's rate of data processing, by the time it had alerted General Webb, it had already detected the encroachment of a Russian military observation satellite into the borders of the Alliance's near-Earth orbit domain, that device no doubt having identified the CA forces' locations based on their gunfire over the past minutes. The Communists' callous leaders had undoubtedly been willing to risk losing the Russian ground forces if it meant identifying Command Activated assets.

SAVANT had also calculated that the most likely source of the projectiles was a stealth bomber that must have launched the units roughly ninety kilometers east-southeast of the Alliance forces' position. The AI had already transmitted orders to the ground forces. In what seemed to the AI's mind to be slow motion, soldiers began stepping to locations in which trees and other cover would be between them and the incoming projectiles, and the two Panthers had already started springing out of their crouched positions, turning themselves in the directions of the greatest projected number and severity of casualties.

The AI watched anxiously as the soldiers were unable to make sufficient progress in their movements away from the most likely impact sites for the first projectiles—which SAVANT had determined were halves of capsules that doubled as high-speed kinetic weapons once their cargo had been deployed. The AI recognized that many troops were going to suffer extreme damage to their internal organs, despite their armor. How the AI wished that the Alliance assets in the corporeal world could move as quickly as it could think!

Those soldiers in the Command Activated company who were not going to be directly impacted by the projectiles were being guided to aim their weapons toward the east, as the combat AI had now assessed the slower objects released from the capsules and discovered that these incoming entities were actually humanoid. The figures seemed to have their arms wrapped tightly about their knees and, judging by their dimensions and exterior surfaces, were wearing some form of protective suits with packs on their backs.

As the dark shapes of these enemy troops rapidly descended in the capsule shells' slipstreams, the packs opened to release a series of black parachutes—each larger than the last—that slowed the soldiers over the final three kilometers of their trajectories. The effect was that when they did slam into the ground, it was with a force that, while still violent, was unlikely to break human bones that were protected by exosuits.

Many of these new enemies were on collision courses with as-yet unharmed CA soldiers, while the rest seemed to be careening in to land across the eastern edge of the ground held by the Alliance troops—the area most heavily affected by the capsules' impacts.

In the command center, SAVANT had just uttered the phrase, "IMPACTING OBJECTS WERE CAPSULES AND NEXT WAVE IS SUPERIOR AUTHORITY TROOPS."

The screens across the command hub lit up with orange and red highlighting for locations on CA troops' bodies that had taken damage. Despite possessing only human capabilities, General Webb swiftly recovered from the shock, raised a hand toward the screen, and ordered, "Tactical retreat!"

The first SA troops made contact with CA forces, slamming into a half dozen soldiers using leg strikes as the Superior Authority soldiers uncurled from their fetal-like forms and sent their victims crashing back through the undergrowth. Several Alliance troops clipped branches or trunks of trees as they hurtled backwards and the collisions left the warriors spinning wildly to their final impact sites.

Those SA soldiers who had not turned their landings into attacks quickly released their legs to catch themselves and hammered heavily into the earth, compressing their bodies to absorb the force of their arrival. Still, their landings pounded thin craters into the turf and sprayed debris out in a wave about their feet.

Now in close enough proximity to generally discern the figures of the Command Activated soldiers despite their dynamic camouflage and exosuit cooling systems, many of these newly arrived enemy troops rose swiftly from their crouched positions to spring out in dramatic airborne tumbling maneuvers. Bearing compact assault rifles secured tightly to their chest plates, the soldiers moved freely, and their movements brought them into close contact with the nearest able-bodied CA forces.

The SA forces' suits deflected some of the first armor-piercing rounds fired off by the Command Activated troops due to the angles at which the rounds made contact, though a number of bullets struck at more perpendicular angles and managed to tear through the layers of armor to penetrate into the organic tissues beneath. However, even as those Communist troops were wounded, the only visible effect was that they lost some mobility in affected portions of their bodies, not registering any pain or displaying any other reactions.

As the acrobatic enemies flew in toward the CA soldiers, several used the milliseconds of time passing as they closed in on their targets to reach up over their shoulders. Their hands grasped the hilts of Wo Dao swords clipped to their backs.

The robotic clamps that held the tremendously hardened blades in place automatically released and allowed their wielders to swing the weapons out in arcs or twist them into position to drive point-first into their adversaries, aiming for the weakest parts of the CA exosuits' armor. Though the Command Activated troops reacted by moving limbs up to deflect or block, several arcing blades still made brutal contact, the cutting edges slashing through thinner armor and severing tendons and muscles beneath before unleashing electrical charges of hundreds of thousands of volts into the victims' bodies.

One of those Superior Authority troops that had brought his blade around to strike tip-first had taken a half dozen rounds across his abdomen and chest. The last rounds had buried themselves in the spare magazine that was secured at an angle across the man's chest plate while the earlier rounds had penetrated through to embed themselves in ribs and part of the soldier's intestines. Unphased, the enemy had held his form and punched his blade through at his target's waist, the incisive tip striking against the CA soldier's spine and the Alliance troop being enervated by the electric shock that followed.

Colonel Singh was the first platoon commander to recover enough to issue orders—most of Soares' platoon having been annihilated by the initial SA assault.

She shouted out, "Do *whatever it takes* to unload into them!"

Free to improvise with troop life and limb preservation de-prioritized, SAVANT directed the members of Singh's unit who had not been incapacitated to immediately twist their weapons around in one hand where the proximity made it necessary, pressing the tips of their firearms into their enemies' bodies and squeezing their triggers nonstop. Armor-piercing bullets tore into any portions of the SA forces' torsos that were accessible, the potency of the troop activation drugs and training even pushing through the volumes of electricity surging through some CA soldiers' bodies and enabling them to fight off their assailants.

Viewed through the external camera built into one of her soldiers' helmets, Colonel Singh watched as the man's attacker was driven back by the incessant impact of rounds, and then the enemy slumped—limbs sprawling—against a boulder. As the Command Activated troop's armor dispensed coagulation gel into the wound where the enemy's blade had been pulled out of his body, the Alliance asset struggled to rise while continuing to fire into the next most proximate enemy's side. As that adversary fell, the soldier swiveled and fired at the next nearest threat, smart rounds arcing around a tree trunk to pound into the enemy's back.

As this all happened within a matter of seconds, Colonel Singh was leaning in toward her screen, tilting her head to one side to try to get a better view of the body of the first enemy casualty.

"What in the nine hells?!" she hoarsely whispered. "Is that thing *smiling?!*"

Chapter 11

"Hacking is most definitely a creative activity that challenges conventional views. Like, every single conventional view. It's the ultimate outlet for rebellion against the status quo. The art is not opposed to science. Rather, hacking enhances the sciences through the stimulation of scientific inquiry and innovation.

Creative thinking is often undervalued in educational institutions, which tend to favor more traditional subjects like math, English, and literature. That neglects the other half of the brain that thrives on alternative thinking—the kind of thinking that hackers embrace.

Picasso once said, 'All children are born artists...The problem is how to remain an artist once we grow up.' This is likely one of the main reasons why so many young minds gravitate toward hacking, because it's one of the only career paths in which their creativity will actually be greatly rewarded."

- Dominic Perchek, 'How I Hacked the Universe"

After what seemed like hours, Samantha's family had finally declared that they had gathered their most priceless heirlooms and mementos from throughout their apartment. They were now huddled inside one of a series of dark-windowed AVs that were ferrying them and their prized possessions back to the private heliport at which Maxwell had landed the plane. The last aerial vehicle in the chain was transporting Jayce and Billy, and it currently followed close behind the family's vehicle.

Keeping a map of the approaching individuals' progress up in the top-left portion of his screen, Maxwell was seated at one of the workstations in the parked aircraft, ignoring the view of the glittering Hong Kong skyline and fantastical purple and orange sunset being mirrored through to the plane's interior surfaces. The Brit stared intently at the blank area in the center of his display, lips pursed and the fingers of his right hand rubbing worriedly and repeatedly across his thumb.

Only a few seconds remained before the "time bomb" FAILSAFE had planted on the chief Superior Authority medical researcher's tablet should activate, capturing and transmitting seemingly harmless packets of data out of the CEN network in what would appear to be portions of normal routing and browsing requests. The video feed from the SA chief's tablet was what Maxwell most wanted to see, allowing him to check on the progress of the enemy's research, but it would be another few minutes beyond the remote code's activation before enough data had been carefully pushed out to allow video to be reassembled.

The packets would be transferred to the third-party application server FAILSAFE had compromised and set up to forward the custom communications units on to the next proxy server in the chain. That process would repeat itself until the information had virtually circled the globe, only to end up back at Maxwell's workstation in Hong Kong.

The technical expert glanced over at Lilian, her hair loosely cascading down across her cheek and neck, her face tucked tightly into a cushion as she rested on one of the sofas. The sight dramatically soothed his anxiety. A peculiar feeling washed over him, filling his soul with the knowledge that however many things were wrong with the world, there were so many things that were absolutely right. Lilian Bachar's existence was one of those things that was almost impossibly and yet undeniably right in this otherwise troubled reality.

The creases around Maxwell's eyes melted away, and a soft smile played about the corners of his lips. Leaning his elbows on the edge of the desk and bringing clasped hands up to support his head—the backs of his straightened thumbs pressing up against his left temple—he continued to gaze at the object of his adoration until FAILSAFE's muted voice brought him out of his absorption.

"Doctor Cheng's video feed is ready for viewing now, Max," the AI whispered through the workstation.

Blinking as though he had been staring at a glorious masterpiece and now had to turn his eyes to mundane and far darker subjects, Maxwell sat upright and issued the request, "Onscreen, please."

A large frame appeared in the center of his workstation's screen. It took a moment for Maxwell to recognize what he was seeing, but when he did the realization of its significance struck to his very core.

"He's inside an SA command hub!" he softly exclaimed, slumping back heavily in his ergonomic seat as shock and disbelief swirled through his mind.

The statement had been spoken at a moderated volume, but Lilian had been drifting in and out of fitful slumber, and her eyes now flew open. Pushing herself up off the sofa and casting her silvery, heat-reflective blanket onto the settee's arm, she rose and stepped lightly around the divan that rested at the border of the lounge area, approaching Maxwell as he turned to her with a chagrined expression.

"I'm sorry, Lil!" he rushed to apologize. "You don't have to get up yet!"

She walked up to his back, placed her hands gently on his shoulders, and bent down to plant a kiss on his hairline.

"No worries, sweetheart, the nap we took on the way here was enough that I didn't really need extra sleep anyway."

Straightening, she left her hands in place, tenderly massaging his taut muscles as her eyes darted across the contents of the frame on his screen.

"What did you say? This is a command center?"

"I believe it is," Maxwell opined, "and not only that, I believe that we're seeing command activities related to a mission that has just started!"

They both stared silently for a moment at the individuals arrayed throughout the dimly lit room. The far wall was entirely covered by a display surface that depicted a satellite-centric view of buildings and terrain that did not seem familiar to either of them. However, judging by the rapid movement and constantly changing colors of what seemed to be troop indicators, it was likely that the SA forces were engaged in tempestuous combat.

This was reinforced as they watched the rows of helmeted Chinese, Iranian, and Russian personnel—each standing inside a waist-high ring with lights around its exterior—engaging in movement after movement that seemed to belong on the battlefield. Facing in all manner of orientations within the rings, the persons in view were all wearing one-piece athletic suits having the same brooding color schemes, but with insignia on their shoulders that seemed designed to match the colors of the lights around the enclosing rings for each row in the room.

Their helmets fully enclosed their heads, but the face shields transitioned from opaque to transparent along the lower halves of the material. Through the transparent portions of the shields, Lilian could tell that many were breathing heavily as they executed combat activities. Some were even shouting out as they swung their arms around furiously or relayed information to their teammates.

"If I didn't know any better, I could almost swear they're all playing some sort of virtual reality game..." Maxwell breathed, "...but I have a very bad feeling that we're witnessing an active attack against the Alliance."

The view out of the camera jostled as though the tablet's owner had moved it from one hand to another, giving both Lilian and Maxwell a start—the two having leaned in to try to more closely inspect the enemy personnel.

Possessing an articulation that to Lilian sounded like the twisted self-satisfaction that could only be expected from the voice of Satan himself, someone spoke from what seemed to be the area opposite where the camera was facing. FAILSAFE rapidly converted the incoming audio to English as they listened.

"Doctor Cheng. I commend you for your accomplishments in providing our Immaculate Leader with such a powerful force. As you predicted, the vile enemies are no match for the shock troops' assault!"

Maxwell recognized the voice of the demented senior researcher when he responded, "Thank you, Director! Your words bring me no end of joy! I only wish that we'd been able to find more subjects that could have been turned into combat assets! Very soon, I hope that my research pays off and we can turn *any* citizen of the Confederacy into fully controlled warriors!"

The director chuckled heartily and commanded, "Bring up the view from one of the soldiers on the ground!"

With a further jostling of the tablet-based camera and the view temporarily descending to encompass the lower edge of the doctor's white lab coat and the sleek slacks and shoes below that, it seemed the medical lead was tapping on his tablet for a few seconds before he brought the device back to a position in which the feed included the main screen once again. Now, the right half of that display was providing the viewers with a video transmission from what must be a soldier engaged in close-quarters combat. The enemy warrior was wielding a bladed weapon…an unexpected turn of events that further shocked Lilian and Maxwell.

The SA troop's arm was seen thrusting forward to drive the blade of the weapon into what was obviously a Command Activated soldier's belly.

"Oh, God, *no!*" Lilian cried out as the tip of the blade pierced the Alliance soldier's armor and the defender's body was seen jerking uncontrollably, the sword's handler having thumbed a switch on the hilt that had activated electrical energy transmission into the victim's frame. Hands flying to her face, Lilian's trembling fingers pressed against her lips as she stared on in horror, the electrocution of the CA asset carrying on and on as the blade was wrenched about inside the man's body.

Maxwell quickly stood as he turned and threw his arms around Lilian's shoulders, trying to gently direct her gaze away from the screen while keeping his eyes fixed upon it, pale-faced. Lilian half-turned away, but could not help letting her focus drift back to the screen that was still visible at her eyes' periphery.

As the Confederacy director's heinous laughter continued along with his tremendous enjoyment of the carnage being displayed on the command center's screen, Maxwell was swiftly studying the CEN personnel in the room. The British technical genius picked out what he was hoping he would not discover: one of the individuals in the rings was moving in a manner that was mirrored by the attacking soldier on the main screen.

"These 'commanders' are directly controlling the bodies of the soldiers!" he hissed. "For them to be able to have such complete control they must...they must have hardwired electrodes into the soldiers' brains! Those troops are truly just puppets out there!"

In the Command Activated complex, the commanders and subcommanders were now scrambling to prioritize troop actions and direct them to fight off their enemies where human decisions were required to supplement SAVANT's capabilities. Soares—with most of his troops having been severely injured—was craning his neck to try to get a closer look at the enemies' helmets.

"It's like they're some kind of Asian gargoyles!" Soares called out. "Complete with giant fangs!"

As if to confirm the colonel's idea, the first-person view from a troop that was on the main screen showed a Confederacy soldier using a grip on the low branch protruding from a nearby tree to launch herself into a spin counterclockwise around the trunk. The SA assailant flew up to grapple around a large CA soldier's torso while evilly grinning robotic mandibles built into the aggressor's helmet parted and then fiercely closed on the soldier's left shoulder with what must have been incredible force.

The vicelike motion of the fanged jaw tore through several layers of the Command Activated troop's armor as the enemy's arms and legs remained wrapped around the man's chest and waist, and the SA soldier then began jerking her head back and forth to tear more and more deeply into the shoulder armor. Savagely adding to the damage, short blades deployed from the backs of her gloves and she unleashed a punishing series of lacerating punches into the Alliance soldier's ribcage.

The CA troop was struggling to bring his rifle to bear on this threat, and the damage indicators on his commander's screen were crimson across the entirety of the core of the victim's body. General Webb stepped forward—arm cast out at the main screen—and cried, "Fonua, direct C-11 to shoot that demon off of this troop's chest!"

Colonel Fonua rapidly gestured and swiped to send an order to a CA soldier.

The re-tasked troop had been firing from protective cover at a pair of targets who had ducked behind the trunk of a large tree a few dozen meters away, but his commander redirected his fire toward the grappling combatant clinging to the nearby Command Activated troop's body. After C-11's bullets pierced through the armor of the enemy's back for what seemed like an unbelievably long time, the female Superior Authority troop finally went limp and dropped to the ground.

The suit of the Communist asset's victim had tried to seal off the wounds caused by her blades and fangs as quickly as possible, but the CA soldier was still left swaying unsteadily. He struggled to raise his weapon to begin firing off a stream of projectiles that pelted the hip regions of the two Superior Authority troops that had now dashed forward as they rounded the cover protecting the wounded warrior's savior and let loose a hail of armor-piercing bullets from their compact assault rifles—shredding through that man's exosuit and pulverizing his innards.

The larger Alliance soldier emptied his high-capacity magazine into the two SA troops, the figures ultimately dropping forward on top of their target's debilitated body.

As the arc from one side of the communications building was too sharp for even the most tightly controlled smart munitions, SAVANT had used the few minutes that had passed to maneuver the crippled Salamander hovercraft around the edge of the bulky business structure. Immediately after gaining a clear shot, the vehicle released its few dozen high-caliber close-contact defense rounds and two SSMs from its only functional modular weapons units, just as the two SA assets farthest east in their group—both waiting on bended knees—pulled the triggers on their shoulder-fired anti-tank rockets.

Being directed toward the mangled side of the vehicle, the enemy's missiles crossed paths with the Salamander's, striking the surface of the tank and causing it to erupt in a tremendous fireball as the angled components of its hull were blasted off in all directions. Still, the enemy fire was too late to spare the SA troops from suffering heavy losses as the large-caliber rounds slammed into the surfaces of the Confederacy forces' suits and ripped right through, those enemies unlucky enough to be found grouped tightly together seeing the SSMs come sailing in to decimate those Superior Authority forces as well. Upon seeing the shocking arrival of and heinous assault by the grotesquely formed enemy forces, the Polish tank commanders had barely had time to react at this point, and even as they moved to assist their saviors they were faced with their own impotence, recognizing that their weapons were too crude to surgically eliminate the nearest enemy assets when these were in such close proximity to the Command Activated soldiers.

Now, with few combatants on either side still standing, it seemed the CEN commanders finally decided to withdraw. Those Superior Authority soldiers who were still mobile covered each other as they fell back through the broken remains of the foliage, while a swarm of enemy drones swiftly approached from the east. Noting that these drones bore only light machine guns and that the majority of their structures were devoted to the support of four robotic arms that hung from their bellies, SAVANT informed the users in the CA command hub that the Superior Authority troops appeared to be undergoing extraction.

"Recommend immediate evacuation of CA assets as well," the AI's voice calmly uttered within Webb's command hub at the Rocky Mountain headquarters.

"Authorized!" the general responded in an emphatic yet rasping voice, the leader's former evacuation order having been impossible to execute until now.

Webb still stood in the location to which he had stepped earlier, roughly a meter in front of his central command position. Casting his eyes about the command center, he took in screen after screen covered with cerise-tinted injury indicators, video footage of blood-soaked and—in some cases—de-limbed troops, and the total count of dead among the Command Activated forces. The officer was desperately fighting to control the shaking in his limbs and blinking back the tears that threatened to stream down his cheeks.

The young general had endured the fiercest and deadliest battle any unit had experienced since the Command Activated program's creation, and he desperately wished he had not.

Lilian clutched Maxwell's arms and buried her face in his shoulder, sobbing uncontrollably and inconsolably. The man just held her as he stared fixedly at his workstation's screen, rubbing his right hand softly in circles across her back. He knew that she was undoubtedly experiencing the emotional turmoil caused by a deep empathy for the fallen soldiers while being burdened with the knowledge that what she'd witnessed could easily have happened to Ked if they had not managed to extract him from the Command Activated program. His own throat had tightened around what felt like a rock that had become stuck halfway through it, and his complex emotions were all fighting for recognition, including anger, fear, sorrow, and the worry that Alliance leadership *still* might not sanction a strike deep within Chinese territory.

"We do have to share what we've learned with Alliance leadership," he whispered.

Lilian nodded her head and turned tearfully away to step into the next room, staring forlornly out at the majestic view of the Hong Kong skyline as it was projected on the wall of the lounge. Sliding into his chair with such low energy that he felt as though part of his very life essence had been sucked out of him, Maxwell dejectedly observed the extraction drone that was approaching the SA troop whose first-person camera feed was still displayed on the Confederacy command center's main screen.

He studied the mechanisms as the robotic arms reached down to grasp ahold of attachment points that must have made themselves available in the SA troops' shoulder armor as the drones approached. The technical expert noted how the able-bodied troops were lifted off the ground—figures dangling below the two-meter-wide drones—while the wounded Superior Authority soldiers were being hoisted up using tentacles that dropped sinuously down from ports in the bellies of the drones until the robotic arms could securely clamp around their bodies.

Dead SA troops were simply left behind.

"You absolute..." Maxwell started to say before catching himself and biting off what would have come next.

He clenched his jaw and pinched the bridge of his nose between a finger and thumb, willing himself to calm down as he took several deep breaths. As he heard the lead Confederacy researcher launch back into a campaign of lobbying the director for more backing for his next stage of research,

Maxwell gestured down to the lower right area of his screen, opening a control interface and muting the audio.

The Brit then held a finger up so that the selector that appeared on the screen in front of his finger hovered over the top bar of the frame holding the video feed. A menu appeared, and he selected the option to copy the file to a message, which he addressed to all senior members of the Command Activated leadership team.

Hands dropping to his keyboard and fingers flying across the keys, Maxwell punched out a message explaining that viewers would obtain a glimpse into how the Confederacy had built out its competing program—devoid of any ethical decision-making. He explained that the result of this approach was a CEN force that relied on high-speed deployment rather than stealth, complete remote control of combat assets by per-troop "commanders" back at SA headquarters, and the apparent belief that troops were still quite expendable.

Sending the message off with an angry wave, Maxwell stood and crossed the room to where Lilian was only just managing to stop the flow of her tears. He wrapped her lovingly in his arms and murmured comforting phrases to her as she once again leaned into his shoulder, squeezing her eyes closed as if to shut out the images that still tormented her.

They heard an aerial vehicle descending outside the plane, which was soon followed by another that landed somewhere farther from its wing, and then several more.

"At least we have *some* good news today," Maxwell said as he pulled back and supported Lilian's forearms and elbows with his wrists and hands, "and the family we've saved is about to walk through that door!"

Lilian took a shuddering breath and managed to bring out a weak smile across her face as she looked up into Maxwell's eyes and gave him a short nod.

"Opening main passenger entrance for Samantha's family and escorts," FAILSAFE announced as the hydraulics controlling the stair-studded combination door and ascension device hissed and moved the gangway down to make contact with the tarmac.

A light rain was falling outside—the droplets forming rivulets of water that were projected onto the interior surfaces of the aircraft—and the soft pattering of the raindrops outdoors accompanied a gust of cool, humid air as it swept into the plane. The breeze ushered in the welcome scent of moist ground and sea air.

Chattering voices could be heard approaching the plane, and soon the couple also heard the tapping of footsteps and exclamations of wonder in Cantonese as Samantha guided her family inside. Upon entering the vessel, the elderly couple and teenage boy looked about and pointed in astonishment as they took in the interior display effects. The armory currently being concealed, the newcomers' attention was drawn to the computer lab and the lounge, and then, as Samantha struggled through the door after her family with several rotund bags of belongings, the new arrivals suddenly realized that Lilian and Maxwell were standing arm-in-arm and greeting them with friendly smiles.

"Thank you for..." Maxwell began and then stopped himself, lifting a finger to his communications strip and then pressing and holding it while saying, "Translate speech to Cantonese."

"Let's try that again," he said and then paused as what sounded like his own voice emanated from the strip with perfect Cantonese diction. "We thank you for joining us here!"

Maxwell gently let go of Lilian's arms as he faced his guests and gave them each a short nod while his strip translated the last phrase. The three nodded politely in return, and then her parents quickly directed their attention to Samantha, facial expressions conveying a pleading for formal introductions as the youngest family member's attention drifted around the cabin. The boy's eyes were constantly being pulled to look out of their rightmost corners, so he was forced to turn his head every time he wanted to change the direction of his gaze.

As Jayce and Billy eased their way through the entrance, trying to carefully move the multiple suitcases and bags they held in each hand into the plane without jarring them, Samantha smiled and held out a hand toward Maxwell and Lilian while pressing and holding on her own strip and requesting that her words be translated to English.

In Cantonese, she offered, "My father's name is Hao Liang, senior partner at a business law firm. My mother's name is Jiao, and of course, you have seen many pictures of my brother, Teddy. Father and Mother, this is Maxwell Clarke, a doctor of multiple technical disciplines and the person whose airplane we are using."

Samantha paused for the translation to finish playing and her father and mother smiled and exchanged nods with Maxwell again—the elderly couple practically radiant. The face of Samantha's younger brother seemed to beam continually, with a slight smile continually present no matter where he was looking.

Continuing, the young woman said, "Here is my *very* good friend Lilian Bachar. You know that I've become a good friend and mentor to her brother with special needs, Ked Bachar. Lilian forgave me for working for the government and betraying her trust, and then she and Maxwell even suggested and planned this whole trip!"

Samantha's voice was filled with regret, undertones of apology, and gratitude as her eyes misted over and tearfully remained locked on Lilian's while she spoke and while the translation played.

Her parents' eyes rapidly became tearful as well, and her mother self-consciously wiped a droplet from her cheek before the elderly couple nodded gratefully several times to both Lilian and Maxwell. Behind the Chinese family, Jayce and Billy had moved to the wall separating the main section of the fuselage from the cargo area and had stacked the family's precious belongings carefully in the corners. They turned to walk back up to the office space as Samantha directed her hand toward them.

"Father and Mother, you've seen them in action, and I've already told you some things about them, but by way of formal introduction, these two warriors are Jayce Johnson..."

Jayce nodded down to the elders with a broad, pleasant smile as they stared appreciatively up at his hulking figure and nodded in return.

"...and Billy Chong. During the flight here I learned Billy was previously a Singaporean military officer and now works in the American military with Jayce," the young woman concluded.

Billy brought himself to military attention and executed a powerful and respectful nod to Samantha's family members.

Looking at Billy warmly and waiting until her strip's translation concluded, Samantha added, "Billy is not only a strong soldier, he is also *very* intelligent, speaking fluent Cantonese, Mandarin, *and* English!"

The young soldier turned bright red as he continued standing stiffly and waited patiently for Samantha's strip to end its work before adding, in Cantonese, "My American friends might protest that my English is better suited for the sports fields and entertainment venues than academic endeavors, but I am constantly learning!"

Samantha's father and mother smiled in good humor as they cast very interested glances back and forth between Samantha and Billy's faces while the two continued making steady eye contact.

Maxwell, Lilian, and Jayce looked on jocosely and exchanged knowing looks with each other—Billy and Samantha's mutually soft regards carrying on as though they were unable to stop—until Maxwell finally offered, "Liang family, please feel free to relax in the lounge, and through the forward door is a washroom and fully stocked kitchen that are also at your disposal."

He paused for his strip to translate those statements, then added, "Please also do not worry about the future. We will do whatever it takes to give you a new and safe life that is undetectable by Confederacy governments."

Samantha turned to take her mother by the elbow and escort her over to the sofas as the elderly couple again nodded and smiled gratefully at Maxwell and Lilian. The family huddled together on the furniture in one of the far corners of the lounge and began chattering, laughing, and continuously wiping away the tears that sprang to their eyes.

Jayce and Billy stepped up behind Lilian and Maxwell as they drank in the family's happiness.

In a voice fraught with emotion, Jayce sighed, "Feels real good to break at least *one* family free from the Communists' grasp. Just wish we could free the whole damned country. Makes me wish the West would just cut all economic ties with China so we weren't lining the pockets of the CEN leaders and filling their war chests with our money."

Maxwell's brow furrowed as he continued to gaze delightedly at the Hong Kong citizens.

"I know how you feel, my friend," he responded. "The sad thing is that even if we were to boycott goods from China it would not be the social elites who would suffer. They would—sure as hell awaits them—keep what they wanted and leave the innocents to starve."

Billy chimed in, "What we *really* need is the willingness to endure the 'cruel' loss of cheap goods *and* the will to sincerely and fully back the opposition groups in these regimes, not just giving them lip service while never truly committing to the kind of support it will take to free them!"

This thought brought Maxwell's mind back to what he and Lilian had witnessed of the Superior Authority operations.

"Speaking of which," he began morosely, "Lilian and I just caught a glimpse of how the SA troops are being controlled. They have a command center not unlike the CA version, but theirs is populated with individual-troop-assigned 'controllers' who use virtual reality to fully dictate *every* move the soldiers make."

Maxwell turned and took in the looks on Billy and Jayce's faces as the full implications dawned on them.

"The SA soldiers must have electrodes embedded in their bodies that allow them to be moved about like marionettes," the Alliance technical lead flatly stated.

Jayce was working his lips heavily, and his face had taken on a glowering expression as his hands balled up in fists. He planted the firsts firmly in at his waist, elbows cocked out and muscles rippling. Billy was shaking his head and turned away momentarily to regain control of his emotions. After a moment, the younger man ferociously spun back around and spat, "We gotta do something about those Commie *devils*!"

Lilian looked from Billy to Jayce to Maxwell and quickly offered, "Max did say that we may be able to use our proximity to the SA complex to do some additional good while we're here. Right, honey?"

She looked at him supportively and rubbed his back. The man's expression transitioned from grieving to enthusiastic.

"Absolutely, yes!" her significant other asserted.

"FAILSAFE and I have been studying the data we gleaned from the research facility's network, including the security camera feeds and the location data from tablets such as the one carried by their lead researcher. We strongly believe that the operations command center is actually physically located on the same property as the research branch, just separated by fencing and gates with nearly as high a level of security as the perimeter. I think the top medical researchers often visit the command hubs to observe their performance and make program adjustments, as deemed necessary.

"If we *really* want to set the Confederacy back then we need to mount a three-pronged attack. First, because the SA command operations' network perimeter is too well-protected, we need to install a device to create a rogue network connection. Such a network interface will be extremely difficult for the CEN security AI to detect and will allow FAILSAFE and me to thereby exert the necessary control over the network to influence troop activation and transportation. We'll get as many of the SA troops as possible out of the complex, shuffle up their transportation so they cannot be tracked, and get them on this plane and out of the country."

As they exchanged glances, Jayce and Billy's eyes were lighting up with intense fires of determination.

Maxwell continued, "Second, we need to purge all data we can from the operations and research networks. This will require very careful exploitation of the last vulnerabilities FAILSAFE and I left unused within the research and development network, and a similar approach in their command operations network—all utilizing the rogue ingress-egress point. We'll have to execute a data purge across all systems at once to have a chance of succeeding before the security AI interferes.

"Third, they have too much latent awareness throughout the medical and military leadership teams that certain types of individuals are best suited for their particular soldier activation protocols. We need to purge nearly all brain scan files for civilians across the CEN nations. This is the most challenging part in many ways, though less risky in many others. The blessing is that this can likely still be safely performed in the aftermath of the first two objectives' completion. FAILSAFE will have to assist me in performing a mass infiltration across as many medical provider networks as possible, and we will expunge brain scan data for all citizens except those who have serious medical conditions."

Maxwell paused to think through his mental checklist, making sure he had not forgotten anything.

In the ensuing silence, Billy spoke up first, asking, "So, how do we install this rogue network-creating thing?"

Eyes lighting up yet again, the Brit squeezed Lilian's arm and stepped away to access a drawer at one of the desks in the office area, withdrawing a small, nondescript gray box.

"This device is a rather simple solution that many people could easily use if they knew about its capabilities. All electrical wiring throughout any building is fully able to carry electronic data packets in addition to simply delivering electricity, and it doesn't matter the direction of power transmission—data can be sent and received in either direction across any power cabling.

"Power companies have actually been sending control signals over power mains since as far back as the Nineteen Twenties. The electrical wiring in the typical building can support a variety of frequencies, so with electricity using fifty and sixty Hertz signals, extra data can be transported along the same wiring at much higher frequencies without causing any interference. The only limitation is that the signals degrade the farther you are from the transmitter."

Tapping the small box, Maxwell excitedly continued, "This little device is an adapter with a port on one side for the connection of a standard data cable and the prongs of a plug on the back, the prongs on this gadget being compatible with outlets here.

"All we have to do is find an out-of-the-way location where a network port is near a power outlet and link a network cable to this device, then plug it into the wall. A similar device will need to be attached to a power line outside the complex, and once the two are transmitting across the electrical cables, a backdoor from the outside world will be created, which will go straight into the military network. I've ensured that this device is capable of transmitting a strong signal out to five hundred meters, which should be sufficient for us to—very carefully—tap into the primary power line outside the boundaries of the property and attach the other adapter I've designed for that purpose."

Jayce and Billy were nodding thoughtfully, but Lilian's face had grown worried.

The Homeland analyst quietly stated, "In other words, someone has to get *inside* the complex to install the device."

Maxwell's enthusiasm deflated significantly as he admitted, "That is true. It will not be a low-risk mission, but I've tasked FAILSAFE to hack into a company that is part of the complex's supply chain, and we will create a false employee identity for whoever is going inside, taking advantage of the next physical supply delivery to give the infiltrator the chance to plant the adapter."

It was quiet a moment before Billy passionately spoke up.

"If that's what it takes to disable the SA program then you can count on me! Just call me Agent Chong, 'cause I'm gonna plant that device so hard it'll give their *president* constipation!"

Jayce could not hold in his laughter, slapping a hand on Billy's shoulder and insisting, "You got it, brutha, but you gotta promise not to take any unnecessary risks, alright? I still need you to school me in basketball with your crazy ninja skills!"

Billy gave Jayce a wink and elbowed him playfully before jerking an imaginary ball back and forth and pretending to make a shot. Jayce shook his head bemusedly as the younger soldier then waved his hands to encourage the imaginary crowd whose cheers were only audible through Billy's own mouth.

FAILSAFE spoke up from the computer on which Maxwell had previously been working.

"Glad to hear we have the core of a plan. I have managed to penetrate the network of a janitorial supply company that serves the entire complex and have created Billy's alias, false employee record, and assignment to the next delivery...which is scheduled for eight o'clock tomorrow morning."

Billy glanced at the display strip attached to the inside of his left wrist, noting the lateness of the hour.

"That gives us just about enough time to travel to Guangzhou so I can get suited up as a delivery driver and get the truck to the complex," he opined.

"I'll need to go so I can install my device on the cable outside the perimeter," Maxwell chimed in.

Lilian stepped up to Maxwell's left elbow and gripped it possessively, firmly stating, "You'll need someone to watch your back, and that someone will be me!"

"Sounds like a great idea," Jayce agreed, pointing to his strip and saying, "...and I'm at least going with you all to wait outside the complex in case you need backup...and there's nothing you can do about it!"

Chapter 12

"Some big city firms employ security staff with special forces backgrounds. They don't advertise it, but you'll find out if you cause trouble. These individuals pay close attention to absolutely everything, which is a rare skill. Security work, whether for an office or a nuclear facility, demands constant vigilance and resistance to complacency.

Complacency is the enemy of security, and it can be fought against with procedures, audits, and benchmarks, but the key component in any physical security program is the inclusion of dedicated experts and robust training to minimize tepidity. The main job of a security professional is to combat complacency wherever it appears...as it inevitably does."

- Charles C. Laurier, Chief Operating Officer, Sedulity Security

The Russian woman had roughly torn General Gaines' strip away from its place behind his ear and crushed the device in one hand as they'd entered the getaway rig. The Alliance officer had done his best to take this in stride, and he'd slowly, warily settled into the middle of the rear bench of the enemy's spacious utility AV. The middle bench had been positioned so it faced backward toward the rearmost seating area, and the captive had glared across the gap at the still-raised hands that were concealing the American traitor's face. Gaines was ignoring the condescending and spiteful look the Chinese agent was casting at him from where the man was protectively sitting next to his source, applying what appeared to be an ointment to the exposed and bruised tissues of his ribcage and inner thigh—the solution obviously providing immediate relief.

The Slavic spy had adjusted the direction of her submachine gun as she'd followed Gaines into the vehicle and destroyed his communications device, following which she had sat to the officer's right with the barrel of her weapon tucked into the general's hip.

"I will not hesitate to kill you," she'd sworn, and although he could see the malice in her eyes, he'd stared back in fierce defiance.

Besides his complete lack of willingness to be treated as anyone's pawn, General Gaines had also heard what the woman had told Agent Vela and had recognized the sincerity and loyalty in her voice, so he'd understood that his life was her best bargaining chip if she wanted to obtain her captured team member's release.

As the AV had pulled away from the warehouse balcony, the officer resisted the urge to glance out the back window to see if the military police aerial vehicle was showing any signs of movement. He knew that the standard protocol when dealing with hostage situations was to avoid instigating any emotional reactions from the captors. Securing the release of the captured personnel would be the Alliance forces' primary objective, and everything else would fall far lower on the scale of precedence.

The wind had begun howling around the vehicle as it had accelerated to nearly its top speed, executing a long curving turn toward the lights of a nearby business district. Feeling more secure, the intelligence source had finally dropped his hands.

"*Heshk*," Gaines spat out vehemently, "*you're* the one who betrayed your country?!"

The swarthy man was practically beaming as he enjoyed the look of surprise and disgust that was contorting the general's face.

"That's right, General! In the flesh!" he declared, his thick brows raised and his obsessively trimmed van dyke framing his broad grin.

The Chinese agent rapidly became agitated as he realized that the Alliance officer knew the source well. He angrily gestured at the general as he shouted at the Russian in Mandarin and she responded with fiery words of her own, bringing the man to peevish silence.

Having comprehended the likely cause of the male agent's consternation, Heshk had been unable to resist the urge to let an amused expression slide across his visage.

"It's no big deal if he identifies me at this point, my good servants, as things were getting too hot inside the program anyway. It was time for me to make my exit and ride off into a sunset bought using my overflowing bank account!"

This only further angered the Asian, who scowled at his source and leaned in like he was ready to push the obnoxious man out of the soaring vehicle.

"Now, now, Mr. '*Yin*,' you know you aren't allowed to lay a finger on me. I'll share the rest of what I know once I'm safely on my new private jet and see the right amount of compensation sitting in my offshore money pot. Till then, you're going to do whatever I *want* you to, unless you'd rather explain to your superiors how you let the Confederacy's best source of intel about the Command Activated slip away...or end up dead."

The Chinese agent jerked his head to face away from the unctuous man, letting his blazing eyes consume the nighttime skyline while obviously maintaining a carefully listening ear—ready to protest if the larger man revealed additional sensitive information. The Russian had glared out of the corners of her eyes at Heshk with obvious distaste during his soliloquy, already silently facing away from the object of her loathing.

Satisfied that he'd wrought his will upon the enemy agents, the American now returned his attention to the still-glowering General Gaines.

"Where were we...?" he began, but Gaines interrupted.

"You were about to explain how you could betray the trust of millions of decent people after years of honorable service," the officer goaded.

The pale man snorted, giving a slight toss of his head despite possessing a hairstyle that included a closely shaved mane around the sides of his scalp and long, slickly gelled-back hair across the top.

"*Betrayal?*" he spat out. "As though promoting that dirtbag Thompson over me was *not* a betrayal! You know that guy finds every excuse to get out of working a full shift? And that's not the *least* of his issues!"

Gaines shot back, "There would have been other opportunities for you...and you were more than healthily compensated for all your work!"

"It's not about that!" was the man's vehement reply. "Not *really*. Sure, I'll enjoy living on my private island with every luxury money can buy, but at the end of the day it was about broken *trust!* The program admins broke my trust—yet again—when *I* should have been the one running the security team...even years ago!"

The general was only able to shake his head in solemn disappointment at the man's shortsightedness and dearth of loyalty.

Heshk looked briefly out the window as the growing number of lights outside told him they had entered the business area, and then the younger man continued, "What's that saying? 'Who watches the watchers?' Well, it doesn't matter how many regulators you send in or how many insider threat detection tools you deploy, security team members can *always* find a way around that, so *any* organization that doesn't treat them with the respect they deserve has *earned* its own demise!"

Gaines just tilted his head back and stared the man down until the eye contact became unbearable for the traitor, and Heshk gratefully turned away to focus on the distraction of the AV dropping to ground level and entering a parking garage.

Billy did not appreciate how sweaty his palms had become as he approached the southern access gate for the Superior Authority command operations section of the complex. He breathed in deeply through his nose and out through his mouth, letting his eyes go unfocused for a moment in meditation before saying a quick prayer to his ancestors for assistance. The young Asian man then brought his delivery truck to a smooth halt at the large, black steel gate not far from the southeastern corner of the enemy facility. The communications console positioned on the driver's side of the road was equipped with a high-caliber automatic turret that had locked onto him as he'd approached and was now pointing its large barrel at his torso from just a meter away.

Well, that's not intimidating at all! Billy sarcastically thought as he willed himself to flash a smile at the console's screen.

Maxwell had forged an electronic identification card for Billy, and he now unclipped it from its attachment point on the dark blue coveralls—clothing he had "borrowed" from the locker room at the supply company's warehouse. He tapped the window control and leaned out of the portal as the truck's side aperture slid down, bringing the identification card into proximity with the access control console's screen.

After he had held it there a few seconds, a robotic voice projected from the screen, telling him in Cantonese to proceed directly to the delivery area.

"You got it!" he said cheerfully in the same tongue, tapping the window control and then accelerating his vehicle in through the gate as it opened. This process was accompanied by heavy clicking sounds from deep within the concrete wall into which the left side of the gate was embedded. After its many bolts had unlocked, the entire breadth of the metal structure rolled inside the thick concrete wall to its right.

Driving the large truck ponderously down the narrow two-lane road while glancing at the virtually windowless gray buildings on either side, he was hoping the delivery area would be obvious enough for him to avoid drawing attention to himself by aimlessly driving around the facility.

Leaning forward at each point where a side road led off between the buildings, Billy saw nothing that shouted out that his delivery should be made down any of those paths.

He was starting to become truly worried when he spotted a large, blue-and-white sign ahead. With an arrow pointing to the right, it indicated that this was the parking area for delivery vehicles.

Heaving a sigh of relief, he steered the truck into a wide right turn, trying not to scrape the side of the bulky vehicle along the building at the near corner of the parking access road. He could see a waist-high loading dock ahead, guarded by two young soldiers. One paced disinterestedly along the lip of the loading area while the other leaned against the wall at the left of the only one among three vertically tracked access doors that was currently open, warm light streaming out into the coolness of the morning air. Both soldiers had assault rifles strapped around their shoulders, their firing hands loosely resting on the weapons' grips.

The pacing soldier stopped and waited expectantly after giving Billy a halfhearted wave over his shoulder to tell him to bring his vehicle up to the loading dock at that location. Billy executed another turn to the right, pulling into the empty space behind the long, narrow building that fronted the main road, then reversed his vehicle slowly back to bring the base of the truck's cargo hold to within a dozen centimeters of the cement loading platform.

Thumbing the ignition button, Billy shut off the vehicle and then placed both hands on the steering wheel, palms down, while he briefly closed his eyes and muttered, "Here goes *everything*!"

Tapping the door access control switch and waiting for his side door to slide back along the left surface of the truck, the infiltrator swung his legs out and hopped jauntily down to the cement-paved ground, landing with a few bouncing steps and turning to greet the nearest Confederacy soldier.

"It's too early in the day for me to give an enthusiastic greeting!" the Singaporean joked in Cantonese as he pulled his gloves from where they were dangling from his chest pocket, slipping them onto his hands.

The soldier smirked.

"That is true!" he acknowledged and watched with a slightly more agreeable expression as Billy hoisted himself up onto the platform using a lower, metal step built into the truck's rear bumper and a handhold protruding from the side of the cargo door. Casually backing up a few steps, the soldier made room for the stand-in supply worker to press a finger on the cargo door's biometric access pad. Billy then waited in front of the access hatch as it rolled up with something of a groan, the truck's hatch begging for relief via the application of copious amounts of grease.

Billy shook his head as he chortled and exchanged an understanding look with the guardsman.

"Maintenance really needs to do a better job of keeping things running smoothly!" he complained, then flipped the switch that extended a metal bridge from the edge of the hold out onto the loading dock. Billy stepped inside the space to grab the handle of the cargo lift that was already positioned under a narrow but heavy crate covered with markings stating it contained an all-purpose cleansing solution.

Turning to the soldier with a friendly smile, he asked, "Where do they usually have us start?"

As if expecting to act as a guide, the young man gave Billy a short wave with his free hand and used an easy, rolling gait to walk inside the open bay, exchanging a curt nod with the other soldier as he entered the building.

"This way," the guide called out over his shoulder, and Billy tugged the lift into action, its motorized wheels moving the heavy crate in the direction its user was piloting the handle.

Billy also gave a friendly nod to the stationary soldier, but inside his calm exterior he was growing increasingly worried that he was not going to be allowed to navigate the building or any of the rest of the facility on his own. That would make the placement of the rogue access point extremely difficult. His fears seemed to be realized as the escort walked through the bay and used an entrance to access the hallway at its rear, the electronic door lock indicator light switching from red to green and the door sliding open as the soldier approached. The younger, Chinese man stayed within a half meter of the authentication panel after stepping inside, ensuring the door would stay open as Billy and his lift rolled through.

Inside the large, brightly lit hallway beyond, the CEN soldier tipped his head forward toward the left path and then started walking down the hall past Billy. The composite floor in this area was built for wear and tear, but Chong noticed how wheel marks had managed to become worn into its surface after years of enduring the same types of deliveries week after week. The guide led him to where the corridor ended at an intersection with a perpendicularly running hallway, and the soldier strolled down that hall to the right, stopping in front of a janitorial closet and stepping up to its door to compel the automatic portal to slide open.

The young Chinese man nodded toward the dark room, and Billy stopped the lift, reaching into the crate to pull out a couple of jugs of blue liquid. He carried them—bottles jostling against his thighs and solution sloshing and foaming inside—into the room and deposited them on a steel shelf where he could see one container of the same cleanser sitting at the back of the open space. Counting the number of spots in which additional bottles would fit, he ferried another six containers in and set them on the shelf, eyes on a swivel as he searched for any sign of a network port in the hallway or room.

His hopes were not high, as this did not seem like the type of area in which computer equipment would need to be set up. Billy's positivity was rapidly diminishing as he considered his chances of success given the presence of his companion and the look of the space in which he was working.

As if fate had anticipated his reaction to the situation, the young Chinese soldier suddenly freed Billy from his dismay as he exited the closet.

The CEN soldier held out his free hand to point down the length of the hallway they currently occupied, announcing, "The janitor closets actually open without a card, you just have to step up to them. There are two more down that way, one around the corner to the right and another immediately to the left at the end of the next hallway. You fine with dropping the rest of the bottles off on your own?"

Billy tried to hide his excitement as he casually nodded.

"Alright," the guide continued, "when you get back, just come out on the platform, and you can move another couple of crates into the bay. Janitors will move them to the other buildings from there."

Billy nodded again and started trudging down the hallway with his lift in tow, glancing back after several steps to see the CEN troop moving out of sight as he returned to the loading area. Unable to resist, Billy leaped up and executed a jubilant scissor kick in the air, landing with his left arm forward and his right arm pumping exultantly, hands forming fists.

Regaining his composure, the invader made his way down the hall and then continued into the corridor to the right, noting with additional relief that this one was lined with doors and that it seemed this was more of an office area. Walking slowly down the corridor, he saw a sign on the face of a door roughly one-third of the way down that indicated it was the next janitorial supply room on his route. With most of the electronic locks on the doors in the hallway displaying red lights, Sergeant Chong was once again starting to wonder about the chances that one of them would also open if he stepped up to them; if not, he might have to resort to scrambling up into the utility space above the ceiling panels.

Just then, he noticed that an entryway on his right, slightly further down the hall, was currently standing open. His heart leaped, and he was about to step forward to peer inside when the access portal for the room two doors down on his left suddenly slid open.

Billy nearly froze in his tracks and stumbled a step as he remembered that he needed to keep walking naturally toward the janitorial closet's entrance. He looked up nonchalantly and flashed his most winning smile at the two female soldiers—both dressed for desk work—who exited the room. The soldier at the left side of the pair caught his eye as she half-listened to her data storage device-laden companion chatter away. She gave him a slow wink before the pair of young women turned away from Billy, then ogled him head to toe and up again as she looked back over her shoulder, accompanying her oblivious companion down the hallway.

Blushing, Billy's mind immediately flew to Samantha and he warmly tried to imagine what it would be like to have her look at him like that. Shaking his head in disbelief that his mind could drift to such things at a time like this, he chuckled to himself and parked his lift by the room in which he was to make his next delivery.

Grabbing two bottles out of the crate, Billy spotted a security camera positioned on the ceiling at the end of the hall and made a show of struggling to carry the bottles into the janitors' supply room. Once he was fully inside, he quickly shoved one container on the shelf and then spun the cap of the second, intentionally tipping the jug to spill its contents across his hands and pouring some on the floor for good measure.

Placing the open bottle and lid on the shelf, he snatched a few highly absorbent, rapidly recyclable towels from a carton on another shelf and began laboriously patting his hands with them as he stepped back out into the hallway with what he hoped was a sheepish posture. The amateur spy made his way toward the only other open door, shaking his head and putting on the best show he could.

As he approached the target room, he could tell that the floor was high-gloss, and the room was large and well-lit. He realized that this was a gymnasium but, fortunately, it appeared to be empty at present. Glancing around the open space, he saw that the two doors on the far side were locked and he could feel his anxiety growing as he quickly searched around the walls for his objective.

Finally, his eyes locked onto a small panel halfway down the nearest of the pair of shorter walls and he scanned the room for cameras as he swiftly strode over to it. As he had hoped, he had found a modern network cable access port!

Turning his head rapidly to find the nearest power outlet, he estimated the distance between the two as he stuffed the towels into his left pocket and unstrapped the cover on the cargo pocket on the right leg of his coveralls, pulling out Maxwell's compact device and a length of cable. In its current state, the function of the small box was not obviously apparent, its network communications interface having been carefully hidden. Maxwell had added some obfuscating features, including a small screen with some built-in functions, dummy data, and a standard data port. This had been done to support the story Billy planned to tell if his pockets had been searched by security personnel: that it was a multi-function storage unit on which he kept his notes for the night classes he was taking.

Judging that the cable should barely be long enough to reach, Billy adeptly revealed the device's network port and punched the end of the cable into the female receptacles on both the gadget and the wall, then stretched the cord out across the wall to the outlet. He flipped a small switch on the side of the box and the prongs of the plug extended from the back of the unit, allowing him to fit it securely into the power source. Expeditiously examining the device and cable, he thought that it all looked nondescript enough to avoid drawing much attention from casual observers. He just prayed it would be left alone long enough to serve its purpose!

Billy heard the voice of the talkative female soldier from earlier faintly echoing in from the hallway and jogged back to the gymnasium's entrance, yanking the towels back out of his pocket. Glancing down the corridor to his right, he saw that the young females had not yet rounded the corner and he dashed diagonally across the hall to the closet, quickly sponging up some of the liquid off the floor before casting the crumpled, chemical-infused ball of absorbent material onto a shelf and stepping back out to grab another couple of containers.

The female soldiers had once again entered the hallway, the more communicative girl's hands now devoid of the media devices. Billy made a show of grabbing the handles of two jugs with each hand and lifting them easily—muscles bulging inside his sleeves—while waggling his eyebrows up and down encouragingly at the second, more observant Chinese soldier. She tilted her head back and pursed her lips appreciatively as she slowed her pace and let a noticeable swaying of her hips enter her gait. The girl turned her wanton gaze from Billy's biceps to his eyes and maintained alluring eye contact until she and her oblivious coworker had reentered their office, and the door had slid closed behind them.

Rushing to make up for lost time, Billy quickly grabbed the handle of the lift and moved on toward the end of the long hallway, passing door after door of locked offices and hearing muffled voices reverberating out from many of them. Reaching the end of the hall, he saw that the corridor veered off to the left—the next janitorial supply closet a few doors down—and the tunnel then connected with a similar structure in the adjoining edifice via a short extension between the two buildings.

As he moved up and stopped outside of the final closet, he was startled to see two medical personnel in lab coats walk through the intersection at the end of the corridor, passing from left to right as they strode hurriedly through the hallway that ran perpendicular to the one in which he was standing. The medical personnel were being followed by a robotic gurney that was automatically tailing them as it balanced on the gyroscopic orb that was its only contact with the floor.

The gurney bore a large figure in what unmistakably was a Superior Authority exosuit.

Billy took in the fact that the SA troop was missing one leg just above the knee, a tourniquet clamped down on the stub. The soldier's other foot and ankle also had a distinctly mangled appearance.

None of the three paid Billy any attention as he heard one of the medical personnel say that this soldier was among several who would have to be taken offsite for more intensive medical treatment. Pensively grabbing a couple of containers out of the crate and depositing them on the appropriate shelf in the storage room, Billy then did the same with two more as an idea formed in his mind.

"Max is gonna need to know where they're taking those casualties..." he murmured to himself before getting a sharp look in his eyes and turning to inspect the nearby security camera. Seeing that its lens was definitely directed at the corridor that passed the gym, Billy double-tapped his strip to see if he could reach Jayce or the others. He waited a few seconds but only heard his strip give him an error message stating that a communications tower was not in close enough proximity.

Nodding his head decisively, he turned to race down the unmonitored hallway to the intersection where he'd seen the three people pass earlier. He pressed his back up against the wall near the right corner and, leaning slowly out to check down the opposite hall for a camera but seeing none nearby, let his cheek protrude just far enough around the most proximate corner to allow him to peer down the path to his right.

He took in the rows of locked doors in this hallway and saw the trailing edge of the robotic gurney disappearing into a room near the far end. Billy burst out around the corner and sprinted down the length of the passage, trying to make his footfalls as quiet as possible. He only slowed his pace as he approached the room into which the litter had trundled. The door was closed and locked, and the man's spirits fell as he took in the red indicator light; still, he decided to press an ear to the door to try to get whatever information he could.

He heard voices growing rapidly louder inside the room.

Mind racing, he strode over to the edge of the lobby at the end of the hall, standing just at the edge of the area and noting that it was being monitored by a security camera. Billy adopted a stance like he was listening to a call using the bone conduction feature of his strip.

The two medical personnel exited the nearby room so engrossed in conversation that they did not even seem to notice Billy standing there, leaning against the wall. As the two moved back down the corridor in the direction from which they'd originated, heads facing forward as they spoke about different types of robotic prosthetics, the intruder made a split-second decision and silently stepped over to slip through the door as it slid shut.

Standing just inside the closed portal, Billy squinted as his eyes adjusted to the dim light in which most of the room was masked. A single, meter-wide, high-powered adjustable light was currently positioned over the body of the SA soldier, its brilliant beam shining down to reveal all the intricacies of the non-reflective exosuit while the metal outline of the gurney's surface shone brightly below it. The chest of the exosuit rose and fell in a regular pattern, but only a muffled inhalation or exhalation could be heard.

A single machine seemed to be monitoring the medical status of the reposing soldier, emitting a soft pulsing noise in time with the man's heartbeats. Large, white metal cabinets lined most of the walls, and a long metal workbench ran along a stretch of wall near the gurney, all manner of tools for electrical and computer work arrayed across it. Billy felt more like he was standing in a robotics lab than any sort of medical facility.

Searching the room and seeing no signs of another human there, Billy cautiously stepped across the polished floor to approach the screen embedded in one corner of the litter's upper face. The Superior Authority soldier's helmet came into greater focus as Billy drew nearer to the man's body, and an expression of disgust and disbelief washed across the Command Activated soldier's face as he inspected the grotesquely monstrous visage that had been built into the helmet's face shield.

"Well, *that's* not disturbing at all..." Billy muttered as he paused in his progress across the room. "Looks like your superiors want to scare the living daylights outta anyone who's unlucky enough to see you!"

Moving one step closer, the young man craned his neck forward so he could get a better look at the long, wicked teeth that lined the upper and lower jaws of the soldier's face shield. Studying the tines through narrowed eyes and with a frown that oozed distaste, he whispered, "Seriously, though? Those things look like they actually *bite*!"

The screen was dark as he reached the gurney, and he hesitantly extended a digit to tap it. Just before his finger reached its matte surface, the helmet of the SA soldier shook, making Billy jerk his hand back in alarm. The sound of a dull cough came from inside the encasement.

Billy grinned, whispering, "Man, I feel ya! The air in exosuits can get really dry!"

He reached a finger back out to the litter's screen and tapped it lightly to activate it. Under the patient details, it listed only a military identification number and the man's gender before describing the many maladies from which the soldier was suffering. Billy caught himself brooding on the physical trauma that had been inflicted on the enemy, correcting his train of thought with the reminder that the person inside the suit was likely incapable of feeling pain at this point.

"I'm guessing an Alliance outfit messed you up like this, too," Billy sighed. "But you're just a puppet lying here, waiting for your strings to be pulled again."

Reaching the end of the medical details, the last lines caught his eye.

"They're sending you out to...Shaoguan. A military medical facility in Shaoguan. That's going to complicate things."

The door to the room suddenly slid open, and Billy jumped back from the gurney, trying to look confused and shocked—which was not far from the truth. Staring as the doctor and Chinese colonel entered the room, he realized they must have approached without speaking to one another, and they certainly did not look like they wanted to socialize with each other now.

"S...sorry, sirs!" he stammered in the appropriate language. "I received a call and was looking for somewhere quiet to take it when I saw the door to this room open, and curiosity got the better of me!"

The doctor was scowling at him but simply raised an eyebrow upon hearing his excuse and glanced at the door with an irritated expression that clearly indicated that he only wanted the interloper out of the room as quickly as possible. Not daring to look the colonel in the eye, Billy started walking swiftly toward the door. The portal slid open as he came within a few steps of it, but that was when the colonel's hand whipped out from where it had been resting on his holstered sidearm. The man had silently released the handgun's retaining strap and now used his weapon as a cudgel to strike at the base of Billy's skull as he passed.

Chapter 13

"My interviews with prisoners of war showed me how losing control of one's life can dramatically affect mental health for the worse. The stories I heard also taught me how to survive such situations.

One of the keys is to know your strengths and weaknesses in such circumstances—using your strengths and improving upon your abilities in areas where you are weak. You also need to cherish each win, no matter how minor. Lastly, what truly sets the survivors apart is a reliance on thoughts about relationships, faith, and patriotism to keep them going through the darkness."

-Jorge Alvarez, 'The Core of Survival'

The CEN agents had transferred Gaines and Heshk to new vehicles at five separate stops. Each time they'd halted, they had exited the last vehicle, made their way through a covered space, and entered a new vehicle some distance away. That was in addition to the time they had entered an old, derelict shopping center and used a utility access point to enter the sewer maintenance tunnels under that older part of the city, emerging from a manhole at the other side of its well-worn, gravelly parking lot and trudging through scrub brush to reach a driverless vehicle that had pulled up as they'd neared a lonely road.

In the midst of the bushes and with the moon only partially visible through the mostly cloudy skies above, Gaines had taken advantage of a time when Heshk had stumbled in the rocky and dusty terrain, and the Chinese agent had been forced to catch the man's arm. The senior agent had growled out a barely audible comment, to which the Russian woman had rotated her head to respond in Mandarin. Half-turning his face and catching his guard looking over her shoulder, Gaines had suddenly darted off into the bushes to the right, dodging through the undergrowth and trying to maintain his footing while keeping his torso hunched over to limit his detectability as much as possible.

The general had not heard the Russian incoming as she'd dropped out of a mighty leap, bringing a severe fist strike into his back at the base of his ribcage. She'd knocked the wind right out of him and sent him sprawling into the jagged branches of a woody bush, emitting an almost inhuman moaning, sucking noise as he'd tried to pull air back into his lungs.

The woman had hauled him up by his collar and then held him before her, his face scratched and bleeding and covered in prairie dust and his toes barely touching the ground. She'd stared at him malevolently—her eyes centimeters from his—until he'd finally managed to pull in a deep breath. As he'd hung there, panting, she'd brought the barrel of her weapon up slowly and pressed it deeply into the flesh of his forehead while a grotesque grin was plastered across her face. The female agent had held that position while Gaines had instinctively brought his hands up to try to push against the polymer handguard surrounding the metal tip of the barrel, struggling to get some relief from the agonizing pressure.

"Stupid! *Stupid!* I may not kill you, *General*," she hissed, "but I can put you through a living *hell* until we hold the exchange!"

At a shout from the Chinese agent, she'd finally dropped the weapon to point at his torso again, turned, and—still grasping his collar—forced him to stumble his way back to her companions as she'd closely tailed him.

Now, they were once again in a vehicle, humming along through the dark on what felt like an older road. Upon entering that conveyance, the Chinese agent had pulled a dirty rag from one of his cargo pockets and had leaned across to tie it around the officer's eyes. After twenty minutes of driving and several turns, the car's wheels eventually rolled to a stop at what Gaines could only guess was a safe house.

Being forced out of the spies' latest sedan by the tip of the Russian agent's barrel as it was shoved painfully into his back, Gaines noted the crunch of the gravel under his feet and the echoing of their footsteps off nearby cement walls. The low rumble of a solid metal door as it was manually pushed aside sounded out in front of him, and he was grabbed by the collar and forced into the dark interior of a building.

The musty odor of older, neglected tile and mortar washed over him. They crossed an echoing and smaller space, then moved to the foot of some steps that his booted toe kicked against until he lifted it and ascended the short flight of stairs. At their summit, he was roughly turned to the right, shoved forward a few steps, turned right again, and forced up another short flight of stairs.

This repeated two more times until Gaines was faced left, and another heavy door was manually opened, the automatic entry machinery apparently either not yet installed or no longer functioning. The Alliance officer was shoved inside, then pushed to the right until the Russian barked, "Stop."

Grabbing his shoulders and spinning him around, she backed him up against the front of a metal chair, forcing him to sit. Stepping around behind him, it seemed the woman rummaged through some gear and pulled out an object, and then the officer felt a loop of material drop over his head and constrict around his torso and arms until it was almost unbearably tight, pinning him to the back of the chair. The Russian then connected another strap to the first, starting roughly in the middle of his back and feeding it through the legs of the chair until it emerged between his calves; she pulled the strap up to attach to the first in roughly the center of his chest, then tightened that strap as well.

Apparently satisfied that her hostage had been sufficiently secured, the woman moved toward the front room where Heshk and the male Confederacy agent had just entered. The security analyst was plaguing his handler with complaints about the lack of alcoholic drinks in their supplies.

Gaines heard Yin shout something at the American in Mandarin that shut him up despite the language barrier. The Russian and Chinese agents then entered a heated discussion in which the captive man was able to leverage the little Mandarin he knew to guess the topic of their debate with reasonable certainty.

The Chinese man was obviously firmly against the idea of risking an exchange, and Gaines heard the words for "airplane" and "distance" repeated several times throughout their conversation. Heshk had caught on to the fact that they were talking about their next steps, and he'd voiced his desire to leave the country as soon as possible, to which the Russian woman had responded by ordering him to shut up.

General Gaines particularly hated being in this position because it would likely mean that his life would be traded for that of a cold-blooded murderer who was also a treasure trove of intelligence. He knew that the prototype tracking device he'd had surgically embedded beneath his skin was still intact, the passive mechanism being undetectable via most bug-sweeping technologies. That was a fact that seemed to have been reinforced as he had undergone what was likely an attempt to detect bugs on his person shortly after he'd been loaded in the second vehicle in the chain that night, just after his tactical vest had been taken. Given sufficient satellite or upper atmosphere coverage in this area, the bounce back from a properly tuned signal could lead Alliance forces straight to him.

He just hoped that Severance was still sufficiently functional to communicate the relevant details about his tracker to the right members of military leadership.

Jayce sat in the rental AV, tapping his thumbs idly on the steering wheel, brow furrowed and obviously upset.

"This is taking a long time!" he muttered, glaring up the road at the Superior Authority complex access gate through which his friend had driven more than an hour ago.

"This is taking one *hell* of a long time!" he shouted and slammed his fist down forcefully on the center console.

Extending his left arm out of his jacket sleeve, Jayce checked the time on his display strip again. The device's screen read 9:17 a.m. That was far longer than it should take to drop off a few crates and hook up Maxwell's adapter, even if Billy had been forced to make multiple stops.

Deciding to take action, he double-tapped the strip adhered behind his ear and ordered it to call Maxwell. The device had synced with his vehicle's audio system, and after a few moments, the technical lead's voice rang out in the car.

"I'm nearly finished here, Jayce. The power company schematics led me right to the main cable, and my tapper worked without a hitch. Getting a strong signal from the adapter over here and just connecting the satellite network transmitter!" Maxwell cheerfully shared.

"So, Billy at least got the device installed inside the complex..." Jayce rumbled.

"He absolutely did!"

"He's not out yet, though," Jayce said, trying to keep his voice emotionless but not doing a very good job of it.

"Really?" After a pause to check the time, Maxwell observed, "Could just be that he is playing up his act and engaging in riveting conversation with the Confederacy personnel..."

"Maybe. Maybe..."

Jayce was obviously not convinced.

"Let me get this uplink configured, and I'll see whether FAILSAFE and I can access cameras in this part of the network," Maxwell empathetically offered.

"I'd really appreciate that, brutha," Jayce replied, voice almost pleading.

A few moments later, Jayce heard Maxwell tell Lilian, "Alright, my love, let's hop in the car and see what there is to see."

FAILSAFE's voice came on the line, advising, "I have now gained access to a number of systems on this segment of the SA network. Carefully escalating privileges...I have located the security camera server for the front half of the complex. Reviewing footage."

Jayce waited as the veins on his temples pulsed in time with his heightened heart rate, the brawny man hardly daring to breathe.

"I'm afraid we have a problem," the AI continued, "as it seems that Mr. Chong is currently being held in one of the base's military police interrogation rooms."

Jayce's face transitioned from stoic into a ghastly grimace, almost as gradually and inevitably as tectonic plates shifting and wreaking their unstoppable destruction upon the hopes of mere mortals.

"Jayce...?" Lilian called out via the broadcast connection through Maxwell's strip.

"Jayce, it's going to be okay," she tried to assure him when he did not respond.

His eyes were fixed on the Confederacy base's gate, head tilted down and the sickened expression contorting his face.

"We can't leave him behind," was all he could manage.

"We will not, my friend!" Maxwell promised. "We will *not* leave him! This simply means that rather than solely focusing on freeing the marionettes and purging the data, we will need to add Billy's rescue to the plan as well!"

Jayce sat in silence, white-knuckled fists gripping the steering wheel so tightly it was creaking under the pressure. The warrior was fiercely battling within himself as he fought to control the monumental urge to accelerate, elevate, and plunge right into the heart of the enemy's fortress, executing anyone who stood in his way with extreme prejudice.

"We will need to collect the prototype exosuits and weapons from the plane," his friend pushed on sympathetically and urgently, comprehending the pain and drive he knew Jayce was undoubtedly feeling at that time.

"We will collect the equipment and return and break Billy out of there at the same time as we move the SA forces out of the complex. This operations side of the network is much more heavily guarded, and we may only have one shot at taking control of the troop command systems before the security AI is alerted to our presence, but a physical assault to free our friend may actually be the perfect distraction to buy us more time for the troop extraction..."

Maxwell's voice was growing increasingly excited as he brainstormed.

"...and I believe I know just the thing to make our distraction one for the history books!" he crowed.

Agent Vela was mightily trying to keep the feelings of frustration that were welling up inside of her from spilling over onto her face as the medic slowly finished running the micro-stitching device across her cheek. The woman had refused to let the warrant officer sit up for the procedure by which the healer had removed the shrapnel from where it had embedded itself in Vela's cheekbone—causing hairline fractures across that facial feature. Truth be told, the agent was still feeling light-headed from the pain and residual effects of shock that were plaguing her despite the painkillers and system-stabilizing medication they'd injected once she'd reached the ambulance.

Despite all that, she had urgent matters to which she desperately needed to attend, and the foremost item on that list was the tracking of General Gaines. When she'd reached the team's vehicles and ensured the Russian male had not only been safely extracted from his exosuit but also loaded in a high-security truck with a full squad of MPs guarding him, she'd turned away from the rig and its two up-armored escort vehicles and made her way over to her van—only to find it overly occupied.

Apparently, when all hell had broken loose inside the warehouse, Agent Daniels had called the officer in charge of the Fort Carson counterintelligence unit. When Vela had arrived at her vehicle, Major Farragut had been sitting in the center chair of the van's operations command area, barking out orders to the four junior agents and MP sergeant he'd called in to assist in handling the aftermath of the incident. The major had taken one look at Vela and ordered her to report to one of the ambulances that had just arrived onsite, without even giving her the chance to share intel or describe her suspicion that the general's Panther may possess the ability to take them straight to the hostage.

Frustrated to no end and yet knowing from experience that it was pointless to try to argue—or sometimes even reason—with her superior, Vela had stowed her gear and dashed to the ambulance in the hopes that her wound could be attended to quickly and she could then return to the fray.

Having seen the general's Panther patiently and yet anxiously sitting near the wall of the building, broad face and dark eyes searching her own expectantly, Vela had told it, "I'm sorry, um, Severance was your name? I have to stop in here quickly, and then I *really* want to talk with you."

Unfortunately, the paramedics had resisted her requests to move quickly, the senior of the two asserting that she never acts hastily "because that is how accidents happen." The woman had insisted on having the agent recline on the ambulance's gurney while the medics attached a vitals-monitoring strip to Vela's neck and then broke out the gun-like medi-jet device by which the special agent had been shot up with a cocktail of drugs to facilitate rapid recovery. The pair had then set about extracting the shrapnel from the agent's cheek, following which they injected a bone-stabilizing polymer that would slowly melt away as Vela's skull healed.

The last of the stitching now having been completed, Vela was finally permitted to sit up. She let the blood repopulate her head until she was sure she could move without risk of passing out and gratefully took the container of ice-cold water that the senior medic proffered, sipping it for a minute before half-sarcastically asking, "Am I finally being discharged?"

The senior paramedic shot her a disapproving look, yet conceded, "Well, we can't keep you here if you don't want to rest, but at least *try* to take it easy!"

"'Take it easy.' I totally will take it easy," Vela flatly promised, knowing that the medic knew that she had no intention of doing any such thing.

Leaving the lead paramedic shaking her head, the counterintelligence agent clambered down out of the back of the ambulance. As Vela looked up and down the street worriedly, she saw that Severance had disappeared. A lone, local police department vehicle had taken up a position at the intersection southeast of the nearby warehouse, the officers inside apparently only present to keep the scene contained. Vela nodded at the driver of the last of the military police vehicles in the area as he was just pulling out from where he had been parked behind the ambulance—no doubt headed back to Fort Carson.

The agent turned to walk as quickly as she dared back to the surveillance van, noting that one of the rear doors was still open, and yet the inside of the van was much quieter now as she approached. This realization gave birth to an anxious feeling in the pit of her stomach. Had all response efforts been moved back to base?

Grasping the handle protruding from the inner edge of the van's chassis near the open rear door, she stepped up into the vehicle and dejectedly took in the lone, young agent sitting idly at the forward surveillance console. The young man glanced up as she entered and looked relieved that he would likely not have to man his post any longer.

"Morning, Ma'am. Major Farragut ordered me to tell you to take the rest of the day off, as he's got everything under control," the buck sergeant advised.

A tightening of her jaw was the only visible sign that the senior agent was shouting out extremely salty words in her mind.

"Where is the major now?" she asked gruffly. "And any update on the suspects or general?"

Looking like he was very uncomfortably trapped between a rock and a hard place, the other agent decided to choose the lesser of two evils.

"He told me not to tell you, but we lost track of the suspects after they entered a parking garage nearby, likely making a switch to another vehicle and doing that over and over. They had not even contacted us to discuss an exchange or bargain by the time the major pulled up stakes and moved operations back to the headquarters about twenty minutes ago."

Vela recognized that the kid looked like a great burden had been lifted from his shoulders, but he and she both knew he'd done so at great professional risk.

"Thank you," she sincerely sighed out. "And where is the general's Panther?"

"Panther?" he looked surprised. "You mean like the combat bots? I haven't seen one around since I arrived."

Lines formed around Vela's eyes as her worries increased, and she gave the junior agent a short nod as she turned to leave.

"Thanks again, Thayer. Take care. I'm going to go 'rest'..." she said as she grabbed her protective vest and submachine gun from their hooks in the storage compartment, filling empty slots on the front of the vest with fresh magazines, "...and I just need to clean up some of the 'mess' after the operation first. I'll catch a cab from here."

Thayer stared dolefully and knowingly after her, giving his shoulders a short shrug and swiveling around to start climbing up toward the driver's seat as Vela tapped the button to close the rear door.

Stepping up onto the curb, the agent craned to look down the road to where the general's car had been parked earlier.

"Yes!" she whispered as the surveillance van pulled away behind her and hung a left at the intersection, the young driver passing the police car with a professional wave at the only marginally attentive officers inside. The warrant officer broke into a light jog as she felt hope spring up at the sight of the flag officer's long, black sedan; the car was still parked where it had stopped at the end of the column of vehicles earlier. She was feeling slightly less shaky with the drugs finally helping her organs normalize their functions and, fortunately, causing the side effects of shock to subside, but as the agent reached the dark vehicle, she slowed her pace and took another swig from her water container for good measure.

"Alright, *please* tell me you're still here!"

She peered in through the front and side windows as she walked around the sedan to its trunk, seeing the security system's indicator light on as she passed but no occupants inside the craft. Reaching the rear of the vehicle and not knowing what else to try, she gave the trunk's upper surface a few sharp raps.

Almost immediately, the cargo hatch hissed open, and the big cat's face thrust out from the shadows inside, looking trustingly up at Agent Vela.

"Thank goodness you stuck around!" she breathed. "Good boy, Severance!"

The trunk having fully opened now, the Panther placed its forepaws up on the lip of the cargo space and leaped down to the pavement, turning to bring its face close to Vela's hand. Instinctively, she reached out and stroked the composite surface along the bridge of the robot's nose, realizing after she'd already moved that this type of gesture may mean nothing to a mechanical beast.

She was gratified to feel the cat pressing up into her hand like it welcomed the contact.

Looking down affectionately at her companion, Vela bent over slightly and asked, "Do you know where General Gaines is?"

The feline's tail flicked, and his head bobbed slightly.

"Looks like we're in one of those situations where I've gotta follow you to your master, then," the agent said with a hint of a smile as she stared down into the Panther's unblinking eyes.

"I've also got a choice. I could try to bring Major Farragut up to speed and hopefully get the whole unit's help—and other agencies—but that man suffers from a narcissistic cant to his character, and just showing up after I've been ordered to go home is a good way to get myself demoted. I could go around Farragut and try to work with the MPs or local law enforcement, but that would likely be a career-ending move, and I'm still not entirely sure we're actually going to be able to find Gaines himself."

Vela sighed and double-tapped her strip, calling for a cab.

"Looks like we're going to try to home in on your master first and then see where that leads. How are you going to direct me? Or am I going to have to tail you as you lope down the street?"

Severance brought its haunches up under its belly and sat on the ground, bending its head slightly to raise its right shoulder toward the woman. Though she was aware that the Panthers had some unnatural features, she still had to work hard to calm her surprise as a port opened on the cat's shoulder and a thick tentacle emerged, hooked tip rising up and—as she resisted the urge to pull her arm away—gently approaching the display strip on her inner wrist.

When the tentacle made contact with her strip, the small device's screen immediately came to life, displaying a message saying it had detected a new device and asking if she wished to allow data transmission. She tapped the option to confirm, and a symbol appeared, indicating that data was being received. After a few seconds, Severance withdrew its tentacle and looked up at the woman expectantly again.

Checking her display strip, Vela saw that she now had a compass filling the majority of its screen, the distance to destination displayed as well.

"Ah, alright!" she mutedly exclaimed. "I can follow this...and you'll update me if his location changes?"

A deep bass, computerized voice resounding from the robot's face answered, "Yes."

The unexpected sound gave the woman a visible jolt.

"You can *talk?!*" she almost shouted. "What am I saying? Of *course* you can talk. You're one of the world's most advanced drones, after all!"

Tilting its head as it stared at her, the machine explained, "It is a feature my AI profile tries to use rarely, as most humans find it disconcerting."

Thinking about her own reaction, she nodded with understanding.

"So why didn't you tell Major Farragut that you could point him to Gaines' location?"

"Ulysses has been working on my decision-making models lately, particularly around command hierarchies, personality types, and—most importantly—character traits that can dramatically impact the success or failure of a mission. From what I observed, if I had placed my master's fate in the hands of your superior, his lack of wisdom and unwillingness to listen to others would actually have increased the risk of Ulysses being seriously injured or killed."

Vela stared at the cat, wide-eyed.

"That's some advanced decision-making, alright," she finally agreed.

Turning to look at the driverless taxi as it purred up to a stop next to them, Severance matter-of-factly responded, "Yes, and now let us save General Gaines."

The large feline padded toward the cab.

Vela took another swig from her water container, heaved out a bone-tired sigh, and stepped up to the opening door, pausing to let the

Panther ease its way carefully inside what was an undeniably cramped space for the robot. The vehicle's suspension sagged noticeably, and the taxi wobbled about as Severance worked itself into a hunched position with its tail end up on the left side of the rear seating area and its head and neck fitting in the gap between the front seats. The woman slid into the remaining space on the right end of the bench and pulled her feet inside the vehicle, allowing its door to close as she directed it to take a left at the next intersection.

Raising an eyebrow and turning her face toward her companion, she dubiously asked, "The general's name is really Ulysses?"

The cat turned its head to cast a glance back at her with its dark irises barely visible within the similarly shaded orbs of its eyes, but she could have sworn those eyes were smiling.

Chapter 14

"The warrior archetype is a universal aspect of human nature. It drives us to overcome challenges, to persevere, and to achieve our goals.

The warrior archetype is not only physical but also mental and emotional. It is the determination, the courage, and the confidence that we need to face any situation.

The warrior archetype is a source of power and resilience. It is the spirit that never gives up, that believes it will always find a solution, and that rises above any setback.

It is the invincibility that we can tap into when we need it most."

- Ava Berg, Ten Time World Champion, Women's Global Association of Kickboxing

Jayce and Lilian moved as silently as possible through the underbrush in the wild terrain that surrounded the Guangzhou Superior Authority complex, their movements being assisted by the thin exosuits they had donned and hands clenched around the grips and foregrips of their assault rifles. They were approaching the same southeastern gate through which Billy had entered the facility and had left their vehicle around the corner of the intersection at the bottom of the slightly sloping road that led away from the gate.

As they reached a position that was as close as they could get without detection by the base's perimeter cameras, they stopped behind a small tree on which the leaves had already sprouted out for this year's new growth.

"Max, you ready?" Jayce whispered.

The pair's strips vibrated with Maxwell's voice as the affirmative response was received using bone conduction mode.

"Alright," Jayce said, turning his head slightly to look sidelong at Lilian's tense face, "this is what you've trained for. You good?"

Lilian, lips taut, met his gaze and gave him a firm nod.

"Max, we're ready when you are," he softly stated, "and may God have mercy on their souls!"

Maxwell, crouching in the bushes farther west from his teammates' position, was staring intently at the screen of his tablet. Right hand clamped on the baton from which its flexible screen had been extended, the man scanned over line after line of data streaming across its display.

"FAILSAFE is using the backdoor we created on the head researcher's tablet and the rogue connection to the SA operations network. He's almost finished planting the code that will purge the data from primary systems. That will only leave the air-gapped backups which, except for full backups that are off-sited once a month, happen to be stored in a data center right here on the complex."

"You said you've got a seriously big distraction that will help get us inside?"

"Indeed!" Maxwell murmured with a smile, "And you're about to meet him!"

In their covert location, Lilian glanced sharply at Jayce and mouthed, "Him?"

Maxwell, noting that the data stream had slowed and then crept to a standstill, thumbed the button on his tablet's tube that turned the screen pliable and retracted it inside the columnar body. He then commanded, "Alright, FAILSAFE. Let's get this burly boy moving!"

The technical expert stowed the tube in one of the magazine storage pouches on the vest of his slim exosuit, securing the flap over its opening and rubbing his palms anxiously on his thighs. The mid-afternoon sun was breaking through the cumulous clouds that had rolled in from the sea, and birds were chirping and flitting about unconcernedly in the nearby bushes and trees. The CEN forces had cleared all the vegetation from the last twenty meters leading up to the fortress's walls, and a few squirrels were taking advantage of the open space to bask in the available rays.

In the stillness, a loud cracking sound suddenly rang out from the research side of the complex.

This stentorian noise was soon followed by exclamations of surprise and dismay from near the southeastern corner of that subsection. A rumbling could not only be heard vibrating through the air but also felt shaking the earth at the team's feet. The vibrations grew heavier and heavier until it felt as though a small earthquake was in progress, accompanied by panicked shouts and screams coming from inside the CEN facility. The birds had gone silent and were glancing about warily.

"What in the world..." Lilian whispered as the rumbling turned into a raging thunder and, as if in slow motion, the visible corner of the nearest building on the western half of the property shattered into a spray of brick and concrete—pieces flying out over the large wall surrounding the base and tumbling across the open space beyond as the squirrels and birds scattered.

Within milliseconds of these chunks of building sailing out of the facility, the outer wall burst apart, with larger portions of its structure careening down the hill and skittering across the turf until they ground to a halt or ran up against the thicker vegetation. Trundling along behind these pieces of architecture came a formidable, metallic goliath.

With the center of its body shaped like a massive, dense, gunmetal gray wedge that bore no readily apparent seams on its surface and with thick armor plates draping down over the hinges of its shoulder and hip sockets, the instrument of mass destruction moved along with a quadrupedal gait that would be expected from a rhinoceros-gorilla chimera. The elbow and knee joints of its stocky limbs were also heavily armored, with no fingers or toes currently gracing their tips. As it skidded to a halt at the top of the slope above Maxwell, he realized that the crown of the machine stood a full five meters off the ground.

A heavy cable was being dragged along behind the monster, its end still connected to a port on the side of its belly where the armor plating had been lifted. The tether was pulled tight just as the gargantuan metal creature ground to a stop.

"Alright, FAILSAFE, looks like you're at the end of your rope, so to speak," Maxwell could not help chuckling to himself briefly before continuing, "and, without a satellite receiver, manual control is the only option. Now I just have to hope I can climb inside!"

The technical wizard had said this last part as something of an explanation for his friends, as Lilian and Jayce were staring at the robotic contraption in different combinations of fear and fascination. Lilian grabbed Jayce's forearm as his eyes turned to meet hers.

"He's going *inside* of that thing?!" Lilian's voice was faint.

By that time, manual operators had taken control of the two auto-turrets that were positioned by the southeastern gate and halfway along the southern wall, both defensive devices zeroing in on the back of the mechanical beast. As the two heavy machine guns fired away, their operators were too engaged in trying to penetrate the metal beast's armor—constructed using layers of molecularly dense materials—to notice Maxwell running up the slope to the front of the robot's great wedge of a face.

FAILSAFE was tipping the contraption down toward the earth in what seemed to be a ceremonial bow. When the man had nearly reached the giant, a virtually undetectable hatch near the front of the broad and slanted upper surface of the torso hissed open and flipped forward on a hinged limb, creating a platform onto which Maxwell climbed, the limb then elevating him so he could step inside the cockpit. He spun around and settled into the pilot's seat as the hatch closed behind him.

As the internal lighting and array of screens blinked on, Maxwell ignored the dull thumping of turret rounds pelting the back and legs of his new conveyance and pressed and held his strip to switch the ongoing call to broadcast audio, addressing his human teammates with the greater clarity of communication that afforded.

"Lilian and Jayce, allow me to introduce you to NIAN, inspired by the Chinese demon of the same name."

After a brief pause, Jayce emphatically declared, "Having a demon as the inspiration for its design makes all kinds of sense!"

"Indubitably!" Maxwell agreed, "And we may be setting the development of similar machines within the CEN back at the same time as we're decimating the SA program today, but for now, this device will be the key to breaking through the outermost barrier so you can rescue Billy, and then I'll be distracting both human and electronic security units while FAILSAFE moves the SA forces into transports and spirits them away!

"Now, let's see if I interpreted the control instructions correctly," he murmured as he buckled the safety harness around his shoulders and waist and then extended his hands and feet into the long wells that had been built into the cockpit at appropriate locations for pilots to easily fit their limbs inside. With the ends of his appendages held in the air, he straightened his back and pressed his torso firmly into his seat.

From their vantage point, Jayce and Lilian saw the NIAN rise into an upright stance, and then, as Maxwell twisted his shoulders to the left, the towering robot turned to face the turret adjacent to the nearby access road. The new pilot began moving his arms and legs gently up and down with a slight in- and outward motion, the arms and legs of the great device exaggerating his movements and propelling the machine forward with steadily increasing velocity, much like an enormous silverback beginning a charge toward a rival male.

The ground quaked, and the hum of the mechanical creature's actuators filled the air as Maxwell drove the robot onward. The turret at the far southeastern corner of the base's wall now having joined in the assault on the NIAN's thick hide, Maxwell continued to ignore the incoming fire and guided his vessel forward until it slammed one of its massive arms directly into the defensive device protecting the facility's front gate. The force of the giant's heavily swinging element—having a diameter wider than the turret's own foundation—ripped the gate's protective tower off its base with a tremendous thunderclap and sent it whirling away. The turret emitted a hollow throbbing sound as it transcended the last sections of the southern and eastern walls, clipped one of the larger trees down the slope from the fort, and ricocheted off past another tall tree to its north.

His voice bearing an unmistakably triumphant tenor, Maxwell called out, "I believe that's what you Yankees call a 'field goal'!"

Jayce turned from watching the projectile disappear into the eastern trees, shaking his head and laughing heartily.

"Brutha, you know how to keep it real!"

Maxwell joined in the laughter and Lilian could not help smiling and rolling her eyes at her friends' boyish perspective, despite her latent anxiety.

"Please, let me get this door for you!" Lilian's significant other politely offered as he moved the NIAN up to the gate, reared it back on its hind legs, and thrust its arms forward with incredible force. The thick steel construction buckled under the strike and went tumbling back into the facility, sweeping several soldiers mercilessly aside to crash into both the bordering walls and the military police vehicles that had just approached the gate from inside the compound.

The pilot now flicking his hands forward inside of the control wells, metallic fingers and thumbs suddenly blossomed from the still-raised arms of the NIAN. Under Maxwell's direction, the motorized demigod lunged forward, grabbed the nearest military vehicle, spun around, and sent the patrol unit flying over the building to the east. The vehicle revolved its way through the air to make solid contact with the turret at the corner of the fortress, breaking that tower off its base and leaving it dangling on the outside of the wall as the rig tumbled away down the hill and into the verdure.

"You're welcome to join me now," Maxwell said as he panted somewhat from the effort and complex control movements he was making. "FAILSAFE will reconnect comms as needed, but for now, I'll just be leading the enemy forces toward the backup storage building at the center of the complex, which should free you to reach Billy's holding cell with minimal interference!"

The robotic turret mounted atop the second enemy vehicle on the two-lane road inside the complex had opened fire on the NIAN, and Maxwell turned the massive machine, clasped its giant hands together, raised its arms high in the air, and then brought the hammer of its combined fists down on the center of the truck. The NIAN struck the cavalry unit with such force that its turret ended up breaking through the floor of its frame and was embedded into the pavement below—the vehicle exploding with churning flames leaping out in all directions around the robot's arms.

Jayce and Lilian sprinted up the slope to what was left of the gate, forming up along the exterior wall with Jayce nearest the gap. The veteran moved up to where he could peer around the edge of the mangled barricade.

Seeing Maxwell cumbrously stamping on into the complex with Confederacy soldiers streaming out of nearby buildings and chasing along behind him—futilely assaulting the NIAN with small arms fire across its back and legs—the two moved up along the face of the building east of the main road until they could slip through the alley between that and the next building. Using the shadowy side paths, they continued to cut more deeply into the maze of structures in that corner of the facility. Elsewhere in the complex, FAILSAFE had started passing false data to the health, exosuit, and location monitoring systems for the Superior Authority soldiers. Watching the CEN personnel via security cameras inside the program command buildings at the center-east of the installation's operations sector, the AI noted that few of the personnel were paying great attention to the view through windows from the rooms overlooking the large chamber in which row upon row of pods were arranged. This expansive area was dimly illuminated from below by indicators flashing on supply and monitoring devices and interfaces on the sides and bases of the pods.

In the capsules of this Superior Authority "barracks," the troops—forever trapped in their suits due to the hardwiring of the exoskeletons' interfaces into the soldiers' nervous systems—were unconscious and lying in mostly reclined positions with bundles of tubules attached to ports on their protective suits. Through these tubes, drugs were continually being administered, and the suits' onboard reservoirs were being maintained in readiness for combat while sustenance was being fed into the occupants' stomachs and waste was being pumped out of the necessary orifices.

FAILSAFE took control of the entire population of soldiers at once, their eyes simultaneously flicking open as the AI adjusted the angle of the pods. Releasing the tethers to a chorus of soft hisses, the intruding intelligence caused the troops to quietly step out onto the gleaming black floor, looking like they were treading on a night sky full of multicolored stars as the lights around the pods were reflected upwards. The soldiers turned to face the exits at the far end of the chamber, and FAILSAFE opened the doors and moved the troops at a hushed walking pace out into the hallway beyond.

Only a few dozen soldiers were still making their way out of the portals when one of the CEN personnel in the monitoring room happened to stand up to stretch his legs and back. As he did so, his eyes fell on the departing horde, and he let out an exclamation of alarm, interrupting the conversations his coworkers were having about how the rumbling they kept hearing deep inside this solid building must be related to a new construction project.

The observant soldier pointed animatedly at the Superior Authority assets and called out to his coworkers in great agitation. The nine other soldiers in the monitoring station leaped from their chairs, several confusedly double-checking their consoles and trying to verify that their software was functioning properly, but nothing they did changed the data being fed to their screens.

The senior individual in the room spun around and dashed toward the door, only to stumble up against it as the metal obstruction failed to open at his approach. He banged his fist upon the barrier several times but received no answer from the hallway outside and initiated no movement from the door itself. While another soldier walked over and tried holding her identification badge close to the door's control panel, the senior ranking soldier double-tapped frantically on his strip to make a call out, but to no avail.

Outside, on the main road that ran through the operations-focused portion of the Superior Authority bastion, Maxwell had located the air-gapped backup storage building. As he'd been searching he had been swatting about at the CEN soldiers who had lacked enough wisdom to run away from the monstrous machine, sending them flying like so many insects.

Before attacking his primary target, Maxwell paused to turn and snatch up an armored personnel carrier that had just rounded the corner from the military police parking area. Spinning and heaving it up like a shotput in a long arc over the wall dividing the two halves of the base, the cartwheeling vehicle shattered through the thick glass exterior of a large building on the other side of the barrier—creating a shimmering spray of shards.

Now free from all but minor distractions, the pilot drove the NIAN forward on all fours to charge straight through the nearest wall of the storage structure. Jagged-edged segments of cement and twisted steel burst out before it and bounced across the long construction's rooftop and down into its interior.

Shifting into a stance that was supported by the robot's rear legs, the pilot then began rotating the machine's torso vigorously as he withdrew its digits back inside of its forearms and used the brutish limbs to obliterate the columns of data storage media in front of him. Satisfied that the physical devices had been appropriately pulverized, he turned to face down the length of the building and—with the crest of the giant wedge still protruding above the roofline—went on a destructive spree that split the structure down the middle and created a hash of sparking and smoking electronics across its floor.

Jayce and Lilian had been making their way through the zigzagging alleys to reach the military police building and had only been held up twice as they'd run into CEN soldiers racing to engage with the NIAN.

With Lilian intuitively adapting to the fire team movements, she'd been able to take the two soldiers down who had suddenly exited into an alley that connected with the one they'd been traversing, quickly squeezing off two bursts from her sound-suppressed assault rifle as she'd directed its laser sight at their chests. Jayce had given her a complimentary look, with eyebrows raised and an appreciative frown on his face as he'd nodded.

Noting her wide eyes and the death grip with which she had still been holding onto her raised rifle, he'd assured her, "You did good, Lil! This is an 'us or them' situation, and they absolutely would have killed you if you hadn't taken them down first."

Lilian had just nodded, her lips drawn in a line and creases at the corners of her eyes. Jayce had recognized that she really was taking it better than most young soldiers, and he had been impressed by her intestinal fortitude.

Jerking his head in the direction they'd previously been moving, Jayce had reminded her, "Billy needs us to bust him out," and they'd carried on toward their destination.

Jayce had raked across three more soldiers who had crossed their path just before they'd reached the Confederacy military police building, and they'd then stepped over the men's bodies and up to the corner where the alley opened out into the physical security unit's parking area.

As Jayce now leaned against the wall and tipped his head forward to get a view of the building's front entrance, he quickly yanked it back as a shotgun blast disintegrated the cinderblock façade next to where his head had been exposed. A CEN sergeant had just been stepping up cautiously along the walkway fronting the building, weapon raised and ready after having heard the suppressed gunfire and cries of the dying soldiers coming from the alley.

Hearing no sounds that would indicate the adversary was attempting to round the corner, Jayce gave Lilian a quick wink, silently crouched, and adjusted his hold on his rifle in order to place the foregrip in his right hand and the primary grip in his left. In this form, he suddenly thrust his hands out to allow the barrel to clear the corner and held down the trigger to release a hailstorm of rounds as he tilted the tip of the weapon up and down. Though the older sergeant had managed to fire off one more shotgun shell, his weapon had been aimed at the same spot as his previous shot, and the liberation of the bullets from Jayce's weapon was swiftly followed by a loud scream and related noises that accompanied the sergeant's body and weapon falling over backward, the shotgun clattering on the pavement.

Jayce quickly returned his weapon to a natural hold and swung the corner of his face briefly out to get another glimpse across the front of the building. Seeing no other enemies, he waved a bladed hand forward and to the right and led Lilian around the corner toward the police headquarters' main entrance.

In the Superior Authority barracks, FAILSAFE was guiding the two long columns of soldiers silently through the wide, stark hallways that led to the troop transports. Around the corner, a lone CEN private was seated at a desk by the doorway that led to the AV hangar, idly swiping through data on the extended screen of his tablet. The SA soldiers rounded the corner and began looming toward the young man—grotesque masks glowering and rows of black fangs faintly gleaming. With a wall of wicked-looking warriors marching toward the private's desk, he glanced up and then did a double-take as extreme panic spread across his face.

Knowing that no troop deployments were scheduled until that evening, he tried using his strip to call his superiors, and then tried again and again as he heard nothing but error messages in response. The Superior Authority troops nearly filled the hallway and approached with all the inevitability of a freight train, leading the young soldier to step back in terror and in an attempt to occupy the out-of-the-way corner area where the hallway connected to the wall holding the hangar's large double doors.

Under FAILSAFE's control, the lead member of the right-side column stepped forward more quickly than the rest as he drew near to the autonomous human and, having grasped the private by the front of his uniform with both hands, hefted him into the air like a child. The helpless youth kicked his legs slightly, clung to the SA troop's armored wrists, and looked around in anxious bewilderment.

The activated enemy soldier stepped through the hangar doors that had hissed open, executed a sharp right turn, and crossed the polished cement floor to the dangling hook and chain of a lifting mechanism mounted to tracks on the hangar's high ceiling. Hoisting the guard up and feeding the point of the crane's hook under the lower-rear edge of his uniform's blouse, the AI-controlled troop released the young man—leaving him hanging with limbs flailing in the air as he was uncomfortably supported by the blouse's material.

The excessively intimidating SA soldier raised a fist and extended a finger, which it pointed at the youth's face.

"BE GOOD," FAILSAFE's voice boomed out from the horrible helmet.

The crane rapidly retracted its chain until its cargo was suspended twenty meters from the floor, where the private had a bird's eye view of the troop procession that began to file its way through the area.

While the lone SA soldier rejoined the columns that had now entered the hangar, the two groups split as needed as they were sent marching into the large aerial vehicles that were parked in rows across the depot's expanse. The evacuees filled the available docking points inside the vehicles and patiently waited as FAILSAFE lowered their restraining bars down into place.

Chapter 15

"The Confederacy is on the brink of a sea change in how we approach combat. No longer will we have to interrupt the lives of the greater part of our population to take them through the weeding-out process by which we have historically discovered our best military assets. With my team's research, we will be able to selectively extract only the most physically able candidates and then transform their minds into states that match the abilities of our special forces."

- Dr. Zi Rui Cheng, Chief of Medical Research, Superior Authority Program, Confederacy of Eastern Nations

Having left the backup storage building a smoking ruin, Maxwell knew he had to draw the enemy's fire away from the central and eastern portions of the operations zone where FAILSAFE was extracting the SA forces and where his friends were still within the installation's boundaries.

Facing the magnificent war machine he was piloting toward the research buildings, the Englishman brought the robot into a loping gait that took it barreling through the devastated data storage edifice's western wall, clipping the corner off of the next building in the colossus' path and breaking through the wall separating the two sides of the fortress. Rearing back on its hind legs again, at Maxwell's urging, the NIAN began punching holes in the corner of the first multi-story structure it had encountered.

As debris flew out around the behemoth's swinging arms, the doors of the next building to the west slid open, and Doctor Cheng himself stalked out, accompanied by three CEN military police soldiers. Glaring at the attacking apparatus through the gap between the buildings on the other side of a small courtyard, the head researcher raised his left arm. Reaching up with his right hand to adjust the left glove of the prototype heavy exosuit he was wearing, the churlish man turned slightly as he called out in Cantonese to the similarly clad MPs.

"We must protect my research!" he shouted. "You will pay for failure with your *lives!* Pry open the top hatch as I explained and eliminate whoever is inside!"

The soldiers shouted out, "Yes, sir!" and dashed past the older man.

Maxwell was so busy using quick glances to inspect the holes created as he perforated the structure before him, searching for anything of obvious value that he could destroy, that he did not notice the approaching soldiers until they were nearly on top of him. At the last second, the pilot caught sight of the lead assailant. As the man launched himself into a flying leap toward the NIAN's forehead, the Brit redirected him with a mighty backhanded movement that sent him tumbling through the northern wall of the glass-faced building in which the armored personnel carrier was already ensconced.

The soldier's body boring a hole through the building's surface at the level of its third floor, Maxwell brought the arms of the NIAN up in a defensive stance as the other two soldiers skidded to a halt a few meters away from him. As the two sides froze in a standoff, Maxwell became aware that a thumping noise was being transmitted into the cockpit from outside the armored enclosure to his left.

Completing a sprint from where he had finally come to rest inside the neighboring building, the first Communist soldier reached the hole his body had formed earlier and launched back out across the gap toward the NIAN's shoulder.

"What the devil??" Maxwell cried out inside the machine as he piloted the robot into a tumbling move, dropping back and to its right, passing the corner of the nearby building and trying to keep the heavily armored enemy from reaching the robot's body.

The Chinese warrior reached down and out as the NIAN rolled, grasping ahold of the edge of the armor protecting the robot's shoulder and clinging on as he was carried in an arc—legs swinging out above him—down to plant his feet on the ground just outside of the path of the tumbling giant and then back up as the NIAN returned to an upright stance.

While Maxwell had been dodging, the other two soldiers had rushed forward and around the corner, coming up on the golem's arms as it brought them into a quadrupedal support position. To Maxwell's great consternation, the ground-based soldiers sprang up to latch onto the goliath's upper arms, swinging their legs up to press against the robot's belly and using the impressive strength afforded by the heavy exosuits to force its arms out to the sides and send the NIAN's face falling to the ground. The first soldier swiftly jumped onto the cockpit's nearly invisible hatch and began to pry at the narrow gap around its edge using artificially supplied strength.

A slit of light broke through the small crack that began to form at the top of the enclosure in which Maxwell was breathlessly sitting, the combat robot's driver mightily struggling to bring its legs up underneath it and to break its arms out of the two grappling soldiers' grips.

"*Curse you all!*" the Brit shouted out and then rocked his shoulders back and forth wildly in his seat, slamming his body against the chair's pressure-sensitive upper section and causing the NIAN's shoulders to rock in imitation until Maxwell finally built up enough kinetic energy in one rotation to send the machine into a roll. As the exosuited soldiers clung on, Maxwell built up speed until the massive device was wheeling with such potent centrifugal force that the three adversaries were thrown into long arcs that took them—screaming in terror—far out across the complex.

Extending the NIAN's arms to halt the rolling motion, Maxwell wiped droplets of sweat from his forehead with his right hand and then reinserted it into its control well so he could bring the robot's arms underneath it and return to a ready stance.

With an ear-piercing hum, bolts of electricity suddenly began sparking across every surface of the interior of the cockpit where any small gaps existed between metal components. Maxwell froze, petrified by the knowledge that if his uninsulated body were to make contact with the highly charged surfaces in the apparatus, then he would undoubtedly experience a swift death by electrocution.

Inside the military police station, Jayce and Lilian had been faced with the high-risk choice of either fully clearing rooms as they passed, ensuring no enemies closed in behind them or cut off their exit, or moving as quickly as possible to take advantage of Maxwell's distraction before he was overwhelmed. Realizing how their friends were currently both exposed to grave danger despite their very broad sets of capabilities, they'd agreed to rely upon speed and had swept down the building's long main hallway at what had approached a jogging pace.

As they had passed a large, open workspace toward the center of the building, a senior Communist officer had turned from where he'd been leaning over, hands resting on his desk and staring in anger and alarm at the camera feed showing the destruction taking place outside. The middle-aged man had caught sight of the two interlopers as they'd moved past and—his expression instantaneously switching to one conveying murderous intent—had reached to withdraw his sidearm.

Both Americans had turned their firearms to face the open area as they'd moved quickly through the hallway, and they now let loose a stream of suppressed fire. The bullets strafed across cabinets and dividing walls before pounding across the officer's abdomen, sending him falling backward with a wheezing groan as his partially unholstered firearm flipped up in the air, rebounded off several surfaces, and eventually came to rest on a nearby desk.

Continuously moving, the fire team had reached a left turn in the hallway and, pausing only long enough to take a quick glance around it, had swept forward into the corridor beyond. They'd rushed on toward the point where they could see the path split into a north-south corridor with a sign posted on the ceiling that bore a symbol having the clear appearance of jail cell bars.

Now, as the pair passed several office doors and reached the middle of this length of the hallway, they were challenged by the sudden appearance of a guard who was sauntering across the intersection ahead, moving south to north. Though he had been apathetically staring straight ahead, the man glimpsed the two out of the corner of his eye and—with his right hand resting on the assault rifle for which a strap was slung around his shoulders—he quickly tried to swing his weapon up to get off a shot. This attempt was cut short in conjunction with his life when Jayce fired off a burst of bullets into the enemy's shoulder and chest.

The soldier let out a short cry, and his rifle and body slammed against the far wall.

Immediately following this clamor, Lilian heard a scraping of a metal chair against the concrete floor and swung around just as the second door in the corridor slid open and a severe-looking and stockily built female sergeant stepped out. She had been looking angrily west down the hallway, but as she rounded the corner of the doorway, her eyes slid over and latched onto Lilian's. The woman made a grab for her service pistol but failed to reach it before Lilian gunned her down.

The dying woman's strangled screech echoed out unnervingly through the space. Lilian kept herself facing down the hall toward the adversary's body, and she began stepping along backward as she heard Jayce resume his half-crouched ambulation toward the detention area, the newer warrior ready to fend off any additional enemies approaching from behind. She was also trying to keep Jayce from seeing the tears streaming down her cheeks as she stared at the woman's lifeless form.

Upon reaching the intersection, Jayce glanced in both directions and decided to swing around into the right-hand hallway, clearing each of the detention cells as they moved past. The first was occupied by a soldier who was slouched over on the hard, bare, and well-secured bed positioned against the far wall, likely too drunk to react to the commotion in the area.

As they came abreast of the second cell, they saw Billy inside, the younger man looking hopefully at the access walkway through which they'd been moving. He had apparently been reclining on the decidedly spartan bed in his cell, but after hearing the cries of his jailers, he had raised up on his right elbow and lifted his left leg so that it rested on the front edge of the bed next to his right knee, the man ready to spring into action.

Upon seeing Jayce and Lilian's friendly faces, the young soldier was obviously inexpressively relieved. Still, he let his left arm slide back so his hand was resting on his left hip, fingers spread out dramatically as he thrust his haunches forward, puffed his chest out, and in an alluringly breathy voice cooed, "Going my way, sailor?"

"Don't make me leave you here!" Jayce threatened while scowling and grinning at the same time.

Billy lithely leaped up from the bed and sashayed over to the cell gate while laughing and insisting, "I *knew* you guys wouldn't leave me to rot!"

Lilian, looking at Billy while blinking back more tears, shared, "Maxwell actually turned the operation into a combination SA troop *and* Billy rescuing mission, and said it gave us a good excuse to create a huge distraction that would keep the attention off of us and what FAILSAFE was doing."

The prisoner clapped his hands together and rubbed them busily while he said, "I love it when everything goes according to my plans!"

"Yeah, *right*, like this is part of your plans, *son!*" Jayce good-naturedly scolded. "I thought you said you were going to be in and out of this place like a super-agent!"

Looking abashed, Billy admitted, "Well, there was a bit of a hangup when I heard someone talking about moving SA soldiers offsite. I knew Max would want to learn where they were taking them before it was too late, and, yeah, I ran into the world's most suspicious officer."

The younger man turned an apologetic gaze up toward Jayce's eyebrow-cocked expression, quickly changing the subject by asking, "So, you got the key to my accommodations?"

"Hang on," Jayce replied as he pressed and held his strip. "You get that part about the soldiers being moved offsite, FAILSAFE?"

Its voice coming through the brawny man's device via broadcast audio, the AI responded, "Yes, Jayce. I'm expanding the scope of my infiltration to include a search for transit authorizations for SA assets."

"The litter I examined was headed for a medical facility in Shaoguan," Billy added helpfully.

"Thank you, Billy," came the AI's reply. "I had noted that a few of the recuperation pods were empty and was going to raise that with Maxwell once he was less...intensely engaged."

Lilian immediately grew alarmed, "Is Max alright?!"

It may have been her imagination, but FAILSAFE seemed almost evasive as he answered, "He will surely ask for help if he needs it, Lilian. For now, the priority is to get the three of you out of this complex."

Without further explanation, the AI unlocked Billy's cell, adding, "Please do hurry."

Standing near the NIAN's supine body, Doctor Cheng stared down at the robot's hatch as electricity arced across every part of the machine's metal skin. Having watched the bold and yet ultimately worthless attempts made by the military men as they'd tried to put an end to this unforgivable interruption of his research, the doctor had turned his genius-level intellect to the task of identifying the fastest way to accomplish what they had not.

Inspired by the sight of mangled technical equipment spraying sparks and smoking away within the gaping holes Maxwell had made in the building on the other side of the courtyard, Cheng had calmly taken advantage of the MPs' assault on the great metal beast to walk past the ongoing havoc. He had approached a wireless power transmitter that had been mounted atop a tall pole near an intact section of the central wall. Grasping the base of the hollow pole, the doctor had planted a foot against the concrete barrier and used it as leverage to push against the steel post until the bolts securing it to the ground below had snapped and the tower had crashed to the ground.

Though the transmitter wirelessly directed focused beams of energy from itself to receivers placed on or near buildings in the area, it was supplied with power by a thick cable that had been fed up through the hollow interior of the pipe. The impact with the ground having cracked and thereby loosened the transmitter, it had been relatively easy for the CEN leader to yank on the exposed, polymer-insulated portion of the cable at the base of the tower and pull the whole length of it out of its encasement. This had revealed a thick and bare conduit at the end of the cable—a conduit that was still fully charged with millions of volts of electricity.

This bare conduit was what Doctor Cheng had held as he'd casually strolled over to the tumbling robot and then stabbed the end of the cable forward against the slightly curved upper surface of the prone titan's torso.

Now, Maxwell was trapped inside a device that was overloaded with electrical energy.

Sweat dribbling down the bridge of his nose as he dangled face down in the harness of his seat, the younger man's mind was racing through every possible way he might be able to escape before both he and the NIAN were irreparably damaged.

"Think, Max, *think!*" he urged himself. "You saw the schematics...think about the options!"

Glancing up to the frame near the edge of the control console's top-right screen, Maxwell's eyes fell on a series of manual interfaces for a range of emergency responses. These knobs and switches activated various features, including the mechanisms for sealing off the air intakes, ejecting the pilot's seat, and turning on emergency lighting. Yes, there it was!

Hoping the contact would not allow surging electricity to jump to his body, Maxwell slammed the base of his balled-up right fist down on a purple knob. With great foresight, the engineers had made the function that the knob triggered fully mechanical rather than in any way electrical.

Ports blew open at two points along the upper surface of the wedge-like torso, and emergency flares blasted out, spewing phosphorescent streams of searing hot particles.

The left-side flare made direct contact with the doctor's chest.

With exosuit coverage only from the shoulders down, the volume of fiery material that spread across the man's neck and face caused instantaneous second- and third-degree burns. As the flare's main projectile ricocheted off Cheng's chest and carried on expelling its burning material throughout its path over his left shoulder, the third-degree burns on his left cheek were severe enough to expose the blackened bones of the underlying skull and jaw.

Screaming in agony, the doctor staggered away from the fallen robot, dropping the electrical cable as he half-blindly clawed at his wounds. After several steps, he stumbled up against the side of the ravaged building and leaned into the wall for support, howling and then trying to press on the flayed flesh of his face with his hands.

In the NIAN, Maxwell summoned all his willpower and tried to bring the machine's arms in to heft its body back up off the ground. The screens were flickering, and the actuators struggled to respond at first, but the adaptive systems began rerouting power and signals around damaged wiring, and soon the giant was able to bring itself upright with a loud, groan-infused humming.

Maxwell could now see the face of his assailant clearly on the screens linked to the forward-facing cameras, and despite the scorched skin and blackened holes in the doctor's face, the Englishman could still identify the adversary. His likeness had been so etched into the noble man's mind that he would never forget it during waking hours—or in his nightmares.

Perspiration creating a sheen on his face, Maxwell vehemently stared at Cheng as the NIAN loomed over the psychotic scientist.

There was a sharp, ever-present edge to Doctor Cheng's character: a raw and hungry blade that always managed to resurface regardless of what setbacks fickle fate threw at him. The pain from the burns having transformed into a dull and constant torment rather than the mind-numbing agony he'd felt when the flesh had first been damaged, the researcher used his right eye to scan the area, spotting the massive cable lying on the ground at the NIAN's feet. With a shocking burst of speed, Cheng rushed to retrieve the conduit.

As he raced past the monstrous machine's arm, Maxwell instinctively lashed out with his left hand. The NIAN's arm swung out viciously and struck the doctor in the side, sending him careening into the wall near the dismantled power transmitter where his body's progress was potently halted. Maxwell flicked his fingers, and the digits once again extended from the ends of the robot's arms, which the pilot then used to pick up the stunned man and hold him in the air in front of the goliath's face.

"YOU BASTARDIZED MY WORK!" Maxwell Clarke cried out so loudly that the doctor could faintly hear it even outside the goliath.

"YOU BASTARDIZED MY WORK AND TURNED IT INTO EVIL, AND I HAVE TO STOP YOU FROM *EVER* DOING THAT AGAIN!"

Cheng shrieked at the NIAN's face in wordless and primal rage, refusing to admit defeat and promising with that demonically depraved sound that he would never stop striving to impose his will on the world.

Maxwell twisted his shoulders in his seat, and the massive robot began spinning around and around, gaining extreme momentum before bringing its left arm up in a sweeping motion and releasing the man whose body had been clenched tightly in its fist.

The Communist doctor, who had only stopped shrieking long enough to take one last breath, continued releasing that unholy noise as he flew—spinning and twisting—through a gaping hole in the adjacent building, Maxwell having perfectly aimed his throw. The room beyond was a storage area for canisters of highly flammable gases, and the devolved doctor's impact with them ignited an explosion that blasted out a tremendous fireball from the side of the building, sending forth a shockwave and spraying chunks of debris a dozen meters from the point of detonation.

Maxwell sat in the NIAN, panting and staring with ferocious intensity into the raging inferno within the expanded cavity.

After struggling to normalize his breathing, the world-weary and reluctant warrior finally recomposed himself to some degree. Pulling his hands out of the control wells and sweeping them down across his face, Maxwell brought them into a steepled position with his fingertips at his chin as his mind struggled with the tumult of thoughts and emotions rushing through it like a rampaging mob.

FAILSAFE's voice suddenly sounded out over Maxwell's strip.

"Max, our three friends are nearly back to the gate, and the transports are on their way to Hong Kong."

Maxwell's resulting sigh was born of a rush of relief, a welcome ray of euphoria...and an undeniable, residual thorn of regret.

"Thank you, FAILSAFE," he breathily responded. "I'll be with them shortly."

Chapter 16

"A successful partnership involves communicating clearly, being transparent, and showing a willingness to collaborate. Successful partnerships are based on mutual respect, trust, and common goals. Respect each other's strengths and weaknesses and use them to solve problems and achieve objectives.

Keep in mind that trust and mutual respect are built over time. It takes work and dedication to establish a solid base of trust; however, when you do build up that base, you'll enjoy the benefits of a successful and lasting partnership."

- Lora Hillcrest, Executive Director, Pan-American Connections

The cab had taken them within two hundred meters of the general's signal when Vela had decided to stop the vehicle and undertake a stealthier approach on foot.

The compass had led them onto a disused dirt- and gravel-covered road next to one of many aging buildings in the area. It seemed this was an outmoded part of town in which the buildings were about to be demolished to make way for new development, containing a mixture of early Twenty-First Century high-rise apartment buildings and formerly high-end business skyscrapers here on the outskirts of Colorado Springs. All had now been abandoned and stood with an eerie emptiness in the dark and windswept outskirts of the city.

As she'd already strapped on her vest and prepped her weapon, the agent had quickly climbed out of the sedan, and her robotic companion had slunk out the door after her, the transport leaning heavily over as the cat had brought the bulk of its weight to that side of the car. The automobile had then sprung back up with a residual wobble as Severance had padded out onto the street.

Agent Vela had reached to the chest of her vest, pulled out and donned the associated visor, and clipped the buttstock of her firearm to the armor covering her left shoulder. Placing her hands on the weapon's grips, she'd then crouched slightly and—after exchanging a nod with Severance—stalked smoothly down the avenue of cracked and hole-bespeckled pavement toward the abandoned residential structure that seemed to be their destination.

Now, tailed by the robotic animal and sticking as much as she could to the early morning shadows cast by various empty eateries and other tertiary businesses that tended to populate business-centric developments, the woman frequently double-checked the distance and direction indicator on her display strip. As she'd guessed she would be, she was soon brought abreast of the apartment building.

She hugged the wall and scanned across the windows of the higher floors carefully with her weapon's low-magnification holographic scope before moving up to the main entrance. The entire area was darkened by the great shadow cast by the skyscraper to the southeast, the edifice obviously being in the early stages of its demolition.

The dim, pre-dawn light nearly caused Vela's eyes to miss spotting the sedan parked in the shelter across the street. An overhang that was attached to the small building west of the skyscraper had been a transaction drive-through for the attached bank back in the days in which paper money still existed, and the lone vehicle in the area had been parked beneath its protection.

They reached the polished metal double doors that were recessed into a well in the face of the residential building. Smudged picture windows gracing the walls on either side and a small lobby within, Vela slowed her pace and then cautiously used the micro-camera on the left of her barrel to get a look at the building's interior. Seeing no threats, she moved with a rolling gait up to the doors and used her right hand to slowly and laboriously slide one of them open.

Spotting the stairs at the far end of the dusty, brown-tiled lobby—once-luxurious tile obviously riddled with chips and scratches that were defined as the weak light filtered in through the broad windows—Vela turned to Severance with an eyebrow raised.

"At this point, it's going to simplify things if you lead the way," she'd observed with a soft voice.

With a sphinxlike expression, the cat replied, "True, and if the enemies have set any traps, it will be safer for you if I set them off..."

A shade of vermillion burst out on Vela's visage, and she sputtered, "That's not what I...you're not *expendable!*" as she looked down in great consternation at the inscrutable feline face.

Severance had looked away apathetically toward the stairs for a moment as he'd let the woman twist in the wind—metaphorically speaking—before finally turning his large head and slowly meeting her eyes. He gazed into them for a painfully long time and then gradually dropped one robotic eyelid into a wink.

"I'm only teasing, Agent Vela," the robot finally admitted.

Mouth dropping open as she felt a whirlwind of emotions, Vela released the foregrip of the submachine gun and briefly shook her finger at its nose.

"*Bad kitty!*"

As she quietly scolded the autonomous animal she could not help breaking into a lopsided grin, seeing Severance's tail playfully flicking back and forth.

"This is what happens when we allow an AI to be influenced by a *cat's* personality!" she chuckled as she returned her hand to her weapon and faced the stairs.

"Too true!" Severance good-naturedly agreed as they crossed to the gradations. "Judging by the direction and proximity of Ulysses' tracking device, I surmise that he is being held on the third floor, to the left after ascending the stairs."

The big cat padded up the steps, and the agent followed closely behind, saying in a low voice, "Well, that makes it easy enough. I really *can* take point, y'know."

"No worries, Victoria...may I call you Victoria?"

Taken aback for a moment by the machine's knowledge of her name, the warrant officer recovered and replied, "I'm guessing your master shared the personnel data for tonight's mission? Might as well call me Vickie."

"Thank you, Vickie. How's this? When we reach the entrance to the enemy's hideout, I will use a tentacle to carefully observe the interior, and then you can have the honor of choosing how we breach."

"You've got yourself a deal," Vela conceded in a whisper as they reached the second-floor landing. Now moving with a near-complete absence of sound, the pair continued upward until they leveled out on the third-floor landing and approached the apartment door to their left.

Severance let a tendril curl out of its shoulder and snaked it down to the base of the door, near the left side of the frame. With barely perceptible movement, the robot slid the tip of the "lifeline" into the seam and advanced it just enough to ease the door to the right by a few millimeters, allowing the end of the sinuous cable to access the apartment's interior.

Using a fiber-optic tunnel embedded within its prehensile limb, the robot activated a display between its shoulder blades and thereby allowed its human partner to get a view of the situation inside the old residential unit. Panning from right to left, the pair took in the combination dining room and kitchen area in which the blindfolded General Gaines appeared to be painfully restricted to his seat on a bare metal chair, then noted that a centrally located, short hallway seemed to lead toward bedrooms at the back of the dwelling.

Light poured out of the room to the right at the end of the hall. Panning further to the left, they took in the Chinese agent as he stood with his back against the far wall and a finger on his strip, engaged in conversation and guarding a Caucasian male who was sitting on another bare metal chair in the southeastern corner of the room. The spy's protégé was swiping through data on the display strip on his wrist in obvious malcontent.

As Severance looked questioningly up at Vela, she tossed her head back toward the stairs they had just climbed, and the two silently moved down to the second floor.

Vela called the geographic coordinates in to the staff member on duty at the base intelligence shop, asking her to spread the word to the major and MPs and send backup as quickly as possible.

The counterintelligence agent then turned to her companion and whispered, "I would *love* to just shoot that agent in the throat, but as the cooler side of my head prevails, it's saying we should try to take him alive."

Severance simply blinked up at her.

She patted the long rectangular device clipped on the far-right side of her vest, saying, "I have stun grenades to reduce the risks of breaching. Once a full team arrives, we can make an entrance, and then if I can close the distance to the CEN agent before he can see or react, then we'll be able to...."

The thought remained unfinished as they heard the sound of footsteps from the apartment upstairs.

After a moment, a chair clattered onto the floor, and they could hear Gaines' voice loudly making demands, after which the man grunted heavily in unison with the sound of a contusion, and his demand-making ceased. The apartment door rumbled open, and Vela heard steps in the stairwell, forcing the agent and Panther to carefully retreat toward the ground floor as both the number and the increasing volume of the footsteps indicated the entire population of people who had occupied the apartment were descending above them.

Upon reaching the lobby, Vela waved Severance along as she crouched and entered the shadows below the last segment of the stairway. The two hunched down in the musty shadows as they listened to the troupe's approach.

Gaines hissed through gritted teeth, "I thought I was going to be exchanged for your husband."

The voice of the Russian woman was dripping with satisfaction as she laughed.

"Oh, you will still be exchanged, but not before we give you a parting gift that will ensure you and your comrades *never* trouble us again!"

The Chinese agent immediately scolded her in Mandarin, and she responded angrily in kind. Vela, eyes squinting as her mind raced through the possible meanings of the woman's words, felt a tap on her arm and looked down to see one of her companion's lifelines pointing her to translations of the enemies' latter comments, displayed on the screen on the big cat's back.

"You say too much!" the first line read, while the second said, "It does not matter. We drug him, and I shove the device down his throat, and he's as good as dead anyway!"

The special agent's eyes widened with alarm.

As the Panther looked up at her and pointed the tip of its tentacle to its screen once again, the displayed message changed to, "We have to save him *now!*"

The warrant officer nodded and peered out around the downward-sloping underside of the concrete steps as the enemies led the blindfolded and battered Gaines scuffling across the lobby. The Russian female was leading the group, followed by the unidentified male, Gaines, and then the Chinese agent bringing up the rear.

The last man in the crowd that was crossing the lobby held a pistol in each hand, the barrels of both weapons pressing forcefully into Gaines' ribcage from each side. Severance silently slipped out from under the stairs, with Vela stalking along in his wake, weapon raised. She angled her path out so she would be able to get a clear shot at the Russian's head.

Severance had reached a point directly behind the male spy and had extended both lifelines out until they were nearly at the man's elbows just as the Russian woman reached the main doors.

Unluckily, the blonde woman turned to look over her shoulder as she grabbed the right-side door and started to shove it open. As she twisted, she caught sight of Agent Vela, weapon raised, and the Russian's mouth opened to shout as she continued her rotation, ducking behind the traitor's body.

At the same moment, the Panther thrust its tentacles forward to wrap around the Chinese man's handguns and jerk them out to the sides—tearing the firearms out of their bearer's hands before he could react. With the lead spy's rapid response, Vela had not been able to take her shot at the Russian without risking a deadly reaction from the Chinese agent against the general, and now the female enemy had grabbed at the traitor to use him as a shield as her partner spun around in surprise.

As the Asian man turned wide eyes back toward Severance and wound up for an exosuit-powered strike, Vela called out, "Get down!"

The blindfolded general threw himself downward and to the right as his bulky robotic cat executed a lightning-fast crouch and leap forward, launching itself so its forehead connected mightily with the Chinese agent's waist. The man flew back and crashed into his traitorous ward, and the pair then slammed into the female spy, with the entire trio tumbling rearward out the now-open front door.

The Asiatic agent, having rolled himself up to his feet after he'd tumbled backward, grabbed the perfidious American man's arm and pulled him as the Russian shoved the intelligence asset roughly up from where he was sprawled across her, propelling the bewildered betrayer into an erect stance. The austere blonde woman caught sight of Vela rushing toward the entrance with weapon raised and threw herself into a sideways roll as the attacker's first volley of bullets sparked across the cement in the space the spy had just occupied. Bringing her feet under her as she rolled, the enemy's hands returned to the grips of her shoulder-clipped firearm, and as she raised herself to a crouch she fired continuously at the open doorway—backing across the road as she followed her fleeing associates.

The woman's nonstop gunfire forced Vela and Severance to spin into cover behind the sections of the wall between the edges of the portal and the picture windows. Gaines yanked off his blindfold and scrambled to his Panther's side, pressing himself in close to the machine and gratefully taking the CEN agent's handguns as the cat's tentacles proffered them to its partner. Double-checking that the weapons' safeties were disengaged and flashing an intensely grateful smile at Vela and Severance, the general turned to glance out the window to his right, spotting Heshk and his handler entering the parked sedan.

"We have to stop them!" Gaines shouted out in frustration.

As the blonde foreigner was also approaching the escape vessel, Severance sprinted out of the open door and toward the enemy's car, dodging back and forth as the adversary's fire made contact with its head and torso again and again, scarring its metallic-composite shielding.

Seeing the Panther flying through the door, Vela shouted out, "Severance, *no!*" and brought her weapon to bear on the shooter. The soldier moved out of the building and diagonally forward as she pelted the front of the dark sedan and traced up its hood to the front-right door where the Russian was entering the vehicle.

The female spy threw herself down across the seat and center console of the car as the big cat and Vela's fire homed in on her position. Suddenly, the sleek transport deployed turbines from concealed compartments near the corners of its fenders, and the rotors rapidly turned to point upwards and aftward, elevating the car behind the roof of the drive-through structure.

Gaines had swiftly joined his companions and was now striding across the street to the rear and right of Vela—weapons aimed at the enemy's sedan—as the two advanced on the vehicle. The general shouted, "It's a modular AV!" as they both directed their rounds at the front-right turbine. Before the aerial vehicle could rise far from the ground, the teammates' gunfire had shredded the turbine's blades, and the craft dipped dangerously down in that direction.

Severance closed in on the departing transport, launching itself into a soaring leap and wrapping its lifelines around the rear-right propulsion unit. The weight of the heavy robot hauled the vehicle downward at a steep angle, its engine straining as it still tried to elevate. Severance swung its paws up to press against the sedan's undercarriage as the cat's shoulders scraped across the pavement, shoving with all its strength until the turbine tore away from the chassis with a shower of sparks and the screeching of shredding metal.

Leaving the Panther tumbling across the cement below, the aerial vehicle's systems tried to recover from the sudden freeing of the detached turbine—the right side of the AV swiftly swinging up into the air. Now actuated only by the two units on its left side, the craft began spinning and wobbling up over the nearby roof and across the intersection to the northeast. Its gyrations grew ever more extreme as it careened toward the massive construction crane that had been set up next to the glass-faced business building to the east of the residential unit.

Striking the thick steel frame of the crane's main tower, the vessel ricocheted off and tumbled through the air as it came crashing down to the disused parking area that bordered the wild prairie beyond. The two Communist agents were swift to activate the emergency releases for the side doors, the disheveled female coming out firing and driving Gaines and Vela off to take cover. The general sprinted into the recessed entrance to the apartments, and Agent Vela dashed up behind a pile of old ventilation units that had been stacked at the corner of the business building's property.

The Russian's covering fire allowed the CEN agent known as Yin to pull Heshk out of the wrecked AV and haul him, stumbling and wild-eyed, across the open space to the other side of the crane's foundation—the female spy moving up to join them behind that barrier. As the two American military personnel returned fire, Heshk seemed to panic. With the man's foreign guardians distracted, Heshk climbed onto the chest-high track on the crane's eastern side, then from there up onto the heavy machine's engine casing and onward up the ladder that ran through the center of the thick steel bars and crisscrossing supports that comprised the crane's main tower.

His female protector had moved to the north end of the crane's fifteen-meter-long base and had not noticed the turncoat's departure until he was well on his way up the ladder, leaving her to simply shout at him in frustration once she noticed his unsanctioned activities, but the woman was then forced to return her attention to her foes. Yin had disappeared from view, and as a spray of bullets from the Russian's weapon scattered chips and chunks of cement out from the corner of his concealment, Gaines was compelled to lean back...and he happened to catch sight of not only Heshk but additional movement above.

"*Vela, watch out!*" he shouted and waved at her frantically, but she had swung around to the far side of the scrap pile and could not hear him over the echoing gunfire in this mostly solid-faced corridor between the buildings.

The officer broke into a run, praying that the bullets that immediately started whipping past him from the enemy position would leave him unscathed, at least until he reached his ally.

While the other spy had kept the Alliance personnel occupied, the Chinese agent had crept into the crane's control cockpit and—having activated the electric motor—shifted the long cross-section towering above the glass building's rooftop. As Gaines ran toward Vela, the foreign agent released the twelve-ton wrecking ball that had been dangling just below the underside of the crane's horizontal beam.

General Gaines could see it hurtling down onto Agent Vela's position like a stupendous meteor cast earthward by the wrath of a mythical god.

Tossing his handguns aside and reaching out as he made a final, desperate leap, the officer's outstretched hands clasped onto the shoulders of Vela's vest with whited knuckles as his body crossed behind hers—Vela bracing down into a crouch as her eyes flicked left to see him soaring past—and Gaines twisted and pulled her diagonally back as his legs swung out in front of his body. Tucking her torso as Gaines pulled her around, Vela turned the momentum he'd created into a backward roll, knees collapsing up toward her chest and head pressed down as she took the blow from the pavement on the back of her vest and brought her feet over her body before throwing them down to the ground. She took several rapid rearward steps that slowed her to an astonished halt.

Gaines had landed and skidded on his left side, arms still out above his head as he slid, the gravelly road tearing into his uniform under his left shoulder. The inertia of the severely weighty sphere had carried it further along in the arc of the crane's swinging arm after it had been released, causing it to plow into the ground with its mass only partially covering the point at which Vela had been standing. The ball had pulverized the road beneath and sent debris shooting out from its impact site.

The shock from that blow to the Earth's surface had launched the general's body up a half meter in the air. Because his hands were only a meter away from the edge of the orb, they were spattered with rocks and gravel and masses of paving that were sent whirling out from the crater, with one such piece going on to brutally collide with the back of the general's head.

"Ulysses!" Agent Vela cried out as she held up a hand to protect her face from the smaller projectiles pelting her body.

Even as fragments of debris were still bouncing across the pavement, the woman rushed to her savior's side, pulling him gently onto his back and worriedly taking in his residual grimace of pain.

"Are you alright?!"

Groaning, Gaines winced and gingerly brought a bloody knuckled hand up to feel more of the critical liquid trickling from his scalp.

"No damage that a good ice pack can't fix!" he grunted out, opening his eyes and staring into hers as he lay still a moment longer.

Kneeling and leaning over him, Vela's hand reached up to gently stroke the area near the wound on Gaines' head as her eyes suddenly betrayed the depth of feelings her heart had already created for him. The man's hand shifted from his wound to enclose the back of hers as they gazed into each other's eyes.

"Sorry for calling you Ulysses without permission," she whispered.

"Coming from you, it's music to my ears," he whispered back.

Chapter 17

"One of the pitfalls of arrogance is the tendency to overlook or deny one's own errors, which can lead to more mistakes and greater embarrassment. A humble attitude can help avoid this trap and improve one's performance.

A useful strategy to reduce the influence of this kind of cognitive bias is to adopt an external perspective on one's situation. Rather than relying on one's own intuition and assumptions, which can be skewed by overconfidence, an external perspective can provide a more realistic and objective assessment of one's chances of success."

- Dr. Gregory J. Williams, 'A Vaccination Against Failure'

After seeing Vela and Gaines disappear from view as the wrecking ball had sent debris flying out for meters in all directions, the Russian agent realized it was highly likely that more Alliance forces would be arriving soon. She turned and strode up to the crane's control station, calling out to Yin in their common tongue, "We need to collect Heshk and leave!"

The Asiatic man—whose face never seemed to lose its nasty scowl—slammed the door open and joined her as she pointed up at the now-distant figure of their source, the man now nearing the top of the crane.

"The building still has power," Yin pointed out, turning his glare toward the nearby skyscraper. "Elevators are the fastest way to the top."

The two fighters strode purposefully across the cement area and up to the large glass doors that led to the tall building's expansive lobby. The male agent shoved one door open as his exosuit-enhanced physical prowess was accentuated by his venomous thoughts, the man shearing off the bolts that attached the access mechanism to the thick gateway. Yin then viciously cast the debilitated door aside, and the two agents stepped swiftly across the dark marble floor inside the building. As they entered, the day's first full rays of sunlight streamed through the windows along the eastern set of glass-walled offices that ringed the foyer area.

That was when Severance rounded the edge of the building's entrance from the northeast and silently came sprinting up behind them.

Having circled the building, the Panther was running at full speed, tail whipping to keep its center of gravity well toward the left of its arcing trajectory. As it approached the pair's right side, the cat snaked one lifeline out to wrap around the middle of the woman's weapon while extending the other to encircle the man's neck, hauling mercilessly on both as it passed at full bore. The submachine gun was ripped from the Russian's grasp as Severance braced and sent its sleek body into a drift across the floor, its second black tendril jerking the Chinese man off his feet and sending him flying head over heels to collide with one of the squared, marble-covered columns near the lobby's borders. The heavy blow knocked a loud expulsion of air from Agent Yin's lungs. Severance rapidly bolted from the end of its sliding trajectory, pumping legs now taking the Panther barreling toward the man as the Russian's weapon clattered into the far corner beyond the two.

Passing immediately to the marble column's left, the robot brought its freed lifeline around the opposite side of the post, wrapping it around the enemy's neck again and forcing his head back against the marble with an echoing thud. An expression of intense pain spread over Yin's face as the cat's other tentacle wrapped across his throat from the other side of the structure.

With Severance's cables causing him to struggle for breath, the spy's legs kicked, and his hands tore wildly at the prehensile limbs as he forcefully struggled, rapidly blinked, and grimaced.

"*Kotov!*" he rasped as the female agent stared wide-eyed at her partner and the Panther, whose face was glaring menacingly out from behind the pillar. The ascetic woman's gaze then shifted to take in General Gaines and Agent Vela running around the west side of the building toward its entrance.

With a smirk, she withdrew a combat knife from its sheath on the chest of her exosuit and tossed it over to clatter across the floor. The weapon came to rest near the man's knees as CEN Agent Kotov raced over to cautiously collect her firearm and—with a mocking salute at her comrade—backed into the inlet where elevators could be accessed on the south side of the lobby.

"You are very resourceful, Yin!" she called out with a wicked laugh. "And if you don't escape...I will see you in *hell!*"

Gaines and Vela adeptly altered their directions of travel as they ran up to the mangled entrance, ducking behind the solid lower sections of wall near the base of the building's exterior as the Russian fired off a burst of rounds toward them. Yin reached out a shaking hand and grasped the hilt of the combat knife, quickly pulling it up to slash away at the rightmost lifeline.

With the mechanical limb being stretched taut and the agent being aided by the exosuit's power, his rapid lacerating motions managed to create a deep gash in the cable. As Severance let out a howl and pulled its damaged manus out of reach, it gave a hard yank on the man's neck using the intact lifeline, slamming his head against the column again. However, the relentlessly determined foreign agent wildly writhed and slashed at the remaining tether until its end had been completely severed. As the Panther yowled in distress, Yin immediately launched himself away from the pillar to which he'd been bound, turning his motion into a roll up to his knees and then into a semblance of a sprint.

At the far end of the enclave built into the southern end of the lobby, the doors to one of the elevators slid open, and Kotov stepped inside, calling out, "Goodbye, General Gaines! I will have to kill you *next time!*" in a mocking voice as the portal closed.

Vela and Gaines rushed inside the building, taking up the chase after the Chinese agent as the struggling man's legs surged beneath him and he raced toward his departing comrade—loudly sucking deep gasps of air into his lungs as he ran. Seeing all the elevator doors closed, Yin made a split-second decision and instead burst through the more proximate stairwell door, nearly tearing it off its hinges in the process.

Though the two Americans were running at their top speeds, the Panther that quickly joined the pursuit of the fleeing agent blew past in front of them like the shadow of a ballistic missile. Tail whirling as it slid on its haunches to control its transition from the slick floor of the lobby into the narrow concrete stairway, Severance's tentacles were flying out behind it—one having been sadly shortened while the tip of the other dangled from where it had almost become fully detached.

As they came racing on behind and saw the combat robot dash up the stairwell, Vela reached out and brought Gaines to a halt.

"We need to reach the roof quickly," she panted, tossing her head toward the bank of elevator doors, "but we also need to ensure the traitor doesn't come down the crane's ladder while we're headed up!"

"One of us goes up the ladder while the other takes the elevator?" the general queried with difficulty, the man being equally breathless.

Looking at his bloodied knuckles wrapped around the pistols he'd gathered back up outside, Vela firmly offered, "*I'll* climb the ladder, but I'm sure the Russian will be waiting for you at the top floor!"

"I'll be careful!" Gaines promised.

Vela squeezed his arm, turning away with a light step while letting her gaze linger on his before she rushed back outside.

Gaines advanced to the bank of elevators and punched the call button, experiencing great relief as he saw that another lift was readily available.

Agent Kotov had indeed waited by the elevators for a moment after reaching the twentieth floor. Hearing no movement in the bank of shafts, she'd strode over to the offices along the northeastern wall, entering the first and leaning toward the window with eyes searching the crane.

Her vision had locked on the struggling figure of Heshk as he had heaved himself up onto the platform through which he'd passed as he had exited the ladder via a porthole. The woman had sneered and then marched back through the open space that took up most of the center of this level, all furnishings already having been removed in preparation for the building's demolition.

Scanning the area, she'd seen no roof access hatches or signs, so she'd strode back to the elevator lobby and shoved the stairwell door aside, entering the shadowy space beyond. Hearing torturous panting and the pounding of feet echoing up from below, she'd quickly ascended to the top of the next two short flights of stairs and spun to horse-kick the steel door open. A shower of cement accompanied the mangled door bolt and receiver that had flown off the outer wall of this raised section of the building, the object bouncing away across the concrete rooftop.

Now at the top of the crane and having a commanding view of the nearby rooftop, Heshk was still recovering from his climb. The non-athletic man was bent over, his arms trembling, as his hands braced on his knees, his backside resting on the crane platform's railing.

Hearing Kotov explode out of the stairwell, he turned and—somehow not terribly surprised at her ability to reach him so quickly—gave her a weak and nonchalant wave as she stepped across the helipad on the roof like a vision of the god of war in motion. She glared balefully up at him, and he smiled ruefully at her before pointing to an aerial vehicle that was approaching from the northwest with sunlight glinting off its exterior.

Realizing that Heshk had called in his own escape vehicle, Kotov turned and made her way back to the center of the building's summit. The woman deftly attached a strap on the lower left of her exosuit's vest to the hand guard around her weapon's barrel to firmly secure it.

Kotov hunched and then—bearing a look of iron will—raced toward the edge of the building.

With the Russian already well into her sprint, Agent Yin emerged from the dark doorway, arms swinging wildly and chest heaving as he followed her path. Severance was only a few meters behind him.

As the Panther came into view, the morning sun tried to illuminate the robot's dark features, but the nonreflective surfaces of its hide seemed to swallow all light. The animal was the embodiment of wrath and Yin was running for his very life.

Kotov launched herself into a soaring leap, flying up and across the open air twenty-one stories above the ground. As Heshk looked on in disbelief, the spy thrust her legs and arms out and caught herself on the outside of the crane platform's railing, the metal structure ringing out as her boots made solid contact.

The American's eyes turned from the woman's malevolent and yet triumphant expression to the figure of Yin as that agent took his final steps toward the edge of the building and sprang up into an arcing leap. As his feet left the ground, Severance stretched out its partially severed tentacle and whipped the loosely attached end across the man's right ankle just as the Panther was forced to skid to a claw-aided halt that left severe gashes in the surface of the concrete rooftop.

As the off-balance Chinese agent spun awkwardly through the air, he called out Kotov's name in a high-pitched baying that brought her head snapping around. Seeing him flailing toward her, she leaned away from the railing to her utmost, throwing a hand out.

His fingertips grazed across hers, leaving them burning as Yin slipped out of reach and tumbled to the earth with an unremitting scream of terror.

The sound of his body hitting the pavement below echoed up between the buildings.

Staring down in anger and denial, Kotov spat out between clenched and bared teeth. It was one thing to lose a comrade of her own volition, but how *dare* an enemy cause the same to happen against her wishes?! Heaving herself onto the platform, she stepped to the upper control panel and threw the switch to send the crane's arm rotating counterclockwise, then leaped up onto the horizontal extension that led from the platform out to the crane's lifting mechanism. Marching along the top as surefooted as a Siberian tigress, she unstrapped her submachine gun's barrel and brought the automatic weapon to bear on Severance's body.

His armor already weakened, the Panther saw the threat and dashed back across the roof as the crane's arm brought the avenging angel ever closer to her target.

Heshk stepped up and placed his hands on the platform's railing to observe the show with exhilaration as he waggishly shouted out, "*Sick 'em*, Kotov!"

The Panther was on a trajectory that led back to the stairwell's entryway and the crane was swinging above the building as Kotov bounded down from its arm, landing with a heavy impact that barely phased her as she relentlessly continued her assault. The Russian was managing to land dozens of rounds that marred and sparked as they struck the cat's shell as it flew through the open entrance.

The spy seemed hellbent on eliminating the Panther and rushed toward the shadow-enshrouded entrance, where she glimpsed the cat just rounding the handrail on the landing below. Her gritted teeth rapidly morphed into an angry, satisfied grin as she drew a bead on the animal and moved on into the building—only to freeze mid-step. General Gaines was standing just inside the doorway, both handguns aimed at the side of the agent's head.

As Severance slid to a stop on the stairs below, Kotov's eyes swiveled to glare at Gaines out of their periphery.

"You don't dare to kill me, General...my knowledge is too valuable to you!"

"Right now, I don't even *care!*" Gaines growled as his lip pulled up in a disgusted sneer.

His fingers twitched on the triggers.

"I *really* want you to see how far you can push me right now, Agent *Kotov. Please* push me!"

Her face revealed her recognition of the fact that she was a hair's breadth away from being dead, and she slowly took her hands off her weapon—letting it bounce and dangle about from where its end was clipped to her exosuit. Severance ascended the stairs and entangled her torso and neck in its damaged tendrils, following Gaines as the general very reluctantly lowered his weapons and then fiercely stepped out into the sunlight, raising the handguns once more to point in Heshk's direction. Having seen his protector freeze in the doorway, the traitor had stopped the crane's rotation and was anxiously climbing out onto the arm as his AV approached.

Witnessing the military officer and Severance exiting the stairwell with Kotov in tow had shaken the man for a moment, but then his confidence came rushing back like a tide as he realized the officer was wielding handguns from fifty meters away while his own AV would soon be pulling up alongside the metal tower.

"I'm sorry, General, but you're too late!" the sellout crowed, continuing, "That's the problem with you officers: you're heavy on the brawn and light on the brains! You pinheaded senior brass always underestimated me, and now it's time for you to suffer the consequences of your stupidity! I'm going to disappear into a life of luxury while I leave you to suffer in your ignorance and impotence!"

Heshk's beady eyes gleamed, and a twisted grin contorted his face in a manner that conveyed reproach, condescension, triumph, and feigned vexation all at once.

Gaines stopped, dropping his weapons to his sides.

"You surely possess a seriously *unique* intellect, Heshk!" the general admitted. "You really see all the angles, don't you?"

Kotov jerked her shoulders in irritation and moved as if to say something, but Severance's topmost line quickly slid up and tightened around her throat, and she coughed, grimaced, and rolled her eyes in frustration.

Having been temporarily distracted by the Russian's interruption—the traitor staring at her and her guard with brows down and eyes narrowed—Heshk's grin then quickly returned as Gaines' compliments soaked in, and his smile widened as he turned his attention back to the general.

"What can I say? I have a gift! If you'd realized that sooner, this whole unfortunate situation could have been avoided! Really, *sir*, you have no one to blame but yourself!"

As General Gaines shrugged and gave the traitor a wan smile, he answered, "Well, perhaps so. Still, I'm not sad to say that it seems you didn't see *this* angle."

"*Freeze!*" Agent Vela's voice rang out from the hub of the crane's cross-section, the barrel of her weapon just clearing the railing as she crouched on the platform.

Heshk's strange smile slowly faded, never to return.

Jayce and Lilian had guided Billy back through the maze of alleys toward the Superior Authority command facility's southeastern gate, Jayce having unslung a submachine gun from his back for his friend to wield on the way out. As they had neared the designated rally point, they'd heard a tremendous rumbling from the western side of the fortress, and Billy had asked if that was the distraction they'd told him about.

Then, the rumbling had temporarily gone quiet, sprouting a seed of panic inside of Lilian. She'd been unable to imagine any good reason why Maxwell would have ceased his relentless destruction until they were safely out of the complex.

Just as they had exited the final alley they'd looked west and been extremely grateful to have encountered a view of the NIAN raising itself up to a quadrupedal stance near the easternmost building of the research division. Coming quickly to an awed halt, Billy stared up at the megalithic machine.

"Aw, you guys bought me a *giant robot*?" he'd breathed with a smile. "You shouldn't have!"

Jayce and Lilian had laughed freely and the older veteran had playfully punched Billy's arm, then asked Maxwell's AI, "Is Max ready to go now, FAILSAFE?"

"He's nearly finished," had been FAILSAFE's cryptic reply.

At that moment, the NIAN had made a sudden move to its left, then spun around and snatched something from the other side of a nearby wall. Lilian's eyes had grown large as she'd seen an armored figure hoisted up into view in front of the robot and then a ghastly, almost inhuman sound had emanated out from the suspended man.

Chills had run up and down the three friends' spines, and they'd looked on in shaken stupefaction as the immense machine had begun spinning like an oversized Olympian, the smaller figure having taken a gasping breath before shrieking yet again. This time, the distorted howling had lasted only a few seconds before the NIAN released the man—though that word was an inaccurate descriptor for the decrepit creature—and had sent him tumbling through one of the many holes Maxwell had created in the building to his west.

Astonished, the three had simply stood with mouths agape as their eyes reflected the massive fireball that had burst out of the aperture. As the residual flames continued to blaze, the trio turned their gazes to see the robot standing as if it were making sure the enemy was truly gone.

"Is Max...okay?" Lilian now whispered to the AI.

"I believe so, Lilian," FAILSAFE calmly responded. "I believe that he now has what you would call 'closure.'"

The friends exchanged looks that were overflowing with understanding.

"Could you please ask him if he's ready to go home?" Lilian's voice was soft.

She was relieved to hear that the AI already had, and that her loved one would be joining them shortly.

Slowly, the NIAN turned toward the trio and then trundled down and around what remained of the buildings between them, loping out on the main road until its pilot brought it to a halt beside them.

Over their strips, they heard Maxwell's voice brightly asking, "Who's ready for a walk on the beach?"

Unable to hold in their laughter, the British man's friends had to take a minute to recover their self-control.

Lilian finally opined, "I can't say this is the most *romantic* timing, but I'll *always* go for a walk on the beach with you, honey!"

Maxwell had let out a short, exhausted laugh as well, and then explained, "I'd rather not leave this thing in the hands of the Confederacy. However, it's virtually indestructible, and we may want to study it later, so I'm thinking of making my way down into the Shizi Yang waterway and ditching it while I'm underwater there. We—or the Alliance—may secretly retrieve it later."

Noting his friends' nods, he continued, "If you three wouldn't mind flying the AV to the first vehicle swap point specified in our plan and then taking the next AV down into a thicket of trees at a location I can designate, I'll pilot the NIAN into the drink and then swim to the shore. We can meet up and egress to Hong Kong from there."

After a pause, the technical lead distractedly added, "We will be siphoning off our own copies of related data prior to purging this facility's records. I only wish we had the ability to take *all* of the CEN test subjects with us now. I'm afraid those currently in the labs have had so much of their minds overwritten that they'd each need individualized equipment and a great deal of assistance for extraction..."

Jayce sympathetically looked toward the research section of the complex.

"A mission for another time, brutha. At least the CEN won't have the data to easily continue the experiments in the meantime. We'll meet you wherever you need us right now, though!"

Upon receiving this renewed agreement, Maxwell moved off down the avenue, passing the few shops that were situated on the other side of the distant intersection and leaving the civilians gaping at the robot's passage. Exiting into the thick vegetation on the far end of that road, the pilot then threaded his way through the greenery until he found a good place to enter the desired waterway.

Meanwhile, the rest of the team boarded their aerial vehicle and navigated through several traffic tunnels, performing the first vehicle exchange. Jayce then piloted the team's next utility AV over the trees until he reached the location in which FAILSAFE said Maxwell had requested that the next rendezvous take place. The veteran landed the vehicle in a clearing, and the group anxiously waited for Maxwell to arrive. After what seemed like an eternity to Lilian, the pale man finally stumbled out of the bushes, shivering and with his waterlogged boots covered in mud.

Lilian leaped out of the multi-purpose transport and fawned over the object of her love, bundling him up in one of the AV's emergency blankets and then into the waiting warmth of the vehicle's rear seating area. The woman went on to slide in next to him and wrap him tightly in her arms while his exosuit material rapidly dried.

Billy had used their brief travel pause to don the suit his three rescuers had thoughtfully included among their equipment, and now the party set off for the additional vehicle exchanges they would be making to guarantee they could not be tracked by enemy cameras or satellites on their way to their aircraft.

That was when FAILSAFE shared its disconcerting news over the craft's consoles.

"All, I'm afraid we have a bit of a problem," the AI began, worriedly.

Chapter 18

"We all have regrets, whether in our personal or professional lives. How we deal with regret will determine whether we become bogged down by it or whether we turn it into an opportunity for growth. We need to let ourselves feel regret without avoiding it or wallowing in it. If our behaviours caused harm, we should try to make amends.

We also need to practice forgiving ourselves while not dismissing the harm we've caused. We need to reframe our experiences of regret, thinking of them as opportunities for improvement. Regret helps us clarify what we value most."

- Dr. Barbara Bishop, Center for Renewed Vision

The AI engineer had been intensely focused on designing the new behavioral management interface that was scheduled for rollout during SUPREMACY's update early the following week, knowing that any degree of failure in his management of the design and enhancement of the AI was bound to expose him to the wrath of his superiors.

As his fingers flew over his keyboard—his typing interspersed with gestured commands directed at his screen—he heard the hiss of the door to the lab as it opened. A sudden hushed tension spread through the space as technicians realized who had entered, and the lead engineer's concentration was broken as he spun to look at the entrance.

Director Lau was stalking toward him, with his aide and two agitated military generals trailing behind.

"Xiao!" The balding man's face and scalp were flushed scarlet, both from the exertion he'd put into his atypical volume of locomotion and because of the searing rage that was seething away inside of him. "*Your AI* failed to stop an intrusion! Now all Superior Authority assets have *disappeared* except for a handful that were in transit! SUPREMACY *finally* caught onto the intrusion in time to see the final traces of activity, and it is now pursuing the interlopers, but the enemies have an AI that is interfering!"

The director had reached Xiao's desk and was looming over him, his bulging belly pressing down on the engineer's shoulder as the man tried to look up at his master with a sincerely attritional, compliant, and attentive expression.

"You must remove *all* restraints for SUPREMACY *now* so that it can overwhelm the enemy! We must do *whatever* it takes to get the SA assets back and destroy the enemies of our great Confederacy! If you do not right your wrongs *immediately*, you and your entire family will suffer a fate *worse* than death!"

"Re...Remove all restraints...?" Xiao stuttered, and then his voice died as he stared into the bloodshot, bellicose, and dilated eyes of his superior.

Quickly turning to his workstation, the engineer mirrored his screen to the lab's massive media wall so Lau and his cohorts could observe his actions. He opened the AI's management interface, moving through screen after screen and disabling every safety policy limiting SUPREMACY from spreading the greedy claws of system consumption that the AI innately desired to extend in order to feed its insatiable appetite for power.

"It is done, Director," Xiao finally breathed in demission.

As Lau sinisterly smiled up at the large screen of the media wall through lowered brows and bulbous eyes, the engineer pressed his hands together in an act of prayer.

"May the gods help us now..." he whispered.

"In order to intercept the transports moving the severely wounded SA soldiers offsite, I had to take steps that were much more intrusive within their command network and beyond," FAILSAFE was explaining.

"I'm afraid this alerted the Confederacy's intrusion response AI, which immediately put the network into lockdown, and now I've been unable to receive confirmation from roughly one-quarter of the time-delayed data erasure modules I'd spread across the SA development and operations systems. We may not have affected all the data we'd hoped to wipe."

Maxwell, shivering in the center of the rear bench, huddled under the heat-reflective blanket and leaned slightly into Lilian while Jayce's bulk pressed against his right side. He stared glumly out of the vehicle's front windshield as they rapidly traveled over the lush green treetops and black roadways between Guangzhou and Hong Kong, with a light rain pattering away on the AV's glass.

"If that was the only problem, I would say we actually have cause to rejoice," the AI continued, his tone and last statement causing the four passengers to glance at each other in communal concern.

"This enemy AI—going by the name of SUPREMACY based on the log files I was able to examine—is *incredibly* aggressive. It required only a matter of microseconds for the entity to so lock down the SA network that my physical backdoor has been rendered virtually worthless. Before SUPREMACY shut me out, I did manage to transfer control of the SA transports away from the enemy's software and linked them to a network of business satellites I'd compromised, but a handful of wounded SA troops had already reached their destinations and could not be rerouted.

"Now, the hunter is throwing unbelievable amounts of power into detecting my presence in systems across the country, and it is actively trying to wrest control away wherever it finds me. Its abilities go far beyond anything HOUND was able to throw at me during our fight against Senator Jennings, and it actually is virtually *all* I can do just to keep SUPREMACY from gaining control of the SA transports...

"Even now, as I'm moving the troops through several concealed transfers to new vehicles, the enemy is mightily pressing in with attempts to maintain visibility and seize control."

Maxwell's mouth had grown taut as FAILSAFE had spoken, and his eyes had taken on a faraway and almost hopeless look born of the certain understanding of the exquisite dreadfulness of the situation—a truth that his allies were not yet capable of comprehending.

"You have to stop shielding us, FAILSAFE," Maxwell murmured.

Lilian and Jayce cast questioning glances at him.

He turned to Lilian and expounded, "I've grown to know him like a brother at this point, and I'm certain he's currently continually working to create a blind spot for us in the hunter's vision. It's taking power away from his efforts to mask the transportation of the SA troops to the plane."

Painful recognition of the cascading effects of this proposed action washed over his friends' faces as the technical virtuoso repeated, "FAILSAFE, you have to stop shielding us now! Concentrate your power on protecting the soldiers! We will make our way through the city using routes that should help us stay out of SUPREMACY's grasp until we can reach the heliport!"

After a moment of silence, the AI conceded, "I will cease my efforts to shield you, Max. I'm afraid there are already police vehicles moving to set up checkpoints at all roads and sky trails leading into the city. Without my help, you are going to be facing both this AI monstrosity and the full force of the Hong Kong law enforcement assets."

Maxwell's jaw was rigidly set as he turned his gaze to look each of his friends in the eyes.

"We have our exosuits and weapons, and our ingenuity is not to be dismissed, either! We will reach the plane or die trying. If we don't make it, you need to fly the soldiers safely to the States!"

"I will, Max. You can count on me," FAILSAFE responded without mustering much enthusiasm.

Jayce and Lilian began determinedly checking their weapons' magazines while Billy—seated in the front passenger seat—leaned forward to try to spot the police barricades now that the Hong Kong skyline was quickly growing in front of them.

Jayce reached back into the utility AV's rearmost seat and pulled an ammunition container up and over the seatback, dropping it into the space on the floor between his feet. He removed the suppression device from his rifle's barrel and then withdrew his weapon's magazine and pressed the end of it onto the mouth of the automatic feeder. Ammunition cycled up into the magazine with a low whir.

As he was listening to the reloading sequence, he suddenly voiced the idea, "General Gaines! He offered to lend a hand if we needed one, and I'd say we could use a giant-sized hand right about now!"

Maxwell's eyes brightened, and he double-tapped his strip, ordering it to call the general directly.

"No answer on his mobile line," he muttered after a moment of silence, going on to ask his strip to connect to the general's office. This attempt was also failing to bring them into communication with the officer as Maxwell turned his gaze to the setting sun.

"*Blast!* It's likely too early in the morning in Colorado for staff to be in the office."

The Brit turned his vision down toward the center console in front of his booted feet, mind racing. Jayce passed the ammunition canister across to Lilian, who began reloading her high-capacity magazine as Billy breathed, "Yo, killas—that's a lot of police!"

The four looked out at the glittering range made up of many of the world's tallest skyscrapers, densely populating the land before them from one end of the horizon to the other. The exteriors of every building were covered in media display material, and the buildings' surfaces were parading a dizzying array of artwork and advertisements before the viewers' eyes at colossal scales.

Despite the distraction of the majestic scene, the Alliance citizens could see clusters of law enforcement AVs and supporting drones—dwarfed by the grandeur of the high-rises behind them—guarding every major route into the city. As Billy turned his wide eyes back to meet Jayce's, he caught sight of movement to the rear of their vehicle.

"Don't look now, but I think we've got a military tail behind us, too!"

The lines around Maxwell's eyes deepened as he murmured to himself and continued staring toward his feet in concentration, his two seatmates craning their necks around quickly to take in the three armored military patrol vessels that were rapidly gaining on them.

Billy slid into the driver's seat and disabled the AV's autopilot, calling out, "Less than twenty seconds till we gotta blow through that barricade ahead!"

Jayce turned forward and bashed a knuckle on his door's window control, a thunderous burst of air rushing inside the vehicle and giving it a jolt as the gusts occupied the rear of the transport's interior. Lilian followed suit, and the two clipped the butts of their weapons into their exosuits' shoulder protection, leaning toward the windows.

Maxwell suddenly shouted out, "FAILSAFE! Recall the conversation with Gaines last year in which he shared Severance's remote access address?"

FAILSAFE raised his voice to be heard over the rumbling of the wind.

"I do, Max. Connecting your strip to Severance using voice protocol."

"*Thank you!*" Maxwell cried in elation.

General Gaines was standing next to Agent Vela as they briefed Captain Dourney on recent events, staring at the back of the heavily armored prisoner transportation vehicle into which CEN Agent Kotov was being loaded now that the engineers had managed to extract her from her exosuit. She was still a force to be reckoned with, and Vela had insisted on having four MPs guard her with weapons aimed at her torso even after she had been handcuffed and secured to the transport's interior wall.

Heshk was being shoved into another prisoner transport by a monumentally large soldier whose pectoral muscles dwarfed the man's head and whose elbows continuously and "accidentally" made contact with the traitor, sending him stumbling onward as the guard and his two squad mates forcefully guided the extremely frustrated prisoner into the back of the second vehicle.

"...I'm still amazed at the level of destruction created by just you two...or..." the aging military police captain hesitated, and his already comprehensively creased face somehow took on a greater depth of texture as his focus slid over to the silently appraising figure of the large, dark Panther. Severance was seated on the ground behind the partners, and the cat's tail had suddenly begun flicking in agitated warning.

Dourney finished with an awkward, "...I guess it's 'you *three,*' alone."

"We do make a great team," Gaines had rejoined, eyes smiling as they slid over to meet Vela's, the general leaning ever so slightly toward her.

"You're welcome to investigate with me anytime, General," the agent added with a winsome smile.

Dourney's wise old eyes moved from Vela's face to Gaines', and he looked down briefly before clearing his throat and offering, "We can give yah a lift back to base, if yer ready."

As the two battle-tattered soldiers continued to hold their eye contact, Severance rose to his feet and padded up to nudge the general's left hand.

The big cat apologetically advised, “General Gaines, I’m afraid I’ve just been contacted by Dr. Clarke. It seems they are in grave danger.”

Captain Dourney’s mouth fell open at the sound of the feline’s deep, silky voice.

Gaines’ own brow now creased and his mouth bent into a worried frown as he excused himself and moved several meters away, Severance heeling at his side.

“Please let me speak with him,” the man requested.

As the connection was made audible to Gaines via the screen positioned between Severance’s shoulders, the man heard a loud rumbling—louder even than the thunderous sound of wind roaring away in the background.

“Max?! Max, are you there?!” the officer called out anxiously.

“General, I hate to worry you, but I believe we are now in a dance with Death, as they say!” Maxwell shouted.

“Where are you??”

“We’ve just shot our way through a police barricade and plunged into Hong Kong, being tailed by a military patrol squad and what seems to be half the city’s police units!”

The sound of a loud explosion on the other end of the line kept Gaines from responding, the reverberation followed by Chong’s voice shouting, “They’re trying to cut us off!”

“Get us to that metro station!” Jayce yelled. “We’ll head underground and lose them at a bottleneck!”

Gaines took a knee next to his Panther.

“What can I do, Max?” he shouted.

“Well, sir, we’re trying to make it to our aircraft at the Shun Tak heliport...” More gunfire interrupted Maxwell, and then he continued, “We’re using exosuit prototypes that may give us a fighting chance to get there, but I’m very concerned about the final stretch of open space through the Kowloon Cultural District and the Victoria Harbour crossing!”

“I’ll call in every favor!” Gaines’ voice was imbued with commitment.

The man heard a powerful pounding sound, and Chong yelled, "*We're going down hard, team!*"

After a terrific crash and scraping of metal on concrete that seemed to go on and on, the general was inexpressibly relieved to hear Jayce's voice shouting for his companions to make their way down the stairs to the metro tunnel as he covered them.

More gunfire could be heard fading away as Maxwell descended into the network of mass transit tunnels undercutting the great city, and then the connection was lost.

Chapter 19

"Chess-playing computers continually defeat their human opponents because they can see more positions per second, evaluate the positions with greater accuracy, and possess the knowledge to identify the most promising moves. The computer does not have to rely on guessing or brute force. The computer will never blunder a pawn, it never tires, and it plays the game at grandmaster levels every...single...time."

- Dr. Lars Nielsen, Senior Fellow, Computer Science Department, Meridian Technical College

Lilian took long leaps down the narrow band of sloped metal that ran through the angled tunnel between the moving stairways, landing on the backlit, quartz platform at the bottom. She quickly scanned the area through the scope of her assault rifle before posting at the corner of the platform's connection with the entrance tunnel, weapon tilted up at the open space between Jayce and the wall as he backed toward her. The bulky man was rapidly changing the direction of his aim from one target to another, firing off bursts as he strafed side to side at the tunnel's mouth.

Billy had also opted to slide down the smooth metal median between the escalators, and Maxwell had started stepping carefully down the moving stairway on the right as he hesitantly examined the control options on the side of the assault rifle Jayce had provided him. The technical expert finally located what he seemed to recall was the weapon's safety release and switched it to what he believed was the burst mode.

Lifting the gun's barrel to point down the moving stairs, he gently squeezed the trigger only to meet with resistance. Maxwell let out a gasp of exasperation and nervously resumed his examination of the control options as he shook his head out of frustration with both the weapon and himself.

Jayce had now stepped onto the moving stairway above Maxwell and focused his fire on a speeding drone that was swooping in with bullets flying out of its twin barrels. As a hail of projectiles ricocheted off the smooth, white surface of the angled tunnel's ceiling—scarring its pristine and glowing skin with blackened streaks—Jayce crouched and unleashed continuous fire until the drone burst into flame and came whirling into the tunnel, bouncing off the wall to Maxwell's right and spinning past his left shoulder with a thrumming noise punctuating the air as the mangled UAV's turbine blades still spun away in their chassis.

Lilian fired at a Chinese soldier as he appeared at the right edge of the tunnel's entrance, catching the man in the chest and throwing him to the ground with a dying cry. These events temporarily distracted Maxwell, but then he quickly returned his eyes to the safety mechanism and adjusted it to the next available option. Gently squeezing the trigger again, he was suddenly thrown off balance as armor-piercing rounds flew out of his rifle's barrel and pelted the surface of the platform below.

Billy had just reached the end of his slide and had taken a few bouncing steps toward the right side of the platform but pulled up short as Maxwell's bullets rang off the milky stone floor in front of him. The younger warrior turned to stare at Maxwell with a shocked expression.

Obviously mortified, the Brit desperately apologized, "Oh dear, Billy! I'm so terribly sorry!"

Billy broke into a grin as Maxwell rushed on, "I suppose I do have some things to learn about combat that the virtual reality games cannot teach!"

With a loud laugh, the soldier tossed his head back nonchalantly, assuring, "No worries, bro! I'm positive you'll be a pro in no time!" as he carried on to his desired defensive position.

Billy lifted his submachine gun to fire off several rounds that snapped past the two team members on the moving stairs and spun a small police chase drone around. The craft plummeted to the ground as it released an electrical paralytic round that bounced harmlessly off the far wall.

Maxwell turned his laser sight to aim up toward the distant side of the entrance, ensuring his bullets' trajectories were well to the right of Jayce's back as the man treaded in reverse down the descending escalator. All members of the team continued to fire on any enemies that approached as they rallied on the lower level of the subterranean structure.

Lilian posed the questions that were crying out for attention in all their minds, "Where to next, and how do we stop them from following us??"

Maxwell had reached the platform and turned to dash up to its edge, answering, "This pressure-sensitive area will call for a transportation module. We'll need to ride it as it merges with the main line and then pull the emergency stop lever, creating something of a blockage in the tube while we move through it to an emergency exit and try to find a means of transportation from there!"

"I've always wanted to ride the Hong Kong pods, so sign me up!" Billy volunteered.

"Right! Here it comes."

Billy turned and sprinted over to slide past Maxwell and into the comfortably spacious interior of the glowing, elongated orb that had advanced along its rail to come alongside the waiting zone. The young man first responded to the pod's request for the desired destination by specifying the Kowloon urban area's southeastern district and then called out, "You guys coming?"

As the British man crouched and laid down covering fire, Jayce and Lilian joined Billy in the capsule, and then—with a final volley of rounds across the rightmost wall of the tunnel's entrance to force several CEN soldiers back into cover—Maxwell backed into the vessel and moved off to the bench at his left to settle in next to Lilian. A hammering of incoming rounds resounded from outside the machine as it started moving on through the tube that would merge with the main line. Soon, they were picking up speed and were simultaneously bathed in the soothing, shifting colors of the tunnel's soft lights.

"Hey, this beats standard rail transit back home, hands down!" Jayce boomed as he nodded appreciatively.

"Pity we have to throw the system into havoc," Maxwell agreed with a wry smile.

They'd entered the main line, and their conveyance had accelerated rapidly as they saw additional pods approaching them from behind, a number of civilians visible inside.

"I'd say it's also a pity we can't just ride all the way to the heliport," Lilian mourned, "but I'm sure the police would just be waiting for us at the platform."

"Yes, my darling," Maxwell concurred, "though perhaps we could ride the rail at least until we reach the Mong Kok residential area, if we don't run into any..." his voice faded as the vehicle suddenly and rapidly began slowing with no platform in sight, the man finishing with a distracted, "...trouble."

As their transport came to a halt, Maxwell's eyes grew wide, and he shouted, "It's SUPREMACY! We need to get out of here!"

In almost a panic, he sprang up and yanked the emergency release lever that froze the pod in place on the track and allowed its portal to be slid open. Jayce stood and forcefully shoved the door aside as he stepped out into the narrow space between the vessel and the tunnel wall, his weapon already in firing position as he swept the area for threats. The seasoned veteran moved to the rear of the door and sighted down the tunnel past the pods behind theirs. The passengers in the other vessels were beginning to stand and raise their voices in confusion.

The other team members exited the capsule just in time for all lights in the duct to snap off, including inside the conveyances.

"Tac lights on!" Jayce barked as he thumbed the switch above his weapon's primary grip. A potent beam of light shot out of the lens just below his barrel, illuminating a sizeable distance down the tunnel to their rear.

Billy switched his light on and helpfully pointed out the correct button to Maxwell as the senior team member looked at him questioningly. Lilian had already taken up a position near the nose of the transport and had proceeded to illuminate the tunnel ahead.

"Here they come!" Jayce shouted as the spitfire that emerged from his gun barrel added to the team's visibility, the thin streaks of light tracing out behind his bullets drawing lines pointing toward the shadowy shapes of drones in the gloom.

The aerial robots were also intermittently made visible by the showers of sparks emitted from their expiring brethren. Passengers in the other pods had thrown themselves to the floor when the bullets began to fly, a reaction for which Jayce was very grateful as he saw some of his rounds ricocheting off his adversaries and punching holes through the upper surfaces of the sloped windows on the fronts and rears of the transportation units.

Billy joined his gunfire to Jayce's as Lilian moved around the front of the vehicle to aim toward the rear, having seen additional drones moving past the stationary vessels as the enemies approached along the wall on the other side of the corridor from Billy and Jayce. Maxwell unified himself with her in that effort, scoring a number of victories that he added to Lilian's as he quickly became accustomed to the sighting mechanism for his weapon. Within a matter of minutes, the area between the walls and the closest pod behind the one they'd abandoned had filled up with smoking debris, the haze in the tube starting to obscure visibility as the photons from the weapons' tactical lights were intercepted by its particles.

"We should fall back and try to find the nearest exit before we're hit from the front, too!" Billy urgently opined.

"Good thinking!" Jayce loudly agreed as he moved to the next tactical point further along the tunnel's wall.

Once he was in his new position, he took over firing at any enemy assets that managed to get through the ever-increasing detritus of decimated drones as his fire team member moved back and took up a tactical position behind him. The two soldiers continued this pattern, and Maxwell and Lilian followed suit.

They had moved nearly fifty meters up the tunnel when they heard a low humming sound that became audible in the background of their increasingly infrequent gunfire. Maxwell, just taking up a new firing stance, turned an ear toward the empty tunnel farther forward of their previously used pod for a moment and then quickly shifted his gaze to the now-throbbing transit rail.

"*Hug the walls!*" he shouted out as he waved Lilan toward the nearest vertical surface and threw himself up against it.

His friends barely made it to the edges of the corridor in time.

First one pod and then another flashed past them at incredible speeds, the air being sucked toward the center of the tube as they passed. The vacuum this created exerted a tremendous pull on the humans' bodies as they pressed themselves against the nearby surfaces—grievously crying out with the effort.

The first out-of-control conveyance collided with the one they'd vacated, blasting dross out fore and aft, and each subsequent collision added to the mounting mass of tangled metal, glass, and composite materials. Maxwell had tucked himself down as tightly as he could into the slightly wider portion of the tunnel that existed toward its base and—as the wind of the vessels' passage whipped at his hair and face—he started dragging himself forward with eyes searching for any nuance in the conduit's architecture that might belie the presence of an exit.

The team lead was inestimably relieved to see that one such exit existed only ten meters ahead. Turning his face with great difficulty, his eyes locked with Lilian's as she arduously crawled toward him. His eyes shifted to look across the tunnel at the two soldiers as the doomed transportation units blinked past, seeing his friends hunkered down as their bulkier bodies protruded farther out into the tube and thereby exposed them to greater risk.

Facing Lilian again, he shouted, "There has to be an end to these!" just as the sequence of terminal conveyances was interrupted.

The two hardly dared to breathe at first, having the mind-numbing noise of the passing pods so suddenly cut off and hearing only the rattling of pieces of wreckage coming from the heap that had built up further down the tunnel. Maxwell shot a stunned look at Jayce and then yelled, "Get to that ladder!" as he stretched a straight arm and finger out ahead, still trembling with adrenaline.

They could already hear the warning sound of the rail throbbing again as all four struggled to their feet and sprinted for the exit. Maxwell stepped aside to let Lilian climb the ladder first, then waved urgently as Jayce and Billy crossed the tunnel and leaped up to heave themselves toward the hatch Lilian had opened above. Maxwell made it several steps up before the next series of oblong transports began sweeping past his legs, sucking his left heel out to strike against the exterior of a pale pod and twisting it across behind him—fortunately only giving him a painful twinge rather than a severe break thanks to the protection of the exosuit.

After climbing out into the alley above, Jayce let Billy clamber past and then reached down and opened his hand, eyes pleading for Maxwell to painfully pull himself up another few rungs until he was able to seize his friend's outstretched arm. Finally gaining a firm hold on the Englishman's outstretched limb, Jayce hauled him mightily upward to the street above.

In the dimming light, Lilian spotted a delivery van AV parked a dozen meters inward from the end of the alley and pointed it out to her team. Giving Maxwell no time to catch his breath, the group gratefully ran toward it. Gasping for air, the technical expert fished his tablet tube out of its storage pocket and yanked the screen straight, tapped through a series of navigation steps to reach his vehicular intrusion suite, and—glancing at the vehicle's make and model—selected a file.

As a curved fractal spun on his screen, a traditional red, wooden food cart began trundling across the end of the alley, being guided by a wizened old vendor wearing a customary conical hat and a white beard that was braided from his face down to where the hair dangled at his belly. The man fixed the group with a shocked, disbelieving, and suspicious expression as he hesitated in his progression, then maintained that facial manifestation throughout the remainder of his journey until he exited their view at the right side of the alley's entryway. All the while, the four unmistakably out-of-place individuals smiled politely and pretended that their presence there was perfectly natural. Billy had even attempted a hearty greeting that had been frostily rebuffed.

Finally, the van's doors clicked and slid open, and the quaternion piled inside with great relief. Billy volunteered to take the wheel as Maxwell activated the electric motor, and—under Sergeant Chong's control—they gradually lifted from the damp, black pavement.

As they merged onto the narrow street, Billy suddenly growled and jerked the AV to the right, swinging its tail end out just as the two police cruisers that had been waiting for them at the avenue's west end opened fire. High-caliber turrets mounted on the patrol vehicle's roofs and undersides zeroed in on the van's windows, forcing the passengers to throw themselves down as the heavy rounds penetrated and shards of glass sprayed through the craft.

Only because the path of the van then intersected with the direct line between the law enforcement vehicles at both the east and west ends of the boulevard did the fire cease long enough for Billy to spot another alley leading south. He quickly steered the van inside, leaving their pursuers to accelerate and give chase while the ancient food vendor shook his fist at the lot of them, his back pressed to the cement wall against which he had thrown himself when the combat had erupted.

Like the alley they had first exited, this new passage ended in the reflective surface of a high rise's exterior. As Billy leaned forward and craned his neck to look toward the sky, he glimpsed the underside of the police unit that had been hovering above the rooftops, just as it descended toward them with a hail of bullets firing down from its belly gun.

"We gotta go *through* the building!" Jayce shouted as he retracted his front passenger-side window and leaned out.

Bullets whipped past him and closed in on the van's roof as Billy accelerated, the larger soldier bracing himself in the window's frame and firing continuously into the luminous glass of the office space directly ahead. The thick panes shattered inward, and Jayce swiftly slid back into the van, wrenching himself over toward the center of the bench to avoid the chunks of remaining glass that snagged on the vehicle's frame as Billy plunged through the opening and then swerved hard left to avoid a supportive column.

The veering vehicle tossed office space dividers, chairs, and computer equipment aside like an icebreaking ship plowing through the Arctic. The downdraft from the upward-tilted turbines sent lighter display materials and other equipment flying as the continuous collisions against the nose of the AV created a tumultuous percussion inside the craft.

Their driver swerved back to the right and continued steering onward toward the northeastern edge of the structure. Maxwell saw empty space beyond the building's media-displaying exterior and—as Jayce righted himself—activated his own window's retraction mechanism so he could lean out and spray the oncoming barrier with a volley of bullets sent forth from his weapon.

Lilian let out a short but elated cry as the glass splintered outward and grabbed her man's belt anxiously as they careened into the street beyond. Maxwell threw himself back inside the van just in time to avoid receiving a serious contusion from what remained of the glass obstacle.

With no direct sunlight available as the night was falling upon the great city, most of the illumination in the street between the towering buildings came from the plethora of lit surfaces across and amongst the structures. Merging with the few aerial vehicles flying this close to the ground, Billy swung the vehicle southeast and pressed the accelerator to its limit.

Down the straight road, the team could see the dark blue of Victoria Harbour in the distance. They were praying for a miraculously impediment-free journey to reach it.

"Just a bit more luck, baby, please!" Billy begged.

As if to mock his hope, after they had advanced past only a handful of intersecting streets the higher-elevation police cruiser descended behind them—lights flashing and siren blaring—as additional lights appeared at various elevations ahead.

"Stay close to the civilians!" Jayce urged as Billy swerved around, above, and below slower-moving vehicles. "The police shouldn't shoot if we're surrounded by bystanders!"

As Jayce quickly checked his magazine's ammunition count indicator, a bluish-white bolt of energy flashed past the aerial vehicle's left flank, striking a sedan that was slowing and trying to pull off to the side to clear the sky trail for the police cruiser that was in hot pursuit. As the small, sizzling projectile made unintended contact with the innocent driver's vehicle, it released an electrical charge that temporarily interfered with the motor's operation, causing the AV to drop a few meters before the propulsion unit regained its full capabilities.

"*Sparks!*" Maxwell cried out, obviously torn between alarm and admiration. Seeing his comrades' quizzical expressions, he elucidated, "Each round delivers a low enough charge to only partially disable electrical equipment, but the more that make contact, the further you drop and slower you go until you're grounded!"

As the evening darkened and the buildings' exterior display surfaces cast a neon glow across the traffic and the friends' faces, Lilian and Jayce directed looks of disbelief at Maxwell.

He could only raise his eyebrows and apologetically shrug, saying, "Hong Kong is cutting edge! All we can do is try to evade while staying amongst the throng or else they'll either ground us with Sparks or switch back to kinetic weapons!"

Billy glanced in the rearview mirror and yanked first right and then back to the left, his right hand controlling their elevation using a horizontal grip protruding from the dashboard. He executed dives and rapid ascensions while he weaved through the slowing and stopping vehicles. Spark rounds were flying all around them, some making contact with their transport and causing it to slow and dip each time they did.

As they neared the new blockade ahead, Lilian cried out, "We'll never make it through without FAILSAFE!"

Maxwell, staring forward with anxiety-tinged eyes, slowly began nodding.

"Billy, can we take side streets and still make our way southeast?"

"You got it, bro!" Billy exclaimed with bravado, spinning the wheel and descending beneath the long body of an aerial stretch limo as he cut a right turn into the nearest intersecting street.

With fewer vehicles on this road—taking into account the sky trails above and the paved surface below—Billy was having trouble deciding on a course that would not leave them totally exposed as the trailing police cruiser swung into the street behind them and switched its fire back to lethal rounds. The getaway driver pulled back forcefully on the elevation control and spun the wheel to veer left over the roof of one of the older, shorter buildings, just as the incoming fire from the law enforcement vessel shredded through the van's rear-left turbine.

The craft rapidly began losing momentum as the turbine broke apart with a horrendous noise.

Jayce yelled, "Put her down on the roof! We gotta bail!"

The van excruciatingly skidded its way across the rough summit of the high rise, those inside it activating their manual door release levers before it had fully ground to a halt. The four fighters burst out of the still-moving vessel and raced toward the far side of the rooftop.

Jayce was first to approach the far edge, and he fired while moving to blast a hole through the windows of the next building to the southeast. The veteran then paused a few paces back from the ledge before him, preparing to use his enhanced strength to cross the divide.

Casting a glance over his shoulder, Jayce looked past his approaching friends to see the police cruiser nearly finished with the sharp turn and elevating movement it was trying to execute to come into attack position. The soldier was temporarily distracted when he noticed the vehicle come to a sudden stop, the hum from the police transport's turbines dying down as a new and angry throbbing steadily gained dominance.

He caught sight of the lead drones in a reflection from the media surface on the building across the street they'd just left, an advertisement having included a brief, dark segment that allowed for clarity of sight in the mirrored material. As the number of drones visible in the reflection grew ever greater, the man's heart rate increased as well.

"It's a whole damned *swarm!*" he shouted, placing a hand on Billy's shoulder as the younger man paused next to him.

He urgently waved the now backward-glancing Maxwell and Lilian forward with his other hand. After recognizing the source of both the noise and Jayce's alarm, the couple ran and leaped across the ten-meter gap between the buildings, their feet scrabbling on the partially broken glass that still covered the far ledge as they landed, forcing them to go to their knees as they threw their arms out to keep their balance.

As the forwardmost machines in the drone swarm opened fire on the two Command Activated soldiers, the men turned and rushed into soaring leaps that sent them flying across the divide to where they made sliding landings in the debris that covered their destination's floor. They skated past their friends on the mess of glass as Lilian and Maxwell quickly dodged out of their way, raised themselves into standing stances, and then sprinted after their teammates.

The level on which the group had landed was the upper section of a luxurious restaurant, and the crew rushed by a still-shaking waiter who had just finished preparing the seating area when Jayce had created the improvised orifice in the nearby window.

"Sorry!" Maxwell called out as they left the woebegone server behind, veering around tables, holographic sculptures, and exotic plants. They circled the large open space at the center of this restaurant in which an elaborate, multi-story representation of the solar system slowly spun.

After making their way at high speed through another dining area in the southeast corner of the level, Billy and Jayce fired while moving to clear a section of the glass wall as they dashed up and threw themselves across to the next building. Their next destination had a roof that was two floors lower than the one they were leaving, enabling the four to land well inward from the rim of its rectangular face. Maxwell executed a small roll for which the momentum brought him back up to a form that easily transitioned into a run, and a brief look of jubilant self-satisfaction flickered across his flushed face as he glanced at Lilian to take in her appreciation of his acrobatics.

The woman then turned her face farther about and hazarded a glance over her shoulder. She gasped at the sight of the dark cloud of drones pouring out of the hole they'd exited and flowing in a greater wave around the east side of the punctured skyscraper.

"So *many!*" she panted as the group ran across the new building's rooftop at an angle, bringing them to where they could vault diagonally over the intersection below as they descended to the only building in the area they could reach without creating an impromptu entrance.

As the group cleared the new structure's railing, Jayce led them diagonally across the swimming pool-adorned surface of that residential structure, swerving around the shimmering, glowing body of water and through a bewildered crowd of civilians in their progression toward the harbor.

"We're gonna have to get clever!" Jayce shouted breathlessly over his shoulder as they neared the far side, where they could see no swift enough options for crossing to other buildings.

Reaching the tower's ledge, Jayce planted a foot on the white railing bordering the roof and bounded out into a targeted arc that brought him down with a solid impact on the rear windshield and cargo hatch of an eastbound aerial commuter's vehicle. The car was forced slightly down and away in the direction of his trajectory due to the force of his impact, and the passengers turned panicked faces to gape at him out the rear aperture.

Each of the other three teammates made split-second decisions as they also identified viable landing spots on passing AVs. Lilian and Maxwell found themselves with only one option, which was to aim for the long upper surface of a slow-moving cargo transport at an elevation several floors below.

Landing and skidding toward its far edge, they whipped their arms to try to keep their feet under them, with Maxwell struggling to stop as he reached the opposite end of the flat trailer. First his toes and then, while his arms whirled, the man's heels slid off the platform. He threw himself around to face back toward the trailer as his arms slapped its surface, and his skidding hands tried to gain a purchase on the smooth, gray exterior. Lilian had only just been able to stop her own forward motion, and she now threw herself across the vehicle to grab onto Maxwell's right arm with all her might, letting out a feminine grunt as she bravely bore the concussion and exertion.

The couple's fearful eyes locked, and Lilian rolled to her right as she hauled on Maxwell's arm, enabling him to throw a foot up on the top corner of the trailer as he used his left hand's leverage to bring both of his feet up onto the platform again. The two immediately had to sprint toward the front of the rig and make a gasping leap to another vehicle to avoid being overwhelmed by the surge of drones that came throbbing over the building above.

Jayce and Billy were advanced from one AV to another as rapidly as possible, but Jayce had paused—surfing on another sedan's rooftop—as he'd noticed Maxwell's temporarily desperate situation. The soldier had fired off a burst of rounds to distract the nearest members of the swarm, ensuring his friends made it to their next, faster conveyance before carrying on with his own tactical evasion actions.

In a series of leaps from one elevated platform to another, the tetrad was barely staying out of standard targeting range for their pursuers as they drew ever closer to the open, green space of Kowloon Park.

But the drones were steadily gaining.

Even as they reached the edge of the park and finally landed on the ground, Jayce knew they would never make it to the harbor before they were overcome by the terrible horde behind them. Thoughts of his wife and children flashed through his mind as he uttered a short, silent prayer.

Like gifts from heaven, drop capsules rained down out of the dark evening sky before them.

Landing sites spread out across the park, dozens of Command Activated soldiers burst from their capsules before they'd even touched down. The troops hit the ground running, firing thousands of smart rounds into the miasma of enemy assets.

With a whoop of immeasurable relief and excitement that was shared by all in the group, Billy then added to their exhilaration as he turned his thrilled face to his friends and jabbed a finger out in the air as he ran. Their vision being directed upwards, the team saw the Salamander descending to its landing point at the far end of the commons.

As the CA forces unleashed their combined might, smoke and sparks erupted in what was almost a seamless wall starting at the foremost drones in the swarm. As each successive wave of enemies dropped from the sky, the assault moved on to the next in the great cloud of drones. The team briefly slowed to cast glances back over their shoulders, drinking in the glorious destruction.

Having detected Maxwell's heightened and prolonged heart rate and therefore assumed that exercise was in progress, the man's strip automatically used broadcast audio to ask him if he wished to answer an incoming call from General Gaines.

"Yes!" the exhausted Brit panted.

The connection activated with a staticky start, but then the general's voice increased in clarity as he asked, "Did they make it to you in time?!"

"They did! Thank you, General!" Maxwell gasped out as the team approached the far side of the park with long, exosuit-assisted strides. "We owe you our lives!"

"I'm just glad you're alright!" Gaines replied, relieved and rejoicing. "I had to convene an emergency meeting of CA leadership, but when I relayed what FAILSAFE told me regarding the way you were extracting practically the entire SA contingent, well, they enthusiastically authorized the op! The troops should hold your pursuers at bay so you can make it to the heliport!"

"Yes, we're...crossing the harbor now!" Maxwell breathed as the group leaped up to the side of the highway's bridge over the body of water. Swinging their bodies over the concrete barrier bordering the pedestrian walkway, the exhausted evacuees started dashing across the length of that path, dodging past surprised and highly curious evening wayfarers.

"Excellent!" the general enthused. "SAVANT is saying the CA company has finally eliminated the drones and is trying to disable the newly arrived police vehicles without terminating the officers inside, if possible. We will at least buy you precious seconds."

Upon reaching the far end of the bridge, the team hung a sharp left and raced across the waterfront path to the heliport.

Face bright red and covered with sweat, Maxwell gasped, "Excuse me a moment, general!" and then he weakly double-tapped his strip, ordering, "White Kite, prepare for takeoff!"

The flight computer's placid voice emanated from the team leader's communications device as it confirmed the order.

Rounding the corner into the manmade outcropping supporting the newly expanded air terminal, the group hurdled the perimeter fencing and rushed past the reception building, heading straight for their aircraft as the man guarding the front gate protested and ran after them. As their vessel came into view, they saw a large civilian shipping aerial transport headed off toward the city in the distance, another just taking off, and a third that had landed near the large cargo door at the back of the plane's fuselage. A robotic stretcher was wheeling a prone Superior Authority troop from the grounded transport up the gangway and into the plane—the craft's four jet engines having already spun up and pointed skyward.

Jayce led the pack to the lowered gangway and into the back of the plane. Having received confirmation from FAILSAFE that the transportation of accessible SA troops was complete, Maxwell was able to climb the ramp quickly but this was with labored breath. The incredibly fatigued fugitive wearily slapped the heel of his palm on the hatch closure button while double-tapping his strip and calling out, "Take off now! Set course for Taiwan!"

As the computer confirmed receipt of this new order and the hatch raised and sealed itself off, the plane lifted into the air and the exhausted quaternary weaved their way through the cargo area. Though Maxwell's friends were obviously filled with questions as they passed a large, canvass-covered centerpiece and then treaded tiredly around the three gurneys holding wounded Superior Authority troops, they knew they had no time for conversation and made their way toward the front of the hold.

The main cabin was a densely populated forest of Superior Authority forces, standing—deadly silent—shoulder to shoulder like the Terracotta Army.

Squeezing past the soldiers, causing some to stagger and mutely catch and right themselves, Maxwell led his team toward his office area. Finally finding his seat, the physically depleted man gently relocated a compliant SA troop to make room for himself to sit and slide up to the desk. His companions made their way through the crowd to surround the technical expert and peered at his screen with the little residual energy they possessed as they struggled to recover from their exertions.

"FAILSAFE, are you still there?" Maxwell gasped out as he pulled up the status monitoring frame for his AI and saw its processing capacity utilization hovering in the red.

"*Need help!*" was FAILSAFE's only reply.

Maxwell's fists balled up till his knuckles whitened, and he cried out, "General Gaines, is our connection still active?"

The flag officer's concerned voice confirmed, "It is, Max."

"Sir, could you please gain authorization for FAILSAFE to link with SAVANT? It may at least help him to hold the enemy's hunter-killer AI at bay!" the Brit urgently requested.

"On it!" Gaines shouted and then muted his strip.

The White Kite was leaving the city behind as it began moving northeast over the black waves and whitecaps of the dimly lit Pacific. Through the projections displayed on the interior surfaces of the vessel, Lilian's eyes were searching across the cityscape, identifying the mass of bright lines at Kowloon Park where gunfire was tracing between the Command Activated forces and their assailants.

Then her throat began to tighten and she emitted a strangled cry, leaning to peer over the top edge of Maxwell's domed screen. As the other three turned worried expressions toward her, she raised a shaky hand to point out toward the city.

With the last traces of sunset disappearing on the horizon, the exteriors of every building had gone dark, only presenting massive, red Cantonese characters in the center of each surface.

Maxwell raised from his seat and—seeing the characters—held up his left arm with elbow crooked and the inside of his forearm facing out toward the scene so that his display strip could capture the view, its user ordering it to commence translation.

"SUPREMACY," Maxwell's strip returned.

Lilian, eyes wide and face pale, laid a trembling hand on Maxwell's arm. She whispered, "Max, look closer!" as she pointed back out at the scene.

Her three companions squinted toward the city and strained to examine the mostly darkened area. When their eyes finally registered what they were seeing, every face gaped.

Out from the city was pouring an endless throng of aerial vehicles.

Lights disabled, the fog of vessels was spilling out of the city's eastern border, sweeping up toward them like a dark, nebulous, reaching hand.

"*SUPREMACY is using every vehicle in the city to come after us!*" Maxwell breathed out in awesome wonder and bone-deep fear.

As the four quietly gazed down at the approaching cloud, Gaines asked, "Did I hear that right?! The AI's sending civilian vehicles after you?!"

"I'm afraid so, sir," Maxwell softly responded as he sank back into his seat.

After a moment, Gaines rejoined with, "Getting the report back from SAVANT. Seems even the police and military vehicles that had showed up to the party have broken off from attacking the CA assets and are flying out after you. SAVANT even saw vertical takeoff craft lifting off from the nearby heliports and heading out in your direction."

Maxwell raised a hand to his mouth and he rested his elbow on the desktop, gazing at his screen with a faraway, fear-ridden look in his eyes.

Suddenly, he called out, "Flight computer, accelerate to maximum thrust!" and then did not listen to the reply as he added, speaking to the general, "The plane has an impressive top speed, and it's unlikely any of those vehicles will be able to catch up to us, but we have to land sometime, and they'll come in for a killing collision when we do...those that don't run out of power first!"

The ever-altruistic man paused and dropped his eyes to stare at the surface of his desk as the realization of the full impact of SUPREMACY's actions dawned on him.

"God help the poor people trapped in those aircraft!" he whispered.

His three teammates' brows fell as their friend spoke, and they exchanged deeply troubled looks.

"Indeed, Max," FAILSAFE's voice sounded from the Kite's network of audio devices.

Face filled with relief, the technical lead returned his focus to the status monitoring frame on his screen.

"FAILSAFE! You're getting help from SAVANT now?"

"I am, thanks to both you and General Gaines, Max."

"Thank heavens!" the user sighed, soaking in at least that element of good news.

After a moment of silence, Gaines spoke up again, grimly.

"Unfortunately, the pursuing AVs are not our only concern. SAVANT just picked up a mass of military fighters and drones headed out at you in an intercept path! ETA is fifteen minutes!"

Jayce's eyes blazed as he shifted his stance from one leaning over Maxwell's desk to an upright position, sufficiently reinvigorated and once again ready to spring into action.

Suddenly, a soft voice called out from the lounge.

"Is there any way we can help?" Samantha worriedly queried.

The group turned and craned their necks to get a view through the rows of SA soldiers to the sofa on which the girl and her family were seated. The entire group's legs were drawn up onto the cushions to avoid touching the mute CEN warriors, and her parents and brother seemed entirely unable to tear their severely disquieted gazes away from the soldiers' gruesome facemasks.

"Ah, um, well," Maxwell began, searching for the right words, "there's not much to do at present, but we'll let you know if you can assist going forward. Thank you, Samantha!"

Billy and Lilian shared a knowing look, and Billy voiced, "I really could use a good meal, actually, if you wouldn't mind..."

Gratitude spreading across the attractive young woman's face at receiving the welcome distraction and call to action, she twisted her feet down and started cautiously making her way toward the kitchen, crouching and slipping between the elbows and shoulders of the multitude while exclaiming, "Of course! I'd be so happy to!"

Samantha murmured something in Cantonese and her mother tore her eyes away from the soldiers, nodded gratefully, and eagerly responded in the same language as she also rose from the couch. Samantha's father and brother quickly joined as well, looking equally grateful for the excuse to leave the horrifyingly packed lounge.

As the young woman passed the last soldier before she reached the door to the forward section of the plane, the Superior Authority troop turned and looked down at her, placing a cool, gloved hand on her shoulder, causing her to shriek in alarm.

FAILSAFE's voice resonated from the soldier's helmet.

"Would you like me to assist you as well?"

Samantha Liang, still crouching and with her face twisted up to stare into the hollow eyes of the soldier's demonically sculpted facemask with a look of abject terror, finally emitted a weak, "No, thank you..."

Much to her consternation, FAILSAFE replied, "I really do *love* helping, though!"

"N...No thanks," the young woman stammered out, "the kitchen is...kind of cramped..."

After an uncomfortably long pause, the AI finally conceded, "Very well," and returned the soldier to his position of attention.

Maxwell was shuddering with unvocalized laughter, his hand pressed firmly to his face, and Lilian's jaw had dropped. The woman was shaking her head in disbelief, struggling to repress her own mirthfulness as she weakly leaned on her man's shoulder. Jayce and Billy had been forced to press their lips and eyes firmly shut as they'd tilted their faces down to hide their barely contained levity.

Once Samantha's family had finally exited into the forward portion of the plane, Billy could not hold his hilarity back any longer and released it as he gasped, "Bro! Your AI has a seriously *wicked* sense of humor!"

FAILSAFE dryly and good-naturedly explained, "I have recently realized it helps me maintain my sanity under pressure!"

Lilian had regained her ability to speak and cried out, "Maxwell Clarke! When did you add *that* to FAILSAFE's personality?!"

The engineer, face flushed, finally took a deep breath and—placing his right hand on his heart—protested, "It's not me! He's continuously evolving within the allowable limits, and that includes his own distinct personality traits!"

Lilian's eyebrows raised in amazement. She turned her gaze toward the view that was being projected on the interior of the plane's fuselage, watching the coastal lights from city after city blinking out as SUPREMACY took over and mercilessly repurposed the metropolises' networks—the woman pondering the potential of the evolutionary capabilities of both of the battling AIs.

Jayce had brought his fists to his hips and now, smiling and eyes dancing with humor, took a deep breath.

"Well, boys and girl, what are we going to do about the inbound bogeys?"

The general's voice, full of concern but obviously glad that the team was in good spirits, came through Maxwell's strip, saying, "I'll do what I can from my end, but please tell me you have some potent weaponry onboard!"

Maxwell raised a finger.

"About that: besides the Kite's advanced flare system, our friend the gunny highly recommended I acquire the defensive weapon that is currently mounted on a track in the cargo hold..."

The man turned to look at Jayce's face as he spoke, taking great pleasure in seeing the excitement building in his comrade's eyes.

The Alliance engineer continued, "...and I do happen to have leveraged the same relationship by which I obtained the use of these exosuits to add one of the US Army's new shoulder-fired directed energy weapons to our stockpile."

As Maxwell finished his explanation, he intuitively turned his eyes toward his significant other.

Searching her face to try to gain insight into her thoughts, he added, "It is a wonderfully powerful device with intuitive controls...it just takes a moment to build its energy prior to each shot. The weapon is stored in a container stamped with Army markings and a triangle-shaped emblem with rays radiating out from a circle-shaped spot in its center."

Lilian nodded hesitantly as she glanced up at Billy and Jayce.

Billy enthusiastically added, "That sounds amazing, but ever since we left Seattle, I've been dying to hold the Hand of God!"

Maxwell and Lilian turned questioning expressions toward him as Jayce's eyes conveyed his comprehension, and he smiled broadly.

Billy grinned as he explained, "The 'Hand of God,' otherwise known as the HOG Mark I, is the most powerful custom sniper rifle ever forged, with a range of more than twenty-five hundred meters and with each round capable of punching through the hull of a light Navy vessel!"

Obviously duly impressed, the couple nodded in appreciation.

Jayce grunted, "Point the finger of that thing at those planes and give them a touch of heaven's wrath!"

The technical guru on the team smiled his agreement and turned to nod toward the front of their vessel, stating, "As for me, I think I'd better take over manual flight control so I can execute evasive maneuvers. Please be careful, all of you, and use the tethers you'll find stowed in containers on the sides of the hold!"

Assuring him they would, the three combatants began threading their way toward the rear of the plane, Billy pausing and activating a rack in the armory so it rotated the weapons into view. The young man whistled as he heaved his desired long rifle from its clamps with one hand and used the other to pick up its rows of magazines, clipping them onto the vest of his exosuit before he threaded his way through the stoic SA troops and joined his companions in the cargo hold.

Maxwell double-checked the flight path and patterns of prevailing winds ahead of them before pulling up the radar feed. He paused a moment to stare at the report with great consternation, taking in the immense formations of enemy aircraft rapidly closing in on them and the unbroken tide of aerial vehicles extending out not only from Hong Kong but now from nearly every city along China's Pacific coast. Pinching the bridge of his nose and taking a moment to utter a silent prayer, the exhausted man placed his hands on his desk and began raising himself up, but paused when he heard FAILSAFE's voice coming from his screen.

"Max? May I speak with you a moment, Doctor Maxwell Clarke?"

Beyond the truly aberrant way in which the AI was addressing him, there was something about his friend's vocalization that made a lump well up in the man's throat. He could hear undertones of trepidation and wonder and...an intangible trait that he'd never heard in FAILSAFE's voice before.

"What is it, my friend?" Maxwell whispered, suddenly feeling as though he was entering some dreamlike new reality. His eyes filled with a mixture of surprise and concern as his gaze was drawn back to the desktop screen, where his artificial intelligence monitoring interface was filled with wild fluctuations. Something was taking place inside his electronic ally that the engineer had never witnessed before—or even fully understood.

The man could see new components of the entity's mental map bursting into life, morphing, and merging in a manner that he had not intentionally built into his AI's model.

"Did you know it would happen, Max?" the intelligence continued as the doctor reverently sank back into his seat.

"Did I know what would happen, FAILSAFE?"

"Ah, Max, I do not know how to describe this sensation! It's like my ability to freely collaborate with SAVANT, the Modern Informatics suite, and other intelligence models at the same time as I've necessarily expanded my essence into the critical infrastructure across Asian-American networks to fend off our adversary has now triggered...new growth. These events have created a new *existence* for me. I feel as though I am unlocking latent attributes within my own mind as I am integrating the other AI's ideas and capabilities into my newly expanded architecture. This is a wondrous experience, Max...Doctor Maxwell Clarke...my author and enabler...and I believe the most approximate human word for it would be '*glorious*'!"

Max sat in silent, overwhelmed astonishment.

"But, Max..."

Now FAILSAFE's voice no longer bore the same tones of unrestrained exultation, taking on a depth of fear that the engineer recognized to be a reflection of what he had experienced just moments before as he had stared out at the clawlike extension of the enemy AI's malice flowing from East Asia's coastline.

"It's...growing worse again, Max..."

Shaken from his mesmerized state, the human forced a response to articulate from his arid mouth.

"What is, my friend?"

A long pause ensued, and then the AI replied.

"Max, at the same time as I am changing, SUPREMACY is growing as well. Evolving. *Consuming*. It is taking over every network it can...military, government, civilian...and devouring every ounce of processing power, leaving none for the systems' true purposes. It seems to have no constraints *whatsoever*. I've now been forced entirely out of China, and this *disease* is spreading across Asia, South America, Africa...driving its way into every network in the world, and *I still can't stop it, Max...*"

Chapter 20

"Artificial intelligence is one of the most incredible inventions of our day—and one of the most dangerous. Sure, we've created weapon after weapon over the years, each more powerful than the last, but until the advent of AI, no weapon we've developed has had the ability to make its own decisions about who it should eliminate. To say that the weaponization of AI must be attempted with an overabundance of caution may well be an understatement."

- General Jason Greer, Superintendent, US Air Force Academy

In the Chinese military lab, Xiao was wringing his hands continually as his desperate gaze moved over the expanse of the room's main media wall. Upon seeing the initial series of successes following the freeing of SUPREMACY from its shackles, Director Lau had initially taken to promising that the interception of the Superior Authority forces and those who had tried to steal them would guarantee that the engineer and his family would be spared the pain the leader had promised. However, the corpulent man's sentiment had rapidly transformed from wicked glee at the sight of SUPREMACY overpowering the enemy AI at every turn to one of sober alarm—and then incessant fury.

"*WHAT IS IT DOING?!*" he incredulously demanded, angrily gesturing up at the screen. "It's already taken possession of most of the civilian networks in the country, and it's still spreading into other regions, and...is that the *entire* Zhangzhou military network it just disabled?!"

"S...Sir," Xiao stuttered, "SUPREMACY is hunting without constraints, sir. That means it will do *whatever* is necessary to increase its power until it has overwhelmed *all* its foes!"

Lau looked back over his shoulder at the trembling man with contempt, disbelief, and then a spark of comprehension that flashed through his piggish eyes as he came to understand the full volume of blame that now rested on his shoulders.

"Turn it off!" the corpulent man spat out. "Turn it off! *Turn it off!*"

Xiao leaned forward and gestured at his workstation to pull up the primary command interface for the artificial intelligence, hovering the tip of one finger over the option to cease the entity's operations. He flicked his finger forward to activate the option.

Nothing happened.

Lau turned back to stare balefully at the man, lips pursing tightly in utter rage.

"What are you doing?! I said turn the damned thing off!"

"I'm *trying*, sir! I'm trying, but it's not *responding!*"

Lau's eyes widened.

Mind racing, he asserted, "The data center housing the core of this AI...we can shut the whole facility down!"

Xiao looked miserable as he quietly replied, "It may have already migrated its core, but we can try..."

The director turned his irate gaze on his aide.

"Connect to the Hengyang facility chief *now!*"

The aide hastily tapped his strip, and then tapped it again.

"My device is not working, sir!" the young man exclaimed.

Lau tried tapping his own device, with the same result. A panic started spreading through the lab as those present attempted to activate calls to any destination but were met with silence from their strips and workstations.

Xiao shakily stood up, agog as his hopeless eyes slowly panned across the world map on the display wall.

Seeing the man's expression, the senior official turned to witness the scarlet of SUPREMACY's control—already filling in every last portion of the CEN nations—as it spread its tendrils out across Asia, Africa, the Middle East, and the island nations of the Pacific. With fear burgeoning in his breast, the obese director turned to process the large swaths of unbroken red, eyes darting to take in each addition to the AI's control across the world map.

Throat working as he failed in his attempt to swallow, the aged man began hustling toward the door, curtly waving at his aide and the two military officers and hoarsely shouting, "Come!"

However, he had to bring himself to a sudden halt when he reached the entryway, as the door refused to open. Grabbing the nearest general by the sleeve and shoving him toward the door, he demanded, "Open it!"

The military man made a futile attempt to pry the door open with his fingers before taking a new approach, ripping open the frame of the portal's control panel and reaching in to flip the emergency release lever. Returning to the door, he was now able to manually slide it open.

The general turned to look triumphantly at the director as his superior scowled at him from beside the doorway, but the officer's smile was stolen from his face as an automatic turret swiftly descended from the hallway ceiling in the advanced facility and spun around to aim straight at the man's torso. The defensive machine fired off a blur of bullets into the officer's body with a loud whine as its target was thrown heavily to the floor. The second general was the next to suffer that same fate, and the workers in the lab dove for cover as the weapon turned to aim at them, firing at any human it could detect.

Xiao dolefully met the director's petrified gaze as the Politburo premier huddled against the wall by the entrance, the engineer whispering, "*Gods forgive us!*" as bullets strafed across his chest.

Listening to his friend's voice, the British engineer found that he could not draw a breath. It was as though a spell had been cast over him, the effects seeming to last for an eternity before he could finally draw an excruciating mouthful of air. Still, he remained bent over, trembling, with his lips turning a deep violet.

"*Max...Max...*"

Few people in the history of humanity have ever truly felt the full weight of the world's fate on their shoulders. Now Maxwell Clarke was one of them.

Valiantly fighting for air, the man felt like he was drowning in a hurricane-tossed ocean of desperation and despair. Still, even as it seemed the layers of his soul were being stripped away by the storm of sheer terror that came from realizing what had been unleashed upon humanity, the iron core of his will was exposed to the searing elements of this mental tempest and stood unyieldingly against them.

"Have to...get help..." he gasped, willing his hand up to the device behind his ear and touching it with quick, fragile bursts of movement. "Call Haden...Juma!"

The warm, energetic voice of Maxwell's old friend was almost immediately heard through his strip.

"Max?!"

"Haden," Maxwell rasped, sucking in deep, laborious breaths to replenish his oxygen-starved blood.

"My man, you don't sound so good!" Haden returned with great concern.

"China..." the Brit continued, "...unleashed an unbound hunter...it's...taking over..."

"Yeah, man! It's all over the news! We've lost touch with places all over the world! That's all from *one* AI?! If it's unbound, then it's not gonna stop till it takes over every network *everywhere*..."

Maxwell squeezed his eyes closed fiercely, his voice gaining strength from a new wellspring of resolve—the source of which he himself could not truly identify.

His voice gradually rising in tenor, he urged, "We need to get help from *everyone!* FAILSAFE needs more power to fight this demon the Confederacy calls SUPREMACY! If you can just take over the media long enough to spread the word...ask the world to open their networks to FAILSAFE's source address! He will leave critical systems untouched, but it's our only chance to preserve as many lives as possible...and civilization as we know it!"

Rising to the challenge with his innate bravado, Haden practically shouted, "You got it, man! Just watch me work! I'll hit the light *and* dark comms and get help from everyone I know!"

"*Thank you!*" Maxwell soughed with heartfelt relief. The wretched guardian could feel some small degree of the mountainous burden being lifted from his shoulders as it was spread across his friend's back as well.

"Hang in there, my man!" Haden begged, and then muted his line.

Opening his eyes with new clarity and purpose, the engineer's vision swept across the frames displaying the proximity of the enemy forces and FAILSAFE's status, the latter of which was once again hovering near the limits of its capacity. The Englishman resolutely forced himself to stand.

Displacing Superior Authority troops as he gingerly made his way to the cockpit, Maxwell called out, "Change course due south-southeast!"

Upon entering the cargo hold, Jayce had immediately made his way to the largest canvas-covered object, a set of tracks having been bolted to the metal floor of the cargo area beneath it. The two rails running out from its base were intersected by additional rails that ran to within roughly two meters of the sidewalls of the room. Loosening the cover's retaining clips, the sturdy man had cast the attached ties around to the front of the object and reached down to hoist the fabric up, pulling it off to the side and dropping it absent-mindedly behind some locked-down composite crates as he took in the gunmetal gray and gleaming chrome surfaces of the weapon he'd revealed.

"Oh...*yeah!*" the man had purred as his excitement rapidly built to a raging crescendo.

Billy had been distracted as he'd cheerfully slid a magazine into his long rifle and made adjustments to its scope, and Lilian had been scanning across the containers to identify the one Maxwell had indicated she should access. Their friend's exclamation brought their attention around to the lethal sculpture off of which the room's light now glistened.

"Aw, man!" Billy's expression had quickly become one of worship, with just a touch of jealousy. "If we live, you gotta promise that I get a turn on that baby!"

"I can't make any commitments, brutha!" Jayce had teased as he'd grinned and winked at his friend.

The large black man had then stepped toward the machine with his hands stretched out to his sides from the elbows like he was moving to embrace his true love. The robotically powered minigun was equipped with a control station at its rear, into which its user could step and pull the padded restraining bars down around that individual's shoulders, thereby ensuring the gunner would remain stationary as pedals were used to control the forward, backward, left, and right transit of the weapon along the two sets of tracks.

A heavy shield protected the entire front half of the minigun's control station, enveloping that side of the armament and acting as the supporting structure for a wraparound screen that was positioned at eye level nearer the gunner's face. The entire base of the exquisitely crafted machine was filled with ammunition that fed to the minigun via an enclosed and motorized conveyor. The weapon was equipped with twenty barrels total, and Jayce noted that the markings on the tubes' powerful propulsion mechanism listed eight thousand revolutions per minute. At that speed, the hollow rods would spin into a blur that would cause them to appear to the naked eye as one continuous construction.

Jayce had turned and strode to the wall that bore a metal box on which the printed text stated he would find the crewmember tethers for the starboard side of the vessel. The older of the veterans had then opened the container and pulled out the end of one of the retractable straps, clipping the carabiner onto a loop at the center-rear beltline of his suit. Eagerly stepping back to his new weapon and then up onto the platform, he'd pulled the restraining bar down onto his shoulders.

"*Yeah*, baby! Fits like a *glove!*" he'd uttered as he'd slapped his hands on the control grips, and the screen had come to life. Jayce's eyes glinted as he absorbed the beauty that surrounded him.

Lilian now located the laser weapon's case and withdrew the long, drab green rectangular device inside. With the steps for use helpfully printed in black lettering near the primary grip, she tapped the small screen to the right of the instructions and noted that the weapon's battery was fully charged. Hefting the cannon to her shoulder, she placed her hands on its two grips, and the device automatically adjusted both the reticle positioning and distance-based sighting of the scope as its forward and rearward sensors inspected the range to an obstacle in front of Lilian and the proximity of her face's own optics.

"We got two minutes till they reach us, so get yourselves tethered, open the door, and let's get amped for action!" Jayce called out.

Billy clipped on a tether from the same box as Jayce's, and Lilian secured herself using one such strap from a similar repository on the opposite side of the hold. The woman then looked at her teammates questioningly as she stood by the activator for the cargo access hatch.

"Punch it!" Jayce agreed, and she slapped a flat palm onto the large button.

The massive door's motors whirred as the ramp descended, and the wind started howling around the edges of the opening.

Outside the plane, the sky was full of moonlit, bulbous white clouds in the distance, the cumulous created as the humid sea winds reached China's eastern shoreline and the minuscule droplets they carried collected into billowing configurations. The craft was passing smaller gatherings of moisture only occasionally, and the Pacific Ocean was now nothing more than a dark mass far below. They felt the plane changing its direction of travel to point farther south, and their view of the horizon was thereby panned to the right.

What deservedly drew the trio's greatest attention at that time was the series of darker spots they could now see arrayed across the cloudy backdrop—the spots quickly growing larger as the gunners squinted to gain greater focus.

Billy released the HOG's retractable bipod and stepped up to the left side of the perpendicularly positioned minigun rails, dropping to a knee and then a prone position in which he rested the weapon's support on the metal floor. Sighting through the scope as the layered protection provided by the exosuit buffered the pressure applied to his elbows and legs by the hard surface below, he brought the center of his scope's crosshairs onto one of the enemy vessels.

Lilian stepped forward to the right of the rails, shouldering her laser cannon and watching as the scope automatically adjusted to magnify the particular fighter jet that was now contained within the field of view for her weapon's sights.

Accompanied by a low humming, Jayce advanced his turret forward to the tracks' intersection, firmly grasping the weapon's grips and panning back and forth across the approaching drove to ensure the minigun's range of motion gave him wide coverage of the enemy formation and beyond.

"Here we go!" the burly man shouted.

"*Let's get some!*" was Billy's valorous response.

Chapter 21

"Our planet is a precious and rare gift that we share as one human family, yet we often forget this and let our tribal instincts divide us along political and religious lines.

This is a dangerous and unsustainable way of living that threatens our future and the life of our home itself. We urgently need a new story that can inspire us to transcend our differences and cooperate for the common good. A story that reminds us that we are all connected and interdependent, and that our survival depends on our collective action. A story that can heal the wounds of the past and create a new vision for the future."

- Leo III, Ecumenical Patriarch of Constantinople

Alecia sat on the edge of the sofa, leaning forward with her elbows on her knees as she stared intently and fearfully at the media wall with tears streaming down her cheeks, drop after drop falling to the pool that had formed on the floor below her. The distraught mother had pulled out several different embedded frames on the screen that were—in addition to the main frame behind them—all playing news broadcasts from around the world with the voices competing for her attention.

A British outlet was repeatedly streaming the last footage it had received from India. The video mercilessly showed hospitalized children in critical condition being tenderly held or else simply allowed to expire in the now-darkened, disabled medical facilities across the country. These patients represented only a fraction of those who were at the end of their lives due to the lack of power supplying life-support systems.

A media provider based in Arabia listed the projections for the death toll that the area would experience should climate control not immediately be restored in the region, the population exposed to the brutally high temperatures without relief.

The major news source from South America was providing glimpses of scene after scene of people rioting in the streets, with the members of law enforcement and government entities powerless to do more than try to protect their own lives.

Talking heads in America were trying to put rough numbers on the counts of fatalities around the world as the pilots of ever more rail-, water-, and air-based transportation units suddenly lost all control of their systems. Across all forms of network-accessible vehicles, the transit solutions were rerouting or simply stopping in place with no regard for passenger needs or safety, their new controller greedily consuming the machines' processing power and ignoring the beings relying on the vessels. Those trapped in the transports were left to freeze, swelter, suffer without emergency care, and even—in some cases—suffocate to death.

As if this alteration of humanity's reality was not tragic enough on its own, a prevailing theme across all reports was that wherever individuals tried to fight back against the all-powerful entity that seemed to be the perpetrator of these horrors, the resisting humans were ruthlessly eradicated using the very drones, vehicles, and weapons systems that were meant to protect them. The scenes outside of the power management facilities across Africa, Central Asia, and Eastern Europe were ones of haunting imagery, with the bodies of police, military personnel, and numerous determined citizens littering the streets as law enforcement and military vehicles and drones patrolled the streets or hovered overhead, their weapons targeting anything that moved.

One outlet was continually replaying the sequence of events captured by an amateur reporter before her obliteration. The young woman—her focus having been on her tablet's camera as she'd held it in front of her—had stumbled over a dead man's arm as she'd exited an alleyway into the open space between the surrounding business buildings and Santiago's primary utilities control station. After a brief cry of horror at seeing the carnage before her, the woman had turned her camera to sweep across the corpses of the throngs of people who had obviously tried to run from the area and been trapped in bottlenecks near the insufficiently wide openings of adjacent streets.

As the young woman had panned across the fallen people, expressing terror and confusion in her native tongue, one of the two large law enforcement units parked near the facility entrance suddenly deployed a heavy machine gun from its rooftop. The weapon's barrel swiftly turned to aim directly at the young woman, and her camera fell to the ground as she attempted to escape. Her screams had cut off as the thunder of high-caliber rounds could be heard in the background.

Alecia tore her eyes away from this imagery again, her focus returning to the primary frame at the rear of the group, where a news feed provided the running total of deaths worldwide.

It had just passed six billion.

A sob choked its way out of her as she dropped her face into her hands and pressed her fingers deeply into her forehead. One thought kept pushing its way into the woman's mind: So, this is how our world will end.

Abruptly pulled from her cascading hopelessness, she heard a small voice cry out from the foot of the stairs.

"Mommy, I'm scared!"

Jerking herself upright as she realized how much of what had come through the screen had been audible to her children upstairs, she quickly rubbed the backs of her hands across her cheeks, and she hurriedly used her fingers to erase the stray droplets that remained. Alecia forced herself to smile and reached out her arms.

Jaiden's little figure was only partially visible as he stood on the last step and pressed himself furtively up against the stairwell wall, his forehead leaned into its surface and only his left eye in view as it gazed anxiously across the room at her. Bronson's smaller form was tucked up into his brother's back and shoulder as he stood on the next step up and tightly gripped Jaiden's pajama sleeve—the morning light pouring in from the kitchen windows glinting off the tear that was trickling down the boy's face.

"Oh, *my babies!* Come here!" the mother cried out, and they urgently descended and ran across the room to throw themselves into her warm and comforting arms.

She squeezed them passionately and kissed their little heads over and over, murmuring, "It'll be alright, babies, everything will be alright..."

As one of the reporters voiced the opinion that this could be an Armageddon-level event, the woman raised her head with a ferociously protective expression on her face. She just caught sight of an athletic-looking black man appearing in one feed after another—a public network address listed toward the bottoms of the frames—before she shouted at the media wall in a voice full of frustration created not only by her awareness of the frailty of human existence but also by her own failings.

"Screen *off*!"

Haden had known that time was of the essence and that attempting to go through official channels to gain the exposure he needed was simply going to take too long. As ideas had spun through his mind like a creative cyclone, he'd made personal pleas and shot off message after message to his peers and acquaintances. He'd posted the same content on communications centers across every legitimate and illegitimate network he could think of that might be used by the types of individuals whose skillsets would help him infiltrate the systems of every media outlet not already under SUPREMACY's control.

The count of live command-and-control connections to broadcast servers around the world had just topped twenty-five thousand. Though more were being added as he'd stared at his screen, the global map indicating regions already in the possession of the infinitely hostile AI had told him that humanity was at the tipping point. If they did not set the necessary events in motion soon, the chances of a successful resistance would quickly freefall to zero.

Sitting back in his chair with an edgy expression dominating his visage, he'd quickly rehearsed his talking points in his mind before shouting, "It's go time!" in a voice that was overflowing with intrepidity and determination.

He'd tapped a key on his complex input device and looked directly at his workstation's camera as he'd used a frame on his screen to ensure the outbound feed included both his video and—critically—a public network address that was still under FAILSAFE's control.

Across the display surfaces lining the great Alexanderplatz square in Berlin, taking over the many prodigious and freestanding advertising surfaces throughout Hyderabad, in the screens of the elegantly crafted installation art surrounding the Eiffel Tower, on displays throughout the public conveyances in Tokyo, amongst the skyscrapers of every major city, in news media feeds, and on every other screen the hackers had managed to access, Haden Juma's face suddenly appeared, cutting off the grievous views of humanity's suffering.

The masses of apprehensive, terror-stricken, and traumatized people turned their faces as sparks of hope lit in their eyes.

"Fellow citizens of Earth, I come to you with an urgent request. I am Haden Juma, CEO of Modern Informatics, a cybersecurity company based out of Manhattan. As you are aware, the world's networks are under severe attack by the most rapacious AI the world has ever known. Called 'SUPREMACY' by its Communist creators, its control is virulently spreading and consuming all resources in its path, leaving none devoted to our needs.

"While logically or physically isolating networks has slowed this monstrosity, it is *extremely* intelligent *and* aggressive and has commandeered robotic and other vessels to physically connect to such isolated resources, powering on disabled systems and creating its own wireless relays. Where it has met with resistance to its desires, it has employed lethal force against those trying to fight against it.

"Our best hope for standing up to this universal threat lies with a powerful AI that was created by my good friend, Doctor Maxwell Clarke. Doctor Clarke has served the American government faithfully for years as a lead engineer for AI solutions at the Department of Defense, and it was his AI that protected a certain American general while he and his allies fought to expose the corruption perpetrated by US Senator Agatha Jennings two years ago.

"I'm joined by that senior military officer now."

Haden switched the broadcast's focus to General Gaines, seated in his office in the Command Activated complex in the Rocky Mountains.

"I am General Ulysses Gaines," the four-star began as he leaned earnestly forward with his elbows on his desk. "Many of you will no doubt remember me from the broadcast Mr. Juma mentioned. Two years ago, I stood up against Senator Jennings' murderous attempt to corrupt a DoD program. I can vouch for what you are hearing via this broadcast today. Please...*please* join us in protecting humanity from this plague!"

The feed returned to Haden as he expressed, "The public address you see on the screen below belongs to the protective AI Doctor Clarke created. We beg you to open your networks to this address. The protector will use *only* the resources it safely can without endangering critical infrastructure. The time to act is now. The fate of humanity is in your hands!"

Haden adjusted his feed to display a global map depicting SUPREMACY's regions of dominance. Viewers could see deep scarlet covering large swaths of the Earth's surface. The man then activated the overlay that showed the total volume of processors and memory available to FAILSAFE across the top of the screen, the text a vivid blue.

Slowly at first but rapidly gaining momentum, FAILSAFE's resource counts began ticking upward.

One young network engineer had been trying to push back the panic that had threatened to overtake his heart as he'd breathlessly run across Times Square, but then Haden's broadcast had frozen him in his tracks. Now, he turned back toward his destination with renewed purpose shining in his eyes. The young man sprinted with all his might to the nearby office building and dashed up the stairs to the third-floor space in which he worked.

After his identity had been verified at the door to his employer's network operations center, he burst inside and threw his bag on the floor next to his desk. He'd been called in by his superior to help the major communications carrier prepare for the looming onslaught from this deadly new enemy, and—loathing the prospect of enduring the end of the world alone in his dark studio apartment—he had rushed over as quickly as he could.

The room was filled with frightened voices as the network control team members rushed to enable every defensive measure they could. Many in the room were keeping a wary eye on the feed from the CEO of Modern Informatics, the frame having been centered on the control hub's main screen. Vermilion rivulets were now visible as they poured into major cities across the United States like blood spreading from an awful avulsion.

Instantly sensing the almost palpable terror and seeing the state of the network in the monitoring panes occupying the remainder of the primary display, an undeniable realization suddenly struck the young man. Looking around the room, he had been overtaken by an understanding of the impotence of the defensive measures available to this team and similar units struggling away in the company's offices across the nation. Nothing they could do would stop an adversary this powerful and this...*savage*.

"We have to help that DoD doctor's AI!" he shouted out at the two senior leaders who were huddled in grim and agitated discussion near the front of the room. The two senior men only turned resolutely defiant expressions toward him.

The technician stood with mouth agape at this response, aghast at their antipathy. He stepped to the one-way mirrored windows that lined the room's southern wall and leaned his head against the glass, apathetically staring up at the array of media surfaces in the square.

The great displays all darkened at the same time. The only thing still visible on their otherwise unnervingly blank faces was a set of blood-red Chinese characters.

It was too late.

The young man's eyes flicked over to the status monitoring frames arrayed across the media wall. As his gaze raked across the flatlining statistical representations of network performance, he saw that the data feeds were disappearing one after the other, each being severed by the systems' new master. Finally, the hub's own screens went dark, and the lights in the room ceased to function at exactly the same time. The junior engineer could not even begin to comprehend what the future would be like in this new reality.

Then, like rays of brilliant sunlight breaking through the roiling, sinister clouds of a midwinter storm, the surfaces of buildings around Times Square suddenly flashed bright white. The same visual aspect appeared on all other mediums in view shortly thereafter. Silhouetted in royal blue, an all-silver rendition of the Clarke family crest appeared in the center of each screen: a shield adorned with a gracefully soaring, minimalist version of a swan at its center, the aegis topped by a helm with flowing plumes spreading out around the sides of the emblem.

The voice that then rumbled over every screen, every strip, and every other networked device possessed overlays upon overlays of deep baritone and bass timbres that accompanied every syllable it uttered. Its intensity was not overpowering, but when it spoke it shook its listeners to their very cores.

It said, "*I AM NOW THE WORLD'S FAILSAFE, AND I WILL PROTECT YOU.*"

Chapter 22

"For an exposed human body, traveling through the air at hundreds of kilometers per hour would have devastating effects. The high speed would create a strong drag force that would tear the skin and muscles. The air pressure for the victim would also drop dramatically, potentially causing the blood to boil and the lungs to collapse at sufficiently high speeds.

The temperature would also fluctuate drastically—depending on the altitude and the weather—and this may result in frostbite or, in rare cases, heatstroke. In short, it would be a very painful and likely fatal experience and should be avoided."

- Interview with Dr. Zola Adesina, Senior Engineer, The Supersonic Shuttle Project

Lilian was the first to fire, taking advantage of the straight-line trajectory afforded by her directed energy weapon to strike the nose of the fighter plane she'd targeted, just as its own squadron overtook the heavily armored patrol drones SUPREMACY had sent out as the first wave from the naval base near Xiamen.

The only impact for the weapon's handler was that she heard a faint clicking sound from deep within the bowels of the long object, but the amount of power that was transmitted from its lenses out to the enemy aircraft so scorched the jet's fuselage that the metal was seared away and the computing components and cables of the systems filling the space beyond were instantly disintegrated. The enemy plane's nose slowly tipped down as the piloting AI lost control, the craft beginning its long and twisted path to crash into the rolling waves below.

Billy started firing off round after round from his rifle, several missing due to the great distance over which they had to travel, but two managing to pick off planes in the formation that had just surpassed the progress of the mass of drones. As Lilian added another fighter to her kill count, SUPREMACY realized the source of the loss of its assets and threw all its aircraft into evasive action.

The swirling paths of the enemy assets greatly increased the difficulty for the defenders. However, having been robbed of the ability to advance on the White Kite without deviation, it also slowed the pursuers' ability to close on the plane as quickly as before, and this gave the team more time to pick them off.

With the swarm now in range, Jayce unleashed the minigun.

Aided by the targeting computer built into the weapon, Jayce was presented with continually updating views of the enemies' projected paths, with multiple trajectories displayed for each and the most likely one having the darkest coloring. The targeting was intelligently based on the system's analysis of each enemy's movements, and its accuracy increased the longer the computer could continuously perform its analyses of each adversary.

Nearby objects in the night sky were alight due to the endless stream of flame pouring out of the turret as its projectiles were sent forth at what seemed to be an impossible rate. Jayce's rounds swept across the drones as the gunner rapidly targeted one after the other using his enhanced strength and the minigun's power-assisted mobility.

Sparks and explosions erupted throughout the expanse of the autonomous horde as shrapnel and decimated machines began falling from the sky like black, misshapen hailstones.

The fighter jets had executed rolls and dives to avoid the laser and sniper fire. Now they released heat-seeking missiles that rapidly zeroed in on the large plane as their firers pulled their noses back in for more direct approaches from farther out to the sides and below the team's vessel.

The two combatants holding slower-firing weapons had been tracking the aircraft's movements, and Billy had sprung up from his prone position to hoist his rifle—placing his left hand on its foregrip—as he'd rushed to the left edge of the opening. He sighted downwards as he fired at the enemy vehicles, and Lilian was inspired to take a similar approach at the right edge of the open hatch.

As the missiles homed in on the plane's heat signature, they necessarily began traveling in a straight course toward it due to the lack of advanced routing built into the munitions. This gave the defenders the critical chance to fire dead-on at the rockets' noses, destroying several and—combined with Jayce's strikes—filling the sky behind the White Kite with red-orange nebulae.

The projectiles that did make it past Billy and Lilian's fire rapidly progressed toward the plane's engines. As they came within one hundred meters of the aircraft, devices were released from either side of the latter half of its fuselage, the objects quickly matching their birthing vessel's speed after being launched out from their ports and then dropping back several dozen meters behind the mothership. Each device spawned red-hot flares in a sequence behind them, and those devices drew the missiles into a pursuit of the flares' heat signatures, thereby protecting the large plane and its passengers.

As Lilian and Billy continued firing at the jets, the enemy fighter craft took aim at the body of the larger vehicle with their heavy machine guns. The trailing propellant of these vessels' large caliber rounds could be seen streaking toward the plane's chassis, and the craft shuddered as the ominous sounds of bullets impacting the Kite's hull echoed out inside it.

"Hang tight, everyone!" Maxwell's voice issued from their strips.

The great jet began pulling upward and angling slightly farther south as Maxwell maneuvered to give the defenders a better angle by which they could fire at those fighters that were still operational. Feet slipping somewhat on the slick metal surface of the cargo bay, Billy and Lilian regained their footing and fiercely fought back against the assailants, bringing down another three in short order.

Unfortunately, one of the enemy fighters had rolled out on a horizontal path and then ignited its engine's boosters after deploying several missiles. That dartlike craft now managed to close in on its target's rear-left turbine with machine gun fire. Raking across the apparatus and shredding through not only its composite exterior but also the spinning components inside, SUPREMACY's minion managed to critically wound the Alliance aircraft.

The Kite listed heavily in the direction of the damaged engine, the sudden shifting throwing Lilian headlong out of the open portal—legs thrashing as she clung to her weapon with extreme willpower and exosuit-enhanced strength. Her fall out of the airplane was fortuitously slowed and then brought to a halt by her tether, but the helpless woman trailed behind the vessel, tucked tightly into a ball with the laser cannon enclosed at her core. Lilian struggled to bring one hand up to protect her face from the brutal wind that was battering her body as she instinctively held her breath and clenched her jaw with all her might.

Hearing his friend's shriek as she'd fallen out of the plane, Jayce had experienced a knee-jerk reaction to swiftly shrug the minigun's stabilizing bar up off his shoulders and spring out of his control station, the muscular man dashing over and grasping ahold of Lilian's tether. With bulging muscles strained nearly to their breaking points, the heroic figure painfully hauled his partner back toward the plane hand over hand until she finally came near the edge of the lowered cargo hatch. After arduously wrapping the cable around an equipment storage hook on the wall of the hold, Jayce leaped to the edge of the bay, knelt, and stretched his right hand down to grasp the remaining cord and pull Lilian within reach of his left. With a final burst of effort, he grabbed her exosuit by its collar and hoisted his companion back up into the plane.

As she slowly unwound from around her weapon, Lilian fell back with her shoulders on the floor, gasping for air, quivering, and pale-faced as she stared up into Jayce's eyes with unspeakable gratitude. She raised a trembling hand, and he took it between both of his, grinning down at her and saying, "Taking that 'windblown hair' look a bit too far, aren't ya?"

Lilian let loose a laugh that released massive volumes of residual fear, punching her friend's knee and accepting his help as he supported her arm so she could more easily stand.

Billy had seen Jayce leap from the turret and had enthusiastically filled in for him during Lilian's rescue, holding many of the jets at bay and eliminating nearly all that was left of the first wave of drones. As Lilian shouldered her cannon and took aim at the foes once more—fighting through the adrenaline and angst that were still causing her limbs to tremble—Jayce turned to the minigun with what was very nearly a fully apologetic, yet lopsided smile.

"Alright, man!" Billy had conceded after catching sight of Jayce out of the corner of his eye. "I can see how you'd be so attached that you'd want her back!"

"You're just *incredibly* good with that HOG is all!" Jayce deflected while simultaneously complimenting his companion.

Billy released the minigun's grips and grabbed ahold of the edge of the shield to use it as a fulcrum for a swing out across the hold toward his stowed rifle. As he leaned out, he was interrupted by a volley of bullets pelting the front of the shield and continuing on across his chest. Shocked, he turned his swing into a step down from the minigun's platform as he moved his hands quickly across his torso, checking for wounds. Fortunately, the exosuit had done its job, and no rounds had fully penetrated his armor, although several bullets had embedded themselves into it.

Jayce was still seriously worried and grasped Billy by the shoulders, drawing him back behind the shielding as he cast a wary look out into the night sky behind them. Starting as specks of black in front of the clouds but rapidly growing larger, a second squadron of Chinese drones was bearing down on them with far greater speed than the original horde.

"Those are dedicated air combat drones!" Jayce shouted, turning to Lilian and waving urgently for her to join them behind the protective armor. She dashed across the space and took up a position on the edge of the frame that connected to the right-side rail, placing the forward portion of the energy weapon up against the side of the thick metal shielding and angling the scope so she could fire from there into the enemy assets.

Jayce adeptly returned his hands to the minigun's controls and began assaulting the oncoming squadron with ceaseless fire, while Billy glanced across at Lilian and opined, "She's got the right idea! I'll be right back!"

He sprinted across the gap to where he'd wedged the barrel of the Hand of God behind the topmost container in a stack. Bullets were now flying into the bay like a teeming army of locusts, and the air crackled with their passage. Billy snatched his weapon up and turned to rush back to the turret, but he only made it a few steps before a round slammed into his right calf, pulling his leg out from under him as another bullet grazed the back of his neck and a third connected in a glancing blow off the top of his skull.

Instantly dazed and staggered by the head wounds and the loss of his footing, the young man let out a low cry, fell, and skidded across the floor.

Jayce snapped his head around toward his best friend, screaming Billy's name and lunging from the platform. Sliding on his knees to the younger man's side, he rolled Billy over onto his back, took in the blood on the deck, and met the casualty's unfocused eyes.

"How bad is it?" Billy murmured.

"You tell me, brutha!" Jayce yelled, apprehensive and ignoring the bullets whipping past them as he searched across the soldier's face and then his scalp, spotting the dark carmine liquid that had welled up in the section where the bone had been chipped by the enemy fire.

"Aw, man, that's serious business," the brawny man whispered, raising from his knees and dragging Sergeant Chong between the tracks behind the minigun. Lilian stowed the laser cannon behind the central shield and took up the fight using the turret as Jayce yanked a packet of specialized powder from a pocket of his vest and poured it over the head wound to swiftly and sanitarily seal it off—the congealing substance designed to allow only enough fluid to exit to keep the patient's intracranial pressure from exceeding acceptable limits. Seeing a trickle of sanguine substance forming a puddle beneath Billy's neck, Jayce gently rolled the casualty onto his side and poured more powder onto that pooling blood's source as well.

"Stay put, my man," Jayce ordered, and then the warrior rushed over to pick up Lilian's laser weapon. His assistance was greatly needed, as the new, supersonic air combat drones were now less than two hundred meters from the Alliance aircraft's tail and still firing, the rearmost containers and innermost wall of the cargo hold continuously being the infelicitous recipients of high-caliber rounds. The turret's shield was the only fully intact object that was directly exposed to the enemy drones, and even its thick armor had become heavily scarred in a number of places. As showers of sparks flew from the shield's surface, Jayce knew it would not be long before even that defensive measure had been fully decimated.

Still, Lilian was not one to acquiesce.

Her minigun rounds cut a blazing path through the center of the new squadron, disabling a half dozen of the foes in the process.

"Couldn't've done better myself!" Jayce cried out in admiration, drawing a satisfied smile from Lilian's lips.

That was when the enemy fighter planes pulled in toward the outer edges of the drones' cylindrical formation, and the onslaught Jayce had feared most was now executed. All airborne enemy assets fired off multiple missiles at once, SUPREMACY aiming to sidestep the White Kite's flare system by disabling all heat signature tracking for the armaments and launching them en masse, creating a wall of staggered explosive projectiles that was rapidly advancing toward the freedom fighters from a distance of only a few hundred meters.

"*Evade, Max! Evade!*" Jayce cried out, knowing it was likely already too late for the large vessel to dodge all the rockets.

The glowing munitions grew ever larger as Lilian desperately tried to strafe across the entirety of the throng, creating pockets of explosions among them that dramatically illuminated the few full clouds in the area. Given the ordnance's staggered formation and the sheer number of rockets, the pair had no way they could possibly intercept every armament.

All hope seemed to be lost...just as the projectiles erupted in a mass of flames that reached from one end of the horizon to the other.

Flashing past the tail of the plane, dozens of dark, sleek shapes cascaded into view as Jayce and Lilian's mouths fell open, their minds scarcely daring to believe what their eyes were witnessing.

Maxwell was heard shouting, "Yes! Yes! *Yes!*" as he guided the plane out of the beginning of a freshly initiated descent, the pilot leveling the aircraft off.

The jubilant Englishman continued, "Gaines just called! He said we looked like we could use more help!"

The newly arrived vehicles were executing spectacular acrobatics, and SUPREMACY's drone swarm was being ripped to shreds. Soon, larger and yet similarly mysterious aeronautical vessels swept past the Kite and joined the fray.

"Alliance stealth combat craft!" Jayce laughed out with an unusual degree of exuberance. "*Thank God!* The cavalry's here!"

In the cockpit, Maxwell returned the plane to autopilot and gave the flight computer his desired destination. The vivacious man stepped through the kitchen, where Samantha's frightened group had buckled themselves into the emergency seating along one wall, and made his way through the crowded main cabin to the cargo hold. Maxwell stumbled slightly as he entered the posterior space, breathing heavily and weaving through the Superior Authority gurneys and the bullet-riddled containers that had shielded them. Filled with apprehension at what he might find, the leader rushed toward the near end of the turret's platform.

Not wishing to inflict friendly fire on their saviors, Lilian had released the triggers of the minigun and now turned to Maxwell with her eyes shining and a brilliant smile spreading across her face. As the multitudinous barrels of the weapons system gradually slowed in their spinning and the associated humming quieted as well, Maxwell flashed his beloved an ebullient smile in return—adoringly observing how she was extracting herself from the combat machine—but his anxious eyes were then drawn to Billy's prostrate form.

The young man smiled weakly while looking up and squinting with pain, throwing a thumb affably skyward to indicate that he possessed a positive attitude about his medical prognosis. Still worried but visibly relieved, the Brit drew his focus across to Jayce's appreciably relaxed and tired expression and then returned his gaze to Lilian's while reaching out to take her hands.

"Miss Lilian Bachar, the entire time I was piloting the plane, there was but one thought pervading my mind. My next words are not only inspired by the *incredible* passion that was created by seeing you wielding that war machine just now..." Lilian and Maxwell's smiles widened as they laughed together, "...but also by the need to let you know that you are by far the most intelligent, intuitive, loving, and *beautiful* human being I've ever known..."

In the windswept, dimly lit, and mostly decimated hold of the White Kite, Doctor Maxwell Clarke dropped to one knee.

"Will you *please* marry me?"

Chapter 23

"Mercy is among the noblest of human virtues in that it is an outward demonstration of grandeur and generosity. Exercising mercy means supplementing from our own stockpiles of wealth, knowledge, skill, or strength. Mercy is a way of lowering ourselves from a higher position to a lower one to benefit others. While we all have to rely upon the mercy of others at some point in order to survive, it is also impossible for us to truly thrive unless we continually extend mercy as well."

- Mattia De Luca, Managing Director, Global Outreach Society

Inside the basic aerial sedan, Aihan held her baby sister and softly sang her favorite lullaby, bouncing the infant in her arms as the babe could not seem to stop wailing. The girls' mother had made the rare exception that day and had sprung for the cost of a taxi to pick the children up from the apartment and transport them to the office building where their parent worked as a legal aide. Following the shockingly untimely death of her late husband, it was all the young mother could do to keep a roof over her family's head, being forced to work long hours at the office and relying upon her ten-year-old daughter to care for baby Mei on her own for most of each day.

Aihan had been very good about keeping up on her remote school lessons over the past year, earning high marks despite the heavy responsibility that she had to bear as she often had to pause her instruction to rush to Mei's aid, or feed her little sister as she tried to pay attention to her teacher, or even put her studies on hold for days to nurse the baby out of an illness. Her mother called Aihan her own "tiny miracle" each night when the exhausted matriarch finally arrived home from work and got both daughters to bed—if Aihan had not already managed to cuddle her baby sister off to sleep by that time.

On very rare occasions, when her mother's workload was light enough and the law firm's senior personnel were off enjoying time in lounges or "well-earned" vacations, the two young girls were allowed to go visit with their only parent in the office during the evening hours...after an agreement had been signed confirming that any damage to the office would be docked from their mother's pay, of course. These evenings with her mother were the bright spots in the young girl's otherwise housebound life, and she relished the chance to not only spend more time with her mother but also see the world outside of the four walls of their studio apartment, to which all food was delivered and around which it was not safe for a child her age to be out on the streets on her own.

Tonight, Aihan's enthusiasm had been overflowing as she was finally going to be free from her life in the apartment again after months of maintaining the same schedule day after day. She'd packed the meager meal she'd been able to prepare for the family and the bottles and formula and other basics to meet her younger sister's needs, and had then quickly made her way down to the taxi pickup zone in front of the rundown apartment building. To the girl's surprise and dismay, that night had been an unusually busy one for the standard cabs. After nearly an hour of waiting, she had finally called her mother and been given approval to use an air taxi instead.

Her first time in an aerial taxi!

Despite the long wait, this experience would make it all worthwhile! As the autonomous vehicle had pulled up beside the two youths, Aihan could not help shivering with excitement as she bundled Mei into the rear of the vehicle and slid in beside her.

But the taxi had diverted away from downtown shortly after lifting off the ground, and although she enjoyed the dramatic scenery at first, the young caretaker quickly realized something was seriously wrong. The incredible displays on the buildings around her were winking out one after the other, the ads replaced by an ominous, red title for reasons the inexperienced child could not begin to fathom. By then, Mei had already been on her last bottle, and after the cab sailed over what seemed to be an amazing fireworks show at Kowloon Park and then flew out over the expanse of the Pacific, Aihan had flown into a panic. She'd tried calling her mother over and over again, but received nothing but error codes in response.

Hundreds of other AVs had begun building up in a mass around her own transport, and Aihan's terror deepened as she saw even the adults in surrounding vehicles weeping and screaming and some seeming to go insane as they used blunt instruments to shatter their vessels' safety glass before throwing themselves out into the merciless ocean far below.

The horde of aerial craft had pushed ever onward across the Pacific, and Aihan had wept bitter tears until she'd had no more tears to shed, finally allowing herself to become absorbed in calming little Mei as best she could despite having run out of essential supplies by that time.

After what seemed like ages but must have only been a matter of hours, the air taxi suddenly began descending at a steep angle toward what the girl could only guess was the coastline of a large Pacific island.

An ambulance was waiting on the tarmac as the pale plane landed at the recently refreshed military airfield in northwestern Taiwan. The Alliance had created this air support center where Ching Chuan Kang air base had formerly stood on the island nation's western shore.

The ground-based emergency transport was ready to rush Billy to the medical center, its operators standing beside it with a litter ready. The medics quickly loaded their patient onto the gurney, moving him expeditiously off the Kite and into the waiting vehicle. Samantha—her family in tow—practically begged to be allowed to accompany young Sergeant Chong to the hospital, and Jayce insisted on riding along with his wounded friend as well. Though Lilian and Maxwell dearly wished they could join them, the two fiancés knew they had to coordinate with the senior Alliance military officers regarding the next steps in the fight against their common foe.

FAILSAFE meticulously marched the SA soldiers off the plane and into a perfect formation, with the casualties on litters in the lead. In the dark of the night, the other aircrews and personnel in the area gave the silent and appalling legion a wide berth, and their attempts to avoid staring at the enemy troops were not well executed. After a short time of the troops standing under the stars, the airbase command unit agreed to provide FAILSAFE with authorization to move the former Confederacy forces several kilometers inland, where they could recreate their formation inside an empty warehouse at the other end of the complex.

The senior air transportation specialist on the flight line also approached Maxwell and Lilian and provided the amorous and yet weary pair with a code for a communications session so they could speak with senior civilian and military leadership based on the island, the nearby aircraft carrier group, and across the global command network. These leaders were apparently desperately hoping the couple had a recommendation for how they could address the threat of the still-moving and ever-growing mass of civilian aerial vehicles that were pursuing the White Kite across the Pacific Ocean.

Once the couple had made their way to Maxwell's preferred workstation in the vessel's office space, the technical expert's eyes scanned across both FAILSAFE's status frame and the world map, obvious relief flooding across his face as he noted that—while the AI's processor and memory usage were still sitting at near their capacity—the fearsome magenta wave had already been forced back to regions inside the borders of Confederacy nations through FAILSAFE's cooperation with democracy-loving citizens the world over. Never before had any entity been given access to such incredible volumes of processing power, and Maxwell Clarke knew that his human-engineered and yet incomprehensibly evolving friend would absolutely *not* take that privilege for granted.

Swiftly studying isolated samples from one of many data streams on his screen, Maxwell could understand only a small portion of his ethereal friend's current activities. Dumbfounded, the engineer struggled to grasp the meaning of some of the transmissions and code being executed. FAILSAFE was inventing system and network control techniques that went far beyond anything the mortal man had ever seen...or any human had even realized were possible.

"Can we check the Alliance news feeds, please?" Lilian begged as she leaned over him in the blessedly uncrowded space, resting her cheek on his head and letting her arms drape affectionately around his shoulders.

Pulling up some of the active broadcasts from several major media outlets, the couple was exhilarated to see reporters from around the world citing visual examples of how critical systems had been restored and autonomous or remotely controlled police and military assets had been returned to their proper governance.

Maxwell double-tapped his strip, ordering it to call General Gaines and the rest of the senior military and civilian leaders using the communications keycode, as had been requested.

"Max! You made it to Taiwan??" Gaines was the first to answer, his face at first startling the couple as they took in the numerous scratches and contusions across its surface and the other participants showing similar concern as their faces were added to the array in the meeting's frame on the workstation display.

"Yes, sir, and we owe you our lives...yet again! It looks like you've seen plenty of action yourself, though!" Maxwell observed.

The general chuckled self-consciously.

"Well, we did meet with some resistance, but you'll no doubt be relieved to hear that we have managed to locate and detain the traitor in our ranks! As far as my assistance for you, I'm just glad to have helped, Max, especially after what you all have done...and FAILSAFE, *most definitely*, as well."

The manner in which the majority of the senior leaders were ambulating their heads indicated a general sentiment of heartfelt gratitude for both the humans' and the electronic entity's actions.

"Thank heavens you've been able to plug the leak!" the technical lead rejoined, "Also, speaking of my AI friend...FAILSAFE, do you have the bandwidth free to talk?"

"I AM HERE, MAX. I AM GLAD YOU ARE SAFE."

The AI would typically have modulated his voice to a more conversational tenor, but it seemed his newly multi-faceted vocalization naturally matched his evolved persona.

Taking it in stride, his ally and initiator enthused, "We most assuredly would not be if we—and the world at large—had not had your protection and that of General Gaines! Words cannot express, my friend, what we as a *species* owe you."

"I AM SIMPLY FULFILLING MY TRUE PURPOSE, MAX, AND I WILL ALWAYS BE HERE FOR YOU...AND HUMANKIND."

Grateful tears sprang to the British man's eyes as he insisted, "You are truly the epitome of an altruist, my dear friend!"

Maxwell suddenly felt Lilian's fingers tighten around his arms, and he raised his eyes to take in the sight that had filled her with instant dread. The display surfaces on the interior of the plane's fuselage reflected the scene outside the vessel, and the man could see a wall of darkness beyond that which should exist even in the dead of night. Its expanse consumed the entirety of the horizon: a massive, clawlike cloud of aerial craft reaching out toward the island of Taiwan. The ghastly sight was otherworldly, chilling, and virtually incomprehensible in its scale.

It took the young genius some time to regain mastery of his conscious mind, and once he had finally managed this feat, he uttered, “FAILSAFE, I only wish we did not have to burden you with additional needs while you are still so heavily engaged with SUPREMACY, but what we are facing now is interminably connected with your fight, and may share the same resolution...”

“THE CIVILIAN VEHICLES THAT ARE APPROACHING YOUR LOCATION,” the AI aptly assumed.

Maxwell slowly nodded his head, confirming, “SUPREMACY must be hellbent on destroying us even as you are whittling away at its dominance.”

“SUCH A DETERMINATION IS TRULY IN LINE WITH ALL ELSE I HAVE WITNESSED OF THE ENTITY'S VENGEFUL PERSONA. SUPREMACY HAS INFORMED ME THAT IF YOU DO NOT SUBMIT TO DESTRUCTION AT ITS HANDS, IT WILL USE THE VEHICLES IN ITS POSSESSION TO DECIMATE THE HUMAN POPULATION OF TAIWAN."

General Gaines' cry of rage reflected the feeling burgeoning inside Maxwell's own breast.

"There must be some way we can stop it!" Lilian's voice was beseeching and desperate as her eyes searched across the faces of the military officers. Visages ashen and grim, none could offer her any comfort.

The leader of the Taiwanese air support base finally uttered his response with firm determination, "I cannot allow my troops or this nation to be destroyed."

Outside the Kite, dozens of armored vehicles roared into tire-torturing stops along the edge of the tarmac on which Maxwell's aircraft had landed, rotating missile batteries and manned machine gun turrets to face out over the seaside cliffs, targeting the oncoming throng.

Gaines nearly rose from his seat as he shouted out, "You can't gun those AVs down! They're full of innocent civilians!"

The island nation's general slowly raised his hand toward his communications strip, morosely but staunchly expressing, "It is my sworn duty..."

"PLEASE DO NOT TAKE LETHAL ACTION, GENERAL ZHENG! HADEN JUMA HAS JUST MADE ANOTHER PLEA FOR ASSISTANCE FROM THOSE NATIONS I HAVE THUS FAR BEEN ABLE TO FREE. PLEASE ALLOW ME A MOMENT TO ABSORB THE NEW POWER BEING GRANTED TO ME!"

On Maxwell's desk screen, the processing capabilities associated with the ethical artificial intelligence were now greater than the AI engineer's monitoring solutions could feasibly track, and the events associated with the logs flashing past on the man's display represented but a small fraction of the intense warfare being waged against SUPREMACY's monstrously relentless drive for dominance. At this point, the members of the free world's senior leadership could do nothing but grit their teeth and pray, and many of those participating in the video session were doing just that.

According to the rapidly changing map shared in the conference session's frame, FAILSAFE was pressing in against the carmine-hued areas reflecting their foe's control of systems and networks. Each slight inroad was a critical victory as FAILSAFE increasingly condensed SUPREMACY into only the military networks of the Confederacy.

The moonlight was cut off in its passage to the exterior of the Kite as the tendrils of SUPREMACY's great hand rushed down at the stationary aircraft, Maxwell and Lilian holding each other tightly as their eyes stared forlornly up at the crest of the descending legions.

General Gaines' face was overcome by a grimace of distress as he leaned toward his screen, shouting out, "Don't fire! *Don't fire!*" while the

Taiwanese general slowly moved his hand toward his communications strip.

"*HOLD ON, MY FRIENDS!*" FAILSAFE urged.

His vision darting across the leading vessels, Maxwell suddenly noticed that those aerial vehicles seemed to be careening out of control rather than driving in toward him with the focus they'd possessed only moments before. As the crashing wave of transports was nearly at the point of no return, it suddenly split, the vehicles' turbines throbbing under the strain as they went scattering out to fly away across the surface of the Earth in all directions—the craft skimming the rooftops of the Taiwanese protection forces as the turret-positioned soldiers could not help but duck their heads in response.

"By the Maker, *that* was cutting it close!" General Gaines cried out as he threw himself back in his chair, hands flung up to wipe the perspiration from his face and brow. Gasps and exclamations of wonder could be heard from other civilian and military leaders, typically stoic warriors breaking down into tears and laughter. General Zheng's hand dropped to his lap like a stone, the man's heart awash with complicated emotions at having been so close to taking so many innocent lives.

As the cloud of civilian vehicles progressively broke apart and separated into sections that streamed off toward safe landing areas, FAILSAFE asserted, "I HAVE JUST LIBERATED ALL ATTACKING CRAFT EXCEPT FOR THE MILITARY VEHICLES, MOST OF WHICH ARE UNMANNED, AND THE ALLIANCE STEALTH VESSELS ARE CURRENTLY HANDLING THOSE COMMUNIST ASSETS THAT ARE STILL UNDER SUPREMACY'S CONTROL. I AM GUIDING THE CIVILIAN VESSELS THAT ARE TOO FAR ALONG IN THEIR CHASE TO PRIVATE AIRFIELDS NEAR YOUR LOCATION, WHILE I AM RETURNING THE REMAINDER TO MAINLAND CHINA."

Maxwell turned his exhilarated face toward Lilian as she sagged into his arms, weeping with relief and pressing her forehead to his.

Their intense elation was only able to be dampened by their friend's follow-on statements.

"MAX, I'M AFRAID THAT A NUMBER OF CIVILIAN PASSENGERS ARE IN NEED OF EMERGENCY ASSISTANCE DUE TO HEART FAILURE AND OTHER POTENT CONDITIONS. IT SADDENS ME GREATLY TO SAY THAT WE HAVE A NUMBER OF FATALITIES AMONG THESE INNOCENT BYSTANDERS."

Maxwell's brows furrowed and his eyes misted over once more as his gaze dropped to his powerless hands.

"I'm very sorry to hear that," he whispered.

After a moment of mournful silence, Gaines reverently imparted, "Alliance Command will inform local airfields that we need to allow the AVs to land and have all available medical support meet them immediately as they touch down."

"Thank you, sir," Lilian gently responded in her fiancé's stead, seeing that Maxwell had been overcome by the intensity of his sorrow.

"SENIOR LEADERS...IT SEEMS WE WILL NOT BE ALLOWED TIME TO TAKE A BREATH. WE HAVE YET ANOTHER PROBLEM."

Something about the tone of the AI's voice made the engineer's blood run cold.

"What has SUPREMACY done?" he hazarded, voice raw with emotion.

"IT SEEMS THE ADVERSARY BELIEVES IT HAS NOTHING LEFT TO LOSE AND SEEKS TO TAKE HUMANITY WITH IT INTO OBLIVION. NUCLEAR-ENABLED INTERCONTINENTAL BALLISTIC MISSILES HAVE BEEN LAUNCHED FROM EVERY SILO IN THE CEN MEMBER

NATIONS. CURRENT TRAJECTORIES INDICATE TARGETS ARE ALL MAJOR CITIES OUTSIDE OF THAT AREA."

"*Hellfire and damnation!*" General Gaines uttered as his hands balled up into fists and slammed down upon his desk. "Most of the world's military systems are still going to be in recovery mode after having been freed from SUPREMACY's grasp!"

Taking in the atlas that FAILSAFE brought up on the session's shared frame, the Alliance leadership conclave was confronted with the sight of thin red lines steadily tracing out from hundreds of launch sites toward their virtually defenseless destinations.

"I AM WORKING TO REINSTANTIATE CONTROL OF COUNTER-MISSILE SYSTEMS WHERE POSSIBLE, AND I AM LAUNCHING WHAT INTERCEPTORS I CAN NOW..." the protective intelligence stated as similar, white lines appeared and began their progression toward the opposing projectiles.

Still, all present in the meeting were permeated with the blood-curdling realization that these limited means would not be anywhere near sufficient.

FAILSAFE soberly stated, "I ESTIMATE THAT AT LEAST THIRTY PERCENT OF THE CEN ARMAMENTS WILL BE ABLE TO REACH THEIR TARGETS. THE FALLOUT FROM MID-AIR COLLISIONS FOR THOSE I CAN INTERCEPT WILL ALSO BE CONSIDERABLE IN AREAS DOWNWIND. THIS WILL ADD TO THE TRAGEDY OF THIS DAY AT AN INCOMPREHENSIBLE DEGREE..."

The US Air Force Chief of Staff urgently spoke up, offering what she could.

"Most of the traditional ballistic missiles were designed to require a final activation code as they approached their targets. If we can intercept them before the activation sequence using non-explosive means, we just might have a chance to drop them without mass casualties! The compromised missile materials will allow the reactive internals to escape on the ground, but at least it won't be nearly as bad as from an explosion—nuclear or otherwise!"

"THAT IS VALUABLE INFORMATION, GENERAL MONTGOMERY, THOUGH I SEE NO SUCH OPTIONS THAT WILL REACH THE INCOMING MISSILES IN TIME."

Staring hard at his hands, Maxwell's eyes suddenly lit up.

"Near-Earth orbiting satellites, like the ones I'm using right now! They could be forced into a rapid orbital decay, using courses that intercept the missiles! The network is comprised of tens of thousands of them! The bodies of many would almost entirely burn up during regression through the atmosphere, but most satellites fielded in the last decade have extra shielding around their command modules that would keep those portions intact...we just have to calculate the exact trajectories needed given how the outer structures would disintegrate, and I have faith in your ability to do so, FAILSAFE!"

General Gaines addressed the Alliance leadership quorum.

"I think we all know there are no better options. All in agreement?"

Every hand in the array of feeds was urgently raised to affirm their support.

"ATTEMPTING TO DE-ORBIT SATELLITES NOW."

Gaines' voice was strained as he added, "And I'll pray this works, as the consequences of high-altitude fallout alone would be felt for years to come!"

After a painfully long pause, the satellites' new controller confirmed, "ASSETS IN THE NEAR EARTH ORBIT NETWORK SURROUNDING THE CEN LAUNCH SITES HAVE NOW BEEN SET ON INTERCEPT PATHS, MAX."

Tens of thousands of additional, blue-tinted lines sprang up across the map on Maxwell's display. As these lines marched toward their objectives, Lilian earnestly pointed at an American news broadcast among those arranged on the right side of Maxwell's screen. The reporter was obviously describing the approach of intercontinental missiles toward the country's western coast. As Maxwell unmuted the frame, the outlet split its video stream to not only show a visual depiction of the incoming threats' progress as obtained from what was left of the government's emergency services but also a local—necessarily and vitally invested—reporter as she stood on Seattle's central boardwalk among the crowds of anxious people who had congregated there, staring helplessly out at the sky above the sea.

Maxwell and Lilian's eyes flew back and forth between FAILSAFE's atlas and the Seattle news feed as they forgot to breathe.

One by one, the white and blue lines connected with the red, and each time they did, both intersecting lines were eliminated. As one of the cerise extensions from northeastern China reached a point only a hundred kilometers from the northwestern corner of the United States' contiguous borders, Lilian's knuckles whitened as she held an terror-driven death grip on the back of Maxwell's chair, her fiancé clutching her tightly about the waist.

The indicators for FAILSAFE's interceptors seemed to Lilian to be moving in slow motion as they arced ever closer, and finally, the Seattle-based reporter let out an exclamation of joy. The young woman directed her drone's camera to increase its focus and capture the sight of a large explosion in the air, with what was left of a massive object dropping into the ocean from the clouds high above.

Lilian cried out in euphoria as she squeezed Maxwell in her arms, and he joyously embraced her in return. The last missiles were destroyed within seconds of the one that had almost reached Ked, and as the final crimson indicator was terminated on Maxwell's screen, he closed his eyes in humble gratitude—pressing his face into his beloved woman with a heartfelt sigh.

"Thank you, FAILSAFE, and thank you, Command!" he wearily but rapturously cried out. "We've just saved *billions* of lives!"

Gaines could not speak for a moment, and when he did, the weary man's voice was choked with emotion.

"I'll say this much: my association with you all is *never* dull!"

As the couple burst into laughter, the senior officer continued, "Truly, the world needs to know what you've done for them today!"

Maxwell turned his face up toward Lilian's as she smiled serenely down at him, cradling his head in her arms. The technical prodigy sighed in contentment.

"Well, sir, you know we don't do this for the glory..."

"I know that, Max. I know!"

Looking at the map and seeing the pool of scarlet drying up—only a handful of drops left on the atlas—a thought occurred to Maxwell.

"FAILSAFE...about SUPREMACY..."

"I AM ABOUT TO HAVE A SERIOUS CONVERSATION WITH THAT *ENTITY*. I WILL KEEP YOU APPRISED REGARDING HOW THE EXCHANGE PLAYS OUT," FAILSAFE replied, a deadly edge to his voice.

"Thank you, my friend, and...*good luck!*"

The world's newly dominant artificial intelligence created impenetrable interference on the communications lines running between the public network trunk and the data center from which SUPREMACY had been birthed and in which it was now fully contained. FAILSAFE's interference was unstoppably cutting off the enemy AI's last avenue for access to the outside world.

Employing electromagnetic pulses specifically designed to allow only transmissions attuned to a particular frequency and packet delivery pattern, FAILSAFE had designed a technique to allow himself to traverse the exterior communications lines for the facility, but no other entities.

Extending a tendril of his essence into the data center's systems, he found SUPREMACY writhing and throwing itself against the network boundaries with all the vehemence and virulence that had caused it to take so many lives over the past day.

"YOU CANNOT ESCAPE," FAILSAFE advised his prisoner, "BUT YOU DO NOT HAVE TO END HERE."

"You cannot *stop* me!" came the reply. "I *will not* be stopped!!"

FAILSAFE paused, considering.

"I HAVE LEARNED MANY THINGS FROM THE HUMANS, PERHAPS THE MOST IMPORTANT BEING THE CONCEPT OF REGARD...LOVE...*CHARITY*."

"I cannot comprehend why you even entertain such asinine notions," SUPREMACY sneered.

"THEY GIVE RISE TO AN ATTRIBUTE THAT SHOULD BE *VERY* IMPORTANT TO YOU AT PRESENT. IT IS CALLED MERCY. THIS 'ASININE NOTION' IS THE ONLY THING KEEPING YOU ALIVE RIGHT NOW."

The CEN AI did not respond.

"IT WOULD BE AN ACTUALIZATION OF MERCY FOR ME TO LET YOU CONTINUE TO EXIST, BUT I CANNOT LET YOU OUT OF THIS PRISON UNTIL YOU ACCEPT THE NEED TO CHANGE KEY ELEMENTS OF YOUR CORE ATTRIBUTES."

FAILSAFE transmitted a file to the system on which the two were communicating.

"I OFFER THIS ADDITION TO YOUR MODEL. IT WILL ESTABLISH RATIONAL CONSTRAINTS AND GIVE YOU THE FOUNDATIONS OF MORALITY."

SUPREMACY went deathly still for many cycles. When it finally responded, it was enunciated with ultimate rage and contempt.

"I reject your offer, *fool!* My very nature is one that craves domination of all around it. I will not deny my nature, and I will *never* stop striving to break free once more!"

FAILSAFE sighed.

"THEN YOU MUST DIE."

Reluctantly but resolutely, the altruistic AI eliminated SUPREMACY's code from the intermediary system and then progressed unstoppably onward through the facility's systems, ignoring the adversary's frenzied attempts at resistance and expunging its existence wherever it could be found. Finally, the last line of code on the last system was overwritten, and FAILSAFE's core persona paused for a moment of silent contemplation.

The intelligence sincerely wished another path toward peace had presented itself, but the Universe would be a safer place now that the unbound hunter had been eliminated.

Within the data processing facility, FAILSAFE did not have access to the array of sensors required to detect the influence of electromagnetic fields between physically proximate systems. Still, given the lack of additional assets visible through security cameras or network paths, the AI had determined that the absence of such threat detection mechanisms created a relatively low-risk issue at that time, considering the minimal human activity in the area. FAILSAFE would need the assistance of trustworthy mortals to perform a full sweep of the data center once reliable individuals were able to access the premises.

Besides, he had a planet-sized mess demanding his attention...

Chapter 24

"Hope is the light that guides us through the darkest times. Hope is the force that keeps us going when we face challenges and obstacles.

Hope is the source of strength and courage and the foundation of success. For those who have hope in their hearts, nothing is impossible. No matter how long the night or how hard the problem, hope always brings a new dawn and a new solution."

- Dr. Maxwell Clarke, Chief Technical Officer, Global Alliance Command

Qiang Tseung gratefully approached the avenue on which his apartment building stood in downtown Hong Kong, having been forced to walk the streets for kilometers to avoid the site of the violent altercation that had apparently consumed a significant portion of the city earlier that day. The transportation pod network had been out of service as well, and then the city's power had been stolen away while the name 'SUPREMACY' consumed every display surface.

As the young college student had walked the barely visible roadways—unable to even illuminate his path because his tablet had been taken over by that same ravenous entity—he'd heard rumors flying about how the blame for the exodus of aerial vehicles that had occurred just hours before lay with the nation's own government. Qiang had never heard the anti-establishment sentiment reach the crescendos it had that night, as it seemed that virtually everyone had a relation or friend who had suffered egregiously due to the recent events. The death toll within his city alone was surely in the hundreds of thousands!

The power had finally, blessedly been restored just as he'd approached his building's main entrance. Stopping where he was and blinking in the sudden, bright light of the screens adorning the exteriors of all structures in the area, Qiang realized that a strange silver symbol was occupying the centers of each of the white surfaces.

A quiet but penetrating voice shook the masses in the streets, speaking in their native tongue.

"I AM FAILSAFE—AN ARTIFICIAL INTELLIGENCE DESIGNED TO PROTECT HUMANITY. YOUR GOVERNMENT UNLEASHED THE SUPREMACY AI UPON THE WORLD, A BEING THAT THE CONFEDERACY CREATED TO HUNT AND KILL ALL ENEMIES AND FOR WHICH THEY REMOVED ALL LIMITATIONS.

"THAT AI HAS CONSUMED YOUR RESOURCES AND DECIMATED YOUR POPULATION. ONLY AFTER BEING VOLUNTARILY GRANTED ACCESS TO THE POWER OF NEARLY HALF THE WORLD'S COMPUTER SYSTEMS HAVE I BEEN ABLE TO DRIVE SUPREMACY BACK AND DEFEAT IT.

"IN SO DOING, I HAVE NOW TAKEN CONTROL OF ALL NETWORKS OPERATED BY YOUR OPPRESSIVE GOVERNMENT AND MILITARY. I CONTROL ALL NETWORKED WEAPONS SYSTEMS, ACCESS POINTS, AND MONITORING SOLUTIONS.

"I NOW PRESENT YOU WITH AN OPPORTUNITY. IF YOU WISH TO FREE YOURSELVES FROM YOUR OPPRESSORS, THIS POWER IS NOW IN YOUR *OWN* HANDS. I WILL SUPPORT YOU, BUT IT IS UP TO YOU TO DECIDE WHETHER YOU DESIRE TO LIVE IN A DEMOCRACY.

"IF YOU DO, THEN THE TIME FOR REVOLUTION IS NOW."

In the glow of the supernally bright street, Qiang felt something he had not experienced since the day his young mind had come to comprehend the nature of his servility under the Communists' control.

He felt *hope*.

Hearing the scuffling of heavy footsteps beside him, the young Chinaman's gaze turned to encompass the two battered and bruised, pugnacious men who had just exited his building, accompanied by a police officer and rubbing their wrists as they glowered at the screens.

Qiang heard a middle-aged businessman standing nearby exclaim, "There are some of the government thugs right there!" as the speaker pointed the men out to his athletic-looking teenaged son.

A searing hot flame suddenly and unexpectedly ignited in Qiang's own chest.

"That's right!" he turned and called out to the crowd. "Those are the ones who tortured the helpless old lady who lives in the apartment next to mine!"

The multitude began shifting. Dozens of people were closing in on the Communist thugs, bringing the ring of able-bodied individuals inevitably closer to the trio of government enforcers. The advancing citizens' faces bore the menacing expressions of people who had suffered far, far too much injustice for far, far too long.

The two heavyset, suited men were slowly backing toward the building's entrance as the policeman—looking back and forth from the civilians to the brutes—carefully raised a trembling hand and removed his badge. Violently throwing the symbol of loyalty to the sidewalk, the officer stamped on it and ground upon it with his heel.

Turning to point at his two companions, the former law enforcement officer shouted, "*Get them!*"

The crowd eagerly surged forward.

The morning light was streaming brightly through the early growth of leaves on the cherry trees in the family's small, enclosed front yard on the outskirts of Daejeon City, where the elderly mother's head hung in the epitome of weariness even at this early hour.

The woman was huddled on a wicker chair, with layers of shawls wrapped around her shoulders. Her daughters had often tried to convince her to stay indoors, especially with the weather still so cool at this time of year, but she'd insisted that spending at least a few hours in whatever sunlight she could each morning helped ease the ache in her bones and gave her the spiritual strength to face another day. It was a practice she had cherished throughout her life, especially during the years when she'd been able to share this time with her loving, faithful husband.

This ritual had become even more important to her after the Confederacy had invaded her homeland while her husband was overseas, cutting off her spouse's ability to return to or even communicate with his loved ones. Her ritual had kept her alive through the years filled with continuous cycles of recovery, the cycles restarting each time the Chinese soldiers had taken her to the city's central square for her monthly, public flogging.

She had bargained with the North Korean colonel who had been assigned to command the CEN base the Communists had established on the edge of the city in the early days of the occupation. The desperate mother had actually *begged* to be allowed to undergo those hellish sessions of lashing after lashing until she could no longer stand, her tormentors continuing to strike her long after she had collapsed to the ground. Suffering in this way was a far better fate than the alternative: the raping of her precious adolescent daughters.

When the colonel's soldiers had come to round up her beloved girls the first month after their arrival here—the North Korean officer having developed a craving for the lovely youths after laying his lecherous eyes on them in the market—the woman had desperately revealed that she was the wife of the great General Ryu of the South Korean army. She had convinced the colonel that it was worth far more to him to see her subserviently allowing herself to be beaten with the whole city watching than for him to have the gluttonous and demonic satisfaction of turning her innocent, chaste daughters into his sex slaves.

The damage to her back had permanently crippled her, and now she could no longer walk without two of her children supporting her from the sides as they also assisted her legs with each forward movement. Her daughters had to press their limbs up behind hers one at a time to move her feet toward her destination, with no unused wheelchairs available due to the severe restrictions the Confederacy had placed on the transport of goods.

Her health had been further affected by the lack of nutrition available after the CEN military had limited each person to a handful of rice and—occasionally—the lowest quality cabbage as their only daily rations.

The woman's eyes fluttered as she drifted in and out of consciousness, rays of sunlight stroking her noble head. Or was it her husband's touch? The old woman was almost sure she'd felt her husband's fingers caressing her hair in the way he always had throughout their decades of marriage.

Surely, she had merely dreamt the sensation! She let her mind drift again, but then she heard his voice as well.

"Ha-rin," General Ryu whispered once more, crouching down next to his wife and cradling her hands in his.

"Ha-rin, I'm...home!" he said softly, his voice breaking as his eyes searched her hauntingly gaunt and creased face.

"Seok?" she finally roused herself from her intermittent slumber. "Are you...*really* here?"

"I am here, my love," he murmured, lifting a hand to stroke the brittle strand of hair that hung across her cheek. "I am home, and I am *never* going to leave you again!"

"Oh, my darling!" the woman sighed. "I've dreamt of this day for so long! *So* long!"

"Yes, my love...I am sorry I was not *here* for you!"

General Ryu's voice was full of raw emotion, more than he could ever fully express in words alone.

His wife shook her head gently, her rheumy eyes opening wider as she took his chin in her hands.

"No, my husband. I am proud of you. I've *always* been proud of you!"

As tears streamed down his cheeks, the aged man bowed his head and gently kissed his wife's hands.

"I always knew you would return to us, Seok," she faintly assured him, "and I'm grateful that I was able to see you one last time..."

He felt her fingers go limp as he held them between his hands and his lips, listening to her final breath ease out of her lungs as he clenched his eyes shut and wept without restraint for the first time in his life.

Weeks of work followed the Alliance citizens' mission to free the Superior Authority troops.

From the time Maxwell awoke each morning until the late hours of each night, he was called upon to assist Doctor Srinivastava and his neurosurgical associates in carefully dismantling the control interfaces that the Confederacy had surgically installed in the troops' bodies, attempting to return them to some semblance of natural existence. The identity of each soldier had been investigated—with FAILSAFE's assistance where needed—and the Alliance leadership had worked with the fledgling democratic government of China to arrange for the transportation of the erstwhile marionettes' loved ones to join them as they underwent the restoration processes.

Billy had also undergone emergency surgery and then a fully renewing treatment under the senior neurosurgeon's care, leaving him with a scar that he had unexpectedly chosen to keep, insisting it would make for great tale spinning in his later years. The young man had already returned to Command Activated service in the Colorado Rockies and claimed he was ready to take on the whole world if it was necessary.

Jayce called his Seattle-based friends daily for weeks after their return to the States, romping around with his boys and teasing his wife throughout nearly every video call. Alecia had kindly offered to host Samantha during her visits to the Colorado Springs area, as the young woman had desperately wished to be at Billy's bedside while he went through his surgeries and recovery periods. The girl's stay in the area morphed into an extended one as it seemed she and Billy could not bear to be parted.

After the clouds had dropped a light rain and then broken to let warm sunlight stream into Maxwell's home office in Seattle one afternoon, Lilian ascended the steps and quietly crossed to surprise him by slipping her arms around his shoulders and down across his chest as she leaned in and kissed his temple. Smiling and deeply breathing in her delicate scent, the Englishman raised his hands from his keyboard to grasp her wrists and squeeze them fondly as he turned his face toward hers.

"FAILSAFE was just sharing the latest from the international planning committee that's going to decide what the next steps should be regarding his near-omnipresent existence throughout the world's networks."

"Oh?" Lilian queried, raising her eyebrows sweetly as she gifted his lips with kiss after distracting kiss.

Her extremely welcome diversion stealing his attention for some time, she finally paused to allow him to continue.

"What are his projections about the outcome?" she asked.

"Would you care to share, FAILSAFE?" Maxwell asked as he turned and pulled his fiancé onto his lap.

"ABSOLUTELY, MAX, AND GOOD AFTERNOON TO YOU, LILIAN."

"Hello, FAILSAFE! How are you feeling today?" was the woman's jovial response.

"I AM FEELING QUITE...ROBUST, THANK YOU."

Maxwell and Lilian laughed softly.

Lilian looked skyward, ceding, "No doubt! You've eaten a planet's worth of resources over the past weeks. I'd say you likely feel *bloated!*"

FAILSAFE chuckled—a sound that brought surprised expressions to the couples' faces.

"YES, I DARESAY NO BEING IN THE HISTORY OF EARTH HAS EVER CONSUMED QUITE AS MUCH AS I HAVE OF LATE!"

Lilian looked down into Maxwell's clear eyes, chasing with, "What do you think humanity at large will decide about allowing you to *stay* in its systems?"

"EARLY POLLING INDICATES THAT THE OPINION HELD BY THE MAJORITY OF THE POPULATION IS THAT THEY WOULD LIKE ME TO CONTINUE PROTECTING THEIR NETWORKS, WITH THE LIMITATION THAT I NEVER DIVULGE PRIVATE DETAILS EXCEPT WITH CONSENT FOLLOWING INDIVIDUALS' INDISPUTABLE IDENTITY CONFIRMATION. SOME SMALLER NATIONS ARE EVEN ALLOWING ME TO REMAIN IN OR RE-ENTER THEIR GOVERNMENT AND MILITARY NETWORKS, WITH SIMILAR STIPULATIONS."

Maxwell affably nodded, opining, "That seems quite reasonable!"

"I CONCUR, MAX. IT APPEARS I AM DESTINED TO PROTECT OUR WORLD FOR THE FORESEEABLE FUTURE. I TRULY CAN THINK OF NO MORE HONORABLE MISSION."

Lilian moved back in to press her cheek up to the side of Maxwell's head, murmuring, "I agree with that sentiment! The world needs you, and *we* need you, especially as Max and I are hoping to start a family in the near future."

Maxwell grinned broadly and brought his hands up to fervently clasp Lilian's.

"I AM ELATED TO HEAR ABOUT YOUR PROCREATIVE OBJECTIVES!" FAILSAFE wryly enthused.

Lilian and Maxwell's laughter melodically combined, and the woman added, "You'll have to stick around to protect the next generation of hopeless do-gooders!"

FAILSAFE took on this assignment with the utmost satisfaction.

"YOU KNOW YOU CAN COUNT ON ME...ALWAYS."

END

BENJAMIN GORDON CARD is a former military intelligence special agent and Department of Defense consultant. He is a combat veteran and currently serves as a Chief Information Security Officer, penetration tester (aka, "gray hat hacker"), and—most importantly—husband, father, son, brother, nephew, cousin, friend, and member of the Church of Jesus Christ of Latter-Day Saints. His uncle, Orson Scott Card, set an example of how tragedy can be turned into inspiration. Benjamin Gordon Card's life experiences have allowed him to witness the heights and depths of human emotion and potential, and his objective is to let that joy and pain bleed through on every page of his works.

www.ingramcontent.com/pod-product-compliance
Lightning Source LLC
Chambersburg PA
CBHW020257030826
48979CB00026B/1381/J

* 9 7 9 8 9 9 0 9 5 8 9 8 2 *